Three Score Years and Ten

Book I of
Give Us This Day

R. F. Delderfield

CORONET BOOKS
Hodder Paperbacks Ltd., London

Copyright © 1973 by Mrs. May Delderfield
First published as the first half of *Give Us
This Day* by Hodder & Stoughton Ltd 1973
Coronet edition 1974
Second impression 1975

Printed and bound in Great Britain for
Coronet Books,
Hodder Paperbacks Ltd,
St. Paul's House, Warwick Lane,
London, EC4P 4AH
by Hazell Watson & Viney Ltd,
Aylesbury, Bucks

ISBN 0 340 18818 9

Aged sixty at his death in 1972, Ronnie Delderfield was best remembered for his very amusing play about life in the RAF, *Worm's Eye View*. But to countless millions throughout the world his name came to be synonymous with the long, intricate and sensitive novels that he came to write in his late years.

GIVE US THIS DAY was the last of these, the last in a series that truly began with the publication of THE DREAMING SUBURB in 1958 and really sprang into popular focus with A HORSEMAN RIDING BY in 1966. Together with its sequel, THE GREEN GAUNTLET, that book chartered the progress of British life and manners in the inter-war years. And its success gave the author the impetus to look further back in time. The result was the trilogy of books of which this is the last part. GOD IS AN ENGLISHMAN began the saga, introducing to the reader Adam Swann in the middle of the Victorian era. Then came THEIRS WAS THE KINGDOM which took the narrative down towards the final years of the old Queen's reign. And interspersed with these books was Ronnie Delderfield's appealing look at school-life in the inter-war years, TO SERVE THEM ALL MY DAYS.

The whole adds up to make for a panoramic vision of the British Isles that may come to stand the test of the next few decades. For Ronnie Delderfield was in essence a storyteller of genius, a teller of tales in the market-place, practitioner of an art that will always be popular and always be influential.

For May

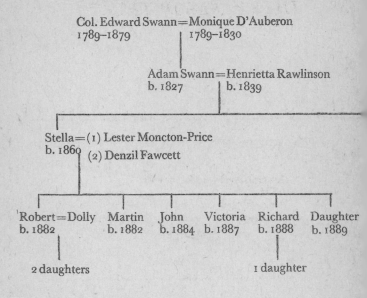

Col. Edward Swann = Monique D'Auberon
1789–1879   1789–1830

Adam Swann = Henrietta Rawlinson
b. 1827   b. 1839

Stella = (1) Lester Moncton-Price
b. 1860 (2) Denzil Fawcett

Robert = Dolly   Martin   John   Victoria   Richard   Daughter
b. 1882   b. 1882   b. 1884   b. 1887   b. 1888   b. 1889

2 daughters   1 daughter

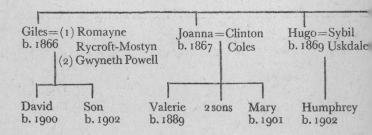

Giles = (1) Romayne   Joanna = Clinton   Hugo = Sybil
b. 1866 Rycroft-Mostyn   b. 1867 Coles   b. 1869 Uskdale
         (2) Gwyneth Powell

David   Son   Valerie   2 sons   Mary   Humphrey
b. 1900   b. 1902   b. 1889   b. 1901   b. 1902

THE SWANNS OF 'TRYST'

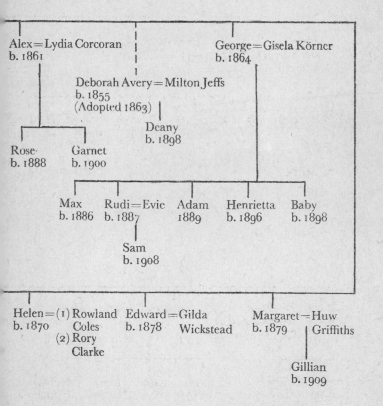

Alex = Lydia Corcoran
b. 1861

George = Gisela Körner
b. 1864

Deborah Avery = Milton Jeffs
b. 1855
(Adopted 1863)

Deany
b. 1898

Rose
b. 1888

Garnet
b. 1900

Max
b. 1886

Rudi = Evie
b. 1887

Adam
1889

Henrietta
b. 1896

Baby
b. 1898

Sam
b. 1908

Helen = (1) Rowland
b. 1870   Coles
         (2) Rory
             Clarke

Edward = Gilda
b. 1878   Wickstead

Margaret = Huw
b. 1879   Griffiths

Gillian
b. 1909

Contents

CONTENTS

Part Three: TOWARDS THE SUMMIT

SWANN·ON·WHEELS
REDEFINED REGIONS

SCOTLAND

Glasgow   Edinburgh

IRELAND

Belfast

Dublin

NORTH
EAST
REGION

Whitby

THE
POLYGON

Manchester

THE
FUNNEL

Macclesfield

Newark

Beddgelert

WEST
MIDLANDS

Derby

Norwich

Birmingham

THE
MOUNTAIN
SQUARE

Worcester

THE
LINK

Pontnewydd

THE
SOUTHERN
SQUARE

London

Cardiff

Tonbridge

Salisbury

THE KENTISH
TRIANGLE

Barnstaple

THE
WESTERN
WEDGE

Taunton

Exeter

TOM
TIDDLER'S
LAND

Truro

PART ONE

Three Score Years and Ten

I

Clash of Symbols

ON THE MORNING OF HIS SEVENTIETH BIRTHDAY, in the Jubilee month of June, 1897, Adam Swann, one-time cavalryman, subsequently haulier extraordinary, now landscaper and connoisseur, picked up his *Times*, turned his back on an erupting household and stumped down the curving drive to his favourite summer vantage point, a knoll sixty feet above the level of the lake over-looking the rustic building entered on the 'Tryst' estate map as 'The Hermitage'.

His wife, Henrietta, glimpsing his disapproving back as he emerged on the far side of the lilac clump, applauded his abrupt departure. Never much of a family man, preoccupied year by year with his own extravagant and mildly eccentric occupations, he had a habit of getting under her feet whenever she was organising a social event and preparation for a family occasion on this scale de-manded concentration.

By her reckoning there would be a score sitting down to dinner, without counting some of the younger grand-children, who might be allowed to stay up in honour of the occasion. She knew very well that he would regard a Swann muster, scheduled for dinner that night, as little more than an obligatory family ritual but she was also aware that he would humour her and the girls by going through the motions. Admittedly it was his birthday and an important milestone in what she never ceased to regard as anything but a long and incredibly adventurous journey, but she knew him well enough, after thirty-nine years of marriage, to face the fact that celebrations of this kind had no real significance for him. Whenever he gave his mind to anything it needed far more substance and permanence than an evening of feasting, a few toasts, a general exchange of family gossip. That kind of thing, to his way of thinking, was a woman's business and such males who enjoyed it were, to use another phrase of his, 'Men who had run out of steam', an odd metaphor in the mouth of a man who had made his pile out of draught horses.

As for him, Henrietta decided, watching his deliberate, slightly halting progress down the drive and then hard right over the turf to the knoll, he would almost surely die with a full head of steam. Increasing age, and retirement from the city life eight years before, had done little to slow him down and encourage the repose most successful men of affairs regarded as their right on the far side of the hill. He had never changed much and now he never would. Indeed, to her and to everyone who knew him well, he was still the same thrustful Adam of her youth, of a time when he had come riding over a fold of Seddon Moor in the drought summer of 1858 and surprised her, an eighteen-year-old runaway from home, washing herself in a puddle. He was still a dreamer and an actor out of dreams. Still a man who, unless his creative faculties were fully stretched, became moody and at odds with himself and everyone about him. In the years that had passed since he had surrendered his network to his second son, George, she had adjusted to the fact that old age, and the loss of a leg, had diminished neither his physical nor mental energies. He continued to make many of his local journeys on horseback. He still followed, through acres of newsprint, the odysseys of his hardfisted countrymen and the egregious antics of their commercial imitators overseas. All that had really happened, when he moved over to make room for George, was the exchange

of one obsession for another. Once it had been his network. Now it was the embellishment and reshaping of
his estate that had filled the vacuum created by his retirement. He still made occasional demands on her as a bedmate, but she was long since reconciled to the fact that
there was a part of him, the creative part, that was cor-
doned off, as sacrosanct as Bluebeard's necropolis, even
from George, his business heir, and from Giles, who did
duty for his father's social and political conscience; even
from network cronies out of his adventurous past, who
occasionally visited him and were conducted on an inspection of the changes he had wrought in this sector of
the Weald since taking it into his head to make 'Tryst'
one of the showplaces of the county. There were some
wives, she supposed, who would have been incapable of
acquiescing to this area of privacy in a man for whom they
had borne five sons and four daughters. Luckily for both
of them Henrietta Swann was not one of them. She had
always been aware both of her limitations and her true
functions and had never quarrelled with them, or not
seriously. To reign as consort of a man whose name
was a household word was more than she had ever expected of life and fulfilment had been hers for a very long
time now. Her place in his heart was assured and their
relationship, since she had passed the age of child-
bearing and become a grandmother, was as ordered as the
stars in their courses. Any woman who wanted more than
that was out looking for trouble.

*   *   *

He paused on the threshold of The Hermitage, doing
battle with his sentimentality. The thatched, timbered
building was a Swann museum, housing practical personal mementoes he had carted away from his Thames-
side tower when he retired, in the spring of 1889. He was
not a man who revered the past but the exhibits in here
symbolised his achievements and it struck him that a man

had a right to sentimentalise a little on his seventieth birthday. He went inside the shady, circular barn and glanced
about him, his eyes adjusting to the dimness after the June
sunlight.

Originally, when he first conceived the notion of a
Swann depository, there had been no more than half-a-
dozen items. Since then many more had been added, the
most impressive being the first coachbuilt frigate the
firm of Blunderstone had delivered to him when he started
his freight line, in '58. It looked old-fashioned now, a
low-slung, broad-axled structure, with a central harness
pole for the two Clydesdales that had pulled it all over the
Home Counties. He had kept its brasswork polished and
the hubcaps winked at him conspiratorially. He glanced
up at the framed maps of the original regions, drawn in
his own hand after that first exhaustive canvass of his
head clerk, Tybalt, probing what they might expect from
haulage clients in competition with the ever-expanding
railways of that race-away era.

The maps seemed to him very crude now, but he saw
them for what they were, the spring from which everything about him welled. Today, with the network almost
forty years old, they certainly qualified as museum pieces,
for George, his son, had abolished the regions as such,
promoting a variety of other drastic changes that had
rocketed some of the older area managers into premature
retirement. The original regions had had queer, quirkish
names, yet another fancy of their creator – the Western
Wedge, the Crescents on the east coast, the Northern
Triangle, where it lapped over the Tweed into Scotland,
Tom Tiddler's Land, that was the Isle of Wight, and the
like. Now these had been condensed into huge areas,
embracing the entire British Isles – South, North, Far
North and Ireland. Prosaic names and very typical of
George, who was still known, among the older waggoners,
as the New Broom.

He thought about George, isolating his good points
and his bad. The good far outweighed the bad, for the

boy had shown tremendous application and a high degree of imagination in the expansion period, although he had not as yet succeeded in banishing the horse and replacing it with one or other of those lumbering, ungainly machines that people in transport said would soon be commonplace on the roads. Rumour reached him that the New Broom had bitten off more than he could chew in this respect. Here and there, egged on by the younger managers, he had experimented with machines spawned by that snorting, fume-spewing monster he had lugged all the way from Vienna ten years before. The older men had jeered at them and their scepticism had seemed justified. Four times in one month waggon teams had to be harnessed to them to tow them home and Head Office had been taxed to explain a pile-up of delivery delays. But George's other changes had been happier. Frigates, the medium-weight vehicles of the kind that stood here, had been all but withdrawn and their teams used to increase the firm's quota of light transport, resulting, so they said, in a wider range of deliveries and a faster service for customers trading in more portable types of goods. George had also made his peace with the railways, contracting with them in every region to offload goods at junctions and then sub-contracting for most of their local deliveries. He had also broken the despotic power of the regional men at a stroke, sub-dividing the depot functions and installing sub-managers answerable, individually, for house-removals, railway traffic and the holiday brake-service. Well, Adam mused, you would look for this kind of thing in a new broom, especially one like George, whose amiability masked a ruthlessness and single-mindedness not unlike Adam's own in his younger days.

He went out of The Hermitage and ascended the tree-clad knoll that gave a view of the frontal vista of house and grounds. It was a prospect that always gave him the greatest satisfaction. Other men had contributed to his founding of Swann-on-Wheels but this, the transformation of a rundown manor house and its surrounding fifty-odd acres, had been his alone, expressing his developing aesthetic taste over all the years he had lived there. It proclaimed the three phases of his life. Young trees, from all over the world, bore witness to his years in the East up to the age of thirty, when he had dreamed of a positive participation in the era and made up his mind to renounce a game of hit-and-miss with the Queen's enemies and the near-certainty of getting his head blown off. The neatness and precision of the layout, with its lawns, spaced clumps of flowering shrubs, belts of soft timber, lake and decorative stonework, signified his middle years and his unflagging passion for creativity within precise terms of reference. The colour, form and enduring mellowness of the scene, with the old, stone house crouching under the spur of rock were indicative of his tendency to opt for the attainable in life, an unconscious compromise between the turbulence of youth and the sobriety of a man who had made his pile and put his feet up. Surveying it, he thought, 'That's my doing, by God! It owes nothing to any man save me,' but he had second thoughts about this. No man, perhaps, but at least one woman, his wife, Henrietta, child of a coarse, comic old rascal now in his dotage among a wilderness of stinking chimney-pots up north. Sam Rawlinson, who had made two fortunes to Adam's one, and thoughts of Sam led directly to his daughter, the tough, resolute, high-spirited girl he had found on a moor and carried off like a freebooter's prize on the rump of his mare.

Regard for her, generous acknowledgment of her fitness for a freebooter's bride, had grown on him year by year. A girl he had married almost absentmindedly, in the very earliest days of the network, who had been able, surprisingly, to stir his senses every time he watched her take her clothes off; even now, at a time of life when a man with a truncated leg was lucky to be mobile, much less intrigued by the spectacle of her wriggling free of all those pleats and flounces.

The thought made him smile again as he remembered a

coffee-house quip of thirty years ago, something about 'that chap Swann reinvesting half his annual profits in his wife's wardrobe'. Well, for anyone who cared to know, he had never been over-impressed by Henrietta Rawlinson dressed for a soirée or a garden-party. He had always seen her as ripe for a bedroom romp, and a ready means of escape from the cares of empire. More of a mistress, one might say, despite five sons and four daughters, each born in that crouching old house under the spur, and a very rewarding mistress at that considering the profound ignorance of her contemporaries concerning the basic needs of a full-blooded man of affairs. All but two of their children had been by-products of these moments of release, but George, and his younger brother Giles, were exceptions.

And even this was odd when you thought about it. George, his commercial heir, had been sired almost deliberately the night of their truce at the one important crisis in the relationship of man and wife. George he had always seen as a tacit pledge between them, acknowledgment that he should look to his concerns as provider and she to hers as gaffer of that rambling house up yonder. And so it had transpired, for Henrietta's maturity had flowered from that moment on, reaching its apogee three years later, with the loss of his leg in that railway accident over at Staplehurst, and the birth, forty weeks later, of Giles, keeper of the Swann conscience.

He turned half-left, glancing across at the belt of fir trees marking the limit of the estate to the north-west, the spot where, in a matter of hours before the accident, the pair of them had found something elusive in their relationship in the way of a hayfield frolic, belonging to a time before the British put on their long, trade faces, their tall hats and that mock-modesty ensemble that everyone expected of a prosperous middle-class merchant and his consort. And out of it, miraculously, had emerged Giles, the family sobersides, whose cast of thought was alien to the extrovert Swanns of 'Tryst', and whose absorption into the firm had proved a counterpoise to George's enterprise. For Giles, to Adam's mind at least, supplied the balance so necessary to any large organisation employing men and materials to make money. Giles was there to safeguard the Swann dictum that every unit counted for something in terms of human dignity and had proved his worth in every area where the waggons rolled. Giles was the adjuster, if that was the right word, between profit and people.

*   *   *

His random thoughts, gathering momentum, descended from the pinnacle of the particular to the plain of the general, so that he saw both himself and his concerns as a microcosm of the Empire, currently preparing for an orgy of tribal breast-beating, the like of which had never been witnessed since the era of Roman triumphs. A Diamond Jubilee. An Imperial milestone. A strident reminder to all the world that the victors of Waterloo and the battle for world markets were there to stay, for another century or more, perhaps for ever.

The papers were full of it. The streets of every city, town and village in the country were garlanded for it. From every corner of the world, coloured red on the maps by conquest and chicanery, a tide of popinjays flowed Londonwards, to share in what promised to be the most emphatic event of the century. Homage to a symbol, the pedants would call it, but a symbol of what? Of racial supremacy? Or trade and till-ringing? Of military triumph on a hundred sterile plains, deserts and in as many steamy river bottoms? He had never really known, despite his diligent observation of the antics of four tribes over five decades. Once, a long time ago, he had seen it all as a matter of trade following the drum in search of new markets and fresh sources of raw material essential possibly for a nation that lived on its workshops. But forty years of trading had taught him that this was no more than an expedient fiction. For now, when inflated jacks-in-office and glory-seekers gobbled up remote islands, he knew that the helmsman was away off course, and that most of these acquisitions would cost, in the long run, far more than they could ever yield.

Gladstone, that self-righteous old thunderer, had told them that years ago and every city clerk who could balance a ledger must be aware of it today. Yet all the time, across the Channel, the laggards, no less greedy and certainly no less vainglorious, were jostling for what they called 'a place in the sun' and he isolated them one by one. There was Germany, led by that loud-mouthed ass Wilhelm; there was France, obsessed by her sense of inferiority since the 1870 debacle; and across the Atlantic there was America with a commercial potential that could, given time, reduce the status of all his rivals to those of nonentities. And thinking this he did what he had always done when his mind ranged far beyond his concerns. He withdrew, thankfully, into the realm of the predictable, represented by his own brood and his own business.

George, no doubt, would forge steadily ahead, pushing the network to its limits. And beside him, as a safety-valve operator, was Giles, placator of ruffled clients, temperature-taker of the Swann work force, adjudicator of every grouse and dispute that came humming down the threads of the network to the heart and brain of the enter-prise beside the Thames. It was enough, he supposed, for a man of seventy that morning, with a tumultuous family dinner party in the offing and little hope of repose until his own and the nation's affairs had steadied. He tucked his unread *Times* under his arm and descended to level ground, sniffing the fragrance all about him and cocking a countryman's ear to the murmurous summer noon.

*   *   *

The wire came within an hour of the family exodus, when the last touches were being added to her Jubilee ensemble and the gardener had delivered the carnations

and roses for the ladies' corsage sprays and the button-
holes the men would wear in the lapels of their newly
pressed frock coats.

Henrietta, her mouth full of pins, could have wept
with vexation as she glanced at the buff slip from Hilda,
her step-mother: '*Father worse. Advise coming immediately*',
a mere five words capable, providing convention took
precedence over inclination, of spoiling an occasion she
had been anticipating for months.

For a moment, without removing the pins from her
mouth, Henrietta Swann weighed the substance of the
message, calculating, on the minimum of evidence, Sam
Rawlinson's chances of hanging on to life for an extra
twenty-four hours or so, long enough for her to sandwich
the Imperial spectacle between the present moment and
a long, hot journey to Manchester in order to put in a
dutiful deathbed appearance.

Almost forty years had elapsed since Sam had forfeited
any affection she had for the old ruffian, for how could
anyone love a father prepared to bargain a daughter for
a scrap of wasteland adjoining his loading bays in the
mill town where she had waited for Adam, or Adam's
equivalent, to rescue her from obscurity. A wily old rascal,
ruthless and disreputable, who had kicked his way up
from bale-breaker to mill owner, who had reckoned everything, including his own daughter, in terms of brass and
done his level best, God forgive him, to mate her with a
simpering nobody. Adam, of course, had forgiven him
long ago, and had even tried, over the years, to soften her
approach, but he had made little or no headway. For her,
Sam Rawlinson continued to stand for vulgarity, male
arrogance and the seediness that attached itself to his
entire way of life, and remembering this like a line out of
her catechism, she removed the row of pins from her
mouth, hitched her petticoat and called, "*Adam!* It's
from Hilda! A wire, saying we should go at once . . .
What *are* we to do, for heaven's sake? Today, of all
days!"

He came out of his dressing-room, took the wire, read it and laid it on her dressing-table among her vast array of bottles and lotions.

"That's for you to say, isn't it, m'dear?"

She said, bitterly, "No, it isn't! Or not altogether. Everything's so nicely arranged. We were very lucky indeed to get that balcony and a thing like this . . . well . . . it's once in a lifetime, isn't it?"

"I fear so," he said, making no effort to keep the chuckle from his voice. "The Old Vic isn't likely to last another ten years even if we do."

He picked up the wire again and took it over to the window, musing. Her frown disappeared then for she knew very well what he was about. Calculating times and distances, as though the dying Sam was an impatient shipper and he had been asked to deliver a haul of goods within a specified time. He said, "I don't know . . . family obligations . . . how would it look, Hetty? An only child, exchanging final farewells in favour of the Lord Mayor's Show?" and hoisted himself round, sitting on her plush dressing-table stool, sound leg bent and tin leg, as he always called it, thrust out.

She knew then he was teasing her as he so often had over the years in this room where few serious words ever passed between them. She said, protestingly, "Really, Adam, it's not a thing to joke . . . !" but he reached out, grabbed her by the hips and pulled her close to him.

There had been a time when his big hands comfortably encircled her waist. They didn't now and recalling this he thought, 'Even so, she's trim for a woman who has produced a tribe of nine,' and his hands passed over the rampart of her corset to her plump behind straining below the rim of a garment that he sometimes referred to as her cuirass. It was an aspect of her that had always captivated him and he pinched so hard that she exclaimed, "Adam! Be serious! We've simply *got* to make up our minds, haven't we?"

"You've already made up your mind," he said, genially.

"All you want now is to shift the guilt on to me. Well, here's how I see it. Sam's eighty-eight and Hilda's a born worrier. But the fact is anybody would find it damned difficult to travel north until the exodus begins, tomorrow night. Nine trains in ten will be heading south-east and most of the upcountry traffic will be shunted to make room for them. We'd best make arrangements to travel on overnight, from London. I'll wire Hilda. Finish dressing. The carriages will be round at noon. If we get up to town by four we'll take a stroll and have a preview of the decorations."

She kissed him then, impulsively and affectionately, and he stumped across to the door to tell one of the girls to bicycle into the village with a reply. But then, on the threshold, he paused. "He's had a damned good innings, Hetty. And any last words he wants to say will be to me, not you. He was proud of you, mind, in his own queer way, but he saw me as the son he never had. Don't let it spoil your day."

2

In the old days the Swanns, in the way of the middle-class, celebrated national occasions *en famille*. As recently as the Golden Jubilee, ten years ago, a small balcony near St. Clement's Dane had accommodated man, wife and such of their family who were still home-based. But in a single decade the tribe had proliferated to an extent that astounded Adam whenever he thought about it. Unlike Henrietta he had never had it in mind to found a dynasty.

Today the royal balcony at Buckingham Palace would have been taxed to accommodate the entire Swann tribe even though two offshoots were out of the country, one in faraway China and another across the Irish Sea. But proliferation was not the only reason for dispersal. In spreading their wings each Swann had swung into an individual orbit, so that their occupations, their associates,

24

indeed, their whole way of life and cast of thought presented a kind of spectrum of Imperial enterprise.

Thus it was that an occasion like this found them, as it were, picketing the royal route, dotted here and there at intervals along its four-mile route. Each of them prepared to cheer certainly, and wave hat, handkerchief or miniature Union Jack, but for different reasons, dictated by private conceptions of what excused this display of self-aggrandisement. Their individual and often contradictory standpoint was highlighted by their acceptance of what the newspapers were already calling 'Queen's Weather', as though, in dominating one-fifth of the world's surface, the British had tamed not merely tribes but elements.

Stationed at Hyde Park Gardens with his eldest daughter Stella, her farmer husband Denzil, four of Stella's children, his own youngest son, Edward, and youngest daughter, Margaret, Adam was content to view it as 'appropriate' weather. There had been times, during his long climb to affluence, when he had quarrelled with the cult of national arrogance but success had mellowed him. At seventy, he saw nothing remarkable about a cloudless day for a tribal rite of these dimensions. It was to be looked for and, in the nature of things, it had arrived. God, he had often jested, was an Englishman. Nothing else could account for the astounding luck of the English since Waterloo. Today the jest was muted. It had to be in the face of the evidence spread below as the procession unrolled, before his eyes, like a vast, vari-coloured carpet. There would come a time, his commonsense predicted, when the balloon would burst, possibly with a Godalmighty bang, but that time was not yet; and it occurred to him, as the throb of martial music was heard from the direction of Constitution Hill, that he might have been over-hasty in his claim that national pride was hurrying towards its inevitable fall. Every race and every creed under the sun was parading down there and at the very head of the procession, mounted on the huge grey he was said to have ridden to Khandahar,

was a small, compact figure, reminding him vividly
of an occasion forty years ago when he and Roberts of
Khandahar had shared barrack and bivouac in an India
torn by strife and had later parted company with a touch
of mutual acrimony, Roberts in pursuit of the new Rome,
himself to join in the free-for-all at home.

Forty years had not blurred the clarity of his recollection of that parting. He had been convinced then that
the little man on the grey was a romantic visionary, who
would soon get himself killed in a village that was not
even marked on a map. Well, he never minded admitting
a misjudgment, and here was the most glaring of his life.
Roberts had not only survived and seen his boyish dreams
translated into fact. He had gone forward to become a
legend in his own lifetime and here were the cheers of a
million Cockneys to prove it. He said, as the grey cur-
vetted below, "He had it right after all then . . . !"
and when Henrietta asked him what he had said he
smiled and shook his head, saying, "Nothing . . . nothing
of any consequence, m'dear. Simply reminding myself
that Roberts and I once rode knee to knee in battles
neither of us expected to survive." But although he
dismissed his association with Roberts in such lighthearted
terms Henrietta took pride in it and showed as much by
squeezing his hand. It wasn't something you could let
drop at a garden-party or a soirée – that one's husband was
on Christian-name terms with the most famous soldier
in the world – but one could bask in the knowledge just
the same.

*   *   *

Half-a-mile to the east, at a tall window looking over
Green Park, Major Alexander Swann, eldest of the Swann
boys, and the only one among them to follow the traditional Swann profession of arms, might have seen it as good
campaigning weather. Under a sun as brassy as this the
ground would lie baked and the rivers would run low,

permitting the rapid movement of troops across almost any kind of terrain, yet there was scepticism in his survey of the colourful assembly that passed, with its companies of colonials, its emphasis on variety, sounding brass, good dressing and spit-and-polish turnout. Alex, who regarded himself as a forward-looking professional, saw it as a circus rather than a demonstration of military might. It was a parade rooted, not in the future and not even in the present, but in an era when his grandfather had ridden down from the Pyrenees to bring Marshal Soult to battle. A single Maxim gun, well-sited and well-served, could cut it to ribbons in sixty seconds flat, and the thought occurred to him, as he watched the company of Hong Kong police step by in their comical coolie hats, that this was mere window-dressing and had nothing to do with the art of war. And it was no snap judgment either. Not only had he fought tribesmen and savages in half-a-dozen Imperial battle areas, his had been the hand that guided the hand of the Prince of Wales to the trigger of the first Maxim gun ever fired in England. He said, voicing his scepticism, "All very pretty, so long as it never comes up against any-thing more lethal than an assegai or muzzle-loader . . ." And his wife, Lydia (she who had transformed him from regimental popinjay to professional) concurred, but, being herself a daughter of the regiment, added a rider: "They'd learn," she said, "just so long as some of us bear it in mind."

*   *   *

A muzzle-loader's range from the vantage-point of Alex and Lydia was the third Swann picket, denied the privi-lege of a first-storey view but not needing one, for he measured six feet three inches in his new boots, and could see over all the heads between himself and the kerb.

Hugo Swann, Olympic athlete and winner of as many cups and medals as Victoria had colonies, would think of it as good track weather, the ground being hard

THREE SCORE YEARS AND TEN

underfoot and it even put the thought into mind. "Hope it holds," he told Barney O'Neill, the celebrated pole-vaulter. "If it does we'll get a record gate at Stamford Bridge tomorrow and they need the cash, I'm told."

It would be difficult to define Hugo's conclusions on the spectacle, other than a spectacle. His father and brothers had long since come to the conclusion that Hugo, bless his thick skull, had never had a serious thought in his life and his presence in the network, where he put in token appearances from time to time, was that of a thirteen-stone sleeping partner. None of them resented this, however, for Hugo, as a Swann advertisement, was worth five thousand a year on George's reckoning. His name appeared on the sporting pages of every journal on Fleet Street nowadays, so that when it cropped up, as it frequently did in coffee house and country house, no one could ever be sure whether the speaker was going to pronounce upon sport or commerce. All one could guarantee was that the name stood for rapid movement of one kind or another, and time schedules had always rated high on the list of Swann priorities.

*   *   *

Four hundred yards nearer St. Paul's, where the procession was channelled into the Strand and marched blaring, thrumming and jingling between phalanxes of hysterical Imperialists (few among them could have said in which continent British Honduras or Tobago were located) was George Swann, managing director and New Broom Extraordinary. He was perched, together with his wife, his family and his host, Sir James Lockerbie, in a window that would have fetched a hundred guineas had Sir James been in need of ready money. And George would have defined the brassy sunshine as ideal hauling weather.

On a day like this, given a fit team, a waggon carrying a full load could make fifteen miles from depot to offloading point providing the teamster knew his business and gave the horses a regular breather. For years now George had taken weather into his calculations but his mind was not on business today. With the yard closed down, and every employee enjoying a bonus holiday, he was wondering what new and plausible excuse he could offer Gisela for not making holiday himself. The problem not only took his mind off his work. It drew a curtain on the procession below so that he saw, not an ageing dumpy woman in a gilded carriage drawn by eight greys, not the clattering tide of blue, gold, crimson and silver of her cavalry escort and not even the Hong Kong police in their incongruous coolie hats, but a diversion that had interposed between him and his concerns since his chance meeting with Barbara Lockerbie a few weeks ago. For the New Broom had lost some of its inflexibility of late and those within close range of it noticed, or thought they noticed, a wholly uncharacteristic irresolution in the way the broom was wielded. A strange, unwonted peace had settled on the network. Dust had been allowed to settle in out-of-the-way corners at Headquarters, and in the regions beyond, so that regional managers who had been at the receiving end of George Swann's barrage of watch-it-and-wait-for-it telegrams ever since Old Gaffer put his feet up, told one another the gale was easing off a point or two and that the Young Gaffer, praise God, was 'running out of steam' as the Old Gaffer would have put it. They were men of the world, mostly, who had been around Swann yards long enough to remember George as a pink-cheeked lad with an unpleasant tendency to pop up in unexpected places when least expected. They fancied, therefore, that by now they knew him as well as they had known his father, but they would have been wrong. For George Swann had not run out of steam. On the contrary, he could have been said to have built up such a head of steam over the years that it became imperative that somebody came forward to open a safety-valve on his explosive energy. And this, in fact, was what had happened the moment Barbara Lockerbie crossed his path. Any steam that remained in George's boilers was now at her disposal, not Swann's.

It was nine weeks since they had met, seven since he had become her lover and a long, fretful week since he had held her in his arms, shedding his packload of responsibilities much as Christian shed his sins and watched them roll away downhill on his journey to the Celestial City. Unlike Christian, however, George had reached the Celestial City at a bound, for Barbara Lockerbie, saddled with an ageing husband and currently between lovers, had an eye for men like George Swann, recognising him instantly as someone in such desperate need of dalliance that he was, in fact, likely to prove virile, generous and unencumbered with jealousy concerning competitors past and present.

She was right. He took what she offered gratefully, without seeking to lay down conditions and without a thought as to how deep a dent she was likely to make in his bank balance. He did not enquire why her elegant boudoir was slightly tainted with cigar-smoke, or who had paid for that cameo set in emeralds that had not been on the dressing table the night before last. He was as eager as a boy, as trusting as a spoiled mastiff, and as uncompromising in his approach as a shipwrecked mariner beached by sirens after years of toil and celibacy. That was why, when she declared these Imperial rites vulgar, and took herself off to her country house in Hertfordshire before they were due to begin, she knew with complete certainty he would find a way of accepting her invitation to join her while Sir James Lockerbie, rival gallants and his little Austrian wife, Gisela, were city-bound by the national junketings. She was not often wrong about men and she was never wrong about George Swann. Before the tail-end of the procession had passed under the Lockerbie window George had composed and rehearsed an urgent summons from his Midlands viceroy. With luck he could make Harpenden by suppertime and a Lockerbie carriage would convey his wife and family home to Beckenham. He rejoiced then that he had granted the network an extra day's holiday in honour of the Jubilee. It meant that no one would look for him until the following Thursday.

3

For Adam Swann, seventy, it was appropriate weather and for Alex, thirty-six, campaigning weather. For Hugo, twenty-eight, it was athletes' weather and for George, thirty-three, hauling and whoring weather. There remained the Swann Conscience, not quite silenced by the jangle of bells and the boom of royal salutes and for Giles, its keeper, it was something else again. Protest weather, possibly, for Giles, almost alone among that vast crowd was not present as a sightseer but as an actor. Evidence, as far as the Swanns were concerned, that all that glittered down there was fool's gold.

His observation post was a first-floor window above the display windows of Beckwith and Lowenstein's, the once-fashionable Strand branch, now set on its slow decline since the carriage trade had drifted east to Regent's Street and Oxford Street. It was almost the last shop in the north façade of the Strand and he was there as lookout on behalf of the forlorn band of leaflet-throwers stationed two storeys above. Among them, at her urgent insistence, was his wife, Romayne, disinherited daughter of one of the wealthiest merchants in the land.

It was not the first foray in which they had been involved but because of the occasion it promised to be the most sensational, certain of earning press coverage, which was more than could be said of earlier protests, even the abortive one they staged at the Lord Mayor's Show last November.

Soper, the fanatical Secretary of the newly formed Shop Assistants' Action Group, had conceived it, a pallid, tireless and, in Giles' view, a very reckless campaigner who had won a majority vote in committee on the grounds

that a gesture of this kind, a challenge thrown at the feet
of the most powerful and influential people in Britain,
was irresistible and perhaps he was right. Few among
those who were offered the Group's standard leaflets
in the street, or at Hyde Park Corner, accepted them, and
even those who did discarded them ten steps beyond.
"We have to move on," Soper had argued passionately,
"we have to force the campaign on the national press and
what more certain way of doing that than putting our
case to the Queen on her way to St. Paul's?"

Put like that it was unanswerable and Romayne, her
imagination fired, shouted "Hear, hear! Bravo!" as
if the proposal of such a bold gesture represented its
accomplishment. But Giles, to her private dismay, had
argued against it, first publicly in committee, where he
had been outvoted, then privately on their way home. She
did not often run counter to him but she did now, saying,
"But don't you *see*, Giles? It's dramatic, something they
can't laugh off in the way they did when we paraded with
placards!"

"It's certainly that," he said, trying to locate the springs
of his instinctive misgivings, "but there's something about
it I don't like. It's not just the risk of arrest on some trum-
ped-up charge – obstruction, creating a public nuisance –
they'd find something if they laid hands on any of us.
And it's not the pleasure of reminding all those popinjays
that there are more important issues than waving flags.
Maybe it's the timing."

"The timing? I don't follow, Giles, dear."

He said, grumpily, "Well, there's no point in us falling
out about it. It was a majority decision and we'll go ahead.
I only lay down one condition. They leave the wording
of the leaflet and the tactics to me."

"Oh, but they'll do that," she said, and he thought she
was probably right. The Shop Assistants' Action Group
did not lack ideas and enthusiasm but it was woefully short
on funds and prestige, both of which Giles Swann, a director of a nationwide haulage network, could provide.

The Jubilee ambush continued to bother him. They lived in a pretty little Georgian house at Shirley, within easy reach of East Croydon Station, and thé back looked over woods and pastures to the Kent–Surrey border. That same night, unable to sleep, he got out of bed and went on to the terrace looking across the fields to the blur of Addington Woods and here, in uncompromising moonlight, his misgivings crystallised. He saw the leaflet raid as a single jarring note in a national overture. It was easy to imagine the wrapt expressions of the Jubilee holidaymakers, each of them revelling in a day's release from monotonous toil to witness an unprecedented display of pomp and martial display in which they would feel themselves personally involved, and a majority, regarding the Queen's personage as sacrosanct, would surely regard the descent of a shower of leaflets on her entourage an act of impiety. It would be irrelevant too, on a day when London was out to enjoy itself, and when every man, woman and child assembled there personally subscribed to the mystique of Empire and took pride in the spread of red on maps hung on the blackboards of the redbrick Board Schools.

Of all the Swanns, Giles saw himself as the only one involved in the present. Alex, George and Hugo were forsworn to the future, to an increasingly modernised army, to the spread of commerce and the triumphs of the sports arena as the might of the tribes increased year by year. His father, who had once had a social conscience, had slipped back into the past, to the battles for franchise and human rights of the 'sixties and 'seventies. But it sometimes seemed to him that he alone was equipped to lift the lid on this treasure chest they called the Empire and examine, piecemeal, the terrible injustices concealed under the plumes and moneybags stowed there. As a child he had witnessed an aged couple evicted and despatched to separate workhouses, and as a youth he had penetrated the galleries of a Rhondda coal-mine and seen, closehand, the filth and degradation of the industrial cities in the

north. Everywhere, it appeared to him, was gross im-
balance; wealth and power on the one hand, grinding
poverty and naked cruelty on the other, but so few
acknowledged this boil on the body politic. They chanted
patriotic music-hall ditties, put their money on the Grand
Fleet and thought of themselves as actually taking part
in an eruption of power and plenty, unique in the history
of mankind. Then they went blithely about their concerns, the privileged making money, gallivanting on
river and race-course, snug under a mantle of rectitude
woven for them by Providence. For the others, who made
all this possible, it was very different. The conditions
worked by shop assistants in the big emporiums were only
one of the blatant contradictions in an age of tremendous
technological progress and the flagrant contrasts within
the system tormented him for it seemed to him that, once
they were publicly recognised and acknowledged, they
could be so easily adjusted. Romayne's revelation was
a case in point.

He remembered her as she had been in their courtship
days, a pampered, highly-strung child of an industrialist,
who had seemed never to comprehend his smouldering
quarrel with the status quo, who had taken all her privi-
leges for granted and had indulged in a fit of temper
whenever anything was withheld from her. But all that
had changed and under pressure of what he looked back
on as absurdly melodramatic circumstances. Unable
to adjust to her selfishness he had jilted her, abruptly and
finally after a scene in an Oxford Street milliner's a minute
to closing time one Saturday night, and had glumly
assumed that the incident marked the end of their bitter-
sweet relationship. Yet it was not so. Something had
rubbed off on her, enough to project her out of her
cushioned surroundings and into the workaday world,
there to test his theories in the light of personal experience.
Eighteen months later, against all probability, he had
found and reclaimed her, earning her living in the cash
desk of a northcountry haberdasher's, and sharing the

34

submerged life of living-in shop assistants working a sixty-hour week under what was really no advance on the lot of slaves. The experience had transformed her utterly, and if that could happen to her it could happen to others, providing the point could be brought home to them with equal emphasis. Yet how to achieve it, without revolution and blood on the streets? Not by protest meetings at Hyde Park Corner. Not by leaflets, placards and parades and letters to the press. Surely by legislation, and the slow reshaping of public opinion it would be possible. There was a lesson here somewhere, for him and for everybody else. Possibly, just possibly, Soper was right. The public needed a shock, a whole series of shocks, and perhaps his underlying misgivings concerning Soper's tactics stemmed from an excessive respect for law and order and an instinctive distaste for involving himself and his family in scandal. Romayne, out of regard for him, had not succumbed to those pressures and remembering this he discerned the real source of her enthusiasm for Soper's paper bombardment. Standing there in the moonlight he thought, forlornly, 'She *did* that. She endured that purgatory for eighteen months, and for no other reason than to prove that we belonged to each other, paying in wretchedness for her tantrums, her ridiculous involvements with grooms and music-teachers, her gross extravagance and the capacity, hardening like a crust, to see the dispossessed as serfs. Well, then, to hell with what I think about the proposal. I'll do it. Not for Soper and not even for the poor devils he claims to represent, but for her.'

He went in to find her sleeping soundly and studied her in the shaft of moonlight that fell across the pillow. A beautiful child, robbed by sleep of the strange contradictions imposed upon her by the past, that included her failure to present him with a child, something she would probably see as a fresh source of inadequacy, although he did not. There were already too many children in the world. Many of them would never have enough to eat.

Many of them would grow into spindle-legged, weak-chested adults with no alternative but to work out their lives at the dictates of some stonefaced overlord like her father or his grandfather. Like his own father, even, despite Adam Swann's national reputation as an enlightened gaffer. He slipped in beside her, still troubled certainly, but comforted, to some degree, by the completeness of her transformation.

2

Paper Ambush

IT WAS DIFFICULT TO RID HIMSELF OF A SENSE OF
melodrama as he went about his preparations, beginning
with the drafting of the leaflet and ending, an hour or so
before the procession was due to pass the corner-site, on
the day itself. It was as though all the time he was planning, counselling, conniving, he was standing off watching
himself masquerade as a nihilist, a Balkan assassin or a
bearded anarchist resolved upon some stupendous master-
stroke instead of what it was, an insignificant discord in
the national overture.

More than once, as the day drew near, he came near
to admitting he was a pompous ass to involve either himself or Romayne in the charade, yet he persisted, partly
because he had his full share of Swann obstinacy, but
more because, below the level of self-mockery, he acknowledged his cause was just. And then, when every last
detail had been perfected, and he was alone in the airless
little annexe, partitioned off from the empty showrooms,
excitement liberated him from the sense of the ridiculous
and he told himself that he would not have been anywhere
else. But it still nagged him that Romayne had insisted,
as the price of his involvement, on becoming one of the
four selected for the perpetration of the actual deed.

They had all wanted a part, even if it was limited to
throwing a handful of leaflets apiece and then running
for it, as Giles and his chosen three planned they should.

37

But four, he said, was the maximum number within a safety limit. Their escape route lay down four flights of stairs, into the corridor between shop and staff entrance, past the janitor's cubicle and out into Catherine Street, there to lose themselves in the crowd. The plan was as perfect as he could make it. There was a more than even chance that they would all be clear away before the distributing point was located and searched, for Soper, himself an employee of Beckwith's, laid long odds that Meadowes, the janitor, would quit his cubicle at the side entrance the moment cheering heralded the vanguard of the procession.

This part of the premises, the western end, was deserted. The entire staff of the emporium, some fifty of them, were now lining the row of windows nearer the Law Courts, and it seemed very improbable that anyone would leave them at the climactic moment, so that the stairs leading to the upper stockroom, where the ambush was centred, were likely to remain free. Soper and his fiancée, a fragile girl with huge, trusting eyes, who served at Beckwith's glove counter, were positioned there, with five hundred leaflets apiece, laboriously blocked out on a child's printing set, for printers could be traced. The wording was direct and, in Giles' view, necessarily inflammable. It ran:

AFTER THE SPECTACLE THE RECKONING! MILLIONS OF HOURS OF UNPAID OVERTIME WERE WORKED BY COUNTER-JUMPERS TO MOUNT THE SPECTACLE YOU ARE WATCHING! THE AVERAGE SHOP ASSISTANT WORKS AN ELEVEN-HOUR DAY ON A SMALLER WAGE THAN AN AGRICULTURAL LABOURER. TAKE ACTION NOW TO ORGANISE THE TRADE AND OPPOSE:
   Low Wages
   Fines for 'refusing'
   Unjust dismissals without a character or right of appeal
   Prison diet, fed to living-in staff
   Abbreviated half-days.

*THESE ARE BUT FIVE CURRENT GRIEVANCES
OF THE MOST EXPLOITED WORK-FORCE IN
BRITAIN.*

Soper and his committee had been ecstatic about this
broadside, embracing, as far as it could on a leaflet
measuring about six inches by eight, most of the major
ailments of this industrial lame duck. Privately Giles
thought it could have been condensed to a point where it
could be read at a glance but there was no time to redraft
so he let it pass, concentrating on the strategy of the
ambush with particular emphasis on the escape route.
And now, in the stifling heat of a room piled with the
paraphernalia of a haberdasher's window-dressing team,
he watched the eddying crowds below, ten deep he would
say both sides of the Strand, with a dribble of latecomers
drifting down sidestreets in the vain hope of finding a
chink in a kerbside phalanx.

Time passed slowly. About nine, as Soper had predicted, the distant throb of drums and the cheers of spectators lured Meadowes, the janitor, from his cubicle and
he went out, leaving the staff door open. Soper's key had
ensured their entry before he was on duty, and Soper and
his fiancée, Miriam, had climbed to the second storey
with their bundles of leaflets. Romayne had been
stationed as signaller on the third landing. His own job
was to watch for the head of the procession, give the signal,
and keep a close watch on the escape route and the movements of the janitor.

Timing, he had insisted, was vitally important. It
would do far more harm than good to throw the leaflets
over the sills before the royal entourage was safely past and
on its way down Fleet Street. He hoped to select a section
of the cavalcade that was marching rather than riding, for
it was always possible that a shower of leaflets would
frighten a horse and cause casualties. If there had been
the faintest hint of a breeze most of the sheets would have
drifted the width of the Strand but the bunting and

flags on the lamp-standards hung motionless and it seemed likely that nearly all would find pavement level on the north side. It didn't matter, so long as Soper and the girl followed his orders and waited for the signal passed on by Romayne. Soper was an impatient chap and waiting there, with the sounds of the drums and brass drawing nearer as they battled with the almost continuous roar of the crowd, Giles wished he had had someone steadier to take his own place as scout in order that he could oversee the leaflet bombers in person. He stepped out and tiptoed halfway down the last flight of stone steps to a point where he could see the empty cubicle, then back again, calling softly to Romayne to tell Soper and Miriam that the janitor was safely out of the way. Then he resumed his place at the window and concentrated on the area immediately below. And it was at that moment, his eye ranging the north pavements, that he noted the movement of the thickset man wearing unseasonably heavy brown tweeds and a brown derby hat.

He was clearly more than a spectator and seemed to have some official purpose down there, for he walked purposefully along the carriageway, head tilted, eyes scanning the façades instead of the carriageway, as though he was some kind of policeman or marshal, assuring himself that all was well among the tiers of patriots massed at the windows of the northside premises. There was no menace about him, only an unwavering watchfulness, and when the blaring bands and the cheering engulfed them all like a tumbling wall of masonry he still sauntered there, turned away from the oncoming procession. By then, however, Giles had all but forgotten him, his attention caught and held by the spectacle in spite of himself, as the royal entourage rolled by, eight rosetted greys pulling the open carriage containing a little old woman under her white parasol, the splendidly mounted and richly caparisoned bevy of royalty in its immediate wake, then the glittering, jingling squadron of Horse Guards, and behind it rank upon rank of blue, scarlet and gold, a thousand or more men with brown faces and martial step, their presence representing the flag at the ends of the earth.

The moment was at hand and he was on the point of turning to call up to Romayne when, once again, the man in the brown derby caught his eye, insistently now for he had stopped sauntering and was standing squarely on the kerb, staring up at a window immediately above. It was the window where Soper and his girl were stationed. With a grunt of alarm, Giles saw the first of the leaflets flutter down, drifting idly and aimlessly, like birds dropping out of the sky, and in the same moment he saw the man below stiffen, gesticulate and run swiftly round the angle of the building and out of Giles' line of vision.

There was really little but instinct to tell him the watcher had spotted something amiss up there and for a second or so he dithered, his eye roving the fringe of latecomers in search of Meadowes, the janitor, but as he hesitated more and more leaflets floated down, separating in flight so that they seemed to multiply out of all proportion to the number printed. Then, whipping round, he heard the scrape of a boot on the stairs and leaped for the landing, almost colliding with a thickset figure in the act of tackling the third flight.

The man must have moved with extraordinary speed. Ten seconds or less had brought him this far but his step, notwithstanding his bulk, was as light as a boy's. In a few strides he would be level with Romayne, staring over the stairwell. A moment later he would have Soper and his girl trapped with his back to the door.

Giles shouted, "Run, Romayne, *run!*" and flung himself at the steps, grabbing the heavy material of the man's trousers, then enlarging his hold on one brown boot, so that the man lurched and stumbled, falling heavily against the iron stair-rail and half-turning, so that Giles caught a glimpse of a red face with heavy jowls, a large moustache of the kind made fashionable by Lord Kitchener, and eyes that glared at him with a baffled expression. He was so occupied with holding the man that he did not hear Romayne's warning cry, or the rush of feet on the stairs heralding the frantic descent of Soper and Miriam, the girl still clutching a double handful of leaflets. He was aware, however, of Romayne darting past or over them and into the store room he had just left and almost at once, it seemed, her reappearance with a dust-sheet that billowed like a sail and all but enveloped him.

Then, amid a rush of movement and a confused outcry, the man he was holding let go of the stair-rail and whirled his fists, aiming a blow capable, he would have said, of felling a prize-fighter had it not been deadened by the enveloping folds of the dust-sheet, but was still powerful enough to knock him clear of the stairs to a point where he cannoned into the scampering Miriam, sending her crashing against the door of the store room. After that all was the wildest confusion, the intruder heaving under the sheet and the four of them arriving in a body at the foot of the stairs and bolting headlong down the corridor to the staff entrance where Meadowes stood, mouth agape and hands upraised to ward off what must have seemed to him a concerted charge. He was swept aside, steel-rimmed spectacles flying one way, peaked cap another, and then they were clear and running through the crowd in the direction of Drury Lane.

There was no immediate pursuit, or not so far as a glance over his shoulder could tell him as they doubled two more corners before arriving at the eastern arcade of Covent Garden, deserted now but shin deep in litter and baskets and barricaded with costers' barrows half seen under their tarpaulins. He stopped then, catching Soper by the arm and saying, breathlessly, "Into the market – a dozen places to hide!" and they both scrambled over the barrows, pulling the girls after them and found cover in the semi-darkness of the grilled caves beyond.

Nobody said anything for a moment. The girl Miriam was grimacing with pain, and holding her right hand to her shoulder where it had come into violent contact with the store room door. Soper was spent but otherwise intact. The white of Romayne's petticoat showed through a rent in her skirt and she was already fumbling in her reticule for safety-pins. Then Soper said, soberly, "My God! That was a close shave! Who was he, Mr. Swann?"

"How would I know? A plain-clothes detective maybe, keeping a lookout for something like this. He seemed to pinpoint the place at a glance."

Soper's eyes widened as he said, "You mean somebody peached? Someone on the committee? He was stationed there waiting for us?"

The narrowness of their escape put an edge on Giles' tongue. "I don't think anything of the kind. He was checking the route and saw something unusual. You and your leaflets probably. Why the devil didn't you wait for my signal like we arranged?"

"We had trouble getting the window open. The frame stuck at less than an inch." This from the girl, still massaging her bruised shoulder.

"But you actually threw leaflets. I saw some go down."

"We broke the glass," Soper said. "We had to, there was no other way," and Giles growled, "Well, at least we know how he spotted us. Not that it matters."

"I'm sorry, Mr. Swann. We muffed it. Most of the leaflets are still up there."

Giles replied, sourly, "You don't fancy going back to finish the job?"

Romayne said, sharply, "That's not fair, Giles! What else could they do in the circumstances? At least some leaflets went out."

The girl Miriam began to cry, quietly and half-heartedly – a child warned that she will be given something to cry about if she doesn't watch out. Giles was suddenly aware of the overpowering might of the forces ranged against them, ranged against everybody in their situation, including the cheering crowds who would soon go home, sun-tired and satisfied with their brief vision of world domination, but expected to make it last until the next

free show vouchsafed by the élite. A coronation, a royal
wedding or a Lord Mayor's Show.

He said, more to himself than the others, "It's no use
... these demonstrations ... leaflets, placards, with everyone involved risking their jobs. There must be another
way, a way that doesn't put everyone at risk." He looked
directly at Soper. "You and Miriam would have been
recognised by the janitor. You daren't go back to Beckwith and Lowenstein's now."

"I don't have to. I've given notice. I told the floor
manager I was moving to another billet up north. I was
paid up last Saturday."

"You've got another billet?"

"No. That was a cover, in case something like this
happened."

"You've got a character?"

Soper shrugged. "I'll use the ones I used to land that
job, ones I wrote myself. I was in trouble at my last place.
It soon gets around if you're a militant."

"And Miriam?"

"She can go back. Meadowes didn't see her."

"How can you be sure?"

"I'm sure," Romayne said. "She was last out and I
knocked his glasses off while she was still in the corridor."

Pride in her took possession of him, going a short way
to soothe the frustration and humiliation of the day. He
said, "You all came out of it better than me. I was
supposed to be lookout but I let him get that far. If
Romayne hadn't been sharp with that dust-sheet none of us
would have got clear. I'm sorry I sneered, Soper. I had
no right to. Your stake is a much bigger one than mine
and I don't have to remind you what can result from using
forged references."

"That's all right, Mr. Swann." He put his arm
round his girl and she winced. "It hurts horribly," she
said. "Do you suppose we could find a chemist open and
get some arnica?"

"You stay here," Giles said. "I'll find a chemist's

and a pie-shop too. You'll be safe enough here until the crowds start dispersing. Then we can all go home. Will you wait with them, Soper?"

"Anything you say, Mr. Swann."

He went out into the blinding sunshine, working his way west towards Trafalgar Square and King William IV Street where, on his way to the rendezvous, he had seen shops open. 'Anything you say, Mr. Swan . . .' They all looked to him for a lead, not because he was more qualified to give one than the least of them, but because he was a renegade from the far side of the barricades, a man who owned his own house, wore tailored clothes and had a famous father. It wasn't good enough, not by a very long chalk, and somehow he would have to improve on it or leave them to get on with it alone. He found a chemist's and bought a bottle of arnica, then a market coffee-stand where he bought four meat pies and four bottles of ginger beer, carrying his purchases back to their refuge in the labyrinthine corridors of the market. Romayne took charge of the girl, coaxing her to unbutton her blouse and expose a great purple bruise above the prominent collarbone. He noticed that she flushed when her neck and shoulders were bared and he turned aside, taking Soper over to the grille. He said, quietly, "You'll never get a billet after this and you know it. Have you any experience of clerical work?"

"I was a ledger clerk at Patterson's, the wholesalers, soon after I left school."

"Why didn't you stick to book-keeping?"

"I got sacked after asking for a rise. No shindig at Patterson's, just a straight case of Oliver Twist on that occasion. Don't bother about me, Mr. Swann. I'll look out for myself."

He liked Soper's spirit and wry sense of humour. Head-strong he might be but if there were three Sopers in every city emporium the rough-and-ready tactics they had used today would be unnecessary. Real solidarity among the helots was what was needed and it wasn't impossible. It

45

had already been successful in the heavy industries up north. Bargains could be struck between the vast numbers of have-nots and the Gradgrinds in their plush suburban houses. But there were not three Sopers anywhere, much less in a drapery store. More often than not there wasn't one prepared to risk his livelihood for a cause of this kind. He said, "I'll get you a billet with my father's firm. I can tell the truth about you to him. It'll be a fresh start."

"And the Action Group, Mr. Swann?"

"We shall have to work for parliamentary backing. It's not impossible. Other trades have achieved it. What we need is some kind of charter to cover all the retail trades."

"That's looking 'way ahead, isn't it?"

"It's better than this hit-and-miss campaign and I'm going to put my mind to it. Have you got enough money to stay on in your digs for a week or so?"

Soper grinned. "For a month. On credit if need be. The landlady's daughter fancies me and she doesn't know about Miriam."

"Where does Miriam live? She isn't living-in, is she?"

"No. She lives with an aunt in Maida Vale."

"Get her home and let her rest. She'd better show up tomorrow and if she should be questioned tell her to give my wife's name as a reference. We'll say she spent the entire day with us and the janitor is mistaken."

He looked relieved at that, Giles thought, and his estimation of Soper soared another point. "You could get married on the wage my brother George pays his warehouse clerks," he said. "It's above average."

*   *   *

They said little to one another on the way home. The heat in the suburban train was insufferable and everybody in the world seemed to be making his way out of the city. It was only later, when they were standing at the window watching the Jubilee bonfires wink across the Shirley

46

meadows that he said, suddenly, "How much does all this mean to you, Romayne? This house, servants, security, comfort?"

"Why do you ask?"

"It's important I should know. Apart from that brief spell, when you ran away and worked in that sweat-shop, you've always been cushioned against poverty. Like me. Like almost everyone we know. We're really no more than salon revolutionaries and I'm tired of facing two ways. But it wouldn't be fair for me to make the decision alone."

"What decision?"

"To throw up the firm and get myself adopted as a Liberal candidate, if anyone will have me. Then work full-time at what I believe in, what I've always believed in from the beginning."

She turned and looked at him speculatively. "You'd do that? You'd walk out on your father's firm for good?"

"I would. Would you?"

"You know I would."

"It's that important to you?"

"Seeing you spend your life working at something you believe in is important. It doesn't matter what. It never has really."

He bent his head and kissed her. "I haven't the least idea how to go about it, but . . ."

"I have."

"*You* have?"

"I've thought about it a long time now but I didn't say anything. It had to come from you. I think I know how I could get you taken up, with a real chance of getting to Westminster."

"If you're relying on your father he wouldn't lift a finger . . ."

"It's nothing to do with my father. It's an idea I had a long time ago, when we were on holiday in Wales, but don't ask me about it now."

"Why not?"

"Because I have to think about it, about the best way of going about it. Just let me work it out and put it to you when I'm ready."

He thought, distractedly, 'I'll never know her. Not really, not like old George and Alex know their wives and certainly not like my father knows Mother. I know no more about her now than that day I fished her out of that river below Beddgelert, when we were kids. But the devil of it is she knows me. Every last thing about me!'

The long day was almost done. From across the meadows came the faint, meaningless sounds of revelry, persistent celebrants sporting round their bonfires, reluctant to write 'finis' to a day they would talk about all their lives. He said, as they settled under the flimsy bed-coverings, "Our joint resources won't run to more than three hundred a year, if that. We should have to sell up and move to wherever I was chosen. A terrace house or a cottage maybe."

"Three hundred a year is six pounds a week," she said. "People bring up big families on that and there's only two of us. Go to sleep, Giles."

It was a clue, he thought, linking her sponsorship with her apparent inability to bring him a child. In a curious way their relationship had shifted of late, ever since her fourth and last miscarriage. Perhaps she saw him as the only child she was likely to have and was determined, in that queer private way of hers, to make the best of it. His arm went round her but she did not respond, although he could tell she was wide awake. He had a sense then of complete dependence on her and with it a sudden and inexplicable onrush of confidence in the future. Perhaps the day had not been such a failure after all.

3

Bedside Whisper

MOST MEN, ADAM REFLECTED, WERE DIMINISHED by deathbeds, but Sam Rawlinson, his eighty-eight-year-old father-in-law, was clearly an exception. Sam, half-recumbent in a bed that had never been adequate for him, looked so excessively bloated that he made the ugly, over-furnished bedroom seem very cramped for visitors, who were obliged to squeeze themselves between bed and wardrobe and then sit very still for fear of overturning the bedside table littered with Sam's pills and potions.

Adam was surprised to find him not only rational but loquacious, as though, in the final days of his long, bustling life, he was in a rare ferment to get things tidied up and sorted out, and he received Adam almost genially, croaking, "Now, lad!" in that broad Lancashire accent of his he had never attempted to convert into the city squeak that many men of his stamp affected once they had made their pile. Henrietta had already been in with Hilda, Sam's statuesque second wife, who seemed, improbably, to be giving way to the strain of the old man's final battle against odds, the only one, thought Adam, he was certain to lose. She warned Adam, "You'll find him low but he's tetchy with it. He's had me on the jump for more than a month now. Try and keep him off his dratted affairs, will you?"

He climbed the gloomy, paint-scarred staircase, reflecting as he went that no one had ever succeeded in keeping Sam off his affairs, for they had been meat and

49

drink to the old reprobate ever since, as a slum-bred lad in Ancoats in the first years of the cotton boom, he had kicked and throttled his way from coal-sorter, to bale-breaker, to the looms and, at thirty-odd, to part-ownership of his first mill where he worked his hands like galley-slaves. He was already a man of substance when Adam met him, forty years ago, and the fact that Sam still addressed him, at seventy, as 'lad', made him smile. Long, long ago they had come to terms with one another, rarely referring to their first confrontation, when Sam had stormed into the Swann homestead threatening to prefer charges against him of abducting his eighteen-year-old daughter. In view of this understanding they were spared soothing bedside prattle, customary in the circumstances. Adam said, bluntly, "Is there anything special you want doing, Sam?" a clear enough indication to a man as forthright as Rawlinson that time was running out.

"Nay," Sam said, "nowt special, lad, tho' I'm reet glad you've come an' no mistake. Couldn't have said what I'd a mind to say to t'lass. Women don't set a proper value on these things."

"What things, Sam?"

"Brass," Sam said, uncompromisingly, "and what to make of it. Eee, they can spend it fast enough, the least of 'em, but I never met one who could put it to work. Now that lass o' mine, she'll have made sizeable holes in your pockets over the years."

"I'm not complaining," Adam said, "and neither should you with an army of grandchildren, and great-grandchildren to spare. There'll be plenty to share whatever you're inclined to leave."

"That's the rub," Sam said, heaving himself up in an effort to make himself more comfortable in the rumpled bed. "Ah've had second thowts about that. One time I had it in mind to see after our Hilda and split t'rest so many ways. Then Ah got to thinkin'. Most o' the bene-ficiaries wouldn't have a notion what to do with a windfall that came their way, so I went to old Fossdyke and drew up t'new will. Hilda'll pass you a copy of it if you ask her."

He was breathing noisily and his broad, battered face had a deep purple flush, so that Adam said, "We don't have to go over it, Sam. You can trust me to follow your wishes."

"Aye," said Sam, emphatically, "I can that. Come to think of it you're one of the few Ah've always trusted, and there's none so many o' them." He paused, as though reflecting deeply. "I were luckier'n I deserved about you but I've owned to that times enough, haven't I?"

"I've been lucky myself, Sam. What do you want to tell me about your money? That Henrietta is getting the whole of the residue?"

"*Nay*," Sam said, clamping his strong jaws, "she's getting nowt, or not directly. Nor young George either, tho' I still reckon him the flower o' the flock."

It astonished him to hear Sam say this, and with such emphasis. He could understand a man of Sam's temperament fighting shy of splitting his money into so many insignificant packages, thereby making it seem a less impressive total, but he had always believed Henrietta, as Sam's only child, would inherit the bulk of his fortune, and that George, who had been championed by his grandfather when the boy threw everything aside to redesign that petrol waggon he had brought home from Vienna, would come off best among the children.

"What are you going to do with it, Sam? Leave it to charity?"

To judge by his father-in-law's expression the question came close to killing him on the spot. He said, gesturing wildly with his fat, freckled hands, "*Charity?* Sweat bloody guts out for close on eighty years to cosset layabouts who never took jacket off for nobody, 'emselves included? Nay, lad, you can't be that daft! You know me a dam' sight better than that! *Charity!* There's too much bloody charity nowadays! No wonder country's not what it were in my young days, when it were sink or swim. Ah'm leavin' the lot to you, to do as you please with. And it'll amount to something when all's settled up, Ah'm tellin' you!"

"Good God, *I* don't want it, Sam. I'm already the wrong side of seventy, and I've got all the money I'm likely to spend!"

"Aye, I daresay, though a man can always do with a bit more. Besides, it's not as cut an' dried as that, as you'll see if you'll hold your tongue, lad. I've had Skin-a-rabbit Fossdyke make a trust fund in your name. That way you can spread it around whichever way you've a mind, so long as it stays in t'family."

"How do you mean, exactly?"

Sam was silent for a moment or two, seemingly occupied in getting his breath and marshalling his thoughts. Finally, he said, "Put it this way. You and me, we had nowt to begin with, but we each of us finished up with a pile big enow to make men tip their hats to us, didn't we?"

"You could put it that way."

"It's the on'y way to put it. Use that brass o' mine to feed any one o' them lads or lasses who shows my kind o' gumption. And *your* kind of gumption. Any one of 'em, mind, man or maid, who'll stand on their own feet an' look all bloody creation in t'face, same as we have. Do you follow me now?"

It made sense, Sam's kind of sense. Bloated and dying, in an ugly house in a Manchester suburb, Sam Rawlinson obviously looked back over his life with immense satisfaction, hugging his commercial success (the only success worth having in his view) as a just reward for his prodigious and profitable endeavours over the years, thereby earning the respect of all men dedicated to the same object and a man with any other objective was a fool, counting for nothing. He would want to see that money well spent and in a way he would spend it if, by some miracle, his youth and vigour were restored to him at this moment. There was a kind of merciless logic in the gesture, for Sam would restrict the deserving to those who, like himself and his son-in-law, backed themselves against all comers. He said, with a shrug, "Well, you might do worse, Sam. I get the drift of it, and you can rely on me to do it your way. Is that all?"

"Nay," said Sam, "it's not all. Ah've been wanting a word in your ear for long enough. Mebbe I won't get another chance."

Adam waited, but for some moments Sam's gaze remained blank. Then, unexpectedly, he rallied and said, very carefully, "It were about young George. Him and that kiss-your-arse manager he sets such store on. What's the name? Same name as that old maid of a clerk you had down there, before you took it into your head to back out and leave t'lads to run your business."

"You mean Tybalt? Wesley Tybalt, the son of my head clerk?"

"Aye, that's him. I got word he wants watching."

It crossed Adam's mind then, and for the first time since entering the room, that Sam was wandering. Wesley Tybalt, the only child of his old friend in the rough and tumble days, had lately established himself as the most dynamic administrator they had ever had. George himself said so, others echoed his judgment and even his excessively modest father, now retired and devoting himself full-time to his East End mission work, agreed with them. Sam had always been keenly interested in the expansion of Swann-on-Wheels but he had never had anything to do with its day-to-day administration. It seemed extremely improbable that now, at nearly ninety, and a housebound invalid into the bargain, he could have discovered anything of importance about the firm's affairs. Wesley Tybalt had served his time up here, but so had everybody else who held a position of responsibility at Headquarters. It was a Swann rule that promising executives should spend six months in every region before joining the London staff so that Sam might well have met and evaluated Tybalt when he was based in the north. That could hardly account, however, for so direct a warning. He said, sharply, "You'll have to be a damned sight more explicit than that, Sam. I'm out of things now, as you well know. George is gaffer, and Giles is next in line. My other two younger sons, Hugo and Edward, are in the network, but I've never once had reason to suppose George wasn't making a thorough go of it. If there was a flaw in young Tybalt I would have heard about it. One or other of the boys would have told me, and asked my advice, no doubt."

"Not George," Sam said, once again clamping his aggressive jaws like a rat-trap. "George is a loner, as you've good cause to know. Your memory's not that short, lad."

That much at least was true. Ever since taking over George had gone his own way without seeking anyone's advice but the business had prospered under him, despite an occasional misjudgment, like the premature introduction of those mechanical vans some years back. As for young Tybalt, Adam had been prejudiced in his favour a long time now, partly, no doubt, because he had received such unswerving loyalty from his father over a period of thirty years. He had met him often during his visits to the yard, a tall, loose-limbed, toothy young man, with thin sandy hair and an ingratiating manner. Not a boy you could like, perhaps, but one who knew precisely what he was about when he came to having charge of the network's clerical concerns. Every single question Adam had ever put to him concerning stock and trends and routes had prompted a concise and realistic answer. He said, doubtfully, "What put this into your head, Sam? Where did it come from? Has George been up here lately?"

"He came once. A few weeks since, when I was still up and about, but he weren't the same lad as back along. There were no flies on him then but there are now. One in particular, I'd say."

"Who would that be?"

"Nay, I can't swear to that. I could've one time, when I was around to put the ferrets in if I wanted to know

anything partic'lar. But I'll lay long odds it's a woman.
He were dressed to the nines and had his hair smarmed
down and smelling like a garding."

"Did he talk to you about business?"

"Nay, he didn't. And that was what made me sit up
an' take notice, for he alwus had before, whenever he
looked in on me. Like I say, he weren't t'same lad at all,
so I got to talking with one or two of the old uns who
dropped in to pass the time o' day wi' me and I got a hint
or two."

"What kind of hint?"

"That Swann's New Broom was cutting a dash wi' the
quality an' leavin' too much to his clerks. I seen many a
good man go bust that way. So have you, I daresay."

"And young Tybalt. Have you ever met him?"

"Can't say as I have but old Levison has. Come to
think on it Levison was the one who tipped me the wink."

"Who the devil is Levison?"

"Levison and Skilly, big warehousemen, Liverpool way.
Done a deal o' business with 'em in my time but they don't
haul by your line. Their stuff goes south on the cheap with
Linklater's outfit. These things get around. They always
have an' they always will among folk who count."

"What got around, exactly?"

"Nowt to speak of . . . ." He was tiring rapidly and his
breathing became laboured so that Adam thought, 'I
can't press him now, although I'd give something to
know what put that bee in his bonnet.' He rose, massaging
the straps of his artificial leg. "I'll think on it."

Sam said, watching him narrowly. "Bloody memory's
not what it were, dam' it!" He fumbled for his hunter
watch, hanging by its heavy gold chain from the bedrail.
"Time for me green pills," he said, vaguely. "Better fetch
our Hilda up, lad. You'll be staying over a day or so?"

"We're staying at the Midland. Hilda has enough on
her hands, Sam."

"Aye," Sam said, listlessly, "she's a good lass, but she
never did the one thing I expected of her." He rallied

momentarily, glaring the full length of the bed at an atrocious seascape hanging on the far wall. "Ah'd have liked a son to follow on. Hetty's litter is well enough but a lass isn't the same, somehow."

His chin dropped and his thick red lips parted. Adam went out, closing the door softly and calling to Hilda that it was time for Sam's green pills. Hetty asked, handing him a cup, "How did you find him, Adam?"

"Very talkative," Adam said, thoughtfully. "He'll soldier on a bit yet if I'm any judge." And then, as if she had expressed a contrary view, "He's a man of parts, is your father. There aren't many of his sort about nowadays."

"There never were," Henrietta said, "even when I first remember him. That was twelve years before you saw him ride a boy into the ground the night they were burning his mill." Then, in a more conciliatory tone, "Do you suppose he remembers things like that now, Adam? Now that he's dying, I mean?"

"If he does he doesn't regret 'em."

"But . . . shouldn't he? I mean, now that he's going? I'm sure I would. You too."

"That's the difference between us and between the times, too. In Sam's day, in my early days come to that, it was kill or be killed. You can't expect a man reared in a jungle to fall to his prayers in his dotage. Not without his tongue in his cheek that is. He asked me to ask Hilda to show us a copy of his will."

"I don't want his money."

"You're not getting any, m'dear," he said, enjoying her swift change in expression that told him that, in so many ways, and notwithstanding her lifelong disapproval of Sam's ethics, she was still Sam Rawlinson's daughter.

2

He was wrong. Sam died in his sleep three days later and they were obliged to stay on for the funeral. In the interval he had chatted with the old chap several times

but neither made further reference to that curious warning
about the dash George was cutting with the quality or the
dubious reliability of his yard manager, Tybalt. Instead
they talked about old times, and mutual acquaintances in
the cotton world, and Adam was not surprised to see
several of his cronies at the graveside, heavy, unsmiling
men, watching the committal of Sam as though his coffin
contained money as well as a corpse. It was not until the
journey home that Adam re-addressed his mind to the
hints Sam had dropped, turning them over and over as
the train rushed southwards at nearly twice the maximum
speed it had attained when he escorted Henrietta, an
eighteen-year-old bride, on her first journey out of the
north. George was cutting a dash among the quality.
George was taking time off to squire a woman, obviously
not Gisela, his pretty little Austrian wife. George was
leaving too much to his manager and the manager needed
watching. It didn't add up to much and finally he asked,
of Henrietta, who was deep in the *Strand Magazine* he had
bought her at the bookstall, "Is everything all right
between George and Gisela, Hetty?"

She looked up a little irritably. "All right? So far as
I know. Whatever made you ask a question like that?"

"Just something Sam said, but he might well have been
rambling. George was there a few weeks back and looked
in on them. 'Dressed to the nines an' smellin' like a
garding' according to Sam."

"Is that all he said?"

"More or less. He hinted that George was gadding
about and maybe neglecting the business, but I couldn't
make head nor tail of it at the time. Do you see much of
Gisela these days?"

"Not as much as I did but that doesn't signify anything.
She's four children now, and a big house to run." She
prepared to re-address herself to her magazine and he
said, with a grin, "Don't you care that much, Hetty?"

"No," she admitted, frankly. "I can't say as I do.
They're all old enough and ugly enough to watch out

57

for themselves, as my nanny Mrs. Worrell would have said. George in particular, for George has always gone his own way. How old is he now?"

"Thirty-three last February." He had a wonderful memory for trivia but he had a special reason for remembering George's exact age. The boy had been born on St. Valentine's Day, 1864, a day when the fortunes of Swann-on-Wheels, near to foundering at that time, had taken a dramatic turn for the better, paving the way for what Adam always thought of as their *sortie torrentielle* into big business. Because of this, and the boy's temperament, he had always seen George as a good-luck talisman. They had never looked back from that moment, not even when he was away from the yard for a whole year learning to walk on one sound leg and an ugly contraption made up of cork and aluminium.

"Well," she said, "there's your answer. He was always a wild one but Gisela knows how to manage him. You've said so yourself many a time."

"So I have. Go back to that story you're reading. It must be a good one."

"It is," she told him, "it's a Sherlock Holmes," and the conversation lapsed, but he continued to think about it, trying to make a pattern out of the few stray pieces but not succeeding, no matter how many times he fitted one into the other, so he fell to marshalling his recollections on the boy's past.

For years now George had been a slave to that yard, devoting even more time to it than had Adam himself in his early, strenuous days. That much was known about George, not only inside the family and firm but all over the City, where men talked shop over their sherry and coffee. It was hard to imagine George as a masher, a gadabout or even a dandy. He had an eye for the girls, certainly had always had, ever since, as an eighteen-year-old, he was all but seduced by one of the manager's wives up in the Polygon. What was her name again – Lorna? Laura? – Laura Broadbent, that was it, who had

a brute of a husband, a man George had ultimately un-
masked as a thief. It was on account of that he had sent
the boy abroad and he seemed to remember that George
had had a high old time in Paris, Munich and ultimately
Vienna, where he lodged in the house of a carriage-
builder, with four pretty granddaughters. One of them,
Gisela, George had married and not before time, if Adam's
arithmetic was correct.

Since then, so far as he knew, George had never had
time to sow wild oats. For two years or more he had been
besotted by that engine he brought home and after that,
when he had proved his point by actually making the
thing run, he had taken over as gaffer at the yard. The
relationship of father and son, once strong, had weakened
over the years. Since his retirement, eight years ago,
Adam had leaned on Giles harder than any of them, but
he seldom talked shop with Giles. Mostly they discussed
politics and social issues, subjects that interested them
both. As for young Tybalt, he would take a lot of per-
suading that a young fellow in his position would play
fast and loose with his future. Wesley Tybalt came from
exceptionally sober stock, and his father was always on
hand to hold a watching brief. It therefore seemed very
unlikely that a man like Levison, head of a shipping
business in Liverpool, could have heard anything but a
rumour to the contrary, and yet . . . old Sam was certainly no fool when it came to a man's commercial worth.

He recalled then that Levison's firm used a rival haulage
line. Linklater's it was, a tinpot outfit, not regarded by
any big haulier as a serious rival and maybe it was there
he should look for clues. A dispute between Swann-on-
Wheels and Linklater's maybe, in which the latter had
been worsted by young Tybalt or George, or both, and
had gone away with a grudge of some sort? A long shot,
so long that it was hardly worth looking into, especially
as he was supposed to be out of it these days. But he knew
he was not out of it, and would never be out of it. Swann-
on-Wheels had been his life for thirty-odd years. All his

possessions and personal triumphs derived from it and a man could never slough off a burden as big as that, certainly not when his own kin were carrying it forward into the new century.

He was glad then that he had arranged for Hetty to travel home while he stayed a night in town to view a furniture sale at Sotheby's. Some choice pieces were coming up, part of the collection of Sir Joseph Souter, and he rarely missed an important furniture, picture or porcelain sale these days. They filled the vacuum caused by his exchange of the roles of haulier and connoisseur. He would drop in at the yard after the viewing, and have a word with both George and Tybalt, scratching around for confirmation of Sam's hints if any was to be found. And having decided this he made his mind a blank, as he had trained himself to do over so many tedious train journeys in the past. In seconds he was asleep.

3

He stood with his back to the familiar curve of the Thames looking the width of Tooley Street at the sprawling rectangle that had been the heart and pulse of his empire since he came here in the steamy summer of '58. A jumble of sheds, lofts and stables, crouched around the slender belfry tower, all that remained of the medieval convent that had once occupied the site. When the Plantagenets had used that bridge, the tower had doubtless summoned a few dozen nuns to prayer. During his long tenure up there it had overseen hauls the length and breadth of the island, a lookout post from which, in a sense, he could see the Cheviots and the Cornish moors, the Welsh mountains running down to the Irish Sea and the fenlands that drained into the German Ocean.

A slum, his wife and customers called it, and technically it was, pallisaded by a tannery, a glue factory, a biscuit factory, a huddle of tiny yellow-brick dwellings and the grey-brown tideway where a thousand years of South

Bank sewage had hardened into a belt of sludge, making its unique contribution to an overall smell of industry that he never noticed, not even now, after he had been inhaling the furze and heather scents of the Weald throughout years of lazy-daisy idleness. He knew every cranny of the enclosure and loved what he knew, seeing it as the powerhouse of the four clamorous tribes that had used this tideway as a base to conquer half the world. Not with sabres and muzzle-loaders like traditional conquerors (although the British had resorted to these times enough) but latterly with merchandise, spewed from their clattering machines and the gold that poured into these few square miles of avarice, expertise and grimed splendour.

He was proud of his contribution, although he would never admit it, not even to his intimates. It was a pride he kept locked away in his big body and restless brain, to be taken out and contemplated at moments like this when he thought, vaingloriously: 'All the others had a part in it. Josh Avery, who traded it all for a Spanish whore; Keate, the waggonmaster and Tybalt the clerk, whose hearts were in piling up credit in heaven; that foul-mouthed old rascal Blubb, who pulled us out of that shambles at Staplehurst and died doing it; Lovell, the erudite Welshman; Ratcliffe, the Westcountry clown and all the other viceroys. *But it was me who created it and set it in motion.* And "the fruit of my loins", as old Keate would put it, are keeping it rolling to this day.'

He crossed the road and entered the open gate that led to the weighbridge and the weighbridge clerk jumped off his perch, giving him the quasi-military salute all the veterans reserved for him after it got about that he had seen the Light Brigade go down at Balaclava, and later helped Lord Roberts, the nation's darling, to empty that stinking well at Cawnpore. The clerk said, "Afternoon, Mr. Swann. We don't often see you nowadays," and he replied, jovially, "No, Rigby. I was seventy this month and I make damned sure you don't! Is Mr. George in his office?"

"No, sir, I think not. Can't be sure, sir, but I think he's off in the regions somewhere. Mr. Tybalt'll know."

"Thank you, Rigby."

He had a continuing liking for the older men, still seen about the yard but falling away year by year now that younger ones were pushing from behind. Lockhart, the master smith was one, directing his four journeymen and three apprentices at the glowing forge. Bixley, the night watchman was another, but he wouldn't show up for an hour or so. Everyone, old and young, greeted him respectfully and it occurred to him that they still thought of him as the real gaffer, despite the New Broom's many innovations, of which there was evidence everywhere in enlarged warehouses, a new exit in Tower Street, the new clerical block where the old wooden stables had stood, now replaced by the red-brick building running the full length of the north side.

His own quarters in the tower were used as a lumber room now and he climbed the narrow, curving staircase, to find the queer octagonal room strewn with crates, sacks and discarded harness, its narrow window, where he had watched many sunsets and not a few dawns opaque with dust and grime. He took a piece of sacking and rubbed a pane, catching a glimpse of the Conqueror's Tower on the far bank and the swirl of river traffic east of the bridge. It was still as heavy and continuous, a never-ending stream of barges and wherries skimming down to the docks where funnels outnumbered masts by about two to one. It made him feel old and lonely up here among debris that was not his any more and he stumped down into the open again, pausing to examine a heavy double padlock on one of the last original warehouses, with its own exit into Tooley Street.

In his day they never locked warehouses in the daytime and he wondered whether this was the result of one of George's edicts, or whether the place contained a particularly valuable consignment. He hoisted himself up on a baulk of timber and glanced through the grilled window but all he could see in the gloom beyond was a tall stack of packaged cotton goods, awaiting shipment to Madras or Calcutta, no doubt. A polite voice at his elbow startled him a little.

"Can I be of service, Mr. Swann?"

He turned, stepped down and faced Wesley Tybalt, sleek and tidy as a solicitor's clerk in his dark, waisted frock coat and high cravat stuck with a gold pin. 'George must pay the fellow well to enable him to dress like that,' he thought, remembering that Tybalt's father had always worked coatless with slip-on sleeves to spare his shirt-cuffs, but he said, casually, "No, no, Tybalt, I was only poking about, taking in all the changes you've made. What's in there, for instance?"

Wesley said, very civilly, "Long-term storage, sir. We've taken to locking the warehouses that aren't in daily use. We had an epidemic of pilfering last year. Mr. George thought it a good idea, sir."

"It is," Adam said. And then, "Do you get much yard pilfering these days? In my time it was limited to waggons making overnight stops."

"We've put a stop to it, sir. No reported case since just before Christmas and then we nailed our man. He's doing two years' hard, I'm glad to say. Can I offer you tea in my office, Mr. Swann?"

"No, thank you," Adam said, wondering what it was about the fellow he didn't like, and asking himself why he found himself making an unfavourable comparison between the spruce Wesley and his fussy little father. "I'm catching the five-ten from London Bridge and merely looked in to have a word with Mr. George. The weighbridge clerk said he was away in the regions."

"Yes, sir, that's so. Since the weekend, sir."

"Do you know where, exactly?"

"Er . . . no, sir, or not since he moved on into Central. He'll let me know, however. He always wires or telephones in when he's away. Any message, sir?"

"No, no message. You'll give my regards to your father when you see him?"

"Certainly, sir. But I don't see a great deal of him now. I moved out to Annerley when I married."

"How often do you see him?"

"Oh, whenever he looks in, sir. Are you sure you won't take tea, sir?"

"Quite sure, thank you. Haven't all that much time," and he drifted off, wondering whether the crumb or two he had picked up during the brief exchange had any significance outside his imagination. There had been that split second hesitation concerning George's whereabouts, and a defensive narrowing of sandy eyebrows when he asked about the pilfering. Nothing much, certainly nothing to justify Sam's comment that Wesley Tybalt wanted watching. All it might mean was that he was covering up for George's philandering and that spelt loyalty of a sort. There was the swanky way the chap dressed, an impression that he considered he had hoisted himself a niche or two above his Bible-punching father, and one other thing that might or might not have significance, the fact that Wesley watched his progress the whole way across the yard to the gate and only slipped out of sight when he stopped to speak to the weighbridge clerk on the way out.

"Are we busy, Rigby?"

"On the jump, sir. Things slacked off during the celebrations but they've picked up since."

He put a spot question, striving to make it sound offhand. "Do we sub-contract to that northcountry haulier, Linklater? I came across him in the old Polygon this week."

"Linklater? No, sir. We used to but they've got their own yard in Rotherhithe now."

"Ah. Well, good day to you, Rigby."

"Good day, Mr. Swann," and he left, stumping slowly down Tooley Street in the direction of the river but stopping opposite what had once been his favourite coffee stall, run by an ex-cavalryman with a long, facial scar, acquired, so he said, serving with the 9th Lancers, known as the Delhi Spearmen after their fine performance in the Mutiny.

He crossed over and ordered a cup of coffee for old times' sake and Travis, the proprietor, greeted him with enthusiasm. "My stars, it's time enough since you looked in, Mr. Swann, sir! Alwus reckoned you was my most reg'lar earlybird in the old days."

"I've taken to lying in at my time o' life, Travis," he said, recalling how often he used to stand there sniffing the early morning tideway reek after an all-night session in his tower. And then, seeing the barred entrance to the yard a few strides up the street, a freak line of enquiry occurred to him and he added, "Did that new exit improve your trade, Travis? I would have thought carters coming and going there would have been your regulars seeing there are two coffee stalls nearer the main gate."

"I thought it would but it didn't," Travis said. "They don't use it during the day, tho' vans call in for stuff night-times now and again."

"Light traffic?"

"All kinds but not your waggons. Stuff you've hauled into town for local carriers. I see one o' Gibson's beer drays waiting there one evening last week. And on'y last night a Linklater two-horse took a load aboard. Short run hauls, they'd be and short-haulers were never much good to me, sir. My best reg'lars were the chaps who had been hauling long-distance and were dam' sharpset by the time they got here. I do see Mr. Hugo from time to time. You must be right proud of him, sir."

He forced his mind away from the disturbing knowledge that one of Linklater's vehicles had been here within the last few hours, despite the weighbridge clerk's assurance that their sub-contract work had fallen off since they opened their own yard at Rotherhithe nearer the docks, and contemplated the new Englishman's obsessive interest in sport. A man like Travis, he supposed, would see

Hugo as the superior product of a commercial family. In his own youth railway kings and engineers had been the popular idols. Now reverence was reserved for muscular oafs who could break track records, kick footballs from one end of the field to the other and hit cricket balls for six. He said, "Ah, Hugo, he's the best free advertisement Swann-on-Wheels ever had, or so my other sons tell me," and finishing his coffee moved off towards the station, his mind still occupied assembling the fragments of information his visit had accumulated.

They were beginning to multiply. George's unexplained absence; Wesley Tybalt's defensive manner; a new gate that wasn't used during the day, although it opened directly on that padlocked warehouse; the weighbridge clerk's ignorance that Swann was still subcontracting for the firm of Linklater, the original source of Sam's information that 'young Tybalt wanted watching'.

It made no sense any of it and he supposed, in the end, he would have to come right out with his suspicions, if his vague uneasiness justified the word, and ask George whether, in his view, there was anything worth investigating. But then another thought occurred to him and he wondered whether, in the circumstances, George was the right one to approach. George might be reticent about his own frequent excursions into the provinces, and almost surely resentful if neglect of duty was implied. What was needed was more detailed information concerning George's alleged 'gadding about', and how much reliance he placed, in his absence, in Wesley Tybalt. The obvious source concerning the first was Gisela, George's wife. As regards Wesley, Tybalt senior would be worth a visit, especially as, according to his son, he called in at the yard from time to time.

He caught his train and settled grumpily into a corner, watching the evening light play tricks with the smoky labyrinth down there under the ugly complex of bridges and viaducts and telling himself that he was an ass, at his time of life, to bother himself with what was amiss, if anything, with the network. He had pledged himself long ago to leave all the worrying to his successors and so far he had honoured that pledge, occupying himself with landscaping and collecting down there in the fresh air. It had kept him out of mischief for years now, and doubtless prolonged his active life, but he began to understand, for the first time since his retirement, that it was really no more than a substitute, and a poor one at that. His real ego, all that he was as a man and creator, had gone into the network, and the merest hint that it was threatened roused him like a man menaced in his sleep. George had made one bloomer over the introduction of those petrol-driven waggons and a dog was allowed one bite, so they said. But not two and not at the vitals of Adam Swann's lifework. Not if he could help it, by God!

4

He had always been a man of action, compelled to put theories to the test at once and after no more than cursory contemplation, so that anyone who knew him would not have been surprised at his decision to leave the train when it stopped at Petts Wood, on the way to Bromley. George had set Gisela up in a fine house here, where the south-eastern spread of the metropolis had petered out and the countryside was still unspoiled. It was a more convenient base than his own, deep in the Weald, and miles from the nearest station. The train service was excellent and George could be in the yard within thirty minutes of quitting his doorstep.

He took a four-wheeler to the cul-de-sac where George's windows looked out over a spread of arable fields and birch coppices, enjoying the prospect of surprising Gisela, for, although a foreigner, she had always ranked as his favourite in-law. She represented nearly all that Adam expected of a wife, concerning herself exclusively with home and children, and making no attempt to fashion her husband into the Galahad brides-in-waiting dreamed about before they had their corners rubbed off. He had never had the least doubt but that she loved his boy dearly, and both he and Henrietta had taken to her the moment she stepped ashore from the Dover packet all those years ago, soon after George confounded them with the news that he was married.

They had four children now, the eldest, Max, aged eleven, the youngest a rosy little bundle born last year and christened Henrietta, just as the third child, Adam, had been named for him. The stamp of the Continent lay heavily on this branch of the family. All the boys favoured their mother, with hardly a trace of their Anglo-Saxon father. Their manners were impeccable and their approach to him reverential. Like their mother, they used the word 'Grandfather' as though it were a title. He had no doubt but that one or more of them would prove a useful addition to the firm in the new century, for they already showed signs of that Teutonic application that had made the Germans Britain's nearest rivals in trade and industry.

The house, taken over from a failed speculator (George had a nose for failures and the bargains that went along with them) stood in its own grounds and was comfortably furnished, although its decor was too Germanic for his taste. Gisela was delighted to see him and pouted when he told her he was only stopping off on his way home, that Henrietta expected him at dusk, and that he was keeping the cab. "I only looked in to find out where I could locate George," he said. "I tried the yard but he's away off somewhere. When do you expect him back, my dear?"

She said, dutifully, that she could never predict George's comings and goings. Sometimes days passed before he turned up, his arms full of gifts for the children. "He spoils them," she added. "It is not good, and I tell him so often. He is very busy just now, yes?"

"It seems so," he said, "but no matter how busy a gaffer he is he shouldn't cut himself off from his base.

Tybalt senior always knew where to find me, even if Henrietta didn't. I was told he had been in the Midlands."

She turned away suddenly, so abruptly indeed that she gave herself away, for his sharp eye caught the droop of the lip. She said, with a shrug, "Then perhaps it is not business this time. Perhaps it is that woman!" He was so taken aback at her frankness that he gasped.

"George keeps a woman?"

"I do not think that he keeps her. I believe she has a rich husband."

"God bless my soul! He's told you about her?"

She turned and studied him with an expression that could have been mistaken for one of patronage. She was flushed, certainly, but he would have said that was due to irritation rather than embarrassment. Irritation not with him but with the entire British race, whose approach to this kind of thing continued to baffle her after years this side of the Channel. "George has told me nothing. How could he, being English, and brought up as an English gentleman?"

"Then how . . . I mean . . . are you telling me he doesn't love you any more? You and the children? '

The pink flush deepened. "I cannot say as to that, Grandfather. He is very fond of the children and spoils them as I said. But there are two kinds of mistresses, are there not? One is a . . . how would you put it? – a toy, he will soon discard. The other is a substitute for a wife put aside, yet without losing her rights." She paused, concentrating hard. "Perhaps 'rights' is not the word. Would 'status' be more exact?"

"Who gives a damn about that?" he burst out. "I heard he had taken to gadding about. The rumour had reached as far as his grandfather, up in Manchester, so it follows I'm probably the last to hear he's off the rails! How does that come about? Why the devil didn't you come to me or the boy's mother? We could have straightened him out. We always have before."

She said, considerately, "Please sit down, Grandfather.

It is not good that you should become so excited over something that is perhaps of small importance."

He sat down, hypnotised by her placidity. 'It's too long since I crossed the Channel,' he thought. 'Here I am, looking at everything through English eyes,' but said, with a lift of his hand, "I don't understand how any woman in your position can take that view, Gisela. George has no right to treat you in this way. His mother would be outraged."

"Then do not tell her, Grandfather."

"I'm not sure I will. I should have to think about it. But I'll tell you this. Whoever she is that woman is making nonsense of his responsibilities at the yard and that's important. To me at all events. It's what brought me here in the first place!" He was rewarded by a frown on the girl's pleasant features, as though he had found a chink in her complacency.

"Ach, that is not good," she said. "You are sure of it?"

"I'm sure of it. Who is this woman? Do you know her? Have you met her?"

"Wait," and she got up, crossing to a huge bureau bookcase that occupied most of the south wall, an item of furniture that he would have thrown out as a baroque monstrosity, better left in Central Europe where it originated. She opened a drawer, rummaged there and returned carrying a copy of *The Illustrated London News*, open at a page of social gossip. There was an illustration of a meet of the Quorn, featuring half-a-dozen celebrities and hangers-on, guzzling their stirrup cup. There was only one woman in the group, a handsome wench with what he recognised as a first-class seat. The caption below told him she was Lady Barbara Lockerbie, wife of the well-known Scottish industrialist, Sir James Lockerbie, 'An exceptionally able horsewoman, whom readers will recall excels not only in the hunting field but in the pursuit of winter sports.'

"If he hasn't told you about her how can you be so sure?" he demanded, returning the magazine and this time she smiled. "George is not a good liar, Grandfather. And I am not a fool."

He decided not to press the point and take her word for it, racking his brains for anything specific he might remember about James Lockerbie, who had bought his Scottish title, they said, with a sizeable contribution to Scottish Liberal Party funds when they were in low water after the last election. He knew nothing at all of his wife, save that she was obviously half his age, for Lockerbie had been prosperous in the days before Swann-on-Wheels surged over the border to capture the Lowlands trade. He made, if he remembered rightly, sanitary units, designed by that slightly risible genius, Thomas Crapper, supreme in the field of water-closets. It all added up to a very bad joke and the taste in his mouth was so sour that he rose abruptly, saying, "You leave this to me, Gisela. When he shows up don't tell him I've been here, do you hear?" But then, recollecting her pronunciation on the two types of women who lead husbands astray, he said, "What do *you* think about her? I mean, is it a passing fancy, or is it something more serious?"

"Ah, I am not qualified to tell you that yet, Grandfather. It began only last March, when he met this woman at the launching of his first trading vessel in Scotland. It is still only July, is it not?"

"But you must have some idea."

She said, pacing slowly across to the window, "All I can tell you is this. When George came to us, as a young man at Essling, he was very gay and nothing mattered to him. Nothing but laughter and picnics and kissing the girls. My sisters, Sophie, Valerie and Gilda, they were his companions at that time, without a serious thought in their silly heads. But then George became interested in Grandfather Maximilien's invention. It changed him. After that, when Grandfather was stricken, he stopped being a boy and we married and he brought me here, as you remember?"

"I remember. You and that damned engine."

"You put him to work, and he pleased you very much, I think. But later you quarrelled over the engine and we went to Manchester to live."

"I remember it all very well. What's all that got to do with George gadding off with the wife of one of his best customers?"

"It has everything to do with it. George has been hard at work for thirteen years. You have a saying for it, 'Nose to the milestone'."

" 'Grindstone'."

"Ah, so. Perhaps he thought it was time to laugh again before he grew old. The way he laughed when he first came to Vienna."

"But he's thirty-three now, and has a wife, four children and a damned great business to watch over. Why can't he do his laughing at home?"

She was still holding the magazine and glanced at it. "Husbands are not horses," she said, so gravely that he suddenly felt like laughing himself. "That horse she is sitting so well was a colt once but somebody took it and trained it and broke it to the bridle. You cannot do that with men like George. One day, for a little time, they will want to frisk again and it is better to let them. At least until they are tired."

He thought, grimly, 'I never did underestimate her. She's got her head screwed on and no mistake . . . !' He said, kissing her, "You're very wise, my dear. I was always fond of you but never more so than now. Would you like me to handle this my way, so long as I keep in mind what you just said?"

"You do what you think is right, Grandfather. George has no right to neglect the business you gave him so generously. As for me, you must understand it is a matter of waiting."

"I understand that," he said, "and I'll promise you something into the bargain. This is between you, me and George, and I'll make damned sure I tread warily, and that he never discovers we confided in one another. Will you bring the children over on Saturday and stay until Monday?"

"Thank you but no," she said, "I would not like George to return to a house empty of everyone but the servants."

She showed him the door and the cabby hastened to settle him comfortably, but he brushed him aside impatiently. "Catch that nine-ten to Bromley and I'll tip you a florin. Miss it and it'll be sixpence."

Suddenly he felt his years.

4

Reconnaissance

As a tactician Adam Swann was decisive, seeing what required to be done and doing it without preamble. As a strategist, working on a long-term plan, he could be both cautious and diabolically tenacious.

In his army days he had a reputation among senior officers as a good man to send out on reconnaissance. His eye seldom missed much of importance. His sketch-maps were models of neatness and accuracy, and it was much the same in the world of commerce. Before he cashed in a looted necklace of rubies, representing his entire working capital, he rode the full length of England, making meticulous notes on local industries, road and railway communications, terrain and a hundred and one other things likely to be invaluable to a haulier. His eye for detail was excellent and his memory phenomenal. He had a few sound precepts from which he never departed and one of these precepts was 'Know your enemy'.

Thus, on returning to 'Tryst' in the first days of July, 1897, he took no immediate action but continued to probe, using his personal contacts, his treasury of social and industrial trivia, and his library of reference books, to follow up his two definite leads, one heading for Barbara Lockerbie, the other concerned with the haulier, Linklater, currently using the Tooley Street exit of the yard to load goods stacked in one of his warehouses. Ten days elapsed before he was satisfied that he had learned all he was likely to learn concerning both.

Barbara Lockerbie was a high-class whore, who had emerged from obscurity with no capital beyond undeniable physical attractions and ruthless self-interest, deploying both to capture a rich and presumably excessively tolerant husband, then lead the kind of life that a selective harlot of her kind found agreeable. That is to say, to spend around three thousand a year on clothes, to stay looking young, to go everywhere, see everything and, more important, to be seen by everyone. She had reached Sir James and his fortune via one husband and many lovers. Even the Prince of Wales was rumoured to be numbered among her admirers but that Adam discounted, reasoning that if half the charmers reputed to have shared a bed with Edward had enjoyed his patronage, Edward would have declined years ago, as enfeebled as a Sultan of Turkey reared in a harem.

Her first husband was an architect and her abandonment of him had led to a soon-forgotten scandal, the poor devil having thrown himself under a train at Liverpool Station soon after her desertion. The woman, he decided, was lethal, and his appraisal of her steeled him to take swift intervention to head off possible disaster, even though he doubted whether the hardheaded George was the type of man who would ruin himself over a woman, no matter how much he was besotted by her. You could never tell, however, in situations of this kind. Avery, his former partner, had been cynical and world-weary at forty, and an experienced roué into the bargain, yet he had sacrificed everything he possessed, and ultimately laid himself open to a charge of double murder, in order to spend himself between the legs of a Spanish music-hall artiste. Adam even recalled his self-justification when they met for the last time, a few hours before he smuggled the idiot out of the country. He had asked, "Have you ever been sexually enslaved?" and when Adam said he had not, "It happens. It happens to the cockiest of us. Take care it doesn't happen to you, Adam . . . A man can turn a blind corner as I did when I first took Esmerelda to bed . . ."

Avery was surely an object lesson for, like him, George's weakness had always been women. He wished he knew more of George's early life in those days when the boy had been opening oysters in the network and on the Continent. The character of Gisela was no real guide to his taste. A man seldom married the kind of woman who could bring him ecstasy, plus a brief escape from care and responsibility. Usually he looked about for something more maternal and mature.

His investigations into Linklater's, the carriers, were more positive. They were a relatively small firm, dealing mostly in sub-contract work, but currently expanding. They had a fleet of about three hundred waggons and bases in a few of the big manufacturing cities in the North and Midlands. Starr, Linklater's partner and son-in-law, had a dubious reputation in the trade. There had been a lawsuit some years back, concerned with the loss of a valuable consignment of agricultural machinery, and Starr emerged from it technically innocent but with his reputation tarnished. The discrepancy between the comments of the weighbridge clerk and those of the coffee-stall proprietor continued to puzzle him, and he decided that it was here he must resume his investigations and that it must be done with delicacy.

George was back at work now, no doubt, albeit temporarily, and a direct approach in the circumstances seemed inadvisable, precluding another visit to the yard. He could have questioned one or other of George's brothers, notably Giles, who was close to him, but he rejected this as putting too much strain on family loyalty. After turning the matter over in his mind he decided his best course was to approach Tybalt senior, who could make innocent enquiries on his behalf, not only about Linklater's, but also concerning the relationship of his son and George, how often George was absent and for how long at a stretch, and maybe the precise function of that padlocked warehouse on the east side of the yard. He told Henrietta that he was going up to town for a day or so to attend sales and she accepted the excuse without question. His only excursions these days were concerned with landscaping and collecting.

He packed a bag and set off for old Tybalt's terrace house in Rotherhithe, where he busied himself with mission work, in company with his lifelong friend, the former waggonmaster, Saul Keate. Tybalt received him rapturously. He had always seen Adam as the temporal equivalent of his nightshirted Jehovah, for whom he was at pains to rescue fallen women, alcoholics and destitute children. His dedicated service to Swann, over a period of some thirty-five years, he regarded as tribute to Caesar, sanctioned in the Good Book, and Adam, while mindful of his idiosyncrasies, held him in high esteem, for he had brought tremendous devotion to his job as chief clerk, sometimes sitting up half the night to trace a missing sovereign or run down a mislaid invoice. He was a small, undistinguished-looking man with a round bald head and huge trusting eyes that blinked nervously behind spectacles. He almost dragged Adam into his house, demonstrating such enthusiasm that it made initial enquiries somewhat embarrassing, until Adam confessed that he was worried about the immediate future of the firm.

That stopped his fussing. He said, looking almost agonised, "Worried, Mr. Swann? But surely there's no need . . . I mean, all the information I have is that we're booming along, positively booming along!"

"Oh, I daresay we are from an outsider's standpoint, and you and I are numbered among the outsiders these days. Financially the firm is sound enough, I can assure you of that. No, it's more specific. You might say a family matter, to do with my son George, as a matter of fact."

Tybalt still looked grave but his concern moderated. "You're telling me Mr. George is trying to re-introduce those mechanical waggons?"

"I wish he was. That at least would indicate he was still absorbed. The fact is, Tybalt, he's fancying himself as the man about town and, to my mind at least, neglecting his responsibilities as gaffer down there."

"I'm very surprised indeed to hear that," said Tybalt, and looked it. "I always thought him . . . well . . . forgive me, Mr. Swann, a bit too go-ahead . . . and, how shall I put it? Experimental? But he's always struck me as a young man with a very astute head on his shoulders, and an absorbing interest in the work."

"Me too," Adam said, "but he's falling off, or so I'm told, from a very reliable quarter."

Tybalt looked evasive and twiddled his neat penman's hands. "I . . . er . . . I earnestly hope that source isn't my boy Wesley, sir. Oh, I know Wesley is very dedicated to the firm, but I wouldn't like to think he's been talebearing. At least, not without seeking my advice first."

"How often does he seek your advice, Tybalt?"

Tybalt looked down at the plush tablecloth, stacked with buff envelopes he had been addressing to mission subscribers. "I'll be as frank as you've been, Mr. Swann. Not nearly as often as I should like. Hardly ever, in fact, since he came in from the regions, and Mr. George appointed him in my place." He paused and Adam looked away. It went against the grain not to take Tybalt into his full confidence but what proof had he got, or was likely to get, that Wesley, in Sam's quaint phrase, 'needed watching'? Time enough if proof turned up. It would likely break the old chap's heart.

But Tybalt went on, with difficulty, "Mind, I don't complain, not really. Wesley's twenty-eight now, and holding an important position in the firm. He's married too, and feeling his feet, I daresay. The truth is, Mr. Swann, all these young people tend to regard our kind as silly old buffers, with old-fashioned notions as to how a business should be conducted. Have you been into the clerical department lately?"

"No."

"You'd be astounded, I think. It isn't at all like it was, not even when I retired, a mere three years since. They've got two of those telephones now, an automatic letter-copying machine, and three young women clacking away at typewriters. I've even seen a little horse-play there when I've looked in, and Wesley has been out and about. I never did approve of young women going out to business. It must present a great moral temptation, even to girls properly brought up."

"Tybalt," Adam said, hiding his smile, "I'm not talking about new business equipment. Or even about a kiss and a cuddle between a clerk and a typewriter operator. I've been given a hint that there's some well-organised hanky-panky going on down there, and the only clue I can give you is that it's centred on that warehouse on the east side, the one they keep locked, even during the day. That, and the exit behind it into Tooley Street, another innovation since our day."

"Er . . . could you be a little more precise, sir?" asked Tybalt, wringing his hands, and Adam said no, he couldn't, because he didn't know anything more, save that the firm of Linklater might be implicated, and he repeated Sam's remark as to his source and the discrepancy between the testimony of the weighbridge clerk and the observations of Travis, the coffee-stall tender. As he expected Tybalt made very little of it. "I'd trust the clerk," he said, "he's one of the old hands. I think that other man must have been mistaken. I knew about the exit, of course, and the padlocking of the doors, but I think you'll find we haven't done business with Linklater for some considerable time."

"Can you swear to that?"

"Well, sir, how could I? It's three years since I handled ledgers and invoices. But Wesley could tell me on the spot."

Adam said, carefully, "I'm not sure that's the right way to go about it, Tybalt."

"Why not?"

79

"Because it implies loss of confidence on my part. Wesley would know I've asked you to make enquiries and I had my own chance to do that when I was there, less than a fortnight ago. I didn't take it because . . . well, because I've got a suspicion that both your son and mine are being systematically hoodwinked by trained thieves, men actually serving in the yard. Wesley told me they had had an outbreak of pilfering but my guess is they only nailed the small fry." He took a deep breath. "Will you do something else for me, Tybalt? Something you might find a little distasteful?"

"I'd do anything for Swann-on-Wheels. You surely know that, sir."

"Yes, I do, but it isn't all that difficult. I'd like you to drift into the yard on some pretext and keep your eyes open. Make it around six, when the clerks are in a rush to be off, and you can get a look at the day-book without anyone knowing. They won't mind leaving you in there. Would you do that, without consulting Wesley? I've a reason for it."

Tybalt said, diffidently, "I think I should know the reason, Mr. Swann. The boy means everything to me now his mother's been taken. We only had the one chick."

"Well, it's very simple. My impression is that Wesley and George are very close, as close as you and Keate and I were in the old days. He'd regard it as his duty to warn George that I was about to pull him up for playing the fool and George is sharp enough to set matters right before I can get at him. What I'm really saying is, I don't want to be left with half a case. If I challenge him I've got to be able to quote an actual instance of neglect on his part and I think I can do it. Does that satisfy you?"

"Perfectly," said Tybalt, and came as close to winking as Adam recalled in their long association. "It isn't easy to show them a pint of experience is worth a quart of enthusiasm, is it, sir?"

"No, but neither is it impossible, Tybalt."

They talked on awhile about old times but when he left

Tybalt he did so gladly. In a way, he supposed, he was cheating the man but there was no alternative so far as he could see. Sooner or later Tybalt might have to face up to the fact that Wesley was either an idiot, being gulled by his own underlings, or was himself a skilful thief.

*   *   *

It was four-thirty when he left Rotherhithe, finding a cab in Jamaica Road and clip-clopping along the familiar South Bank that had so many lively memories for him. It was here he had walked with the giant waggonmaster, Keate, in search of Thameside waifs, whom Keate later recruited as vanboys and a happy notion that had been too. At least a dozen of the gamins, dredged from the mud, had gone on to hold responsible positions in the firm. One had become a regional manager and was still entrenched in what had been, in his time, the Southern Square, and recalling that Rookwood was now a man of substance, with a grown family of his own, nostalgia assailed him. He thought, 'I told myself I could slough it off when I marched out, and left George and the others to get on with it, but it's not so easy as all that. There's something to be said for taking one's ease but I miss the rough and tumble of life down here in the thick of it.' And in a curious way he felt grateful to George and Wesley Tybalt for drawing him back into the swirl of the enterprise.

The cab dropped him off at his hotel in Norfolk Street, the Strand, and he went up to his room with the evening papers, wondering how he would pass the time while Tybalt did his probing.

The city editors, after a surfeit of national junketing, seemed to be turning their attention to the outside world again. One had almost forgotten its existence this last month and it was now seen to be in its customary turmoil. There was trouble in the Balkans again. Germany was yelping over the murder of two of her missionaries in

China. France and Russia were getting together, with a view to giving Kaiser Wilhelm something to worry about. The Americans were slamming high tariffs on imports, in order to stimulate their own industries. They were a restless, quarrelsome lot, with no clearly defined purpose, of the kind that had brought Britain to the fore-front, that unwavering conspiracy among homebased men of affairs to make money and let politics take care of them-selves. Germany had the commercial potential and if she concentrated on trade, instead of trying to get herself elected bully of Europe, she could soon learn the tricks of underselling her competitors. That was the source of real power, not a rabble of clockwork soldiers marching here, there and everywhere, like overgrown children. But they would never learn, or not while that grandson of Old Vic was in charge, insisting that everybody referred to him as The All-Highest.

He turned, impatiently, to the inside pages, where a domestic item caught his eye. Trunk telephone wires were being transferred to the General Post Office, a sure sign that the contrivance Tybalt had spoken of slightingly was now generally accepted and would soon, he supposed, link every business concern in the country and perhaps, given time, every home as well. He hadn't installed a telephone at 'Tryst'. With half-a-dozen servants to run his errands, and the telegraph system in the village, it hadn't seemed necessary, but perhaps Henrietta might like to think about it, if only to gossip to her friends about her interminable round of fêtes and croquet parties.

On the following page was a news item of more relevance to him, a debate on the Employers' Liability Bill, aimed at making hirers of labour responsible for injuries and compensation to men injured on their premises during working hours. He wondered if George had given any thought to it. Swann-on-Wheels had its own provident scheme covering this contingency, a measure he had introduced years ago, so that once again he saw himself as a pioneer and preened himself a little as he shaved and changed for dinner. They would all come round to it in time – that precept of his that a man's profits were directly related to the way he treated his work force – but for years most city men had regarded him as an eccentric and a radical in this respect. You never got much out of men you regarded as animated tools of the trade. You had to isolate them as individuals, and invest them with some kind of dignity, and Giles had seen to it that his well-defined policy in this respect had survived his father's retirement.

He thought about Giles for a moment, asking himself if the boy found fulfilment in his job at the yard and deciding, not for the first time, that he hadn't, and probably regarded his post there as a stop-gap. Not that it was, of course. He was a necessary counterpoise to George, his ideas equating more with Adam's own than with any of his brothers. 'I should have made a parson out of him,' he thought, 'for money doesn't interest him and never will. He's always seen himself as some kind of standard-bearer and standard-bearers need a sound organisation at their backs if they are to survive.'

Thus ruminating, and in a relaxed frame of mind considering his purpose here in town, he took a constitutional along the new embankment, winked up at Boadicea's statue, wondered again at the incongruity of Cleopatra's Needle, returned to the hotel for a nightcap and finally toddled off to bed. Tybalt might well draw a blank at the yard tonight and, in any case, he was very unlikely to report in until tomorrow. It would be interesting, to say the least, to learn if the old chap had uncovered anything about Linklater's.

He already had his nightshirt on, and was in the act of opening the window to get a breath of riverside air, when somebody rapped at his door and he called, gruffly, "Who is it?"

"Me, Mr. Swann! Tybalt! Could I have a word with you, sir?"

He opened the door and the clerk was on the threshold,

looking, Adam thought, as though he had met a headless spectre in the corridor.

"I was just going to bed. I didn't expect you tonight, man!"

"I'm sorry, sir, but I didn't feel I could leave it. Might I . . . might I step in, sir?"

"Of course. You look about done. Would you like me to ring for a drink?"

"No, Mr. Swann . . . no drink, thank you . . . but I had to see you and came as quickly as I could. I did what you asked, I went down to the yard tonight. It was a few minutes to six and everyone was leaving. I said I'd lock up and give the keys to the watchman as usual, so I had the place to myself."

"Well?"

"You were right. There is something queer going on. There's no mention in the current ledgers or day-books of a sub-contract with Linklater's, but I wanted to be quite sure, so I had a word with that coffee-stall proprietor and he confirmed what he'd told you. He said one of Linklater's vans had been there again last night, about nine-thirty. It stayed about ten minutes, no more, and was backed in so tightly that he didn't see what was offloaded or taken aboard."

"What then?"

"Well, seeing that the man seemed so positive I looked in at Linklater's yard on my way home. I pass near the gate, it's in a cul-de-sac off Jamaica Road. There were several vans in the yard so I . . . well, Mr. Swann, I slipped in and I looked inside a half-dozen of them. Most of them were empty but the last one was fully loaded. There were several of our crates, Mr. Swann, with our brand on them."

"What was inside? Did you get a chance to look?"

"No, sir. I was going to, even if it meant prising one open, but then two men came out of the shed across the yard." Tybalt paused, drawing a deep breath, and blinking twice a second. "One of them was Robsart, our yard foreman. I didn't know the other. It was getting dusk then so I thought it best to slip away behind the vans and make my way out. I signed Robsart on myself, sir. He'd been with us four years on suburban runs. I remember I was surprised when he told me Wesley had promoted him yard foreman. There were several men there with more experience but later Wesley said Robsart was the brightest of the bunch and thoroughly up to the job."

"He's certainly up to something," Adam said. "Did you come straight here after that?"

"Yes. Though I had it in mind to do something else."

"What was that?"

"Take a train out to Annerley to talk it over with my boy."

"I'm glad you didn't, Tybalt."

He turned away, moving over to the window. The night was clear and there was very little river mist about. The light of a thousand lamps reflected on the sliding Thames and the muted roar of the city came to him like the long roll of muffled drums. He had little doubt now but that Wesley Tybalt was implicated, and that some really massive 'shouldering' was going on down there. He remembered coachman Blubb introducing him to that word, a phrase the old coachees applied to the practice of picking up passengers at intermediate stops on a regular run, dropping them off one stage short of the terminus, and pocketing the fare. Only in this case it was not passengers but goods that were being shouldered, and suddenly two-thirds of the pattern became distinct to him, incorporating Sam's hint, the leak from Linklater's Northern headquarters, that warehouse with an unobtrusive exit that they kept locked, back and front, during the day and Travis's reports of vans calling after the yard had closed and only one or two men would be on duty.

The goods, he imagined, would start out from Northern

and Midland bases in Linklater's vans, to be offloaded close to the starting point and hauled South in Swann's waggons, stored in that warehouse, uninvoiced of course, until one of Linklater's vans could collect them, with nobody a penny the wiser save a sprinkling of rascals in both firms operating the swindle. He said, quietly, "You realise there must be at least half-a-dozen of our chaps involved in this, Tybalt. Waggoners from the original depots would have to be squared, as well as the yard men like Robsart. They've been making a very good thing of it, I wouldn't wonder, and it must have been going some time to develop to this stage."

"You're saying we've hauled hundreds of pounds' worth of goods into London for Linklater, Mr. Swann?"

"That's putting it very mildly."

"But it's the most outrageous confidence trick I've ever heard of! To do that, openly, night after night . . . A regular smuggling run, practised on that scale? I simply can't imagine what Wesley could have been about to let something like that happen under his nose! I mean, the boy must be a complete fool not to have checked the contents of that warehouse from time to time."

"What about my George?" but Tybalt went on tut-tutting, so that he thought, miserably, 'He'll have to know but I'm damned if I can tell him. How the devil does a man convince an old friend that his own child is a cutpurse heading for gaol? No wonder Wesley covered up for George that time. That young fool's whoring must have been a Godsend to him. I daresay he stages a pick-up every time he knows George is off somewhere with that woman . . .' He said, "I'm very indebted to you, Tybalt. For the time being let's face the fact that both your son and mine are hard at work proving neither one of 'em is fit to put in charge of a waggon, much less a fleet of 'em. I'll locate George tomorrow somehow, and lay it all on the table for him. There's nothing more you can do except go home and go to bed. It was sharp of you to check on Linklater's yard. I'll see that place has its shutters up before another twenty-four hours are past."

"There's no possibility of some other explanation?"

"None that doesn't nail your boy and mine as victims of a three-card trick, Tybalt. Are you sure you won't take a drink?"

The little man shuffled, then threw up his round head. "I've faced a good many upsets in my time, Mr. Swann, and I've done it on tea."

"Then let me order you a pot of tea," and without waiting for Tybalt's assent he rang the bell and summoned a waiter. When the tea appeared Tybalt poured, his movements as precise as an old maid's, and Adam thought, dolefully, 'I wish to God I hadn't involved him now. This is going to hit him damned hard,' and he urged the clerk to drink up, get a cab and go home to bed.

When Tybalt had left he sat in his nightshirt at the window looking over the river, musing on his tactics from this point on. He had a penchant for French metaphors and one occurred to him now, *offensive à outrance*. There was no point in nibbling around the edge of this un-savoury mess. George would have to be located and brought back, by the ear if necessary, and both he and Wesley would have to be confronted with the situation as far as he knew it. That foreman Robsart would have to be threatened until he told all he knew. The thieves would have to be run down, here and out in the network, and sent packing. There would be prosecutions, no doubt. Charges would have to be formulated against Linklater and Linklater's operators. It was likely to be a long, sordid business, with half the yard men under suspicion during the investigation. He lit one of his favourite Burmese cheroots, a solace granted him over the years, ever since, as a youngster, he and Roberts, and other men long since in their graves, had ridden across the Bengal plains. Beyond his window the roar of the city subsided to a soft, insistent murmur.

He had his first piece of luck next morning. He was dawdling over his second cup of coffee in the breakfast-room when a waiter brought him a message that a Mr. Giles Swann had called, but could only stop a short while. Adam said, eagerly, "Tell him to come in and fetch some fresh coffee, will you?" Giles, dressed for travelling, entered from the foyer, taking the seat indicated but saying he only had twenty minutes as he was anxious to catch the ten-ten Westcountry train from Waterloo. "I'm going down to clear up that Gimblett claim," he said. "That old Scrooge is still bucking at paying up, although the adjudicators declared for us a month ago. That collision at Taunton was his liability."

"How the devil did you know I was here?" Adam asked, and Giles said, smiling, that he was always here when he was in town, and Hugo had word from Henrietta yesterday that he was off on one of his junk-buying jaunts. "My words, not his," he added. "I think you've got a collector's eye."

They talked as equals, something he was unable to do with his other children, but Giles, unlike him in so many ways, had a maturity that the more extrovert of his family lacked. "As a matter of fact, I'm here to ask a favour, Father. A small one."

"It wouldn't have to do with George, would it?"

"No. Why should it?"

"I don't know. Just a hunch. Is George at the yard?"

"No, he isn't. He hasn't been for a day or so."

"Where is he? I can never find him these days. He's here, there and everywhere and I particularly want a word with him while I'm up here."

"He's in the regions," Giles said. "They expect him back sometime tomorrow."

"Do you know where in the regions?"

"No, but Wesley Tybalt would tell you."

"I don't think he would." He looked at Giles narrowly. "How do you hit it off with that chap, Giles?"

"Not all that well," Giles said, looking a little puzzled. "He's a first-class yard manager, according to George, but I don't find him as likeable as his father. He's a bit of a know-all, and talks down to the men and up to us."

"My sentiments exactly," Adam said, "and he resents my poking my nose in when I feel like it. He probably takes his cue from George in that respect."

He toyed with the notion of taking Giles into his confidence but quickly decided against it. All his life he had been jumping on people for coming to him with untidy briefs and his own was far from complete. "What was the favour, boy?"

"It's about a chap called Soper. I promised him we'd take him on. He's out of a billet and I'm obligated to him. He's a member of the Shop Assistants' Action Group and has had about as much as he can take from the drapery trade."

"There's more to it than that, isn't there?"

Giles hesitated. "Yes, there is. If I want your help I owe you the truth. Did you read about that leaflet raid on the Jubilee procession in the papers? Fleet Street end of the Strand?"

"Yes, I did. A very juvenile business, to my mind. That sort of gesture is spitting into the wind. Did Soper get the sack over it?"

"He can't go back. And he's nothing put by to keep him while he looks for another billet."

"He won't get one without a character."

"That's why I'd like to help him." He looked Adam in the eye. "How do you feel about the shop assistants' cause, Father?"

"Sympathetic. If I was in drapery it would have been a bomb not a leaflet. Time they organised themselves like other trades. But that's their business. It certainly isn't mine at my time of life."

Giles said, slowly, "I'll not keep anything back. I organised that 'spit in the wind'. I was there at the time. Me and Romayne."

Adam wasn't much surprised. He knew Giles was mixed up in various campaigns, all of which were probably as abortive as this one. He said, "It's the wrong way to go about things, boy. Old Catesby, up in the Polygon, could have told you that. He was your kind, always chasing the millenium, and even went to gaol for it in his time. But he learned and started from the bottom up. Got a proper trades union organised, and then went right after parliamentary representation. You don't get far over here, marching around with banners and distributing leaflets at public assemblies. People are too lazy and too indifferent. Legislation is the only lever the British will accept. Germany excepted, we're ahead of others in capital and labour relations. This chap you're telling me about, is he the wild man type?"

"He wouldn't be if he worked for a firm like yours."

Giles always gave him the impression he was only helping out at Swann-on-Wheels, that he had never been fully integrated, like George, Hugo or even young Edward, and that his post as Claims and Provident Scheme Manager was a stop-gap while he went on looking for a purpose in life. Yet his work had never been in question. Adam had heard George say that Giles' tact and patience was worth five thousand a year to the network, if only on account of cases settled out of court, thus saving a sheaf of lawyers' bills. Adam said, "This Soper, has he had any clerical experience?"

"Yes. Before he became a floor-walker at Beckwith's."

"George would have signed him on on the strength of your recommendation."

"In a case of this kind I'd sooner approach you, Father."

That was another thing about Giles. He still addressed him as 'Father', instead of the more familiar 'Gov'nor', used by his brothers. It stemmed, he supposed, from the boy's attitude towards him since the time they had first begun discussing history and politics when Giles was a child of thirteen. Adam always had the impression that

Giles still regarded him as his mentor in these fields and would see that as far outweighing his vast commercial experience.

"If I'm to catch that train I must hurry," he said. "Here's Soper's address." He wrote rapidly in his notebook. "Maybe you could find time to call and look him over."

"I don't need to do that," Adam said. "I'll tell George he's been highly recommended to me by an old customer and I want him given a chance. Good luck in the West, boy. Wish I was coming with you. I always liked that part of the country."

"Why don't you? I'll be returning first thing to-morrow."

"Things to do," Adam muttered and escorted him into the street, where Giles had a hansom waiting. He watched him get in and responded to his hand wave, thinking, 'Queer chap, old Giles, but so likeable . . . lovable even. More brains than any of 'em if he'd put 'em to better use but you can't have everything . . .' Then he climbed up the stairs to his room, still undecided on his next move in the confrontation he knew must occur within twenty-four hours.

He sat thumbing through his notes on Barbara Lockerbie, dismissing as improbable the possibility that George was engaged in genuine network business, gambling on the likelihood that they were off together somewhere and telling himself that his first priority was to intercept George before he turned up at the yard. He had Sir James Lockerbie's town address, in Sussex Place, but it was unlikely George was holed up there. He had a country place somewhere but Adam did not know where it was, so he went down to reception and buttonholed the manager, whom he knew well, demanding to know if Sir James Lockerbie was a telephone subscriber. "I can soon find out, Mr. Swann," the man said, "for I keep a list here," and he popped into his inner office, re-emerging a moment later with the information that Sir James was listed as subscriber two-seven-five in the London area.

"Could you connect me?" Adam asked, "I've important business with him and don't want to waste time calling on him if he is out of town."

"Certainly, if you'll step into my office, Mr. Swann. The hotel telephone is in there. Very few of my guests ever seem to have need of it."

"That doesn't surprise me," Adam said, "we managed well enough with pen and ink in the old days," but he followed the manager into the office and watched him twirl the handle before asking the London exchange for number two-seven-five. After a few moments he offered Adam the earpiece. "Speak slowly and distinctly, sir," he advised, "and don't hold the mouthpiece too close. No one will disturb you in here," and tactfully he left, closing the door.

A disembodied voice at the end of the line said, "Sir James Lockerbie's residence. Who is calling?"

"Swann," Adam said. "Director of Swann-on-Wheels. Is your master in town?"

"No, sir," the voice said, "he's abroad. Could I send a message, sir? Is it social or business?"

"Social," Adam said, heading off a switch to Lockerbie's London headquarters. "Is her ladyship at home?"

"I'm afraid not, sir. This is Medley, the butler speaking. Her ladyship is in the country."

"Well, see here, Medley," Adam said confidentially, "I'm very anxious to send her an invitation she's expecting. Could you oblige me by giving me her country address?"

"It's not usual, sir. Mr. Swann, you said?"

"Yes. Your master has been doing business with me for thirty years and my wife is extremely anxious that this invitation reaches Lady Lockerbie by today at the very latest."

"I see. Well, Mr. Swann, I think I would be exceeding my duties by withholding the country telephone number.

I think you'll catch her there later, sir. After six, I would say, for I understand she's attending the local regatta today."

"I'd be uncommonly obliged," Adam said, trying to keep the jubilation out of his voice. "What is it?"

"Swanley Rise, number six, sir. It's in Hertfordshire and you get it through the Barnet exchange."

"Thank you very much indeed," Adam said. "I'll get in touch with her before dinner," and he hooked the earpiece on to its gilded standard, reflecting that he might have been unjustly prejudiced against telephones. They certainly saved time and trouble on occasion.

He went out into the sunshine, wondering how to pass the hours until early evening. He intended staying clear of the yard, where his presence, twice in ten days, would certainly alert Wesley and there were no auction sales advertised that he cared to attend. He had no wish to run over to Gisela's either. The wretched girl had enough worries, without him adding to them, and momentarily he was at a loss as to how to put in the time. Then his eye caught the destination board on the front of a 'bus – 'The Tower & Minories', and fancy jogged him like the elbow of a playful uncle. The Tower of London. The grey pile he had stared across the river at for thirty years when isolated in his Thames-side eyrie, but had not visited since he was a lad. He said, aloud, "Damned if I won't look in there, like any gawping provincial. Why not? I need something to take my mind off my worries for an hour or so," and he moved out into the crowded roadway and swung himself aboard.

The 'bus set him down on Tower Hill, where some of his favourite characters from the past had taken their final glimpse of the world in the upturned faces of ten thousand Cockneys, assembled to witness a spectacle that was even more popular than a bear-baiting or a cock-fight. Strafford, who put too much trust in Princes, old Lord Lovat, for his share in the Jacobite rebellion, and that nincompoop Monmouth, who died gamely they said, but

93

only after crawling on his knees before that bigot James. Well, they managed these things more discreetly nowadays, and he wasn't at all sure that the condemned thanked them for it. He had a notion that a man needed an audience on occasions like that and might even look for a chance to show his paces at the last minute. He went down to the public entrance and past the Traitors' Gate, once again making a character assessment on the men and women who had climbed those slimed steps from the river. Tom Moore, too holier-than-thou for his taste, Tom Cromwell, the prototype of many a crafty merchant he had bested in his salad days, and young Elizabeth, who learned her lesson well during the period she lived here in the shadow of the headsman. Then up to Tower Green, where a raven gave him a speculative eye, as though the old ruffian queried his purpose there.

He stood for a minute beside the slab marking the spot where the scaffold had stood, remembering the luckless Ann Boleyn and rekindling his lifelong resentment for the least likeable of England's monarchs, who had her pretty head lopped by the Calais executioner. They said the damned scoundrel (Adam had never regarded Henry as anything else) waited outside the city wall for a cannon shot, announcing the fact that he was a widower, before riding off to Jane Seymour, and he wouldn't put it past him.

He looked in at the tower that had held so many state prisoners, thinking: 'If you played for high stakes in those days you earned anything you took away from the table.' Then he tackled the winding stair to the horse armoury, peering at the exhibits with the eye of a man who had seen more carnage than most and afterwards stumped down again and crossed to the battlemented walk overlooking the river, where Raleigh was said to have spent most of the daylight hours during his long imprisonment here. He must have been in a particularly fanciful mood today for he found himself thinking of Raleigh as a kind of Giles, a man full of promise who somehow never achieved much, perhaps because he attempted too much, and never learned the trick of concentrating his energy. Yet anyone who could write that valediction of Raleigh's was a man of parts, surely . . . What was it again . . . ? A few lines that had appealed to him so strongly when he learned it at school that it had remained with him all these years:

> E'en such is time that takes in trust
> Our youth, our joys, our all we have
> And in the dark and silent grave
> When we have wandered all our ways,
> Shuts up the story of our days.
>
> But from this grave, this earth, this dust,
> The Lord shall raise me up, I trust.

It occurred to him to wonder how much store his own family set upon hope of a personal resurrection. Not much, he would say, for all their regular church-going when they were youngsters. Henrietta, he knew for a fact, never let herself contemplate death, her own or anyone else's. Alex, professional soldier, would have come to terms with it long ago. George wasn't the spiritual type, or Hugo either. The one might see Paradise from a Turkish janissary's standpoint, a perfumed garden, full of houris, and the other as a super sports stadium, where he won every event on the card. Giles was more difficult to predict. He was too intelligent not to have renounced conventional doctrine long since, but, like Adam, he had a powerful belief in man's potential and in the never-ending struggle between good instincts and bad. As for the girls, they had almost certainly given a great deal more thought to their clothes, looks and figures than they gave to their souls, and not for the first time he envied men like Raleigh their deeply-rooted faith in an all-seeing, all-caring Creator, universal at the time, he supposed, before tiresome fellows like Darwin and Huxley set about confusing everybody.

The sun was moving down towards the higher reaches of the river now and he glanced at his watch, taxing his long memory regarding the likelihood of one or other of his many business cronies about here who would be likely to possess a telephone and let him borrow it for an out-of-town call. He decided on Crosby, a timber importer, with offices in Cannon Street, and went out on to Tower Hill again where, after some tea and a cake in a bunshop, he whistled a hansom and gave the cabbie Crosby's address. A few moments later they were threading their way through westbound traffic, very thick about here, and not getting any better, despite so many road-widenings since he had become a regular user of these streets forty years ago.

The man set him down outside Crosby's place at the very moment a three-horse fire-engine dashed past, moving in the direction of the bridge, the epitome of urgency with its clanging bell and rattle of equipment, gleaming brass and straining greys, moving over the ground as though they were quite aware of the fact that they took precedence over drays, four-wheelers, hansoms, bicycles and even the odd motor in the press. The driver's handling of the team was a pleasure to watch and every-body did his damnedest to give the vehicle clearance. Then, in its wake, came another, and finally a third, so that the cabbie said, "Someone's in trouble, sir. Looks as if it's on the South Bank. They usually manage with their own brigades," and he pointed with his whip at a blur of smoke hanging in the clear air above the south-eastern angle of the buildings.

"That'll make traffic worse," Adam said, recalling the clubbed approaches to the bridge on that side whenever anything of this kind was afoot over there, but then his quick ear caught a single word shouted by a newsboy at a customer buying his paper a few yards along the kerb and he almost ran over to the lamp-standard where the boy had his pitch.

"*Where* did you say? *Where* is it?"

"Swann's, sir, the carriers . . . Going well, they say . . . !"

Adam threw himself round and caught his cab in the act of turning, shouting, "Get over the bridge! Half a sovereign if you make it in ten minutes . . . !", and dragging open the door he flung himself on to the leather cushions he had quitted a moment since.

5

River Scene

THE MAN EARNED HIS HALF-SOVEREIGN. TAKING
advantage of every chink in the traffic, and three times
mounting the pavement with his nearside wheel, he
brought Adam to the junction of the Borough High Street
and Tooley Street in eight minutes. As the cab drew up
yet another fire-engine clattered up from the direction of
Southwark so that to Adam, scrambling from the hansom
and hurrying breathlessly as far as Grubb's glue factory,
the yard was seen to be ringed with fire-engines and arched
over with hissing jets from their hoses.

The confusion about him was that of a city captured
by storm. Great banks of yellow smoke gusted towards
the river on the light breeze, more and more sightseers
arrived every minute, some of them scuffling with the
harassed police, and trapped vehicles from the Old Kent
Road side tried to fight their way out of the press, striking
one another glancing blows so that their drivers' oaths and
shouts of warning added to the general tumult. And
beyond it all, like the continuous crackle of musketry,
came the menacing sputter of the flames at the heart of
the fire some hundred yards lower down the street.

He stood there a moment dazed by the uproar, telling
himself that it was all a mistake on the part of that newsboy, that it was someone else's empire that was burning
and that his presence here was part of a nightmare. But
beyond this the core of his brain kept reminding him

that the fire was no coincidence, that the crooked trail he had been following ever since Sam Rawlinson had croaked out his warning, led directly to this scene of destruction and the suspicion, close to a certainty, made him swear aloud as he chopped his way through the press of spectators, shouting, "I'm Swann! I own the damned place . . . ! Let me pass!"

The police nearer the bridge gave way to him but halfway down Tooley Street, at a point where he could see the pulse of yellow and crimson flame beyond the weighbridge gate, a sergeant caught him by the arm and said, "Don't go in, sir . . . They're driving the horses through! The stables have caught," and he watched, appalled, as four Cleveland Bays dashed through the gate heading directly for the section of the crowd held at the junction of Tower Bridge Road. At the same time he saw a terrified Clydesdale caught by a triumphant urchin outside the scent factory and led away, to await receipt of its captor's tip.

He said, to the sergeant at his elbow, "How bad is it? How much of the yard is involved?"

The policeman replied, "Bad enough! It's only been going forty minutes and look at it. All this side is well alight but they say the Southwark brigades are getting a grip on the other side."

"How did it start? Does anyone know?" and the man glanced at him. "How do they ever start? Carelessness nine times out of ten, and Mr. Nobody's the culprit! Stand *back* there! *Jarman! Hoskins!* Stop those fools crossing the road!" and he bustled away, fully absorbed in his job of controlling the ever-increasing swarm of spectators, now surging in from the bridge and all the side streets connecting Tooley Street with the Old Kent Road.

A moment later Adam saw his youngest son, Edward, wild-eyed and stripped to his shirt and shouted, "Edward! Over here, boy!", and the youth spun round, knuckling his eyes and exclaiming, "Gov'nor! How did you get here? I thought . . ."

"I was in Cannon Street and heard of it. Were you here when it started?"

"Yes, in the clerical section . . . Somebody rushed in and said a warehouse was well alight . . ."

"Which warehouse?"

"Number Eight, that new one behind the tower. There was a frightful panic. Everyone rushed out and did what they could but it was little enough until the brigades got here. We only had the hand-pump and buckets. Then the roof of the counting-house went up . . . must have been sparks."

"Are either of your brothers around?"

"Hugo is. Over on the far side, turning the horses loose. The waggon-shed and forge are alight and two other warehouses, I believe. Everything was as dry as tinder, sir!"

Adam said, "Keep by me, I'm going in," and taking advantage of the sergeant's back he slipped across the road and through the dense smoke shrouding the weighbridge.

It was a little clearer beyond, where the river breeze was driving the smoke to the west and he was able to make some assessment of the overall scene. The heart of the fire was in the immediate area of Number Eight warehouse, the one they kept padlocked, but there seemed no hope of saving the counting-house, or the stable block and forge that ran at right angles to it. Three pinnaces, one-horse vans that served the suburbs on short-run hauls, had been dragged out of the waggon-shed and were burning in isolation in the centre of the yard. Maddened horses clattered past on either side, making by instinct for the main exit. A group of helmeted firemen were playing four jets on the counting-house but even as they watched a superintendent detached them to concentrate on the stable block, leaving the one-storey building to burn itself out. Smoke from the gutted warehouse set them both coughing and wheezing and all around the steady crackle of the flames proclaimed the certainty that Swann's headquarters, as he had known it over half a lifetime, was doomed.

He said, grimly, "Where's the yard manager? Where's Wesley Tybalt, Edward?"

"I don't know, sir. George is away, and Giles too . . . Shall I try and find Tybalt?"

"Yes . . . you do that. I'll stay as close here as I can. They seem to be containing it about here."

"Hadn't you better get back to the street, sir?"

"Do as I say. Find Tybalt, and if you can't bring Hugo."

The boy dashed off, moving in a way that reminded Adam of Henrietta's claim that, of all the Swanns, only Edward favoured her father Sam. It was true. He had Sam's big head and squat, squarish frame, Sam's bustle and air of guarded alertness. In a matter of seconds he was lost in the swirl of smoke from the stable block but he re-emerged a few minutes later with Hugo in tow. It was the first time Adam had ever seen Hugo blown, despite his string of triumphs on the running track. He gasped, "It's a regular shambles, Gov'nor. All happened so quickly. Never seen a fire get a hold like that. But we got the horses out. All seventy of 'em."

"Anybody hurt?"

"No, sir, I think not. But the superintendent says he can't save Four and Five warehouses. He's concentrating on the others, giving them a rare soaking. The waggons are our property but there are customers' goods in all the sheds."

"Water will spoil what the flames don't get," Adam grunted. "How about Tybalt? Is he over there?"

"I haven't seen him," Hugo said. "Come to think of it I haven't seen him all day."

"I have," Edward volunteered. "He came into the counting-house and went through to his office some time in the afternoon."

"When was it? Think, boy, think hard!"

"It must have been about an hour or so before the alarm was given."

"You didn't see him go to the key rack?"

"No, sir, but he doesn't have to. He has duplicates in his office over there."

"Where, exactly?"

"In a rack on the wall behind his desk in the annexe," and Edward pointed to the butt end of the clerical building, the one portion of the block that was still more or less intact. Even its window, facing the yard, was unbroken.

He said, "Come with me, Edward. Hugo, go back and tell the superintendent to make his major effort on the warehouses. You're quite right. The waggons are fully insured but we've only minimum cover for goods in transit, once they're stored in the yard!" As Hugo hurried off he led the way to the abutting end of the clerical section, Edward following with a bewildered expression on his pink, squarish face. There was a pinnace axle-tree resting against the brickwork and Adam lifted it, smashing the frame and the four panes of glass with a few swift blows. The heat here was intense but under the wall they were protected from the dense clouds of smoke issuing from the burning half of the building. He turned to the boy. "Scramble in and look at that desk and key rack. Jump to it. Desk first . . ." and Edward dived through the aperture and was at once shrouded in smoke.

He called back, "All the drawers are open or thrown down. He must have saved his papers."

"Are his keys there?"

"Yes, sir, I think so."

"Bring 'em out, boy. Sharp about it," and Edward came tumbling out, his hands full of keys, each with its oval label.

"Shall I give them to the firemen?"

"No, I'll take them. They'll hack their way in if they have to but it mightn't be necessary. You say the desk was cleared?"

"More or less. There were papers on the floor."

"Right, now listen here. I'm staying in town, at The

Norfolk, and there's nothing I can do here. Tell Hugo where I am, and tell him to notify the brigade chief and the senior police officer. I need a drink and a good wash while I'm at it. You and Hugo watch out for yourselves, and don't take chances saving property. We can always replace property," and he walked away, leaving the yard by the main entrance and pushing roughly through the ranks of sightseers now contained behind a rope barrier. He was more than halfway across the bridge before he saw an empty cab going his way. He said, clambering inside, "Norfolk Hotel," and settled back in the interior, his mind juggling with so many factors that it finally abandoned any attempt to relate them. The stench of woodsmoke clung to his clothes and he had inhaled so much of the stuff that he felt sick and muddleheaded. But then, as he stretched his legs, he heard the keys jangle and thought, sourly, 'That was a bonus, anyway. I don't know as it will prove anything but it's a lead having regard Tybalt's jumping the gun in order to empty that desk.'

2

His over-riding desire, before he so much as ordered a drink, was to have a bath. The stench that hung about him was not merely unpleasant. It darkened his thoughts to a degree that the fire could not have achieved. The depression was at a different level, the deepest level of his consciousness. He probed its source, asking himself why a fire, even one so fierce and destructive, should make him feel lonely and desolate. Then it came to him in the whiff of his jacket as he peeled it off, a stink of frustrated wretchedness and personal degradation that took him back to a time years before Swann's waggons roamed the high-ways, to places on the far side of the world. It was the once familiar reek of burning towns, the stench of Delhi, Cawnpore, Lucknow and Jhansi, ravaged, looted and fired. It struck him that the nose was the best barometer of the spirit, that certain smells one associated with hope and happiness, and others, like this one, with bitterness and defeat.

He muttered, "Here now this won't do! You're responsible for it in a way, so keep your nerve and see what can be salvaged from the mess!" and he spread the keys Edward had given him on the bed, examining each label carefully.

There were seventeen in all, eight giving access to warehouses, two to the main entrances of the yard, one to the head clerk's office, one to the clerical building itself, one marked 'postern' (he assumed this opened the new Tooley Street exit) and four belonging to other sectors of the yard, the tack room, the waggon-stores and the forge. He set aside all but the warehouse keys and studied these again, marking off in his mind the buildings they represented, the row of one-storey warehouses facing his old tower that were used, in his day and since, for goods awaiting shipment and onward transmission into the Kentish Triangle and Southern Square.

At first the set seemed complete but then it came to him that one was missing. The key to that smaller, newer warehouse across from the counting-house, with its exit at the rear, and the significance of this occurred to him at once. It told him that Wesley Tybalt, slipping into the office to empty his desk, had hooked this key from the rack and used it to further some purpose of his own.

Cautiously he pondered that purpose, forgetting his need for a wash and a drink but sitting there in his shirt-sleeves, his mind reviewing every factor in the case.

Wesley had not been seen about the place all day, save for that fleeting visit to his office. Wesley had been nowhere around when the fire started and gained its hold. The fire had begun in that quarter of the yard. Wesley had not returned the key, a golden rule at the yard all the time it had been Swann's headquarters. It pointed, he would say, to two certainties. One, Wesley was the last to visit the small warehouse, and two, Wesley had been warned by someone that the hunt was up and he would be required, within the next twenty-four hours, to answer a number of awkward questions. Concerning himself and Robsart, seen in Linklater's yard last night, and concerning, above all, the contents of that warehouse and the invoices representing the goods inside. Dramatically a pattern emerged revealing so much that it had the power to make him leap up, putting so much reliance on his tin leg that he stumbled.

'Great God, the fellow's not only a thief but an arsonist, covering his tracks!' he thought, and almost choked with rage, calling himself an absolute fool not to have spotted the grand design days ago, or at least last night, after Tybalt senior told him about the Swann packages in the Linklater waggon.

His first impulse was to contact the police and put them in touch with their colleagues at the seat of the fire. His second, on the heels of the first, was more complicated. It involved not only Wesley Tybalt, but Tybalt senior and maybe a dozen subverted men at headquarters and out along the network. Detection on this scale called for skilful timing and absolute secrecy if the entire gang was to be rounded up and the network purged from top to bottom. And he was unequal to the demands of that task right now, when he was tired, hungry and filthy.

He looked at his watch, surprised to find it was coming up to eight o'clock, four hours since he had stampeded over London Bridge to the burning yard. He shrugged off the rest of his clothes, put on his dressing gown and slippers, took his towel, soap and razor and went along the corridor to the bathroom, an innovation up here, for until recently guests had made do with tin bowls and cans of hot water carried up three flights of stairs. For half an hour or more he soaked and scraped, turning the finer points of his assumptions over and over in his mind and then, feeling ready for battle, he sprinkled himself with lavender water and went back along the corridor to his room.

He had not locked it and on crossing the threshold it

seemed that the place was full of people. He drew back, rubbing eyes that were still smarting from smoke and yellow soap. Then he saw that there was only one person in there but the man by the window was so huge, and possessed such a commanding presence, that he seemed to fill the room. It was Saul Keate, his former waggon-master, who had been his friend and confidant since that first summer evening in '58, when Avery had introduced him as the likely recruiting sergeant of a South Bank work force. A gentle giant, standing six feet six in his socks, with a great, slabsided face and mild blue eyes, a man who had searched the docks night after night for lost souls with potential that could be channelled into the network. Another Bible-puncher, certainly, and a prude who winced every time he heard a carter swear, but a person of immense positiveness for whom he had always entertained the greatest respect.

He said, "Have you just come from the yard?" and Keate, surprisingly, said no, although he had heard about the fire from one of the men who lived in his street. "According to him there was little I could do," he said, "so I thought it best to come here and give you this, sir. It had this address on it or I would have travelled down to 'Tryst', late as it is." He handed Adam a sealed envelope addressed to him in Tybalt's hand and marked '*Urgent and Personal*'.

"Where did you get it?"

"At Tybalt's home. It was on his sitting-room mantelshelf when I called round for some mission funds appeals he asked me to collect this afternoon. His front door was ajar but he wasn't there. I called up the stairs and then made enquiries. He lives alone, as you know, except for a woman who comes in and does for him since his wife died. I found her eventually. She told me he was there at midday, when she left, but she hadn't seen him since." He waited in his grave, self-effacing way that recalled so many orders-for-the-day sessions down the years.

Adam said, "Very obliging of you, Keate," and carried

the envelope over to the window, opening it, taking out two closely-written sheets and reading them with his back to the light.

The first lines made him catch his breath for Tybalt began:

My dear Mr. Swann,

When you read this I shall have moved on, and I pray God Almighty finds it possible to forgive me for what I am about to do. But I thought it only honourable to admit that I did not follow your advice last night. I was far too agitated to let it rest until morning. I took a train to Annerley to discuss this grave matter with my son, and try and discover whether he had remained in ignorance of the fact that Robsart and others were robbing the firm. I learned a great deal more than I bargained for.

He looked up, glancing across at the impassive Keate. "You say you couldn't locate Tybalt? You're sure he wasn't somewhere about the house?"

"As I said, I called, sir . . ."

"Then listen to this, Keate. I'll read it first and explain on the way over there. You and I are going back as soon as I've got some clothes on . . .

". . . You will understand, Mr. Swann, how excessively painful it is for me to write this, so I do not propose to go into details. You will do that as soon as you confront my boy, Robsart and that scoundrel Linklater. The truth is, in a word, Wesley was implicated so deeply that he heard me out and then offered me a substantial bribe to forget what I had seen and deduced, saying he could concoct some plausible explanation to satisfy you and dispose of Robsart and his associates overnight. I do not think I need tell you I spurned his offer and counselled him there and then that there was only one course open to him now, to lay everything before you and Mr. George, and throw himself on your mercy.

"At first he brushed this aside, saying you would make certain he went to prison, but I went on and he finally promised he would consider taking this course, provided I would allow him a few hours to make up his mind. It seemed to me I owed him that, or rather I owed it to his wife and child, so I left and went home. No words of mine can express the shame I feel on his behalf. I can only assume he was a far weaker vessel than I thought and was led away by Linklater or Robsart, but one thing he did add and I pass it on for what it is worth. The pickings were trivial at first but when Mr. George took to travelling more, and gave Wesley a free run of the yard, he plunged deeper and deeper into wickedness and began organising big-scale runs from the North and Midlands, roughly along the lines you suggested – that is to say, our vehicles making the long hauls and Linklater's onloading from that warehouse whenever the occasions were propitious.

"I can only add that never, under any circumstances, could I look you in the face again. Our long association has been, to me at least, a very happy one and I will carry with me to the grave a deep appreciation of all your trust and kindness since I came to work for you in the earliest days of Swann-on-Wheels.

"I remain, sir, your very humble servant, Hubert Tybalt."

He had never seen Keate so blanched and tense. The big man seemed dazed with shock and when his lips moved no sound issued from them for a moment or so. Then he said, hoarsely, "He can't . . . he wouldn't do anything so . . . so foolish, so dreadful, Mr. Swann?"

Adam said, sharply, "He certainly will if we aren't lucky enough to run him down and persuade him a man can't take upon himself the guilt of others, no matter how close they are. Go down and get a cab. Pick the youngest horse in the rank and tell the cabby we want him to risk his neck in a dash to Rotherhithe. Don't say anything more now, we haven't time. I'll be with you in less than five minutes." And without waiting for Keate to leave he tore open the wardrobe and threw his spare suit on the bed, struggling out of his dressing gown and flinging himself into his clothes. He went out in such a hurry that he left the door open and the bed strewn with keys.

3

Traffic had eased off at this hour but the journey seemed a tedious one, for it did not take him long to acquaint Keate with the basic facts of the situation and afterwards, following a futile speculation or two, the pair of them jolted on in gloomy silence. It wanted a few minutes to ten when the cab drew up beside Tybalt's little house and he bundled out of it, calling to the cabbie to wait. Keate was close behind him and they paused in the narrow hall to light the gas, then went on into the front-room, where Tybalt's mission appeals lay in neat stacks on the red plush tablecloth. He said, gruffly, "You stay here. I've got to make sure before we alert the police. I'm pretty certain it'll be the river, and I only hope it takes him a long time to screw up his nerve!", and he clumped upstairs, finding a candlestick on the tiny landing and lighting the wick.

Tybalt's bedroom, tidily done over by the woman who looked after him, was empty, and the bed had not been disturbed, but that meant nothing, for she had been here until midday. He went back across the landing and examined the other two rooms, scarcely more than boxes. One, that was furnished, had been Wesley's all the time he was growing up here, and a text hung over the bed, one of those framed Biblical quotations that hung in the homes of all men like Tybalt. It read 'I am the Way, the Truth and the Light'. He went out and was beginning to descend the stairs again when he noticed a door midway between the bedrooms that he had mistaken for a cup-board. He now saw that it was not a cupboard but a recess, converted into a water-closet. On impulse he turned back and flung open the door, holding the candle high above his head.

Tybalt looked back at him, a baffled, outraged expression in eyes that were wide open, as was his mouth. His feet reached to within about six inches of the floor. The knotted cravat about his neck was hooked over the trigger of the cistern and entangled, somehow, in the short length of chain and even as he stared the final irony of the situation jumped at him in the form of the raised lettering on the cistern. It announced that the water-closet was the product of James Lockerbie & Company, Ltd., Sanitary Engineers, Glasgow, the man George was cuckolding. George had given Wesley Tybalt so much rope that he had succeeded in hanging not Wesley but Wesley's father.

He would have thought himself proof against the shock of witnessing a violent death but this death was more than violent. It was obscene, a bizarre and shuddering mockery of all the man hanging there had believed in and practised throughout his blameless life. It was as ritualistic as the death of a terrified savage, willed to destroy himself by a witch-doctor and it was acknowledgment of this, rather than the spectacle itself, that made him recoil retching, steadying himself by throwing up a hand to grasp the lintel of the makeshift door frame.

In that moment Keate was beside him, the pair of them crowding the narrow door frame as Keate said, quietly, "Leave him, sir. I'll see to him. Go down, sir, I'll not be a moment," and Adam turned and groped his way down the stairs to the front door, standing there with his back to the hall gulping the river breeze and telling himself that he was past this kind of thing, long done with meddling in other men's affairs, and yearned only to be safely back at 'Tryst', with Henrietta, his trees and his flowers.

He was still standing there when Keate came down,

saying, in the same steady voice, "Take the cab and get along home, sir. Leave everything to me. I'll inform the police and do what has to be done," and when Adam made a gesture of protest, "He was *my* friend, sir! The best a man ever had," and practically propelled Adam to the cab, calling to the driver, "Back to the hotel but take it steady this time. The gentleman is in no hurry now."

But later, an hour or so later, Adam decided that Keate was wrong. He was in a hurry, a tearing desperate hurry to call George to account, and he only waited long enough to down a couple of stiff brandies before searching through his notebook for the number that butler had given him earlier in the day, a day that seemed to have stretched itself into a month and a month in which disaster piled on disaster in a way that was somehow new to him, and that after a lifetime of adventure. He went down to reception and saw the night manager, asking if he might use the inner office for a private telephone call, and when the young man had ushered him inside and offered, as was usual he supposed, to get the callee for him, he waved his hand, saying impatiently, "No . . . I'll get it. I know how to work the damned thing. Mr. Irons showed me this morning."

It took longer than he thought, a matter of ten minutes or so, and he was close to giving up when a woman's voice said over the wire, "Who is it? Who is calling?"

"Is that Lady Lockerbie, ma'am?"

"Yes it is." The voice was snappish and decisive, the voice of a woman who did not suffer fools gladly. "Who is it calling?"

He said, very meekly, "You won't know me, Your Ladyship, but I'm calling on very urgent business. This is Mr. Wesley Tybalt, yard manager of Swann-on-Wheels. I was given this number by Mr. George Swann and told to use it in emergencies. There has been an emergency, Your Ladyship. I'd be very obliged indeed if you could put me in touch with Mr. Swann."

He waited, counting the seconds and perhaps ten elapsed

before she said, carefully, "What *kind* of emergency, Mr. Tybalt?", and he said, eagerly, "A fire, Your Ladyship. I'm afraid I have some bad news for Mr. Swann. Half the yard has been burned down. The brigades are still there."

That rattled her a little. He heard the swift intake of breath but the voice was casual when she said, "I think I might be able to locate Mr. Swann for you. He is one of my house guests."

"You could reach him soon, Your Ladyship?"

"Possibly. I'll pass your message to him."

"I'm sorry, ma'am . . . at the risk of sounding impertinent it is essential I locate him as quickly as possible. I could wait while you enquired for him."

There was a longish pause. Finally she said, "Very well, Mr. Who-is-it?"

"Tybalt, ma'am."

"Tybalt."

She went away and he settled himself as comfortably as possible in a cane chair that was too deep and too small for his bulk and customary sitting posture. Minutes passed and he yawned, trying to keep awake by equating the faraway voice with that lovely imperious face of the horsewoman Gisela had shown him. Presently a polite male voice enquired, "Did you get your subscriber, sir?" and he said, "Yes, I'm waiting." Slowly, as minutes passed, the exhilaration the success of his ruse had injected into him waned, the mild glee insufficient to hold at bay the memory of Tybalt's baffled eyes and short legs dangling six inches from the closet floor. His head nodded and the confines of the uncomfortable chair enfolded him in a way that made him yearn for release. And presently, against all probability, he dozed.

6

Return of Atlas

THE GARDEN-HOUSE, A PRETTY, TIMBER-CON-
structed building, set in a secluded part of the grounds
of Sir James Lockerbie's country home, was his wife's
favourite resort when she was temporarily disenchanted
with cities. It was comfortably furnished and out of
sight and sound of the big house, an ideal place to re-
enact a kind of Marie Antoinette Arcadian fantasy, and
Barbara Lockerbie was given to fantasies. Indeed, she
would have argued that fantasy (judicially translated into
fact whenever the opportunity offered) had been responsible for her spectacular climb from the daughter of an
Irish emigrant, to the late Victorian equivalent of a
Regency courtesan. George himself would have acknowledged this. In fact, every young spark and kept doxy in
London's second-grade society acknowledged it, and it
was generally assumed that even Sir James Lockerbie
must have adjusted to it, for there were certain commercial
advantages accruing to the husband of one of the most
talked-of women in London. It kept the name of Lockerbie in the eye of men with money to burn, especially in
a society where, despite so many impressive technical
achievements, the earth-closet and the close stool were
still much in use, where few country houses boasted a
bathroom and the habit of daily bathing was still regarded
as a mark of eccentricity.

Thus Sir James, who spent a great deal of his time

travelling, and whose ambition it was to die the wealthiest man in Scotland, gave his wife a notoriously long leash and appeared to pay little heed to gossip concerning her virtue. She was gay, undeniably pretty, an excellent hostess when he had need of her services as such, and wore a romantic halo that went some way to encourage tolerance regarding her alleged shortcomings in other respects.

Her father, it was rumoured, was a Kerry landowner, whose gambling debts had obliged him to live abroad where he subsequently married a Portuguese heiress. Her mother, some claimed, was a Polish ballet dancer, and had been a mistress of Czar Nicholas II who had married her off to a British embassy official. She had, according to other random tongues, been born in Trieste, in an Indian garrison town, in the American West during the '49 gold rush, in Bergen, in Egypt and any number of places with exotic connotations, like Samarkand, Baghdad and a village high in the Caucasus.

Not one word of these colourful stories was true but this was no loss to romance. Real romance resided in her survival, and promotion to a position where she could pick and choose wealthy lovers and receive them, more or less openly, at the Garden House, on a Hertfordshire estate of four hundred acres, or in her apartment in the Avenue Wagram, in Paris. Promiscuous she undeniably was but she was not a fool and London had never been the setting for a single indiscretion. She had more than enough commonsense to realise that nobody moving in her circle credited the fact that anything important, including an act of infidelity, could occur outside London. Incidents rumoured to have taken place across the Channel, or in the British provinces, could therefore be dismissed as fiction.

As to the truth concerning her origin, perhaps she herself had never known it and had been obliged to invent a pedigree. In fact, she was the illegitimate daughter of a scullery-maid, employed on an absentee landlord's estate in County Mayo at the time of the Irish potato famine, and Bab Casey, as she began life, was the deferred price paid by a starving girl for one square meal a day. Her mother must have had a certain shrewdness, however, for she at least prevailed upon her lover to give her enough money to emigrate to Canada on one of the Cork coffin ships, and the scullery-maid must have been hardy, too, for she and her child survived when three-fifths of her fellow passengers died on voyage, or during the quarantine period in the St. Lawrence River, where they were buried in mass graves on an island before the survivors were set ashore at Montreal.

It was here, in the shanty town, that Barbara spent her brief childhood until she followed her mother's example and ensured her own survival by sailing away as the fifteen-year-old mistress of a German sea captain, later drowned off the Newfoundland Banks. She next turned up in Liverpool, as part of the travelling equipment of an animal trainer, who exhibited at one-night circus stands in the cotton towns of the North-west. It was here, while assisting her employer in his alligator act, that she attracted the attention of a professional gambler, who took her to Glasgow, graveyard of many a gambler, and his too after Barbara moved from half-world into broad daylight by leaving him and marrying a Paisley architect of respectable family.

From then on her career was at least on record. She divorced her husband when she was twenty-three and married Sir James Lockerbie a few months after his wife had died of jaundice. Few women could have come this far without learning the basic rules of survival in a world shaped by men for men and Barbara learned more than most. Her philosophy was simple, and based on the assumption that a busy man, obsessed with the business of coaxing a good living from a gullible public, may prattle a lot about domestic felicity but invariably ventures beyond the range of his own hearth in search of it during his brief intervals between stints of hard grind. Another thing she learned about men was that few of them ever matured, as a woman matures. From adolescence until senility the simple gratification of their senses was more important to them than all their wealth and status and almost any man, however thrustful and ambitious, is a slave to his carnal appetites. It was therefore in this direction, and no other, that a personable woman should look for advancement. Had she been asked to summarise her conclusions in this field she would have said that a help-mate, however dutiful and accomplished, invariably lost the battle to a bedmate, providing, of course, that the bedmate knew her business as well as Barbara Lockerbie, alias Mrs. Creighton, alias Barbara Tracy, Barbara Villeneuve, Barbara Schmitt and so on, all the way back to little Babs Casey, fighting to stay alive in a Canadian shantytown.

*　　*　　*

She had tested this theory on a string of lovers, some chosen for gain and lustre, others, as she passed the thirty mark, for diversion, and her involvement with George Swann, head of a national transport network, was proof that her theory was sound. George attracted her for a variety of reasons, chief among them being his indifference to competition. It was as though his headstart over every other haulier in the country equipped him with an ability to discount her other admirers, past and present, and this added up to a kind of amiable arrogance that she found very agreeable. George took what she had to offer boisterously and gratefully, but he left it at that, using her, she suspected, much as she had used a succession of men in her rise from the gutter. He never probed her past, or speculated on their future as lovers, seeing her, no doubt, as a prolonged holiday treat and, God knows, the poor man badly needed a holiday when she ran across him at his ship launching last April. As far as she could decide he hadn't had one for years and was not even aware that he had earned one, and it might have been the memory of this that prompted her to lie about the telephone bell that broke in upon their idyll towards midnight the day of the regatta.

He was shaving now in the tiny dressing-room adjoining the bedroom and from the bed she could hear the rasp of razor on stiff bristles that required him, so he said, to shave night and morning. She felt very much at peace with the world after a tiring and somewhat boring day on the river, for the regatta and the sunshine had brought everybody out, and she had had her fill of chitter-chatter with local sportsmen and their frumpish wives. George, thank God, was not a sportsman, and had no interest in fashionable games and pastimes. He evidently enjoyed his work and manifold responsibilities. He must have done, in order to keep his nose to the grindstone ever since he took his father's place as head of the network, but he had no social ambition and this in itself was refreshing. He was, she would have said, a man who preferred to save his vitality for his network and her, and she was not disposed to let him go until she had exhausted all his possibilities.

She now lay spreadeagled on the silk coverlet of the bed, speculating whether the long day by the river had exhausted him as much as it had her, and how this was likely to affect his performance as a lover. She was clinically interested in such performances, and his, a little storming and clumsy at first, was improving rapidly under her tuition. She even thought he was aware of this and gave her the credit for it, and this was very exceptional in the male animal. She called, lazily, "Do you know why I'm always pleased to see you, George?"

He called back, "Because you don't have to flatter me."

"No," she said, "although that's a point. It's because you're the only man I know who doesn't decorate his face with a lot of bristly undergrowth."

He said, laughing, "Got it from the Gov'nor. Never seen him with a beard or whiskers."

He often mentioned his father, usually in terms that

implied they got along much better than most reigning monarchs and their heirs apparent. "You're very fond of him, aren't you, George?"

"I've got a hell of a lot of respect for him."

"Does he keep a mistress somewhere?"

"He's turned seventy, woman."

"Did he ever keep one?"

"Not to my knowledge. Personally I doubt it. All his energy went into the network. He started from scratch."

He drifted in, dabbing his tanned, good-natured face with a towel, and contemplated her a moment before lowering himself on the edge of the bed. He was in no hurry. He never was nowadays and this was something else she found rewarding about him.

"What's your mother like, George?"

"You're not interested in my mother."

"I'm interested in any woman whose husband reaches seventy without him getting goatish."

He said, thoughtfully, "Come to think of it, I daresay you're right. She probably had a good deal to do with it."

"How, George?"

"I always got the impression she wilts every time he comes into the room. She still does."

"That wouldn't account for it, would it?"

"It would in her case. She never troubled to conceal the fact and that has a steadying effect on a man."

"Tell me."

"It enlarges his domestic conscience. Makes him feel shabby when he does cut loose."

"Your wife thinks a deal of you. Do I bother your conscience?"

He said, quite seriously, "Yes, from time to time. But then I tell myself that a man must have fun sometimes. I had a good deal up to the age of twenty-one but not much since."

"Where did you find your fun, George?"

"In Munich."

"Tell me about Munich."

He told her something of his time in Munich, where a statuesque German widow, almost old enough to be his mother, had seduced him before he was twenty. He still remembered Rosa Ledermann with great affection. It was she who had shaped his tastes in women. He had a preference for well-covered women, with generous hips and busts, and now that he looked at Barbara Lockerbie he realised that it was her figure that had attracted him, even though she had delicate features and a beautiful skin. He said, voicing his thoughts, "If I had met you a few years ago I wouldn't be here dancing to your tune. You were skinnier then, or so I've heard. Is that so?"

"Yes, it is so," and she subjected him to a long, careful scrutiny, noting his jauntiness and the half-smile about his clean-shaven lips. She thought: 'He could keep me quiet for a year or more, I daresay. Maybe even longer, providing he didn't begin taking me for granted.' Aloud she said, "Kiss me, George."

"I'll do more than that. Move over."

Her arms arched over his strong neck, pulling him down and pressing his mouth to hers with a kind of playful determination, as though willing him to take the initiative. And when her mouth opened he did, losing his jauntiness and letting his hand run as far as her thighs but it was never her habit to yield to the first overtures. As his head came up she turned hers sideways and he saw that she was laughing.

"What's the joke, Babs? Is it us? Saying good night all round and slipping away here?"

"No, not that."

"Something that came to mind unexpectedly?"

"That's very sharp of you, George. Sometimes you're a little too sharp. I was thinking of that poor little man on the other end of the telephone."

"What little man? You said it was your town butler, ringing about tomorrow's enquiries."

"Well, it wasn't. That was a wicked lie."

"Why?"

19

"To keep you here. It was someone who works in your yard. A man called Tybalt."

He sat up, instantly attentive. "*Wesley* Tybalt? My yard manager?"

"Yes, and it was very naughty of you to give him this number to use in emergencies."

His face clouded now as he said, "Tybalt's had that number ever since our first time up here but he's never used it. What was the emergency?"

"I'll not tell you."

"You damned well will tell me!"

It was a long time since Barbara Lockerbie had felt menaced and the experience was rare enough to excite her. She said, "Now listen here, Mr. Waggonmaster, you might be God Almighty in your network but here . . ." but he cut in, taking her by the shoulders in a grip that would leave bruises.

"I'm not fooling any longer. It might be very important, so you'll tell me why Wes Tybalt rang."

"It wasn't important."

"You let me be judge of that."

She had learned, over the years, precisely how much teasing a man could stand. There was no sense in antagonising him beyond a certain point or he might turn sulky and sulks in a lover meant a dull evening.

"All right, let me go. It was a fire at the yard."

"What kind of fire?"

"How should I know? He said a fire, and asked if I could get hold of you."

"And you left him on the end of the telephone?"

"The line is still open."

"But good God, I heard that bell tinkle when I started shaving fifteen minutes ago. You had no right . . ." and he would have made for the landing where the telephone was but she felt challenged and grabbed him by the hand, throwing her full weight against his arm so that he staggered and fell on her.

"Let go, Babs! I've got to talk to Tybalt if he's still there."

"He's waited fifteen minutes. He'll wait another ten. At least long enough to prove I'm more important than a transport yard," and she tried to enfold him in a way that would have delayed some men even if the bed had been on fire.

She got a real shock then, of a kind that was unique in her experiences over the last few years, although it was by no means the first time she had been manhandled. He got his right hand under her chin and pushed with sufficient force to break her embrace and throw her against the bedhead where the impact made her teeth rattle. And then, before she could regain sufficient breath to swear, as only Barbara Lockerbie could swear given provocation, he was gone and she heard him snap, "*Tybalt?* Are you still there, Tybalt?", and after that, while she was deciding whether she enjoyed or resented being rough-handled by a man again, a sharp exclamation on his part followed by a long, mystifying silence.

2

The voice reached Adam like a hail from the top of a mountain. George's voice certainly, but distorted by distance and his own drowsiness so that it was small as a child's yet charged with a child's urgency.

"Is that you, Tybalt? Tybalt, can you *hear* me?" and he dragged himself fully awake, stared down at the earpiece still held in his numbed hand, and said, "It's not Tybalt, George. Tybalt's skipped." And the gasp at the far end of the wire reached him as the ultimate in surprise and apprehension.

He was alert now and wondering how he could have slept so soundly without relinquishing his grasp on the heavy earpiece. There was a sour taste in his mouth, the straps of his tin leg had cut into the flesh of his thigh and he could still smell that damned smoke.

"*You*, Gov'nor?"

"It's me, George. Come on home you young fool, and get about your business."

"What . . . what's happened? I heard there'd been a fire. How bad a fire?"

"As bad as a fire can be, short of loss of life. Two-thirds of H.Q. is in ruins but that's the least of your troubles, lad."

It was rubbing in salt but he didn't care. If anyone had sat up and begged for punishment George had over the last few weeks.

"Two-thirds? What *could* be worse?"

"Your credit. And the life of someone who gave everything he had to the network."

"But you said no one was hurt . . ."

"Not in the fire. I'll give it you short and sweet, George. Young Tybalt's made a monstrous fool of you. He robbed the firm right and left and his father caught him at it."

"*Old* man Tybalt?"

"Yes, *old* man Tybalt. He was one year junior to me. What the devil has his age to do with it? He was so damned ashamed that he hanged himself before I could get to him and I hold you responsible for that. Can you still hear me?"

"I can hear you."

"Then I'll add something to that. Do you know what Tybalt used to anchor the cravat that strangled him? One of Lockerbie's flush cisterns. Go in and tell that woman as much. I daresay it will make her laugh. Then come home and don't waste time doing it, d'you hear?"

He replaced the earpiece on its hook and put his hand to his aching thigh, massaging it with the slow circular motion he had employed ever since he wore an artificial limb. The night manager looked in.

"Were you able to get your subscriber, sir?"

"I got him and I'm obliged to you. Put the cost of the call on my bill and make it up for the morning. I shall be leaving after breakfast."

"Certainly, sir. Good night, sir."

"Good night."

He climbed the stairs feeling older than Pharaoh and as oppressed as Atlas. There was no satisfaction in bludgeoning George in that ruthless way but it had to be done. Only a shock of that nature would bring the boy to his senses and even that might fail when he surveyed the ruin of the yard. He might see it as something hardly worth redeeming.

*　　*　　*

She was still sitting on the bed. Naked now, her back to the bedrest and slowly combing her blue-black hair as though, by unmasking all her batteries, she could be certain of capitulation on the spot. He was stubborn but not as stubborn as all that, or not unless the sum total of all she had learned about men was less than she had assumed all these years. She said, gaily, "Well, George? Did the little man tell you to report back for duty?"

"The little man wasn't the yard manager. The little man was a very big one."

"Oh? Who would that be, George?"

"My father."

She was not so much alerted by that as by his changed expression. It was drained yet glowering, as though news of the fire had reduced him to total insignificance.

"But he's retired, isn't he? How does he come to be mixed up in it?"

"No time to explain," he said, thrusting his legs into his trousers and hitching his belt so tightly that it emphasised his small waist and the impressive breadth of his shoulders.

"Listen, George," she said, earnestly, "I'm sorry I kept it from you but I really couldn't imagine you would be concerned to that extent. After all, what do you pay men for if it isn't to run the place when you're away?"

"Wesley Tybalt did that all right," he growled. "He's been practising large-scale fraud and coinciding every fresh haul with my absences. If I ever run across him he won't live to betray anyone else who trusted him!"

"How much has he stolen from you?"

He glared down at her. Her promise seemed to arouse in him no more interest than if he had been looking at a bale of merchandise.

"What the hell does it matter? I get a message that my place is in ruins, that my manager has skipped with everything he could get his claws on, that Tybalt's father, one of my Gov'nor's oldest colleagues has hanged himself for shame of it. What the devil do you expect me to do? Call it a day and snuggle into bed?"

"*Hanged himself?* You mean the manager's father was involved?"

He paused, at least long enough to give her a pitying glance. "How could you understand? Some people have scruples. You might be amazed to learn it but they do. Wes Tybalt's father worked for Swann-on-Wheels from the day it sent its first waggon out on the roads. It was his life, and he lived to see it in ruins at the hands of his son and successor. It's no use asking how you might feel in those circumstances. You probably wouldn't feel a damned thing, not being put together that way. But *I* feel something. I feel it wouldn't take much to put me in the frame of mind of old man Tybalt!"

He was scrambling into his clothes all the time he was talking. She said, with a shrug, "Well, you still have to be practical. There's no transport out of here until morning. All the servants are in bed, the stables are locked, and there isn't a train to town until six in the morning."

He paid no further attention to her so she climbed off the bed and put her arms around him. "George, dear, think! I can arrange for you to be driven to the station in time to catch the first train. I daresay it's a shock, and naturally you'll feel yourself needed. But for heaven's sake . . ."

He freed himself from her with an air of resignation.

"I'll walk to the main road and hope to hop a night

haul into Covent Garden. Market gardeners pass through the village from time to time." He gave her a final, searching look. "This is goodbye, Babs. I'm wide awake now and you aren't likely to catch me napping again. Good hunting."

The flatness and finality of the parting stunned her, striking a shattering blow at her vanity, so that, for the moment at least, she felt as vulnerable as the fifteen-year-old waif who had staked her future on Captain Schmitt, in the St. Lawrence River, all those years ago. She said, wonderingly, "Don't I count for anything any more?"

"Not a thing, my dear, but it's not your fault. Like I say, it's the way people are put together and you're patchwork mostly."

She had no answer to this, and stood there, hands on hips, watching him go. The front door slammed and she listened to the scrape of his feet on the wooden steps leading to the lawn. He was a man entirely outside her experience and her sense of humiliation, although overwhelming, was tinged with curiosity. She went over to the window and pulled aside the curtain. In the light of the waning moon she saw his shadow cross a gravel path and melt into the coppice that shut off the view of the big house. She realised then that she would never see him again and the certainty of this generated in her a yearning that was more urgent than anything in her past. She would have given all she possessed to have been able to will him to turn about, re-enter the room, throw her on the bed and share his strength with her for a few riotous moments, absorbing a little of the ethos of the first real man she had ever held in her arms. Frustration welled in her to a point where she could have screamed and hurled things about the room but she lacked even the spirit to do this. Instead she sat astride her dressing-stool, staring into the gilded mirror and seeing there a parody of the woman who had purred back at her reflection an hour ago.

3

Adam stood in the narrow casement of the tower looking across an acre of desolation at the familiar curve of the river, finding a crumb of satisfaction in the knowledge that the stone-built belfry had survived while all about it were heaps of ashes and charred timber, broken here and there by the rotten tooth of a chimney-stack where the stoves of the various buildings had been centred. Here, on this side of the yard, his tower was all that remained. The Tooley Street warehouse, the counting-house, the waggon-shed, the forge and even the high clapboard fence had been consumed, together, he assumed, with a hundredweight of documents, ledgers, invoices and records of goods in transit to the docks and goods awaiting transit in the network. How did one set about sorting out a mess on this scale? Old Tybalt could have attempted it but Tybalt was lying under a sheet in the Rotherhithe mortuary.

At right angles to the main gate the stable block was all but destroyed and two of the original warehouses, timber-built, were roofless and windowless. Of the rest, on the far side, where the Southwark brigades had been first on the scene, warehouses had been saved but it was likely half the goods inside had been spoiled by jets played on the roofs and through the windows. Tiny eddies of smoke still rose from a jumble of waggons at the centre assembly point and word had come that a total of forty-seven vehicles had been destroyed or damaged. All the horses had been saved, thank God, but to use them someone would have to borrow transport from Southern Square, The Bonus and the Kent Triangle, dislocating all the schedules in those regions for as long as Blunderstone the coachbuilder took to replace what was lost.

He heard footsteps on the stairway and turned back into the room as George came in. His face, clothes and hands were smudged and blackened. He looked like a man who had himself narrowly escaped death in a blazing building.

He said, "They told me you were here at first light, George. Is that so?"

"I was lucky. I got a lift as far as Barnet in a market gardener's van, then caught a train around four."

"Have you had any breakfast?"

"I've no appetite for breakfast, Gov'nor."

"You'd best have some, none the less. Send one of the men over to the coffee stall. You've had a good look round?"

"I've seen all there is to see." He glanced round the octagonal room, littered with debris that might just as well have been burned. "I'm glad this place is intact. It means a lot to you, doesn't it?"

"Aye, it does." He lowered himself on a crate, spread his legs and rested his hands on his knees. Pity for the boy was beginning to invade him. He had never seen George look or move in this listless way. "It's not the end of the world, lad. You'll make it all good, I daresay, providing you pull yourself together and go back to that nice gel of yours. There's not much you can do here until the assessors have had a look. Why don't you go home to her. She'll be right glad to see you."

George said, "I can't get two things out of my head. How I could have been so wrong about Wes Tybalt, and why his father had to take it so hard."

"As to the first," Adam said, "young Tybalt fooled us all, me included. I never liked the chap. He was too smarmy for my book. But it always seemed to me he knew his business."

"He knew his business all right," George said, savagely. "It's hard to estimate but my guess is he's taken us for thousands, apart from the fire. I screwed that much out of Robsart before the police took him away. I got a list of his confederates too. These fellows have no more loyalty to each other than they have for us."

"How many are involved?"

"Eight. Three in Northern Region, three in the Midlands and two in the South. Robsart told all he knows and I think he's telling the truth. Probably too scared to do less. I've sent wires to lay the others by the heels, but they're small fry. Tybalt was the brains behind it. Robsart says he even organised Linklater's side of it and where the devil are we to start looking for him?"

"Overseas, I'd say. Providing you want to."

"Don't you?"

"No," said Adam, "I don't think I do. He'd be hard to find, anyway. He probably had it planned and is heading for some country without an extradition treaty. He might be snug on any one of a thousand vessels by now. My guess is he crossed to France last night and will keep moving from there. Take my advice. Don't spend yourself chasing Wesley. You've got more than enough to keep you occupied."

"That isn't the reason, is it? I mean, not the reason you don't want Wesley brought back and charged."

"No. The real reason is the loyalty I owe his father. Used to bully him unmercifully in the old days, when he came up here fussing about one thing and another. But Swann-on-Wheels owes him more than it owes any single man and if I could have reached him in time I'm sure I could have talked him round. However, there it is. Any fool can chart a course when he's home and dry. It never occurred to me he'd go to his son and give him a headstart in that way."

"Do you really think he started the fire, Gov'nor?"

"He started the warehouse fire. Probably didn't intend to do more than destroy what was in there, so that we should have trouble proving anything. Unsupported evidence of men like Robsart wouldn't have convicted him."

"Then why didn't he stay and brazen it out?"

"He slipped up admitting as much as he did to his father. Or maybe the size of the blaze scared him, or someone saw him entering or coming out of the place. Who can tell? Forget Wesley and take a look at your own affairs, George. Care to tell me how it started? I'm not poking about in a midden heap. It might help to talk to someone other than your wife."

"Gisela won't even refer to it. Most English women would but a Continental goes to the heart of the matter."

"Isn't that woman Lockerbie the heart of the matter?"

"No, Gov'nor, not really. There was nothing permanent about that relationship. What happened here in the meantime is what counts."

"You're saying you were never in love with that woman?"

"I've never really understood that phrase . . . 'in love'. Have you?"

"Not in the way poets peddle it. Love? I suppose I've always seen it as a crop raised by an association between a man and a woman after they've been trapped by their senses. Your mother and I were like that. I didn't 'love' her in that sense when we married. And she was far too green and too flighty to know what she was about, apart from choosing a wedding gown, and having some kind of status conferred upon her. But she fancied me and I fancied her, and we grew important to one another, the way people do when they find 'emselves saddled with shared responsibilities." He beetled his brows and stared at the floor. "If you had to cut loose for a spell why didn't you go to the places men frequent when things get on top of them?"

"It wasn't that kind of need."

"What kind was it?"

George said, slowly, "I was twenty when I met Gisela. I'll tell you something I never told anyone else. You've met her tribe of sisters. They were all as pretty as pictures, and very saucy with it in those days. I might have settled on either one of them, or all three of them maybe, if it hadn't been for old Grandfather Maximilien and his engine. He steered Gisela my way. Quite deliberately. You probably never did believe our eldest boy was a seven-month child."

"You married her on that account?"

"I didn't even know she was pregnant."

"Then what's all this got to do with you staking every-thing you worked for on a frolic with a high-class whore, like that Lockerbie woman?"

"As I say, it goes all the way back to Max and his engine. Until I found myself hooked to that, life was all cherry pie. Afterwards? Well, it was never quite the same again. I put everything I had and hoped for into that brute Maximus and I still think I was on the right track. About transport, I mean, about petrol-driven vehicles being much more than fussy little toys, replacing the carriage and pair. Then, when I thought I'd made a breakthrough, you handed the business to me on a plate and the fact is I wasn't ready for it. I had no idea how much it involved, and how many demands it made on a man."

"You seemed content enough. You appeared to be making a rare go of it."

"I was content, and I was making a go of it. But then, one day last spring, I suddenly realised it was taking over. To the exclusion of everything else, including Gisela and the children. It was my bad luck that this should hit me in Barbara Lockerbie's company. Do you want to hear the rest?"

"Only if you want to tell me."

"We met at that launching of mine. The Lockerbies invited me to spend a weekend with them at their lodge in Skye. Have you ever been to Skye?"

"No, though I've looked across at it."

"It's a magic place. Or it seemed so to me at that time and in her company. Sir James didn't turn up and I see now she planned it that way. We were out on the lower slopes of a mountain and the weather was fine and warm for the time of year. I suddenly realised what I'd been missing all these years and that soon I'd be forty. It all stemmed from that realisation, a matter of letting off steam, I imagine. The trouble was I didn't realise, until I heard your voice over the telephone last night, how much steam was there. That, and the fact that women have always been more important to me than they seem to be to you and Alex and Giles and the others. I don't mean all women. I mean lively, high-spirited women like Barbara Lockerbie, and that landlady of mine I once told you about in Munich."

He understood. Far better, perhaps, than George knew, for in her own way Henrietta was such a woman. Had it been otherwise it seemed probable that he too might have needed a change when he was George's age. The trouble lay, he supposed, in the fact that Gisela was a serious-minded little body and wouldn't know how to coax him out of such a mood, whereas Henrietta would, and had done so time and again without him being fully aware of it until now. He said, "Well, some of us drive ourselves hard and when we do there's generally a price to pay. You've paid yours, lad, and been overcharged to my way of thinking. I'm glad you told me as much as you did, but where do you go from here?"

"I know the answer to that," George said, "but I haven't the gall to tell you. Maybe I'll tell you when this place is ticking over again."

"No, tell me now. You've laid all your other cards on the table. Play out the hand."

George said, with a ghost of a grin, "You'll kick me downstairs I daresay, but I'll chance it. I need a longish spell clear away from this place. Not to blow off more steam, at least not that kind of steam, but to follow a dream. Your kind of dream."

"Something new?"

"Not entirely. We went over the same ground when we parted company that last time. As I say, I've never ceased to believe the real future of road transport is in the mechanically propelled vehicle but everything I've attempted so far has gone off at half-cock and I know why. You can't approach a job as demanding as that with half your mind on a business this size. You need isolation, and time to concentrate on every last detail, every

modification, every scrap of information that comes in
from the States and the Continent. Steam waggons aren't
the answer, not for our kind of work. But there *is* an
answer and I'd find it if I had the time and money."

"You've got the money, haven't you?"

"Not really. All I've put by is earmarked to pay share-
holders what Wesley Tybalt filched but I could scrape by
on next-to-nothing until I had a blueprint that satisfied
me. Do you remember Jock Quirt, that Scots mechanic
I had by me, when I was working on Maximus up at Sam's
place in Manchester? He was an ugly little chap, with
very little to say for himself, but he was a bit of a genius
to my way of thinking. He's still working on that prototype up in the north."

"You're suggesting you set him to work right here?"

"No, I'm suggesting I go to him and we work on it
together, but it would mean someone who really knew the
ropes taking over here until next spring. I think I could
guarantee results by then and we'd have motor transport
that would give us a two-year start over every haulier in
the country. I've absolutely no right to ask this . . ."

"But you are asking it?"

"Yes."

His head came up and the quick gesture reminded
Adam again that, of all his children, George came closest
to the Adam Swann who had made his grab on the
strength of three guarantees. The yield of a looted necklace, sold to shady rascals in the city; a dream, not unlike
George's; and an invincible belief in his own star. He
said, doubtfully, "I'm turned seventy, George, and past
it. Go ahead with your dream if you have to and you'll
be no use to me or anybody else if you don't. But find
someone else to sort this lot out and get things moving
again."

"There isn't anybody else. And you aren't past it.
It's my belief you don't really think you are either."

"I wonder."

He turned and crossed to the narrow window and this

time he did not see the desolation below but the broad curve of the river and the many-turreted tower he had explored only yesterday. He stood there a long time, thinking back and assessing himself in terms of profit and loss, failure and achievement, hopes fulfilled and un-fulfilled. He thought of 'Tryst' too, and the showplace he had made of it in the years that had passed since he turned his back on this slum. He would miss that and he hadn't much time to squander. How would Henrietta think of it? What would his doctor have to say about him shouldering a packload like this at his age? But did it matter what Henrietta, or the doctor, or anybody else thought? He did a kind of equation with the various factors of the case. A headquarters burned to a cinder. A criminal prosecution in the offing that would expose him and his as fools, milked by their own employees. George himself, at a crisis in his life, wanting desperately to atone but in his own way and on his own terms. He thought, distractedly: 'I wonder if he's right and whether I'm right to sympathise with him? I was wrong about mechanical transport. It's plain enough it's almost here now. I might even live to see the day they put the last of the horses out to grass and clutter the roads with clumsy galleons, like his precious Maximus. Everyone said I was mad to carve up the area the new railways had neglected but I saw further than most of 'em. Maybe George does now, for he's my flesh and blood, and there's a lot of old Sam Rawlinson in him. But none of these things count in the long run. The heart of the matter is, would I care to come back here and spend a St. Martin's summer in this room, gathering all the loose ends together and adapting, if I could accept them, to all the changes he's made already?' And suddenly his heart gave him the answer and he understood that, in an odd, clownish way, he would enjoy the exercise enormously, would relish being fully extended again and needed, not only by George, but by all those Johnny-Come-Latelys George had planted out along the network, cocky youngsters

mostly who had long since written him off as an old cod-
ger, well past his prime. He said, "I'll do it, George.
For one year from today. And God help the whole boiling
of you if I prove unequal to it, for then you'll all be in a
worse mess than ever. As to money, well, you don't have
to worry on that score. Your grandfather didn't trust
any one of you come to the end. He left his pile to me,
with orders to dole it out as I saw fit, and you'll get your
slice of it. If you want to pour it down the drain in some
murky workshop that's your business. I only want two
pledges from you and here they are. You'll be back here to
take over twelve months from now, hit or miss. And you
take that wife of yours north with you."

"Gisela won't leave the family."

"You can dump the family with Henrietta. It'll keep
her out of mischief while I'm slumming it right here."

George said, eagerly, "You won't regret it, Gov'nor.
Not when the final score is totted up."

"I'm not so sure about that but I've followed my nose
in situations like this all my life and I'm too long in the
tooth to change. I see too much of myself in you, George,
and that's a fact. Though I do flatter myself I had better
brakes at your age."

"Giles will back you."

"Oh no, he won't. In case you haven't looked hard
enough, Giles has a dream of his own and it doesn't run
on four wheels. As for Hugo, well, I've never seen him
as anything more than Swann's barker in the market-
place. Young Edward is more promising. He showed his
mettle yesterday. I'll take him under my wing for he's
merchant through and through, I wouldn't wonder."

He got up stiffly. "Go down and get a wash under the
pump and we'll drink to it before I catch my train. I've
still got to break this news to your mother. She won't
have heard of it, tucked away down there."

George went out without another word and a moment
later, watching from the window, Adam saw him splashing
head and shoulders in the pump trough. He thought,

'I don't know . . . I could have wrung his neck twelve hours since, and here I am, giving him his head again just as if he was all I had to show for my years here.' And suddenly, as clear as a picture on the wall, he had a memory of coming home to 'Tryst' one frosty February night, in 1864, and being greeted by the news that Hetty had been delivered of her third child and second boy, and going upstairs to look down on a merry little bundle in the cot, wide awake, knuckling his mouth, and staring back at him with an expression he could only describe as conspiratorial. And then, he recalled, a droll thing had happened, reminding him of the pact he and Hetty had made nine months before, after he learned from his father she had gone off the rails in his absence and come near getting herself seduced by a gunner who had fancied her. As if the baby in the cot was aware of the circumstances accounting for his presence, he had winked in a way that made Adam laugh aloud. He understood then why George was so easy to forgive.

7

A Titan, Fishing

THE NARROW COASTAL ROAD, REACHING THE
tiny village of Llanystumdwy, crossed the boulder-strewn
river Dwyfor by a humped-back bridge, just beyond a
cottage on the right. Where the bridge wall was broken,
giving foot access to the river below, she stopped the dog-
cart, saying, "Down there, Giles. That cottage is his old
home but I learned from that man back there he'd gone
fishing. He spends a lot of time fishing when Parliament's
not sitting and he can slip away up here."

He looked at her with amused incredulity. "I can't
just buttonhole him in that way, Romayne. Not him,
not a man with his reputation. He'd snub me and I'd
deserve it."

"L.G. has never snubbed anyone in his life. Sat on
them, talked them down and carried them along in his
wake, but not snubbed. It's not his nature and I should
know, for I'm one of his constituents seeing that Beddgelert house is still in my name. You do as I say. March
right up to him and tell him what you have in mind and
he'll admire you for it. Nobody in the world is cheekier
than Lloyd George."

"Let me see that letter again."

Romayne opened her reticule and took out a single
folded sheet, straightening it and passing it to him. The
secretary's reply was couched in a single paragraph on
House of Commons paper. It said:

Dear Madam,

Further to your enquiry concerning your husband, Mr. Giles Swann, Mr. Lloyd George has asked me to say that he will be in your area for one week when the House rises and would be happy to see Mr. Swann if he could come to Llanystumdwy before midday between Monday, 15th, and Thursday, 18th.

Nothing else but the signature was written on the paper.

He said doubtfully, "It's a bit chilly, isn't it? A chap like that must get hundreds of similar requests and if he's on holiday . . ."

"Trust me, Giles. I know exactly what I'm about!" and he thought, 'Well, I can stand a snub from a stranger, and afterwards, maybe, she'll let me go about things in my own way.' And he got down and went through the gap to the steep, fern-clad bank where there was a tiny path, hardly more than a rabbit run, leading inland through close-set trees growing above the stream. He had only gone about fifty yards when he saw him, sitting on a rounded boulder holding what looked like a boy's fishing rod made from a bamboo cane and a ball of twine.

He recognised him instantly, not only as the rumbustious politician who was always getting into the news and its backspread of photographs, but at a much longer remove – a jaunty, rather cocky young man he had encountered all those years ago at the door of the empty Chamber of Commons, on his very first visit to Westminster, the incident that had inspired Romayne's impulsive letter to the member for Caernarvon Boroughs.

He recalled the circumstances vividly. Himself a shy, thirteen-year-old, awed by the place where he stood; the young Welshman, brash and confident, despite his sing-song accent and country clothes. Slightly patronising yet friendly and informative, with his talk of the miserly wages Llanberis quarry-workers were paid and his intention, implied rather than uttered, of doing something about it if the opportunity offered. And since then he

had, proving that his talk on that occasion was no adolescent boast but the pledge of a man already aware of his
potential.

All that, however, had happened eighteen years ago
and since then 'Mr. George' (who had dismissed the
hallowed Chamber as 'crabbed and poky') had moved on
to capture headlines as the noisiest, wittiest, most tren-
chant member of the Liberal Party whereas Giles, by his
own reckoning, had stood still looking on.

He went down the narrow path until the fisherman,
hearing the crackle of dry twigs, looked up and smiled,
calling, in a slightly moderated brogue, "Lovely morning,
Johnny Peep! Come and join me in the sun. The fish
aren't rising. I did much better here as a boy poacher!"

He still wasn't sure of his welcome, despite Lloyd
George's jocular greeting. 'Johnny Peep' implied an
intrusion and he could pinpoint the source of the gibe:

> *Here I am, Johnny Peep,*
> *And I saw three sheep,*
> *And those three sheep saw me.*
> *Half-a-crown apiece pays for their fleece,*
> *And so Johnny Peep goes free . .*

It was a verse quip of Robbie Burns, who had used it to
win an evening's entertainment from three northcountry
drovers.

He said, "I'm Giles Swann, Mr. George. My wife wrote
for an appointment and later persuaded me to follow you
here. I realise that's a liberty but she seems to think you
don't mind seeing constituents."

"I never mind meeting an old acquaintance, Mr.
Swann."

"You remember me?"

'Perfectly. A small, over-awed boy with knobbly knees
and a reverence for politicians they don't deserve."

It was astounding, he thought, that he should recall
their first meeting but the politician had another surprise

for him. "Why do you suppose I addressed you as Johnny Peep?"

"That was understandable, me dropping in on you in this way. You must value the few hours you get to yourself."

"Not all that much. I never did care for my own company. The truth is I like an audience. Anyone about here will tell you that. As to recalling you, it came back to me the moment I saw the name 'Swann' on your wife's letter, and why not? It's a very famous name and you mentioned your father's profession on that occasion." He laid his improvised rod aside. "So you know the identity of Johnny Peep?"

"It was Burns, wasn't it?"

"One of my best stories. Robbie was a rare spirit. Do you read him still?"

"Not in dialect," Giles said. "He's too broad for me." Then, "I . . . er . . . didn't see my wife's letter. To be frank, she wrote it without my knowledge and sprang it on me when she got a reply."

"Sounds an enterprising lass, Mr. Swann."

"She's Welsh."

"That accounts for it. Join me," and he made room on the boulder. "I take it you know what she wrote *about*?"

"She knew that I was anxious to be considered by the Liberal Party as a prospective candidate and thought a direct approach to you was the best hope. I must be frank again, however. I live and work in London. We have a holiday house up here, and come as often as we can. We met about here when we were eighteen."

"Where exactly?"

"I fished her out of the river at Aberglaslyn. I thought she was drowning but she wasn't, just fooling. She's the daughter of Sir Clive Rycroft-Mostyn, the industrialist."

The politician whistled softly. "Dynastic alliance?"

"Far from it. My father-in-law and I are not on speaking terms, and haven't been since before Romayne and I married, eight years ago."

"Political differences?"

"Not really, although I never did care for his way with people. He's a big Tory subscriber."

"Yes, he is," Lloyd George said, thoughtfully, "and a bad man to work for they say. But your father is a radical, I'm told. Did he bring you up the way you should go?"

It was difficult to withstand the man's charm, even though, behind his amiability, there was irony, and that hint of patronage, as though Giles had been a small public meeting of the faithful. He had the most winning smile Giles had ever seen on the face of man or woman and he could understand why he had a reputation with the ladies. His personality played over you like a warm draught, but a searching one at that, Giles thought, telling himself that it would be dangerous to be less than frank with a man whose shrewdness showed in his eyes – merry, teasing eyes, but feeding every impression back to the calculating brain in that big, proud head. He said, "You've probably heard about my father's methods. His above-average pay-scale and his provident scheme. He was a pioneer in that field and many City men dislike him on that account."

"But he never tried to enter politics?"

"No. He's a merchant first and foremost."

"Probably more useful to us in that capacity," Lloyd George said, chuckling. "At least he's demonstrated that it isn't necessary to chain his workers to the oar in order to balance his books." He broke off, looking down at the tumbling water with a relaxed but watchful expression. "And how about you, Johnny Peep? Are you a convert, or have you always had a conscience? No, that's not what I'd like to know. Put it this way. Suppose we found you a constituency to nurse, and after times out of mind addressing lukewarm audiences in draughty church institutes, the walls of Jericho fell and you clawed us another seat from the privileged? What qualifications would you claim to enter that pint-sized chamber where we met and make your maiden speech to gentlemen who weren't listening?"

It was not at all the kind of interrogation he had been

expecting. The man's complete lack of formality and touch of irony ran contrary to one another, so that it was difficult to decide whether he was posturing or deliberately seeking to discourage. Giles said, finally, "I've had far more administrative experience than most applicants. I'm in charge of a provident and pension scheme for two thousand hands and I've read most of the social prophets in my time, deeply enough to quarrel with most of them."

"That's a point in your favour. Nearly all were theorists. Anything more?"

It was a time, Giles thought, to gamble and he had the advantage of having Celtic ancestry on his mother's side. Irony was a weapon in this man's armoury but it wasn't the one he employed very much in his attacks on every aspect in the system where he saw, and bitterly resented, injustice and inherited privilege. Colourful detail and dramatic licence spiced every public address he had ever made, either as courtroom solicitor or a member of Parliament and it followed that he would be likely to respond to his own stock-in-trade. Giles said, "When I was a boy of ten I watched an elderly farm labourer and his wife expelled from a tied cottage and sent off to separate workhouses. I never forgot that. It had a direct bearing on what I read and what I thought about when I was still at school. The month I left, thirteen years ago now, I walked from North Devon to Edinburgh to see things for myself. One incident made a deeper impression on me than anything else. It was on the deepest level of a Rhondda coal-mine. A young miner had his foot crushed by a runaway tub and I visited his parents that same night."

"Well?"

"They saw the accident to their son as a piece of rare good fortune. It meant he could still earn money but in safety, on top, a cripple with a sporting chance of survival. If we can't do better than that, as the richest and most powerful nation on earth, something's wrong with our thinking as Christians."

He saw at once that the gamble had paid off. The politician was looking at him with interest and the gleam of mockery behind the eyes had gone. "That's what we're looking for, Johnny Peep. But I wouldn't have expected it from a man with your background. Where is your holiday home in Beddgelert?"

"On the Caernarvon Road, about two hundred yards this side of the village. It's called 'Craig Wen'."

"The white rock. I know it. Might I invite myself to call and have tea with you and your wife tomorrow?"

"My wife would be delighted, Mr. George. But you could meet Romayne now if you wish. She's waiting for me in the dog-cart up on the bridge."

"Ah no," he said, "that would be taking advantage of the lady. Anyone sharp enough to write that letter and steer you here would want to do the honours. Tomorrow. Around four."

It was a polite dismissal and he got up, extending his hand. "You've already been more patient than I had any right to expect."

"And you've been more entertaining, Mr. Swann. Constituents who buttonhole me as you did usually want to talk about the disestablishment of the Welsh church, or get a shilling off their rent. Good day to you."

He shook hands, casually, and picked up his amateurish rod and line. When Giles looked over his shoulder halfway back to the bridge he was still hunched there. He looked very boyish for someone they said would end his career in the Cabinet or in prison.

2

Neither of them ever forgot one detail of that first visit of the Welsh Cyclone, as some of his admirers were calling him, to the pleasant house under the chain of mountains that enclosed the Nant Gwynant Pass all the way to Capel Curig, and on through the softer Vale of Conway to the sea. It was a house that had happy memories for him, for it was here, when he was no more than a schoolboy, he had lost his heart to the lovely restless girl Romayne Rycroft-Mostyn had been in those days.

The memory of the visit remained a red-letter day for him because it was here, rather than beside the tumbling Dwyfor, that he fell under the hypnotic spell of this strange, magnetic being, a force rather than a man, embodying, as Giles saw it, the romantic fervour of the Celt and a shrewdness that was Norman rather than Celtic and served the purpose of brake, spur and generator of a man whose life, up to this point, had been a calculated advance towards the limelight and the source of power. For Romayne it had deeper, more personal significance. She saw Lloyd George's patronage as the first practical attempt she had ever made to channel the potential of Giles Swann into a course where others, as well as herself, would accept him as a teacher and interpreter of his own uniquely compassionate philosophy. That, and the first real opportunity he had ever had of justifying himself in his own eyes.

For two hours by the grandfather clock, the Welshman talked about himself. Not vaingloriously, and certainly not tediously, for it was like listening to a saga out of the remote past where a king without a kingdom set about searching for his destiny. He told them of his obscure but happy childhood in these hills, fathered by a shoemaker uncle who emerged from the tale as a kind of Chiron preparing Jason for the Argosy. He told how, having decided to make his protégé a solicitor as a first step, his Uncle Lloyd had coached him in Latin by first learning Latin himself from a sixpenny grammar, bought on a bookstall. He laughed over his adolescent exercises in oratory, in the pulpit of a Welsh chapel, his early forays into journalism and the dramatic incident that made him famous throughout Wales when he successfully defended quarrymen flouting the law by forcing churchyard gates and burying a Nonconformist father beside his child in ground forbidden to Dissenters.

The rest was familiar, at least to Giles. His challenge, at the age of twenty-six, of the local squire at the hustings, his early days at Westminster and his rise to prominence as a politician who paid scant tribute to parliamentary procedure in his onslaught on the social sicknesses of his age.

But then, as the sun passed beyond the mountain summits in its swing down towards the Irish sea, he returned briskly to the purpose of his visit, the possibility of settling Giles in a constituency where hard work and, as he put it, the gathering might of the people, would elect him to Parliament and enable him to help convert Britain into a real democracy instead of a sham one.

"For mark you, it's almost here," he prophesied, with one of his extravagant gestures, "this landslide that will sweep us into power and enable us to implement reforms centuries overdue. Five years, ten at the most, but not more I promise you, and maybe you'll be there, Johnny Peep, to hammer out a constitution based on principles of justice, merit and equality of opportunity."

But it was not all rhetoric. He had a shrewd eye, for instance, for advantages to be wrung from the fact that Giles Swann bore a nationally-known name in commerce and it was while questioning Giles on his father's secure foothold on the southern perimeter of the region that he pounced on one specific area as an ideal jumping-off place.

"Pontnewydd?" he exclaimed, after Giles had told him the name of the valley where he had descended a coal-mine in the company of Bryn Lovell, for so long his father's viceroy based on Abergavenny, "I know it well and I've heard tell of Lovell, too. Isn't he the man who hauled a Shannon pump to the flooded shaft, and saved the lives of nearly sixty entombed miners? Why, man, it's a legend down there and legends are stock-in-trade. Pontnewydd is in Usk Vale country, that will likely fall to us after a couple of campaigns. Evan Thomas, the candidate down there, is over sixty and I doubt if he'll weather it."

He was silent and contemplative for a moment. Then

he said, "It would mean full-time campaigning, lad. Over a period of years unless you were exceptionally lucky. How dependent are you on your father?"

"I've money saved and my holding in the Swann Company would bring me a small income. But wouldn't it be possible to campaign up to the next election on a part-time basis?"

"No," Lloyd George said, uncompromisingly, "it would not. Winning a seat in Parliament was once a rich man's hobby but it isn't any longer, praise God. People stopped playing at politics when Gladstone broadened the suffrage. In a place like Pontnewydd it would be a fight with the gloves off, much like my first fight against Squire Nanney up here."

"Couldn't he be chosen as a North Wales candidate, Mr. George?" Romayne asked and he said, smiling, "No again, my dear! He's an Englishman, who doesn't speak a word of Welsh. In the south that isn't important. They've had the English on their backs for so long they're half Anglicised themselves I'm told, although they wouldn't admit it. We might try for an industrial seat in England, but I wouldn't have much influence there. Many English Liberals regard me as a potentially destructive element. The more respectable among them have already joined the club."

"What club is that?"

His eyes danced. "One that I hope you'll avoid if you ever get to Westminster. The Pro-Consul's Club as I think of it, where the lions lay down with the lambs. Or the wolves. Dramatic personality changes occur in revolutionaries, once they've put on the Westminster strait-jacket. You might even have difficulty distinguishing them from their opponents after a year or so in that hothouse. It's a rare place for raising hybrids." He looked at his watch. "I'm due in Caernarvon for a constituency meeting at eight and must leave you now. May I take it you're prepared to put yourself in my hands? Well, you might do worse in your situation, for I've taken a rare fancy to you, Johnny Peep. A little more fire in your belly and you'll emerge as a very promising recruit to my way of thinking. A Tory-orientated young man, with everything to gain by accepting the advantages conferred on you by a rich background and good education, who accepts the radical as the arbiter of the twentieth century." He turned to Romayne. "You can play your part, my dear. The role of a politician's wife isn't easy. You'll soon learn that, I daresay. In any other profession a man can use what cover is available. Out there in the arena he's a sitting target and it isn't only his hide that takes a walloping from time to time."

They were both well aware of what was explicit in the warning. As recently as last July Lloyd George had been cited in a divorce suit that threatened to topple him but he did not act like a man under a cloud. His denigrators, Giles decided, would have to get up long before sunrise to catch David Lloyd George napping.

*　　*　　*

Adam was in his tower working by lamplight when Giles came to him with the letter. An invitation to present himself at an Usk Vale constituency meeting, where preliminary steps would be taken to replace the retiring Liberal candidate at a rally of the Executive in the new year. Evan Thomas, a local councillor who had fought three unsuccessful elections had stepped down earlier than anyone expected on grounds of failing health. Almost certainly, Giles decided, he had been nudged by younger elements of the party in the area, men working in close liaison with Lloyd George, who was already accepted by the thrusters as the real leader of the Welsh Liberals.

Giles had kept Adam informed to date but there hadn't been much to pass on and, in any case, his father's energies were fully absorbed in the gigantic task of reorganising and rebuilding headquarters while still exercising control of the provincial network. Giles had not been able to help him much. His own experience was confined almost wholly to welfare on the one hand, and the investigation of claims on the other, and he rarely spent more than two days a week in the capital. But Adam had not complained. Indeed it had seemed to Giles, through those busy autumn months after the New Broom had vanished from the scene, that his father relished the task thrust upon him by George's leave of absence, and the havoc wrought by the fire.

"You'll be going down to look them over, I take it?" he said, and Giles reminded him that it was more a case of being looked over.

"Swanns do the looking," the old man said, half in jest.

But Giles replied, "Oh, I don't give myself much of a chance. They'll be sure to choose a local man in favour of a candidate who can only pay flying visits to the valleys," and failed to notice his father's abstracted look as he took the letter and held it closer to the circle of lamplight. "I thought I should let you know I'll be out of touch Monday and Tuesday of next week. I'll get those Swansea claim forms from the clerks and deal with them over the weekend."

Adam said, sharply, "Wait on, son. Don't be in such a confounded hurry. I need time to mull this over. Pour me a noggin and help yourself to one while you're about it."

"But you're swamped with work. Look at that desk."

"I'm getting on top of it."

Giles went to the wall cupboard his father had reconverted into a cellarette. Ever since he could remember his father seemed far more relaxed in this queer octagonal chamber than in his more comfortable surroundings at 'Tryst'. The place still had the air of a bivouac, tenanted by a campaigning general with spartan tastes and a passion for work.

"How do you feel about going the whole hog, boy?"

Giles looked at him, encouraged by the smile plucking the corners of his mouth.

"You mean shifting down there permanently? Leaving you to cope with this mess alone?"

"I'm not alone. Keate has come back four days a week. And that young brother of yours is a damned quick learner."

Giles noticed he said nothing of old Hugo. He had always been disposed to dismiss old Hugo as an amiable oaf. Anywhere outside a sports stadium, that is.

"One of us ought to stand with you, apart from a kid Edward's age."

"Not you, boy. For one thing your heart's never been in it and for another this letter tells me you've got bigger fish to fry. Well?"

"I don't know. I as good as told Lloyd George I couldn't accept a full-time candidacy."

"Question of money?"

"No. We could get by on a modest income down there."

"That won't get you far, son."

"How do you mean?"

"The Liberals are not only short of young talent at the moment. I happen to know they're desperately short of ready money."

"I didn't promise them any money."

"You didn't have to. I'm not saying that chap Lloyd George doesn't recognise good political potential when it comes knocking at his door, but it wasn't that that got your foot in the door. If you could bring the local party a sizeable annual subscription they wouldn't give a local man a second look. I know that much about party politics. You've got your share of Sam's residue. It's more than enough to win that seat, backed by hard graft."

"Isn't it a bit like buying your way in?"

"You have to buy your way into everything, son. You always did, even in my day. Only now it's twice as expensive. Only those Keir Hardie crusaders see politics in any other light and they'll come around to it as soon as the Labour Party settles down."

"Lloyd George got himself elected without financial backing."

"So he did. But who keeps him there, pitching away at the coconut shies? His family practice mostly. I've had that on good authority."

"It still doesn't entitle me to leave you in the lurch."

Adam sipped his brandy. "Tell you something I've not told anyone else, Giles. Something I wouldn't admit to your mother, if only for fear of hurting her feelings. I'm happier here, back in this slum, than I've ever been ever since the day I walked out on it, and turned my hand to making something of 'Tryst'. That was a challenge while I was doing it, but now all that's left for me to do is to watch the trees and shrubs grow and I'll be gone before they mature. Oh, I daresay George regards what I'm doing here as a sacrifice, and I mean to let him go on thinking it. It might help to keep him in line, after that silly business with that Lockerbie woman. The truth is I put myself out to grass before I was used up and it does a man a power of good to realise that when he's seventy and get a chance to prove it. Lift your glass, boy, and drink to the first Swann to make laws. They've been busy bending 'em ever since Agincourt. It makes a change."

Giles finished his brandy, reflecting that nobody ever stopped learning about the Gov'nor. His queer passion for this squalid place. His unquenchable faith in himself and his potential. His gruffness, forthrightness and swift, unexpected touches of kindness, gentle as a woman's. He said; "If I won a seat, would that make you glad? Proud, perhaps?"

The old man crossed to the cupboard and poured himself another measure. "It's important I should know, sir."

The 'sir' arrested him. Like his brothers, even young Edward had stopped calling him 'sir'. It was Gov'nor or Father, according to their estimate of his mood.

"Glad? Yes, I'd be glad for your sake. Proud? I'm not so sure. You've got respect for that place and I once had. But most of it has leaked out my boots over the years."

"It's still the best governing instrument in the world, isn't it?"

"Yes, you could claim that I suppose. But looking round the world nowadays I sometimes wonder if we couldn't have set a better example."

"Because other democracies are younger and greener?"

"Not necessarily. Put it another way. Ours should be better than it is by this time. We had a long start over everybody else and I'm not sure I like the use we're making of it nowadays. 'Strutting' doesn't become us."

He knew what was in his father's mind and it was not merely the recent exercise in what he had dismissed as 'tribal breastbeating'. It was an attitude taken for granted by almost every living soul in the islands, from tiara-wearers, walking the red carpet between ranks of cooing shopgirls outside Devonshire House, down to the hardest-driven slavey in the basements of their town houses. It was in their ditties and their folk lore, and taught alike in their redbrick elementary schools and ancient seats of learning. It could be heard in the clamour of their half-penny press and seen in the swagger of their sailors on shore leave. You could see it reflected in stock-market quotations and hear its voice in the rattle of money pouring into a million tills. It decked itself in feathers and pearl on Hampstead Heath on Bank Holidays and in scarlet and gold in garrison towns all over the world, and perhaps Adam was speaking for his son as well as himself when he added, "It's not all bad, mind you. The devil of it is most radicals would throw out the baby with the bath-water. There's a lot here worth saving but it needs pruning and we'd best set about it ourselves before some-body does it for us. If you get into that place, give 'em a prod from me, will you?"

"If I ever did get there," Giles said, "I'd look to you for a briefing before I threw my hat in the ring."

Adam watched him cross the yard as he had watched

his brother George go, thinking, 'Well, that's another of 'em. It's lucky Hetty wouldn't call "whoa" when I wanted to, for we're going to need reserves before we're through,' but this didn't depress him unduly. Swann-on-Wheels had been his life's work and the patrimony was there for the taking, providing any one among his five sons was equal to it. But he wasn't a man enslaved by the notion of seeing his own flesh and blood dedicate themselves to it, in the way he had done when he had turned his back on soldiering and took the plunge in the 'fifties. He would see that as vanity and although reckoned as proud as Lucifer by friends and enemies alike nobody had ever called him vain. He drained his tot, stumped round the end of the desk and settled himself in his wide-bottomed chair. Outside the evening sounds of the yard reached him, muffled in river fog. A Goliath, or fully-loaded man-o'-war creaking in from the Midland sector; a vanboy's quip as he leaped down from a tailboard; the dolorous hoot of a tug heading down river towards the docks. Sounds that were the symphony of his life and enterprise about here, able to comfort him as he settled back to his work.

8

Swanns at Large

SHE THOUGHT ABOUT THEM ALL A GREAT DEAL.
The big old house was quiet as a convent these days and
seemed half-empty too, despite its four indoor and four
outdoor staff. Adam and Edward were away at work all
day and the only one on hand was Margaret who, notwithstanding the fact that she had put her hair up four
years ago, and was now an unusually pretty child of
eighteen (it was natural that Henrietta should think of
the youngest of nine as a child); she was inclined to be
solitary and spent so much of her time painting.

Sometimes, indeed, whenever Henrietta pondered it
deeply, she resented his decision to return to the yard,
having come to believe he was done with all that. It was
only after that long gossip with Deborah, when her
adopted daughter returned here for a holiday in August,
that she adjusted to his abrupt return to the city.

There had been the unlooked-for bonus in the permanent presence of George's four children, Max, Rudi,
Adam and her namesake, Hetty, the first of her grandchildren she had a chance to spoil, but they were all so
like their mother that they did not seem children to her,
more like a quartet of little adults, with their impeccable
manners and ingrained habits of obedience instilled into
them by their Austrian mother. Familiarity with Gisela's
children led her to reflect upon the curious choice of
mate made by the most extrovert of her sons. She would

have thought George would have sought out a very
different girl, pretty possibly but fashionable and as self-
willed as himself, whereas Gisela was by far the most
complaisant of her daughters-in-law.

Henrietta knew all about that shocking lapse of his by
now, although the menfolk had done their best to fob
her off with half-truths. Secretly it hadn't surprised her
much. In so many ways he was more like Adam than any
of them, and she imagined Gisela's placidity would have
exasperated him in time and set him thinking of more
exhilarating romps between sheets. A man of his type,
and Adam's, needed more from a woman than
acquiescence, and she even went so far as to discuss this
with Deborah when they held a stimulating inquest on the
scandal in August.

She had always been able to confide in Deborah, ever
since that awful time after the Staplehurst rail crash, when
she would have gone out of her mind had it not been for
the child's unwavering faith and ability to communicate
it to others. Deborah Avery, a love-child of Adam's
former partner, Josh Avery, had never seemed less than
a daughter to her, and marriage to that nice young journalist, Milton Jeffs, had done nothing to weaken their
relationship. She had taken it for granted that Deborah,
with her quick brain and ready access to Adam, would
know more about George's wobble than she did and she
was right. Somehow, although Deborah lived in far-off
Devonshire, where her husband ran a local newspaper,
she was in possession of all the facts – George's shameful
neglect of work, wife and family, his scandalous affair
with the wife of Sir James Lockerbie, his misplaced confidence in that scoundrel Wesley Tybalt (who had since
disappeared from the face of the earth) and finally that
awful fire that had drawn Adam back into the network.
What Henrietta wasn't sure about was Adam's motive in
letting the boy have his head about that obsession of his
and this Deborah had been able to pass on, saying, with a
chuckle: "But it's so characteristic of him, Aunt Hetty!

He isn't really a stick-in-the-mud, you know, he just likes to pretend he is. He knows George is absolutely right about the advantages of getting a flying start with mechanical transport, and I think he did it for Swann-on-Wheels rather than George."

She had been surprised by that, thinking that Deborah would have had more sense than to assume the time was fast approaching when Swann's merchandise would be rattled about the country in horseless vehicles, of the kind George had played with for so long in the old stable across the yard.

"You can't mean to say you agree with him, Debbie? You can't think we'll soon be selling off all those Clydesdales and Cleveland Bays?" and Debbie had replied, laughingly, that of course she agreed with him, and that George's sense of dedication, when one thought about it, was another Swann characteristic.

"Adam looked far ahead when he threw up soldiering to start the network in 1858, didn't he? Everyone thought he was daft then. Even you, I suspect, when you married him. Come now, be honest, Auntie, you would have much preferred to marry a boneheaded soldier in scarlet and gold, wouldn't you? Uncle Adam always declares that you would and tried to persuade him to stay in the army."

"Adam Swann has too long a memory for my liking," Henrietta grumbled, remembering this was true at the time Adam rescued her from a shepherd's hut on a rain-soaked moor. "But surely, a haulier's business with teams and waggons is one thing and that snorting monster George brought home from Vienna is quite another. I mean, it's really no more than a toy, is it? Oh, I know we have motors on the roads nowadays, and there are even one or two about here, although whenever I see one it's always being towed home by cart-horses."

"That's what I mean. Until now motors have been regarded as expensive toys, even by their inventors, but that won't last. They're getting better and faster and more powerful every day and it's quite obvious they'll have to be used for much more than road racing and one-day excursions to the seaside. But I didn't come in here to talk about motors or George either, Auntie. I've got a piece of family gossip that you'll be the first to learn, but you must promise me you'll keep it a secret until I give you the word. Even from Uncle Adam."

Henrietta fidgeted. All her life she had relished secrets, and had been flattered when one was entrusted to her. So rarely, however, had she kept faith with her confidante that fewer and fewer secrets came her way now that she was a grandmother many times over.

"Tell! You know I won't breathe a word to anyone."

"I doubt it but I'll take the risk. I'm going to have a baby."

The shock was so great that it precipitated Henrietta out of her chair. "A *child! You*, Debbie? But goodness gracious me, you're . . . you're *forty-one* by my reckoning."

"You don't have to shout about it. Yes, I'll be forty-two in November, and Milton and I had long since given up hope, but it's true, thank goodness. It will be born in late January, and there's no more doubt about it. In fact, that's one reason why I came up without Milt, to see a specialist. I've never spent a night away from Milt until now."

"Eight years!" Henrietta exclaimed. "Eight years and now . . . now *this*?", and an expression of anxiety crossed her face, so acute that it touched Debbie. "Aren't you scared half out of your wits?"

"Of course I'm not. It's unusual, I'm told, but it's not unique. All the medical men I've seen – and Milton has fussed no end in that direction – tell me I'm exceptionally healthy and, given luck and good care, I'll be all right. It might have to be a Caesarean section but they can't be sure until nearer the time."

Henrietta gazed at her with awe. Debbie had always seemed so wise, even when she was the child Adam brought in here out of the snow thirty-odd years ago. She had heard vague and rather frightening talk about Caesarean sections at her croquet-party gossips but she had never met any woman who had one or even anticipated having one.

"Well, it would scare the living daylights out of me! I'm pleased for you, of course, for I've known all the time you longed for one. But after eight years trying . . ."

"Trying is about right," Debbie said, merrily. "I'm sure nobody could have tried harder," and saying that brought Debbie even closer, for Henrietta would have been too inhibited to talk this way with any of her daughters, even Joanna who had been pregnant, stupid girl, when she ran off with that young scamp, Clinton Coles.

"Have I *got* to keep this a secret?" she wailed, and Deborah said she had, for at least a month, for if anything happened between now and January she would prefer to nurse her disappointment in secret.

"Oh, I'm sure nothing will," Henrietta declared, slowly adjusting to the stupendous news and finding herself able to share Debbie's pleasure. "To think you'll be ahead of Giles and Romayne after all and Romayne only thirty!" and she kissed Debbie on the cheek and begged her to write soon and give her permission to confide in Adam and the girls.

"And now you tell me all your family gossip, aside from George," Debbie said. "Gisela's tribe will be in to lunch any minute and we shan't get another chance. Has Margaret got a beau yet?"

She recounted all the Swann trivia, the kind of detail Adam would never bother to pass on, for she suspected he and Debbie discussed nothing but politics whenever they met. No, Margaret hadn't got an admirer, and didn't seem to want one. Instead she spent hours and hours painting about the estate, and never had much to say for herself at a soirée or fête. Alex, the eldest son, was in India now and so was his wife Lydia, of course, for she accompanied him everywhere. Their daughter Rose, and son Garnet (named for Sir Garnet Wolseley, Alex's commander in Egypt) were expected home soon to get their education here but Alex was on a five-year tour and would be forty before she saw him again. It was very depressing, she admitted, to have to acknowledge a son of nearly forty, but there it was, she didn't feel fifty-eight, and she didn't think she looked it when she was well corseted. Giles and Romayne led a strange, bizarre life, bereft of all social occasions and as obsessed with politics as George was with his engines, surely the two dullest preoccupations on earth if one discounted cricket. Stella, eldest of the brood, was apparently content with her peasant's life over at Dewponds and her tribe of mop-headed peasant children and that lumping husband of hers, Denzil Fawcett.

"The girl really let herself go after she married a second time," Henrietta said, "and I can never understand why. She turns the scale to twelve stone now and never wears anything but straw bonnets and gingham. It's odd, for you remember how fashionable she was when she was growing up here, and how she could have taken her pick from the hunting set in this part of the county. But there it is, it's her life, I suppose, and when I remember that frightful first marriage of hers, I really ought not to grumble. Denzil still treats her as though she was one of those Gainsborough ladies, stepping out of a picture frame." Then there was Hugo, still a bachelor, and likely to be, poor boy, for he never stood still long enough to fall in love, although his sisters told her girls swooned at the sight of him. As for young Edward, Adam seemed to think he had a rare head for business and a passion for work, and *that* was a comfort, now that George had disappointed everybody.

"And how about Joanna and Helen, Auntie?" Debbie prompted, remarking privately that Henrietta had always been disposed to dismiss girls as afterthoughts.

"Oh, they might just as well be dead for all I see or hear of them. Joanna is stuck in Dublin with Clinton and their family, and Adam seems well satisfied with all he hears of the Irish branch. And poor Helen and that stuffy missionary she married are in China. They moved on there from Africa last Christmas and she's written saying Rowland is worked off his feet, for they have all the diseases in the medical dictionary out there. I *do* wish she'd make him throw it all up and buy a nice practice here in Kent. He could well afford it. His father is rich as Croesus and it can't be doing the girl any good in all those terrible climates. She lost her first baby, you remember, and never had another. I've only seen them twice since they married."

"She's probably happier with a man absorbed in what he's doing," Debbie said, "and from what I remember of Rowland Coles he isn't a husband to be 'talked' into anything." She glanced at Henrietta shrewdly, adding, "Anyway, who are you to advise a wife to take the initiative? You never did, save that one time when Uncle Adam lost his leg and wasn't around to keep you in order."

"Ah," said Henrietta, unabashed, "but nobody in their senses could compare Clinton or Rowland Coles with Adam, could they? I mean, he's a very remarkable man, isn't he, and I'm not alone in thinking so, am I?"

"No, Auntie, you're certainly not," Debbie said, laughing, "but even if you were nobody could persuade you to the contrary."

Out across the paddock Phoebe Fraser's lunch-bell jangled and as Henrietta bustled off Margaret came in, wearing a sun-bonnet and a linen dress plentifully bedaubed with paint. She held a sketch under her arm and Deborah said, "Let me see it, Miggs. And don't tell me it isn't finished."

"Finished or not it's no masterpiece," Margaret said, and held it up, to reveal what Deborah at once thought a very colourful and exceptionally strong watercolour of a corner of the paddock wood, where the path ran under a stand of beeches towards Adam's Hermitage. The picture centred on the beech clump but the foreground was a riot of colour, composed of one tall foxglove, some yellow toadflax and a sprinkling of trefoil. The composition was uncontrived and the painting of the leaves, petals and seed-pods impressionistic, yet definite enough for individual flowers to be identified.

"It's very good indeed, Miggs. And I believe you think it is."

"Oh, I'm coming along," Miggs admitted, "but this is far too free to impress a professional. An Academician would dismiss it as woolly."

"I think half the pictures they exhibit are woolly," Debbie said, "and all paintings should be 'free' as you say. At least, they should give that impression. Do you ever paint in oils, Miggs?"

"Not landscapes and never outdoors. Foliage and flowers require softer treatment, I think. At least, mine do. I should concentrate on oils if I was a real painter."

"But you *are* a real painter, Miggs. You've got a very individual style. Why, I've seen hundreds of amateur flower paintings and landscapes and I'd sooner have this one on my wall than the best of them."

She noticed the girl's cheeks flushed, and thought, 'Poor Miggs! Growing up here among all these Philistines. It must be very discouraging for her sometimes,' and said, "Have you ever sold a painting, Miggs?"

"Good heavens, no! Who would buy one?"

"I would. I'd buy this if you'd sell it. It would remind me of growing up here every time I looked at it."

"Then I'll give it to you."

"Oh, no, you won't. People only value what they pay for. I'll give you a sovereign for it," and she took a purse from her dress pocket and extracted the coin.

Miggs said, "But I'd sooner give it to you, Debbie . . ." But Deborah pressed the coin into her hand and closed her fingers on it.

"At least let me frame it for you. There are plenty of frames in the old Colonel's cupboard." Deborah recalled then that the old Colonel, Adam's father, had spent his old age down here painting and then she remembered something else that struck her as singular, Henrietta telling her, in an expansive moment, that Margaret had been conceived the night they buried the Colonel in Twyforde Churchyard. Well, maybe it proved something, for who else among the Swanns ever put brush to canvas, and now that she thought about it Margaret was the spit of that French wife of the Colonel's whose portrait hung in his old room in the east wing.

She had a few minutes before lunch so she went upstairs, moving along the wainscotted gallery to the eastern side of the house, pausing here and there to wonder at all the laughter, loving and heartache that had gone on between these old walls since that old pirate Conyer built his house on this spot. She remembered a great deal of it herself, since that winter's day Adam winkled her out of the convent and brought her here to live among his own sons and daughters. What would have happened to her if he hadn't? Not long after the place was closed down and the nuns went back to France, and she had never set eyes on her own mother. Adam was, as Henrietta claimed, a very remarkable man.

She moved on into the old Colonel's room, glancing up at the portrait of Monique d'Auberon, Adam's Gascon mother and the old Colonel's Peninsula and Waterloo trophies. The cavalryman's busby, with its numerals, '16th Lt. Dragoons'. The field-glasses through which Cornet Swann had looked across the Bidassoa at Marshal Soult. The sabre that killed the cuirassier who lopped two fingers from his hand at Waterloo. Henrietta would never have any of his things moved nor allow the room to be used by any of the children, and Deborah, knowing her so well, could understand why. The old chap had championed her when his son brought her home on the rump of his mare all those years ago and Henrietta would see him as the sponsor of her marriage and all that emerged from it. It was a pleasant thought and did her credit.

She went out and moved back towards the broad staircase, thinking of all the children she had seen scampering
and quarrelling along these waxed oak floors. Stella,
Alex, George and Giles, and the post-accident spread,
Joanna, Hugo, Helen, Edward and Miggs. All but the
two youngest were scattered and although the house was
very old, and full of ghosts, her recollections of the Swann
tribe belonged in that category now for what did she know
of them today apart from scraps of information contained
in their occasional letters or comments on the small change
of the day? They wrote or said little of their secret hopes,
fears and frustrations and nothing that singled them out as
nine men and women, born in that master bedroom across
the gallery. All the same, she experienced the strongest
urge to give birth to her own child in this house for it was
a house of high adventure and anyone born in it would
be inoculated against dullness and mediocrity. She
smiled at the notion and went down to lunch, wondering if
Milton would understand why the place exerted such a
pull over her at a time like this and whether he would
dismiss it as a pregnant woman's fancy.

2

Deborah's guesses concerning latterday Swanns had
substance. Each of them, in their own way, was an
adventurer, with a strong dash of their father's enterprise
and their mother's tenacity of purpose.

George, at that moment in time, was working against
the clock alongside his acolyte, Jock Quirt, a fierce,
wholly dedicated man, whose approach to the apparatus
of his trade was that of a pilgrim handling fragments of
the true cross. They were making rapid progress up here,
in the oppressive heat of a Manchester summer. Yet the
ten months left to them, before Adam's ultimatum expired,
did not seem long enough to surmount so many hurdles.
Once embarked on a project like this there was no knowing
how many blind alleys one had to explore for a means to

increase power while stripping down overall weight, and grappling with repetitive problems like overheating, friction, warped metals and technical anticipation of the fearful shaking and jolting inseparable from the passage of a vehicle over roads that had served the coaching era. There was a new mountain to be climbed each day and a desert of speculation crossed after dark, so that he was now very glad indeed that Adam had persuaded him to take Gisela but leave the children behind. Released from them she could play a woman's part in the undertaking, appearing at regular intervals with hot food and drink and in between running his errands to every forge and workshop in the city.

It was thus a new Gisela he came to terms with up here, a person as resolved as himself to assemble something practical from this jumble of rods, bolts, brackets, wheels and cannisters, and when, after a twelve-hour stint he was ready to peel off his filthy overalls and take a bath, she was always there, even-tempered and giving, so that one night, holding her in his arms, he was moved to say, "I must have been mad to take you for granted all these years . . ." And she replied, in her modest way, "Hush, George. A man has his work, and his own way of going about it, and I'm a part of it now. It's something I've always hoped to be since the time Grandfather Max found you a purpose . . . sleep now." So he had slept, dreaming of a time when they were skylarking beside the Danube, and he had isolated her from her fun-loving sisters, put his arms about her and decided that here was a woman who could reveal to him his inner self and nurse such creativity as he had inherited from that ageing Titan beside the Thames.

*　　　*　　　*

Thousands of miles east of George Swann's north-country workshop, Alexander Swann, who after the Jubilee had been posted to India, wrestled with frustrations that were akin to those of his brother, inasmuch as they were concerned, in the main, with marketing a piece of hardware to his generation. But perhaps Alex's task was the more formidable, for his circle of activity was that much narrower, one in which prejudice and ridicule was the norm.

For years now, urged on by his wife Lydia, daughter of a military buffoon, Alex had been hard at work convincing his masters that increased fire-power was the only guarantee to success in confrontation with the enemy – with any enemy, be he savage, armed with sword and spear, or with a Western rival, who was also busy perfecting his own means of aggression.

Specialising in small-arms, particularly the new Maxim gun adopted by the British army after Alex himself had fired the first prototype on the Wimbledon ranges, he had never ceased to advocate the multiplication of the quota of two guns per battalion, arguing that outmoded weapons like the lance and sword, and the use of cavalry as anything other than reconnaissance troops, were as archaic as Hannibal's elephants once the Prussians had annihilated the Painted Emperor's legions at Sedan, in 1870.

That was already twenty-seven years ago but so few professionals above the rank of major appeared to have learned the lesson inherent in the arrival of the breechloading rifle. They continued, confound their sluggish wits, to think in terms of headlong charges against infantry equipped to mow them down like so many partridges, and most of them did not even think as far as that, seeing an army career as an eternal round of polo matches, pig-sticking forays and the maintenance of a military etiquette that belonged to the time of the Black Prince. Sometimes it was like battering one's head against a wall or journeying on through a morass of Lyle's Golden Syrup, and he was already aware that his unquenchable enthusiasm was regarded as a bore in the messes.

Yet he persisted, not only because he was his father's

son but because, at his elbow throughout all those years of sapping and mining, was the counsel of his wife, Lydia, she who had rescued him from permanent involvement in among those self-same regimental pigstickers. Year after year he persisted, hawking his hardware and his theories from Africa to India, to Egypt and back again, until regimental wags found a derisive soubriquet for him – 'The Barker', the chap who, due to a touch of the sun maybe, had evolved into a travelling salesman trudging from fair to fair with a packload of nostrums and cure-alls on his back. Yet all the time Lydia continued to sustain him, sometimes locating an eccentric colonel, or a major-general, who would at least listen to him, but more often counselling patience with her prophecy that one day he would be seen to be right and could make history as the unsung saviour of the Empire.

*   *   *

Stella Fawcett, once Stella Swann, was untroubled by opposition. In her own tiny world, bounded by the fron-tiers of a three-hundred-acre Kentish farm, the word 'Mother' (as everybody thought of Stella now) was holy writ. Denzil, titular master of Dewponds, had deferred to her ever since he had installed her as mistress of the farm she had helped him to rebuild and everybody else, the straggle of children, the farmhands and even the whole-salers who bought Fawcett crops, took their cue from him, so that it became a matter of; 'We'll see what Mother has to say about it', or 'Go to Mother and get your orders from her unless you want to do it all over again.'

She was thirty-seven now, as broad in the beam as one of her own butter churns, and with massive freckled arms that could, so they declared, have boxed the ears of a fairground prize-fighter, yet she was not all brawn and maternal majesty. Under her direction Dewponds, almost alone among local farms, had ridden out the agricultural depression of the early 'nineties, and the

Fawcetts, it was rumoured, had money in the bank as well as the best strain of beef cattle in the Weald. For Stella too was her father's daughter, although she had been late to discover as much and came near to foundering at the time of her marriage to a dissolute wastrel over the Sussex border. Denzil it had been who rescued her from that impasse and when her marriage was annulled, and Dewponds had been rebuilt brick by brick by the pair of them, he had married her, or, as village gossips preferred, Stella Swann had married him, carrying him off like a prize turnip and using him to sire a spread of blue-eyed children, between their stints of labour on the farm.

Did she ever think, as she waddled between farm-kitchen and henyard, of her brief, inglorious spell as the Honourable Lady Moncton-Price, in a ratty old country seat some twenty miles from here? Did she ever remember being spied upon through a knot-hole by a homosexual husband and his lover? Had she completely erased from her memory that climactic night when old Moncton-Price, her father-in-law, had prodded and pinched her as though she was a horse at a fair, and gone on to propose that she lived on as his doxy, while maintaining the farce of a marriage with his son? If she did she gave no sign of it, but perhaps the subconscious memory of these terrible humiliations prompted her outward respect for Denzil and the fact that, at intervals of less than two years, she presented him with a lusty son or a rosy-cheeked daughter. Possibly she still saw him as the bearer of that storm-lantern under the lambing copse, that had been her beacon light the night she fled from the Moncton-Prices in a tearing south-westerly. It may have been so but it is open to question. Strong in Swann obstinacy and will power, she was woefully deficient in Swann imagination.

*   *   *

Far to the north-west, across the breadth of the shires, the mountains and eighty miles of Irish Sea, Joanna Coles, *née* Joanna Swann, was living in much more ease and comfort than her older sister. Joanna was an essentially lazy woman, who needed a definite stimulus to deflect her thoughts from clothes, race-meetings, fox-hunting, and her husband's prospects of promotion in the Swann hierarchy. For it was generally assumed the Irish branch was a managerial proving ground.

Clinton, who shared her enthusiasm for race-meetings, had taken her along to the Curragh that afternoon and she was not much surprised when he excused himself on the grounds of placing a bet on the three-thirty but went instead to pay his respects to the handsome Deirdre Donnelly, this season's toast of Dublin. Joanna did not resent his devotion. She had long ago taken the measure of Clint Coles (still referred to as 'Jack-o'-Lantern' by her father, on account of the elopement nine years before), confident that he was unlikely to compromise himself with a woman like Mrs. Donnelly. For one thing she was much sought after, and Clint was too sure of himself to compete for favours. For another she was the wife of one of his best customers and Clint had his eye on the main chance over here where the branch had thrived under his management.

It was true that Clinton, left to himself, could be dangerously impulsive and she should know this better than anyone, but Joanna reasoned that impulsive men kept on a tight rein were those most likely to bolt, even if they waited years to do it, and over here it was generally accepted that husbands were free to flirt at all sporting assemblies. Wives, too, if opportunity came their way.

There was no harm, however, in reminding him that she was not stupid and had not been taken in by that excuse for leaving the enclosure. So, after making sure there was no man of her acquaintance in the stand whom she could use as a light foil against Deirdre Donnelly, she scrawled a note on a page of her pocket-book, and tipped a steward to give it to Mr. Clinton Coles on his return. The note told him she could be reclaimed in the mixed refreshment buffet. It would bring him there at a run, she calculated, for although Dublin etiquette was more relaxed than across the water, it was unusual for ladies to enter either of the buffets unescorted.

On the way through she passed a cheval-glass and caught a glimpse of her reflection, finding it moderately pleasing for a woman of thirty, eight years married and the mother of three children. Her mother had always declared her the flower of the flock as regards looks and elegance, and Joanna noted with satisfaction that her figure had not suffered as a result of her last pregnancy. She did not look more than twenty-five and her best feature, a wealth of soft tawny hair, carefully arranged under a wide picture hat, was as arresting as it had always been. Her complexion was good too, for the Irish climate suited it and she gave herself a little nod of encouragement before passing into the pavilion and looking round for a waiter to bring her tea.

Several men glanced at her approvingly, among them Tim Clarke, owner of 'Spanish Flyer', placed third in the last race. Like everybody in the Pale she knew Tim, a rare character in a city teeming with characters, and wealthy to boot, having made his fortune as an importer of Continental wines and spirits, of which he had what amounted to a monopoly hereabouts. He had two famous sons, she recalled, Rory and Desmond; the first an M.P. for a Meath constituency, and a prominent fillibuster in the Home Rule campaign at Westminster, the second holding a commission in the 2nd Dragoon Guards, a brilliant steeplechaser who had twice come close to winning the Grand National at Aintree. Thus old Tim, fat as a wine vat and oozing a geniality that ran counter to his reputation for striking hard bargains, had a foot in both camps. Rory's fiery speeches at Westminster established him as a true patriot, and Desmond's profession, plus his sporting reputation in England, ensured the goodwill of Dublin Castle. Tim was also said to have a gallant reputation with the ladies and at once proved it by being the first to catch her eye, doff his hat and take advantage of the fact that she was the only unaccompanied woman in the buffet. He said, with a bow, "Mrs. Clinton Coles, I believe! Allow me to get you something. Glass of champagne, eh?" And without waiting for assent he snapped his fingers and two waiters came at the double.

"Tea, if you please, Mr. Clarke. I'm parched for a cup, and I've lost my husband."

"You mean he's lost you and it's mighty careless of him," he said, ushering her to a seat. "Why, if you were my wife, Mrs. Coles, I wouldn't let you out of my sight at the Curragh. A rare lot of garrison mashers on the prowl today, ma'am."

"He went to place a bet," Joanna said, enjoying the small stir she seemed to be causing in here.

"He didn't back my horse, I hope," Clarke said.

"No, indeed," Joanna said, matching his sauciness, "Clinton said Spanish Flyer isn't due to win until next time out, Mr. Clarke," and he laughed heartily, his sharp blue eyes lost in ripples of rosy flesh.

"Very spry of him. Tell him I'm saving the colt for something better but I'm not such a fool as to be more explicit in here, my dear."

He somehow managed to imply that a few moments privacy with her might prove a worthwhile investment and it suddenly struck her that she could exploit this encounter to her own and Clinton's advantage. She recalled Clint grumbling, only last week, that he had underquoted for Tim Clarke's all-Ireland distribution but still lost out to an Irish haulier, Brayley. She also remembered what Clint had said on that occasion, telling her that old Clarke would not risk his son's displeasure by putting money in English pockets. She thought: 'If I can put in a word for the firm with someone of his standing, Clint is going to look very foolish when he shows up here as soon as he's done flattering the Donnelly filly,' and she said, carefully, "I'm not sure I should be civil to you, Mr. Clarke. My husband tells me he pared an estimate to the bone on your behalf last week, and you accepted Brayley's tender in spite of the fact that his quotation was higher and his service far less reliable."

The thrust seemed to delight the old fellow. He wheezed for a full half-minute before saying, "Bless my soul, Mrs. Coles, you're a chip off the old block and no mistake! I knew your father when he opened up over here. Shrewd man. He brought haulage costs down with a bump and not before time. The Dubliners were holding the lot of us up to ransom. Now when would that be? Five years ago?"

"Eight. My husband replaced Mr. O'Dowd as Irish manager, soon after we were married. Now be so good as to tell me, Mr. Clarke, why did we lose the contract? I have to know, for when Clinton finds I've been talking to you he'll quiz me all the way home. Was it simply because Mr. Brayley is an Irishman?"

The attack, pressed home in this way, momentarily disconcerted the wine merchant, so that he welcomed the respite granted him by the arrival of the tea-tray. But then, before he could counter, Clinton arrived out of breath, and not seeing Clarke at once, scowled his displeasure and said, "Really, my dear, wasn't it rather silly to disappear like that? I wasn't gone but ten minutes . . ." but broke off when he became aware of Clarke's grin across the table.

Tim said gently, "Come now, don't scold her, man. She's only here to argue your case and how many wives would do that in public? Especially young and fetching ones like yours. Here, let me buy you a drink to take the sour taste of that contract out of your mouth," and again he summoned a waiter, this time ordering two whiskies and sodas. "I know that's your tipple, Coles. It's my business to know these things. Don't let your tea go cold, my dear."

Then followed, for Clinton Coles, one of the most bewildering intervals of his sojourn in Ireland, for it soon became clear that a man whose patronage could mean as much as two thousand a year to the firm and who had resisted all his efforts (including costly backhanders to warehouse clerks) to point custom Swann's way, had taken a great fancy to his wife and was vulnerable on that account, if half they said about Tim Clarke's galli-vanting was true. For ten minutes they talked horses but they soon got around to business, and the upshot of the occasion was a promise from Clarke that he would review the contract when it came up for confirmation at his quarterly Board Meeting next month.

By then the last race was run and they had downed a couple of whiskies apiece while Joanna sipped her tea and concentrated on looking excessively demure. It was when they rose to leave, however, that Clinton Coles became fully aware of his wife's potential as a business asset. Clarke said, "If you're thinking of attending the garrison supper-ball on Thursday week, could I prevail on you and your charming wife to join my party as my guests? The fact is, I'm short of young people this year, and we ought to take advantage of a gel as decorative as Mrs. Coles."

Clinton murmured that he would be delighted to accept and Joanna, glowing with triumph, added that they would anticipate the occasion with the greatest pleasure. She reasoned that old man Clarke would have no means of knowing that year after year had passed without the Coles having received a coveted invitation to the liveliest event of the Dublin season.

They were bowling homewards before Clinton, slowly recovering from the shock of acknowledging his wife as an emissary extraordinary, squeezed her hand and said, feelingly, "My dear, you were sensational! We've as good as hooked that old rascal and it's all your doing. How did it come about? You went into that buffet in a pet, didn't you?"

"Oh, not really," Joanna said, generously, "I was aware you were one of the wasps buzzing round Deirdre Donnelly's jampot, but why should that bother me? I really did need some tea, and as soon as the old goat started sidling up to me I thought I'd take advantage of it. After all, where's the harm? He's over sixty and only playing games with himself, isn't he?"

"Well, I wouldn't go as far as that," Clinton said, chuckling. "They tell me he can still give a very good account of himself with the barmaids, and seeing how dashing you look today no one can blame him trying his luck. I would have thought, however, he'd turn glum as soon as I appeared on the scene. Maybe he reasoned I'd turn a blind eye for two thousand a year."

"Ah, and would you?"

He looked outraged. "Good Lord, woman, you surely don't mean . . ." but she laughed and pinched his knee, underlining the tolerant and cheerfully sensual relationship that had developed between them since she and her sister Helen had switched beaux at a Penshurst picnic in their youth. She knew very well that he was not in love with her in the way she had been with him since she had surrendered to him on a Kentish hillside, but she flattered herself that she could still make him forget the Deirdre Donnellies of this world when she had him in her arms.

"I'm only teasing," she said, "and you surely know it. Well, we didn't back a winner, but, taken all round, I'd call it the most profitable day we've had at the races, wouldn't you?"

"I would indeed," he said, "and it isn't over yet, my dear."

Neither was it, in the sense he implied. That night, in their pleasant bedroom overlooking the Kingstown busy harbour, he was a boy again and she reflected that he was never likely to be anything else, despite his cares of office and a propensity to spend rather more than they earned each year. And yet, in the event, she was wrong in assuming today had been a profitable day for the Dublin branch of Swann-on-Wheels. She had no means of knowing that her chance encounter with Tim Clarke, at a Curragh race-meeeting, was the very first detonation in

a chain of explosions down the years that would, by the
spring of 1916, divide her loyalties and Clinton's, and that
the wounds inflicted by the breach would not be healed
until Dublin itself was a battlefield.

*   *   *

Two months' voyaging and a week's uncomfortable land
trek from the Dublin Pale, where the London Mission
had its pitch under the walls of Peitang Cathedral in the
Imperial City of Peking, Helen Coles, once boon companion of Joanna, and sister-in-law to Clinton was also
recalling the famous picnic on the wooded hillside above
Penshurst Place, in April, 1888, an event that had led to
her marriage with Rowland Coles and her presence here
in the enervating summer heat of the Chinese land mass.
The heat, the smells and unceasing clamour of the great
city were factors that disinclined her to continue the battle
to persuade herself that she had the best of the bargain on
that occasion.

In the years of trapesing that had followed her acceptance of Rowley's proposal, she had made sustained efforts
to convince herself that she was very privileged to be the
wife of a man whose sole ambition in life was to relieve
suffering, teach aliens the rudiments of Western hygiene
and bestow upon them the benefits of a Christian way of
life. Having her full share of Swann tenacity, however,
she stuck gamely to her endeavours, but here in Peking, a
mild improvement on their billet in East Africa, she was
conscious of losing ground rapidly. Her temper was not
improving and neither was her health but, what was
more depressing, she was coming to terms with the certainty that she was thoroughly unsuited to the life of a
medical missionary dedicated to his calling, and was
wishing heartily that something would stifle her yearning
for a humdrum life in the company of Europeans, living
out selfish lives in a comfortable background. And this
made her feel shamefully disloyal to poor Rowley, whom

she still cherished, but in the way one might cherish the chief of a tribe, or the austere and remote father of a large and indigent family.

She had come to look upon Rowley in this way by slow and arduous stages, signposted over nine years of marriage by his expectations of her as a helpmate and deputy, rather than someone licensed to release him, from time to time, of his fearsome responsibilities, but she had proved miserably unequal to the task and awareness of this made her a failure in her own eyes.

She knew, at the deepest level of consciousness, that it was not her fault, that no mere woman could wean him, even momentarily, from his resolve to work miracles among the heathens, first upon their bodies, and then (providing he had the time) upon their souls. She learned this very early in their marriage, possibly by the manner in which he made love to her on the rare occasions he could be coaxed from this quest in savage, fly-pestered backwaters for his personal Holy Grail. On all occasions, even when on leave, and at a remove from his flock, it was she who had to initiate each encounter and remind him shyly that she was his wife as well as his dispenser, and when he acquiesced, in his quiet, grave way, he performed his marital functions absentmindedly, as though he was carrying out some repetitive task, with a particle of his mind. Then he would lie flat on his back, pondering some problem concerned with the spread of typhus, or the contamination of drinking water, or an antidote for the bite of some lethal reptile, and was quite lost to her in the physical sense until the next occasion.

It had a very depressing effect on her, this withdrawal, as though, each time it occurred, he was saying that she was incapable of stimulating his senses, and fleetingly, with a kind of terrible nostalgia, she remembered the frolics of other, less exalted men, who had embraced her in dark corners of 'Tryst', sometimes letting their hands stray over her breasts and buttocks, proclaiming what she had always assumed a male compulsion to fondle and be fondled. Sometimes she found herself envying his convert nurses when he lost his temper on account of their clumsiness or dilatoriness and snapped at them in a way that sent them scuttling. It would be gratifying, she thought, to goad him to a point of fury where he would unhitch his belt and thrash her and make her smart and cry out, for this would at least establish that she stood for more than a mute, unpaid assistant in the wards where his patients queued for a few moments of his time.

All the other missionaries' wives, and there were more than a dozen here in Peking, seemed to adapt to this passive role, but mostly they were middle-aged, with complexions dried and skins wrinkled by equatorial suns, whereas she was still only twenty-seven and could never banish from her mind the greenness of Kentish hopfields and the freshness of meadows and coppices in the Weald. The death of their child, after a few sickly weeks of life, had been a double tragedy for her. Its survival might have prevailed upon him to send her home to await his next leave. As it was, he seemed to take it for granted that she would remain as isolated from civilisation as a female Crusoe, and she had begun to doubt whether she had the hardihood to endure a three-year stint at the Peking Mission.

The possibility of their being shifted, she gathered, was remote. Nothing dramatic ever happened out here, as China pursued its timeless journey down the centuries. The Chinese had developed a way of life that nothing could hope to alter, and the great powers, Britain, America, Germany and Austria, enjoyed their limited concessions in this incredibly old city. She discounted rumours of a growing opposition to the foreigner building to northern and eastern provinces. The wily old Empress would never be so stupid as to challenge the might and technology of the West and any move against isolated missions and trading outposts would be savagely repressed by Imperial troops.

She re-addressed herself to the monthly task of writing

to Joanna in Dublin, the only member of the family with
whom she maintained a regular correspondence. 'My
Dear Jo . . . Nothing much to report . . . kept busy from
dawn to dusk . . . thank you very much for the dress
patterns but I don't know whether I shall ever find time
to make anything . . . Rowley very well, although I
must confess I feel drained of energy in the summer . . .
my love to Clint and the family . . . I do envy you two
boys and a girl but perhaps I shall be lucky soon . . .'
Random, inconsequential thoughts that were hardly worth
committing to paper yet her sole link with a world that
sometimes seemed as remote as the stars.

* * *

George tinkering with machines; Alex peddling lethal
hardware. Stella dominating a dutiful array of sons,
daughters and farmhands; Margaret filling her canvases.
Joanna as a Swann emissary in Ireland; Helen eating her
heart out in Peking; Hugo touring the country from one
sports meeting to another; Edward following in George's
footsteps, it seemed. Henrietta saw them all as a queer,
rootless, self-centred lot, not in the least like the orderly
spread of soldier sons she had envisaged when, as a girl
living in a rackety industrial town, she had dreamed the
hours away, waiting for a prince to ride over the hill.
She granted them a rather breathless individuality,
and a trick of fixing the attention of whoever looked in
the direction of any one of them but they lacked, to her
mind, a common theme, a resolute and clearly defined
purpose that had been hers all the years they had been
growing up in this old house on the spur. Their various
aspirations confused her, for they were not, she would
have thought, the ambitions that should activate con-
ventionally reared sons and daughters. Their fulfilments
to date eluded her. The best she could do was to number
off their progeny and hope that a coherent pattern would
emerge from the following generation. But having

settled her mind as to that she went about her chores contentedly enough, cocking an eye at the clock now and again to remind herself that a predictable husband and youngest son would be home soon, wanting their supper.

But Adam, in his stone eyrie above the sliding Thames, did not view them in these slightly censorious terms and did, indeed, perceive a pattern in their collective pursuits, seeing them as children of their tribe and times, widening an ever-larger circle in a way that soldier sons would never have done and on the whole he was not displeased. 'At all events they're *positive*,' he thought, 'every last one of 'em, and that's as much as a man has a right to expect at my time of life.'

The verdict mellowed him, leaving his mind free to pursue his self-imposed task of restructuring the network and going about it in a way that would probably astonish George when he scrubbed his hands and re-addressed himself to paperwork. For this restored to him his pride and pride, to Adam Swann, was a power-house that set all his other generators to work and helped to balance the nation's books. He seldom gave a thought to his grand-children. The past he had renounced at the age of thirty and the future was not his business. All his nervous energy was engaged with the present on a purely day-to-day basis and on that basis Swann's waggons would continue to roll.

PART TWO

Tailtwist

I

Breakthrough

THE VALLEY WAS NOT AS GILES REMEMBERED IT.
When, as a scholar-gipsy, he had first passed this way
on his marathon walk from Devon to Edinburgh in 1884,
he had seen it as a monument to squalor that yet retained
a few subtle undertones of an older Wales, when unsullied
streams ran between folds in the hills and islands of green
showed on the ragged escarpment behind the town. Dirty
and depressing, especially under lowering skies, but raising
a few of its tattered banners of the time before the English
first came here with their mail-clad men-at-arms, later
with their prospectors and surveyors, finally with their
armies of scavengers to claw the wealth from the ridges
and darken the mountain with spoil.

Today, a mere thirteen years later, the whole area was
given over to the money-grubbers, with no vestige of
green remaining and tips everywhere, dark against the
sky on the northern edge of the town. Housing had proliferated as the mines expanded and more and more
Welshmen yielded hard-won acres to the thistles and came
out of the interior to earn their bread. The winding gear
was silhouetted against the winter sky, a stark symbol of
Anglo-Saxon dominance, like a gallows in the market-
place of a conquered town. The steep terraces of the tiny
dwellings began higher up and stretched all the way down
to the grey-black blob that was Pontnewydd, where there
were a few grubby shops and a rash of chapels, each built

like a fortress of local stone. The overall picture now was one of stupefying drabness, and yet, knowing these people, Giles was fortified by the certainty that this was not the whole picture, only its frame and outer edges. Down there in the heart of the place, and up here on the serried terraces, there was warmth and comradeship that one could seek in vain in more wholesome places. There was human dignity too, a plinth for loyalty, courage and the dreadful patience of men and women who, while admitting defeat, had never signed the articles of unconditional surrender.

Lovell, his father's former viceroy about here, found them the house, one of the few about here with privacy, for it stood at the end of an unsurfaced road running at right-angles to Alma Terrace and ending in a cul-de-sac under the lowest ridge of the mountain, the house, Lovell said, of an official of the Blaentan Company, that could be bought for a couple of hundred pounds. Stone-built and four-square to the winds that cut their way through the northern passes all winter and the south-westerlies that blew in from the Atlantic in spring and autumn. A three-bedroomed house, reckoned grand by Pontnewydd standards, for it had a small, walled garden front and back, and a rear view of the mountains of mid-Wales.

Lovell said, giving him a steady look: "Sure you want to buy it? Will your wife care to bide here, within washing-line view of cottages and tips? Pontnewydd is the central point, I'll grant you, and will shorten your journeys about the constituency, but we could find something more salubrious if we looked nearer the coast, and you'll have the horse and trap to get you around."

"I'll hang out my sign here," Giles told him. "If I'm to represent these people I've got to know them both in and out of the mine. Where else could I hope to do that?"

"It's not you I'm thinking of," Lovell said. "You were always something of a Romany, even when you looked in here as a schoolboy, and talked me into taking you down a pit. But Mrs. Swann deserves some consideration.

With a man like Rycroft-Mostyn for a father, and eight years soft living in London, she'll not take kindly to slumming, will she?"

"She might," Giles said, smiling. "You can decide that when you meet her," and on impulse told Lovell the story of her flight on the eve of their wedding, and how he found and reclaimed her, working for a few shillings a week in a northcountry drapery store.

"I never heard that," Lovell said, wonderingly. "What made her do a daft thing like that?"

"All manner of motives, adding up to a need to break free of her background. In fact, I might as well admit that, but for her insistence, I wouldn't be here now, throwing my hat in the ring. She seems persuaded I'm tailor-made for the role."

"Ah," Lovell said, nodding, "that tells me more about her. I've had the same notion ever since you looked in on me on that tramp of yours." He mused a moment, toying with the heavy key of the front door. "Tell you something else. You'll win this seat, in spite of Carey's grip on the farming and docking interests further west. In a year or so the Tories will have shot their bolt about here. Maybe you're right to camp on the battlefield. It might help overcome the prejudice against the English. That'll be my line of attack, anyway."

"You'll come out of retirement to be my full-time agent?"

"I will and gladly," Lovell said, "and I'll tell you something I never dared tell your father. I did my best about here, and made a success of the branch, but trade was always second best with me. I always did have a hankering to get at their throats. Any true Welshman has and I'm free to please myself now that I'm a widower and the boys are grown and off my hands. I'll see Hughes Brothers about the house. They'll need a deposit, for a place like this wouldn't stay on their books long."

He led the way into the open and paused at the rusted iron gate between the two stone pillars of the front patch. "Christ Almighty!" he said, "but they've made a rare midden of it, haven't they? I used to fish down there as a boy. All you could catch now would be an old boot and a tin can. I wonder if they'll ever go away again?"

"They'll go, when the seams run out. Meantime we'll give as good as we get, I promise you."

*　　　*　　　*

The weather had broken when he drove her up here for the first time. The valley was screened in a curtain of slanting rain and the mountains were unseen under great grey banks of low cloud. It was a pity, he thought, that she couldn't see the one redeeming feature of the landscape, but she made no complaint, following him round the squarish house that was littered with crates, a few of which he had already unpacked, for they had planned to move in at once and be on hand for the adoption meeting on Saturday. He had chosen the back room as their bedroom on account of the view it offered but now that he entered it the drabness of the vista depressed him a little. He said, "You're sure about this, Romayne? After all, as Lovell pointed out, we could look about for a more cheerful aspect beyond the main line. There's a belt of agricultural land there and one or two stone-built villages."

"With populations of a hundred or so?"

"No more. Almost everyone about here works in the pits. The electoral roll shows a population of around twenty thousand in Pontnewydd alone."

"Then here is the place we start. Anything less would be a compromise, wouldn't it?"

"Well, yes, I suppose it would, but you'll spend a good deal of your time up here and you ought to have the final say in it."

"It was all my idea, remember? So now that it's shaping up don't apologise for it, not ever. To do that is cheating, Giles."

"Cheating who?"

"Me. This is the first worthwhile thing I've ever done
for you, to bring you up to the point of making a clean
break and I want to remember that, always. It's a fresh
start for me too. Those years in London were no more than
an interlude."

She walked slowly round the little room, with its peeling
wallpaper and brass bedstead set against the inner wall
between sash window and door. Most of his unpacking
had been done up here. The folded bedclothes were piled
on the mattress. A bedside table had been set up with its
oil-lamp and there was a new dressing-table in the opposite
corner, looking like a piece of furniture that had come in
here out of the rain and been unable to find its way out
again. "I'll tell you something, Giles, that might convince
you that this isn't a fad of mine . . . settling here, I mean.
This place, this house, is going to mean a great deal to
me. A new beginning for me as well as you, for we've
never been man and wife in the full sense of the word or
not until this moment. No, don't quarrel with that for
you know very well what I mean. We've loved each other,
yes, but neither one of us has ever been . . . well . . .
fulfilled, in the way those miners and their wives are fulfilled in those brick boxes down the hill."

"You're talking about children?"

"Partly. I'll give you children here. I feel it, inside
here," and she touched her breast. "But I'll give you
more besides and the feeling that I can makes me happier
than I've ever been. Safer, too."

He kissed her mouth, surprised by the eagerness of
her response. She said, "Let's not unpack anything more
up here. Uncrate some of the kitchen stuff and light the
fire. I'll make the bed up and cook supper. It will only
be bacon and eggs and cheese but I'll improve on that
without a cook. It won't do for you to have people waiting
on us up here. Just a woman to pop in and help clean up
in the mornings, that's all I want from now on," and she
addressed herself to the blankets and pillows, going about
it so briskly that he had to remind himself he had never

seen her make a bed before. He went down the narrow
stairs and soon had a crackling fire going with sticks and
a bucket of coal he had brought up in the trap. By the
time supper was cooked and eaten, and the crocks scoured
in a sink half-full of water boiled on the hob, darkness had
closed in, pressing against the uncurtained windows. She
said, "Do you want to tackle those voters' registers now,
or shall we make an early night of it?"

"I'm doing no paperwork tonight. I was travelling
from first light this morning, putting in the time getting
to know the beat until your train arrived."

"Give me fifteen minutes," she said. "There's something I've a mind to do," and she slipped away upstairs,
leaving him with the impression that they were alone for
the first time in their lives. When she called down he
damped the fire with dust, extinguished the lamp and
went upstairs, pausing on the threshold of the bedroom
and blinking into the lamplit room. It was a room magi-
cally transformed. Rose-pink curtains screened the
window. Rugs covered the shredded linoleum. The bed
had been made up and turned back and she was sitting
at the dressing-table mirror brushing her hair.

"Well, bach?"

"It's marvellous! I've never seen those curtains before."

"I made them and the rugs were set aside before the
inventory was made out at Shirley. It's cosy, isn't it?
Much cosier than I expected. The heat comes from that
chimneybreast and it'll stay warm all night, so long as the
fire stops in. Feel here."

He put his hand on the chimneybreast and found the
bricks warm. "I think you got a bargain," she added.
"This place is far better built than Craig Wen but that's
because it was built by Welshmen for a Welshman. In
Beddgelert they were just fleecing the English."

It amazed him how quickly she was adapting, but
then he remembered that she was pure Welsh on her
mother's side. "I daresay you'll end up speaking Welsh
fluently," he said. "You've got the hang of it from old

Maggie, up in Beddgelert." And as he said this there came
to him, fresh as a rose, the memory of that first morning
she had led him into her father's house in his dripping
clothes, and Maggie had scolded her in Welsh and dried
him off while Romayne, full of mischief, had changed into
a gown of crimson velvet, with gold facings and rows of
gold buttons on the bodice and sleeves. She said, "What
are you remembering now?"

"Your 'Camelot' gown," he said, "and how you looked
when your hair was cut short and combed close to the
head, so that it matched the gold buttons on the sleeves."

"You've forgotten something not so far back."

"What's that?"

"Today's our wedding anniversary."

"My God, so it is! And I *had* forgotten, although
how . . ."

"I didn't," she said, triumphantly, and reached beyond
the bed and pulled out first a stone hot-water bottle,
wrapped in her nightgown, then a bottle of champagne
and two glasses. "There," she said, "but it's not fair to
crow over you because I made up my mind our first
night here would have to be a special occasion. That's
why I persuaded you to leave me behind to finish the
packing. Open it, but don't let it shoot over the bedclothes. They're all we have until the van gets here."

It was years, he thought, since he had seen her in this
mood, as sparkling as the child she had been the day they
met. She was wearing a blue silk dressing gown he had
bought her on their first visit to the Continent, a dashing
affair, trimmed with Lille lace and sashed with blue
velvet. He drew the cork and filled the glasses, saying,
"What do we drink to?"

"To winning Pontnewydd from the enemy!"

"No," he said, "to us, and to you especially, for I've
never seen you like this since . . ."

"Since before I ran off?"

"Since before that really, for we seemed to squabble
our way through that interminable engagement. Since

that day on the mountain just before you went back to
London to be presented. You flew into a temper because
I argued against us getting married right away."

"I remember and I was right. You should have taken
me at my word. My father would have agreed, he was so
relieved to find anyone who would take me off his hands.
At least we should have been spared all those silly
squabbles."

"But you wouldn't have seen how the other half lived
and then we shouldn't have been here at all."

"That's so. I'd forgotten how it began."

She drained her glass and set it down on the dressing-
table, crossing to him where he sat on the edge of the bed.
"It's permanent," she said. "You believe that, don't
you?"

He unhitched the bow of her dressing gown, slipped
his hands behind her and ran them lovingly down her
back and over her thighs. "I not only believe it. I feel as
if we were beginning our honeymoon, with all the
benefit of experience. There's Welsh magic left in this
valley after all. Those tips haven't been able to banish it."

She slipped out of her gown and threw it across the
only chair in the room. "Stop making speeches," she
said. "They'll be needed later. If we're on our honeymoon
let's get on with it, bach," and she kissed him, lifted the
hot water bottle from the bed and slipped between the
sheets.

The pleasant languor of her body encouraged a state
of mind enabling her to isolate the uniqueness of the
occasion in a way that had never been possible in the
past. For then, like a heavy shadow, the shame of her
encounters with other men prompted by curiosity on her
part and uncomplicated lust on theirs, had stood between
her and physical fulfilment in the arms of a different kind
of man, one whose chivalry and essential tolerance had
been recognised by her from the first day she met him.

He knew of those earlier follies, of her seduction, before
she was seventeen, by a groom and later a Belgian

musician. She had allowed them to fumble her with clumsy fingers, then possess her for a few sweaty moments in isolated corners of the house. Her father had made sure that he did know when, washing his hands of her, he was still resolved to use Giles Swann as a go-between in his relations with his work force. He had laid the un-savoury facts before him like items in a police report but it had not freed him from the need of her, nor scared him off, as it would have scared most men. Rather it had enlarged his area of compassion so that their subse-quent relationship had never been soiled by the know-ledge. As for herself, her lovers, if you could call them that, had never come close to teaching her anything of the least significance about the way to search out a relation-ship that promised to assuage the loneliness of spirit that had clouded her childhood and adolescence. Indeed, it was not until this moment, the culmination of the long haul that had led them to this unremarkable little house overlooking a ruined valley, that she recognised the act of physical fusion, even with a man she could respect, as little more than a starting point in the journey of the soul towards personal fulfilment. It was imperative that she should acknowledge this and acknowledgment was made with a gesture. She reached out and found his hand in the darkness, lifting it gently and mooring it under her breasts. Its presence somehow confirmed her full acceptance of the active role in their partnership.

2

George versus the Clock

FOR GEORGE THE WORK WAS REMINISCENT OF
housebound hours spent over jigsaw puzzles in the nursery at 'Tryst', a methodical sorting and shifting of seg-
ments of a battle scene, or a farmyard, until the four
cornerpieces were in place, and the straight edges in
approximate alignment, so that a start could be made
towards completing the picture but the analogy went far
beyond that. Just as, bent over the tray holding the puzzle,
the selection of a fragment was suddenly seen to be the
correct one and a segment slotted into place, so it was with
the third prototype of Maximus, whose assembly presented
so many experiments, frustrations and disappointments.
There was a penalty of error too. On the workshop floor
a misconjecture could represent a wasted day, perhaps a
wasted week and he was working against the clock.

He had been through it all before. Once beside the
Danube, sorcerer's apprentice to old Maximilien Körner
assembling his giant carriage that had ultimately crawled
through the morning river mists like Jupiter's war-chariot,
and later during his earlier severance from the firm, when
he had improved on Max's model to a degree that had
half-persuaded his father that the days of the dray horse
were numbered.

But now the challenge was more immediate. All over
Europe and the Americas men were bending brain and
will to the solution of these selfsame problems, although

a majority of them still regarded the mechanically propelled vehicle as a substitute for the brougham rather than the waggon and dray. He made the fullest possible use of their discoveries, however, adapting and often blending gleanings from word-of-mouth information, sketches and sometimes spare parts, run down by the indefatigable Scottie Quirt, who had spent ten years drifting about the north and midlands, hiring his skills to whoever would pay for them.

Like a jigsaw, yet he sometimes saw his task in a more majestic light. A range of mountains, with a few major peaks and innumerable smaller ones, each presenting a peculiar challenge of its own. Nothing was predictable in this wilderness. Sometimes the loftier peaks were easier to scale.

One such peak represented the ratio between thrust and laden weight, another the variation of gears to adapt to gradients, including a reverse gear, for without the ability to reverse a vehicle was as cumbersome as a barge fighting a strong current. He estimated that he should be able to generate sufficient power to haul a five-ton load, more than any load Swann's four-horse or two-horse waggons could haul over indifferent roads and this had been achieved by constant modification of the carriage until the overall weight of the vehicle was reduced to a point where its chassis did not fracture under the strain. The main structure of a Swann man-o'-war, the heaviest category in use with the exception of purpose-built Goliaths, was of oak, four inches thick in places. A petrol-driven Maximus of corresponding strength would be impossibly heavy, so he switched to nickel-steel that was found equal to anything Swann was likely to haul, excluding heavy machinery. The gear changes operated through a gate, with a retaining bar to prevent reverse gear being engaged in error.

The third and fourth mountains to be scaled, however, presented greater challenges. They represented overheating, and a tendency for vital parts to be shaken loose by vibration and passage over uneven sections of carriage-way and he was assaulting these most of the winter. Over-heating was eventually cured by the introduction of a perforated jacket made of copper and the summit of the fourth major peak was reached on the unforgettable day that he and Scottie fitted their double semi-elliptic front and rear springs, affording the first real flexibility Maximus had ever achieved.

There remained the minor peaks, each with a range of problems of their own, so that it was sometimes like inching his way up a shingled incline sown with brambles and quickset thorn. They represented braking, solved at last by internal expanding shoes operating in drums, uneven transmission, overcome by a new type of carburetter intake copied from a French model, lubrication and a hundred and one other problems, each of which proved desperately time-consuming. Even so, by late April, ten months from the day he had stripped son of Maximus down to its last rivet in the Salford yard, he had done what he had set out to do. He had, he told himself, a vehicle capable of hauling a sizeable load south to H.Q. in two days, averaging seventy-five miles a day from the final testing ground, a mile east of Macclesfield, to London Bridge.

"Will you take me with you, George?" Gisela asked, when he was ready for the gamble, and he said, regretfully, that he could not. A passenger meant extra weight and, aside from that, the driver would have to face a formidable buffetting. It was a silly risk to take in view of the fact that she was now five months pregnant.

"Then I shall go by train," she said, "and it's a great pity. I should enjoy your father's expression when he comes down from that tower and finds a Maximus in his yard."

"Oh, you could still do that," he said, anxious to acknowledge her loyalty and invaluable help over the past ten months. "Set out by train the day after I leave and when you get there wait for me in the yard of the old

'George', somewhere between five and six. If I break down I'll telephone Bendall's factory in the Borough and he'll send someone over with a message. In that case catch the train on to 'Tryst', but say nothing about the trial run. I'll catch them bending or not at all."

She said, gravely, "You will make the journey, George. If you had doubts you would not set out."

"But this is a pure gamble."

"No, George. Your father, he is a gambler but you are not the same. Your father would gamble on his luck, but you? You would not put one pennypiece on a horse unless you owned it, trained it and rode it in the race. That is the difference between you."

It increased his confidence to hear her talk that way and he went blithely about his final preparations after Scottie Quirt had left them to take a holiday with his family in Glasgow and she had packed her things to follow him to London. She saw to it that he should lack nothing for the journey that was in her power to supply and it was while she was baking pasties for him, the night before he was due to set off, that he said, "I'll make it up to you, Gisela, I swear it."

"Ach, but you already have, George. I have been very happy up here. It has been like the old days, when grandfather Max was alive. Will you travel loaded?" she replied.

"Part loaded. I'm taking two tons of rice down to the Madras Trading Company, in Cheapside."

"Why rice?"

He grinned. "Proof, of a kind. A four-ton load is due to go south by road tomorrow. I've shipped half of it aboard and given Carstairs, the yard goods manager, instructions to despatch the other half at seven o'clock, the same hour as I leave."

"And you plan to get there well ahead of him?"

"We'll see. I've worked out a route and my worst gradient is one in twelve, but I'm still scared of over-heating."

She said, "Suppose the motor is as good as you think it is and suppose you prove it to all of them, what are your plans when you take over from father again?"

"A fleet of 'em," he said, briefly, "with all the four-horse waggons withdrawn and their teams allocated to frigates and some extra Goliaths, for it'll be years before we can develop a non-rigid vehicle to haul the really heavy one-piece loads – boilers, generators and the like. There's only one thing I should enjoy more than making it in two days."

"And what is that?"

"Grandfather Max to wish me luck."

"He's here," she said, "I dreamed of him last night. Both of you, locked away in that stable at Essling." Then, remembering how Max had died, "There's no danger, is there?"

"None for me. Plenty to oncoming traffic. I'm resigned to being cursed by every carter from here to London Bridge."

* * *

The rice had been loaded the day before and every foreseeable contingency guarded against. Twenty gallons of fuel was stowed in ten-gallon drums forward and he had even shipped a water-cask in case she boiled at a point on the route where no water was readily available. He had a spare tyre too, although, if one left the rims, he was doubtful of replacing it without Scottie's help. After he had run the vehicle out and warmed her up he went over all his preparations again, while it stood there trembling like an over-trained racehorse at the tape. He thought of the Swann-Maxie as female, although he had seen its two predecessors as male. Maybe it was because she was so much trimmer, or perhaps because all the months he had sweated over her she had reminded him so often of the maddening unpredictability of a woman. He thought, 'Maximus doesn't suit her now and Maxima doesn't sound right. If we do build a fleet on this model it will have to have a trade name and Max ought not to be forgotten.' He finally settled on a hyphen-ated name, 'Swann-Maxie', and looked up at the clear April sky, praying for propitious weather, at least as far as Market Harborough or Kettering, where he planned to let her cool off for the night, depending on his progress.

The first leg of the journey, as far as Cheadle, was encouragingly uneventful. Gradients rather than mileage had dictated his choice of route and the roads thus far were level and fairly free of traffic at that early hour. He averaged seventeen miles an hour over the first thirty-five miles, and she seemed to be behaving impeccably. In all the villages crowds of boys ran alongside shouting up at him, some of the bolder ones in ribald terms but the older folk just stood by and gaped, and only one old chap, mounted on a spirited bay, shook his crop threaten-ingly when the horse reared at a farm gate. He thought, 'There'll be plenty of that before people get used to motors. I daresay a majority would like to see that damned Red Flag Act back on the Statute Book but that won't happen. It's already cost us the lead we might have gained over Continental mechanics.'

It was after Cheadle, as he was following the valley of the Trent in a south-east direction, that he had his first scare. He had tackled a long incline at a slow walking pace and breasted the summit with a great sense of relief. Below him, curving eastward in a wide, scimitar sweep, lay the white road running between low hedgerows, with a straggle of farm buildings at the bottom where the river was crossed by what appeared, at this distance, a shallow ford. He thought, gratefully, 'Well, here's a mile or two of coasting,' and changed gear, forgetting for a moment the down thrust of the load behind him but sensing its compelling weight when he realised the slope was much steeper than it looked.

There was nothing to give him an accurate indication of his speed but by the time he was two-thirds of the way down it seemed to be far in excess of the limit he and Scottie had agreed upon when they were planning the route mile by mile. His teeth rattled every time the wheels struck a dried-out puddle crater, where underground springs had been at work all the winter, and then, as the road flattened out, he saw a herd of cows crossing from left to right, and it seemed to him that nothing could prevent him ploughing into them.

He had rigged up a handbell on a short length of rope, the bell itself fitting into a bracket on the canopy support, and he took his left hand from the spokes of the steering wheel to ring it furiously so that an aged cowman, emerging from the nearside gate with a pair of yapping collies at his heels, glanced up and saw his approach at a distance of about eighty yards.

George had never seen a man look more astounded and for what seemed like seconds he stood there, hand on gate, mouth wide open. But then, with remarkable agility for a man of his years, he turned and ran up the hedge, diving head first through a clump of ash saplings that grew there and disappearing in a flash while his cows, unimpressed, pursued their leisurely progress across the road to the opposite gateway.

A violent collision seemed inevitable, even though only two or three cows still remained on the road, and a collision would certainly have occurred had it not been for the dogs. Almost equally terrified, but more conscientious than the cowman, they bounded forward nipping the heels of the laggards, while George threw his entire weight on the brake lever without, it would seem, doing much to check the thundering onrush of the Swann-Maxie, for now it was as though the weight at his back was propelling man and vehicle down the last stretch of road straight into the river.

And then he saw something else, the narrow entrance to an old packhorse bridge marking the ford, and he knew that to stay on the road was to gamble the entire enterprise on his ability to steer a straight course between the stone parapets. He did not possess that much faith in his own skill. There was no more than an inch or so to spare on either side and in response to a split-second decision, he chose instead the nearest of the two ford approaches as looking the shallower of the two. He shot off the carriageway at an angle of about sixty degrees and the sheet of water that rose on impact enveloped him, rising in a solid column like a waterspout. And then, without so much as a lurch, Swann-Maxie stopped dead in about a foot of water, and people came running from all directions, converging on both banks and dancing and gesticulating as the hiss of steam from the radiator sounded the knell of his odyssey.

There was no one to blame but himself. No rustic cowman could have anticipated the onrush of a monster weighing some five tons laden weight on a country byroad miles from the nearest city, and no medieval builder could be blamed for building a bridge only inches wider than the largest haywain then in use. The fault lay with himself, for changing gear at the summit and putting too much reliance on his powerful handbrake, and he climbed down into the current cursing himself in German, still his favourite language for abuse.

The water rose to the level of the hubcaps so that he saw at once it was not a matter of the engine being flooded but rather doused in that first surge of water. As he realised this his spirits lifted for he reasoned that the automatic inlet, the valves, the surface carburetter and the ignition tubes could be stripped down and dried, although the process would occupy him at least two hours, even if no vital piece of mechanism had been dislodged by the jolt.

An enormously fat man in a moleskin waistcoat and a hard hat seemed to be in authority among the wildly excited group of onlookers on the far bank and George called, "Can you tow me clear on to level ground? I'll pay a sovereign an hour for the labour and the hire of horses."

The fat man swallowed twice, licked his heavy underlip, pushed his hat brim an inch higher on his forehead and said, ignoring the offer, "Christ A'mighty! Whatever iz un?"

"It's a petrol-driven waggon," George said, impatiently. "Can you do what I ask? I've got to make Leicester by dusk."

At that the man removed his hat altogether and passed his hand over the full extent of his balding skull, saying, "I thowt at first it were a locomotive running loose from up the line. A horseless carriage, you zay? But that'n iz ten times the size o' the doctor's," and at that George's heart leaped and he said, eagerly, "The doctor here owns a motor? Will you send for him? He'll have the tool-kit, no doubt. Will you do that? For an extra half-sovereign?"

"Christ A'mighty," the man said again, "youm pretty free with your coin, maister." And then, after ruminating a moment, "Arr, I'll vetch 'im, for he'd give me the length of his tongue if I didden and he missed this carnival. *Ben!*", and he whirled about and roared aggressively at a gap-toothed boy beside him, who was still surveying the vehicle as if it were a stranded dragon, "Stop gawping and rin an' vetch Doctor Bowles. Look sharp about it! Seed 'im go in Fanny Dawkins', minnits back. Tell 'em us've something in the river he'd like to zee!" His speculative gaze returned to George. "A sovereign an ower, you're offering?"

"That's what I'm offering but every minute counts. If I'm out of here in less than two I'd add to it, sixpence on every minute saved."

The bribe now seemed to animate the man who shook himself in a way that caused his gross body to quiver. In less than five minutes two enormous Percherons were trotted out, yards of plough harness were produced, and with a single, squelching heave Swann-Maxie was dragged out on to dry ground and into the lee of a barn where the horses were unyoked and led away, and George crawled

under the vehicle for a close inspection of the complex
of tubes and rods assembled there.

No damage was visible but every part dripped water
and he was already removing the feed pipe to the carburetter when a cheerful voice greeted him from the
offside, calling, "Hey, there! Come on out, man, and
tell me what happened. Maybe I could help, although
this is a new one on me. Is it a Daimler?"

George crawled out, leaving one end of the feed pipe
uncoupled, to see a man about forty in a neat broadcloth
suit that at once distinguished him from the rest of the
crowd still gathered about the machine. "Desmond
Bowles," he said, extending his hand. "Anything shaken
loose? Or is it a case of stripping down and drying
out?"

George shook his hand and although time pressed on
him like a goad he found the doctor's smile so engaging
and his interest so obvious, that he decided the least he
could do was to introduce himself and his product.

"My name is Swann," he said, "and I'm in transport.
You'll know my firm, no doubt, the hauliers, Swann-on-
Wheels. I'm making a trial run to our London head-
quarters and planned to get as far as Leicester tonight.
Do you own a motor, doctor?"

"Yes, I do. A Panhard-Levassor," Bowles said. "I
brought her over from the Continent last year but she's in
dry dock at the moment so I'm back to the buggy, confound it. Do you mind if I crawl under and have a look?
I've done a lot of tinkering with petrol-engines. It's a
hobby o' mine. These people think I should be put away,
of course, and the same probably applies to you. I've
never seen anything like that before, however."

"Nobody has. I only finished work on her this week.
She's purpose-built for commercial work and not designed
for joy-riding as you can see. Have you got a tool-set
with that Panhard? A smaller screwdriver is what I need
to detach the intake pipe from the carburetter. That's
where the damage is, if any. One drop of water through a

joint and I'm stuck unless I can clear it," but he was addressing no one in particular for the doctor had slipped out of his jacket and scrambled underneath the rear wheels where his findings reached George in a series of short, authoritative pronouncements, as though he was diagnosing a patient.

"No need to remove the intake pipe. Not yet anyway. We'll try blowing bubbles first. Been stuck here myself but in far worse trouble. Your chassis is much higher and your casing took the brunt of it. Damned good idea that casing. Bellows might help." His head emerged, and he bellowed at Ben, the boy who had summoned him, "Slip across to the forge, Ben. My compliments to Vosper and tell him I need his hand-bellows again!" The boy darted off as Bowles said, "Dry the externals with the bellows. Done it myself and it works sometimes. You're right about the intake, though. She's blocked. Grit washed in, I wouldn't wonder. That or an airlock. It can happen crossing a puddle sometimes. Come on under, Mr. Swann."

George joined him and found him supporting the loosened end of the intake, holding it between finger and thumb of his gloved hand. "A steady blow," he said, "can't use the bellows on here. Careful, she's piping hot. Use your handkerchief," and George fascinated by his air of knowing precisely what he was about, found his handkerchief, wrapped it round the detached end of the intake and blew gently and unavailingly for a moment until, with a faint plopping sound, the blockage cleared. He said, excitedly, "I can dismantle the carburetter with the tools I've got already, Doctor Bowles. Then dry 'em out piece-meal. Will you give her an overall dusting?"

"The moment Ben gets back with the hand bellows. My stars, but she's a powerful brute! How far have you come today?"

"From Macclesfield. I've planned a two-day haul to our London H.Q. If I can make it, I'll be building a fleet to replace our four-horse vans," and the Doctor sat up so abruptly that he dinged his hat on the crank casing. "*Build!* You built this yourself? It's not patented?"

"Parts of it are. It's my third prototype, based on an Austrian model built by a man called Körner. He was quite unknown, but I happen to be related to him. She's been running sweet as a nut up to here. You can blame this on my damn foolishness, taking that hill too fast."

"Here, I'm teaching my grandmother to suck eggs," Bowles said. "I took you for an engineer. 'Swann' you said. You're *the* Swann's son?"

"I'm more than that. I'm his managing director," George said, smiling, "and I'm extremely grateful for your help in spotting the trouble at a glance. I should have wasted an hour eliminating various factors. Here's your bellows, Doctor," as a breathless Ben joined them, carrying a brass-nozzled bellows of the kind found in every forge in the country.

"Pity you can't stop over," Bowles said, methodically setting to work with his bellows on every exposed section of the engine. "Between us I daresay we'd have my Panhard on the road again in a jiffy. You're sure you can reconnect that intake with tools you've got?"

"I'm already doing it," George said, gaily, congratulating himself on his luck, and they worked on in silence for ten minutes or so, drying out and dusting off every section of the engine with the bellows and clean pieces of sacking supplied by the obliging Ben.

"That'll do, I'd say," Bowles said, squirming out into the open. "Crank her up and see if she turns over," and George followed him out, reaching into the driver's cabin for the heavy crank lever and noting, as he slotted it in and prepared to swing, that the crowd, now grown to about a hundred, edged away leaving himself and Doctor Bowles alone in the clearing.

He brought all his concentration to the first swing, remembering to cock his thumb inside on account of the powerful back-kick the engine produced on several occasions, once putting Scottie in hospital for close on a week

The initial cough was one of the sweetest sounds he had ever heard, and then, using the full strength of his arm, he swung furiously and the engine burst into a stuttering roar, gloriously sustained and magnificently full-throated, proclaiming that Swann-Maxie was no worse for her ducking.

"Are you going to risk stopping her?" roared the doctor, above the beat of the engine.

And George shouted back, "No, by God! I'm off, while I've got the chance! Where's that fat chap in the moleskin jacket? I owe him a sovereign."

"I'll give it to him," Bowles shouted through cupped hands, "up with you and the best of luck," but the fat man, seeing George on the point of climbing aboard, overcame his caution and waddled forward, pointing to his watch that showed the delay had cost George fifty minutes from the moment he plunged into the stream. He threw the doctor a coin and engaged low gear, heaving at the steering column and regaining the flint road at about four miles an hour. Bowles waved his dinged hat, the crowd edged forward and a ragged cheer sped him on his way over the level stretch to a fork in the road where a signpost indicated the ways to Derby and Lichfield. He bore off to the right and slowly built up his speed to around twenty miles an hour, presently seeing the triple spires of Lichfield Cathedral away to the south-west and calculating (he had his father's trick of memorising routes, mileages and local products) that he was now within a hundred and twenty miles of London Stone and reflecting that Swann's waggons had been hauling beer and market produce from this area for forty years.

Tamworth, Atherstone and Hinckley – he skirted them all, adding a dozen or more miles to his journey to avoid the risk of getting caught up in a traffic jam in busy streets and around five o'clock, after one brief halt for a cool-off at Polesworth, he was heading almost directly eastward towards Market Harborough, sixteen miles south of Leicester, and eighty-one from London.

There was still an hour or more of good daylight but it seemed like pressing his luck to push on, taking pot-luck when he stopped for the night and, in any case, his head was aching and his eyes were sore with dust, so he pulled on to the broad grass verge short of the little village of Sibbertoft, ate two of Gisela's pasties and spent an hour carefully rechecking tomorrow's route sheets. He had a yearning for a pint of country-brewed ale but he dared not leave the vehicle unattended and nobody came by whom he could tip to go to the nearest tavern, so that he was about to make do with water when he remembered Gisela had put tea, sugar and condensed milk into his knapsack. "Just in case," she had said, when he told her he wouldn't have time for a picnic. "You may find yourself stranded miles from anywhere and be glad of some tea while waiting about for spare parts to arrive."

In a few minutes he had a roadside camp fire going downwind of Swann-Maxie and brewed his tea in a billy-can he kept among the tools. He was grateful for Gisela's forethought then, for never had tea tasted so good, easing the ache from his brow and washing the dust from his throat.

It was dusk by then and to stretch his legs he walked along the country road as far as a stone monument, pausing to read its inscription and learning that he was camping on the field of the battle of Naseby. He thought, grinning, 'Old Giles will laugh at that and see something symbolic in it – *The old order changeth, giving place to new*. He'd remember the Johnny who wrote that too, but I'm hanged if I do.' He lit his pipe and leaned against the memorial, inhaling the freshness of the evening breeze and the scent of the hedgerows for it seemed he could never free his palate of dust motes and fumes of Swann-Maxie's exhaust.

His progress, despite the mishap, had been remarkable. By the route he had come he estimated he had travelled over a hundred miles in ten hours. With ordinary luck he should now fetch up at The George Inn, Southwark, about tea-time tomorrow. No other experience could have taught him so much in such a brief span of time and he reviewed the lessons learned one by one. Somehow the steering would have to be lightened and some means would have to be found of extending the range of gears, for gradients far in excess of one in twelve would have to be faced when the vehicle went into mass production. The vibration, although greatly reduced by the new springing system, was still a source of anxiety and that plunge into the river had set him thinking hard about the hazards of descending hills as well as climbing them. Shoe-brakes were adequate to check the progress of the vehicle itself but when one added on the thrust of a load it was asking for trouble to tackle gradients commonplace in many areas of the country. There were aspects, however, that encouraged him. Transmission problems seemed to have been overcome, and over-heating, although a factor that had to be watched, was not the ever-present menace it had been on the two earlier models. He knocked out his pipe and went back to the machine, draping it for the night in a tarpaulin, then crawling inside and making a nest for himself on a palliasse wedged between fuel drums and rice sacks. In a few minutes he was asleep.

*   *   *

He made a dawn start in the morning. Before the chill was off the air he had brewed himself tea, breakfasted on chocolate and apples and refuelled with the help of a watering-can fitted with a funnel. To do this, in the stiffish breeze that was blowing, he had to make a wind-shield out of the tarpaulin, for a gust was sufficient to spray the spirit in all directions and he could not discount the high risk of a fire caused by a spark from a roadside fire. This set him thinking about the positioning of the fuel tank, so that he mused, 'The devil of it is you can only go so far in a workshop . . . The real solution to every problem is out here on the open road, where theory and practice merge. I could improve on this model in a dozen ways right now and I suppose that will be the way of it from here on . . a slow climb towards perfection, if it's ever possible to perfect a wayward brute like this. Well, now for the physical jerks!' He took the starting handle and swung and swung until he was scarlet in the face and sweating freely, despite the nip in the air. On the twenty-eighth swing, when his arm felt as if it had been stretched on the rack, she started with the now familiar stuttering roar and he tuned the engine and moved off, taking the road to Dunstable.

For two hours his progress was smooth and uneventful, apart from the sensation his appearance caused in villages and one or two small country towns. It was just short of Letchworth, after passing over a particularly rough stretch of road, that disaster struck again. Part of his cargo had shaken loose, promoting a snaking motion on a mild descent that ended in a hump-backed bridge, where he pitched so heavily that he had to slew the vehicle hard right on to the verge. In that swerve the nearside tyre left its rim.

He managed to stop almost at once but the damage dismayed him. The tyre was twisted into a loop and half-severed by the iron rim and he saw at a glance that it would have to be cut away and replaced with his spare.

He was still wondering how this could be done without lifting gear when the knife-grinder appeared, riding a trap with a high, hooped canopy and a sad-looking cocker spaniel crouched on either side of him where he sat on the box. The man was a singular-looking wayfarer, tall, spare and narrow-faced, with sad, brown eyes to match those of his dogs, a Romany no doubt, who preferred his own company and obviously lived in his ancient two-wheeler.

His professional apparatus was stacked in a tailboard box or suspended from the canopy struts on short lengths of string, so that it jangled and rattled as the trap approached. Unlike most of the wayfarers George had encountered, however, he seemed to find nothing menacing about Swann-Maxie and looked her over with mild interest before pulling in, tying his horse to an overhanging bough, and saying judiciously: "You'll have to cut that loose, brother. And you'll need something more business-like than that clasp knife." He foraged among his tools and produced a murderous-looking butcher's knife. With a few swift slashes he rid the wheel of the ruined tyre which he then examined, with what seemed to George a professional interest. "The best Malayan rubber," he said, sniffing it, "and you've given it a rare pounding, brother. Do you carry a replacement?"

"Yes," George told him, "but to fit it I'll have to raise the front wheels at least four inches and muscle won't do it. I'd gambled on this happening near a farm or a forge where I could hire labour and borrow levers. By my reckoning I'm still five miles short of Letchworth."

"Four and a quarter," the man said, "but I have something better than a lever," and he went back to his tail-board and dug deeply into it, dragging out what appeared at first to be a large bench vice but on closer inspection was a multi-purpose tool with both curved and flat expanding surfaces, operated by large butterfly nuts, a marriage between a bootmaker's last and an anvil. "A legacy of my father's," the grinder said. "He was a Jack-of-all-trades and made his own tools. He was a file-cutter at one time and I find this useful for straightening agricultural implements. Scythes mostly and plough-shares. Do you carry a heavy wrench, brother?"

The man's serious, methodical air made an immediate impression on George, so that it crossed his mind that the country must be teeming with inventors and would-be mechanics, grandchildren of the Industrial Revolution with inherited skills of every variety. He fetched his largest wrench and the grinder selected a section of the front axle as an anchor for his expanding vice, spinning the heavy butterfly nuts with long, supple fingers until the tool was about one-third extended. Then, together, they applied the wrench and George was greatly relieved to see the rim inch from the ground until it was spinning free, after which they took a breather before tackling the job of fitting the spare tyre George had trundled out.

The man said, incuriously, "What would you be hauling south, brother?" When George told him it was Madras rice he said, "Now there's a queer thing to be taking into London, and London is your destination, no doubt. Wouldn't rice come in by sea and be offloaded on the spot?"

"Not this consignment. It's an assortment of high-grade samples and came ashore at Liverpool. I only happened to stow it because it was there. I could have made up the weight with anything handy." Although time was pressing he felt obliged to give the man an explanation of his presence here on a country byroad, with a stranded vehicle and two tons of Madras rice. The traveller was a difficult man to surprise. All he said was, "To replace the draghorse, brother, you will need to do one of two things in the new century. Either you will have to prevail upon a niggardly Government to surface every main road in the country, or you will have to find a means of cushioning those wheels in a way that will enable them to absorb the shock of every dip on your route. Springing alone won't do it, although you have some powerful springs there. Are they making any progress with heavy, air-inflated tyres, on the lines of those fitted to the latest bicycles?"

"If they are I didn't get to hear of it," George said, "and I made enquiries everywhere, here and abroad. The weight of a vehicle like this would be enough to puncture air-inflated tyres every mile or so, except on a first-class Macadamised road. This kind of mishap could happen twenty times a day."

"Ah," said the grinder, thoughtfully, "God is a great husbander of secrets, brother. He will reveal that one, no doubt, when the time is ripe. Will you join me in a short prayer, brother?"

"For the patenting of air-inflated tyres for heavy vehicles?" asked George, too surprised to smile.

"Why, no," said the grinder, gently, "for God's blessing on the remainder of your journey."

"I should be obliged if you pray on my behalf, brother," George said, not in the least disposed to laugh now, whereupon the man closed his eyes and said:

"Lord God, please to look kindly upon this traveller, and grant him a safe arrival. He is about Thy work, I think, and is not prompted by usury. Amen." And, while George was still debating whether or not the grinder was correct in his charitable assumption, the man picked up the spare tyre and began to fit it to the rim of the wheel, motioning George to hold on to the spokes while he inched the taut rubber in place with the help of a broad-bladed file he had fetched when he brought his winch.

It was the work of a few minutes to lower the chassis and when it was done George said, "I'm uncommonly obliged to you for your help. I hope you will allow me to pay you for your time and trouble."

But at that, for no particular reason, the more sedate of the two spaniels gave a short, scornful bark and the knife-grinder said, "The dog rejects your offer of payment, brother," and said it without the merest hint of a smile, so that George had no alternative but to suppose the grinder found nothing whatever surprising in his dog's ability to form moral judgments or, for that matter, to understand every word that had passed between them.

He shook the man's hand warmly, thanked him again, and went on his way in a mood of quiet exaltation, boosted not so much by the man's skill and kindness but by his evident belief that the horseless carriage came within the orbit of the Almighty's plans for mankind's progress. 'My stars,' he thought, as he moved off towards Dunstable, 'you learn a thing or two on the open road. I daresay that's where the Gov'nor learned most of his lessons. He'd relish that chap, to be sure.'

By noon he was skirting St. Albans and an hour later, on Barnet Heath, he was drinking a pint of ale and munching beef sandwiches, sparing a thought, as he refreshed

himself, for the woman whose home lay a few miles to
the north-east and who had, in a sense, shown him the way
home again. His entanglement with Barbara Lockerbie
seemed to have happened a long time ago and yet, in
terms of the calendar, it was only ten months since he
had walked out of her summer-house and begged a lift
on a market cart to the scene of what could have been,
but for his father's tolerance, the wreck of his fortunes.
And the thought of surprising Adam, with eight weeks in
hand, added zest to the final stage down the old Roman
road where carters, waggoners, bicyclists and a few
horseback-riders gave him a wide berth and sometimes
shouted a jest into the wall of sound isolating him from
other traffic.

At three-fifty-five by Cricklewood Church clock he
was moving through traffic that reduced his speed to a
crawl. By four-thirty, he was traversing Oxford Street
to approach London Bridge from Cheapside, crossing the
river and edging into the yard of The George at precisely
four-forty-five. And there, on the flower-decked gallery,
sat Gisela with tears in her eyes, so that he forgot Swann-
Maxie for a few moments, abandoning her to a crowd of
stablemen and urchins who approached her less reverently
than his rustic audience north of Lichfield, for hardly a
day passed now when a motor or a mechanically-propelled
waggon of one sort or another did not turn on the cobbles
where coaches had discharged their passengers in the
days before Stephenson laced the country with his gridiron and made the 'Shrewsbury Flyer' as obsolete as a
chariot.

She said, "It doesn't even look out of breath . . . and
you're ahead of time. I hadn't expected you until dusk
and ordered dinner for seven-thirty. Shall I cancel it,
along with the room, George?"

"Not on your life, my love, for if she's none the worse
for it, I am. I could eat a five-course meal and sleep the
clock round but I'm not foregoing the spectacle of the
Gov'nor's eyebrows lifting half the length of his head

Have you got a wrap and a veil?" When she nodded he told her to fetch them. Fifteen minutes later he had swung Swann-Maxie in a wide arc, repassed the arch of the inn and was heading for the yard.

2

Adam was in his eyrie when Edward rushed in, almost incoherent with excitement; and this was enough to bring Adam to his feet, for Edward, a dour boy, went about his work with the air of wary concentration characteristic of old Sam Rawlinson when he was satisfying himself that a customer got what he had paid for but nothing in the way of a bonus.

For a moment he could make little sense of the lad's jabberings but finally he gathered it was something to do with George and said, "Hold it, boy! Start from the beginning. What's George been up to now?"

Edward, pointing to the window, said, "He's here. With that petrol waggon and a load of rice for Dickenson's!"

"George here? With Dickenson's rice . . . ?" and following the direction of Edward's finger he hastened round the end of the desk to the window. What he saw made him grunt with surprise for there below, in a tight circle, was every waggoner, clerk and farrier on the staff, all gazing up at his son and daughter-in-law, enthroned on a streamlined version of the juggernaut he had seen thunder past his holly bush ambush on its test run up in Cheshire nine years before. The boy was right about the rice too. The tailboard was down and already a couple of jubilant warehousemen were offloading Dickenson's sacks.

He called, scarcely less excited than Edward, "*George!* *Gisela!* Wait, I'm coming down!" as if he expected them to vanish in a cloud of blue exhaust gas, and in reply to Edward's "Hold a bit, Gov'nor, I'll fetch 'em up here!" snapped, "Nay, you won't lad! This is one time I bend

the knee to George! He's two months in hand, by God!"
He followed the boy down the winding staircase, sniffing
the unfamiliar stink of engine oil that introduced an
entirely foreign element into the blend of smells about the
yard. He called, as George handed Gisela down, "Hi!
How far have you come in that thing? When did you set
out?" and Gisela answered, saying, with just a hint of
triumph, "Yesterday morning! He left Macclesfield at
seven a.m."

"You're telling me he took *you* along?"

"No," she said, descending and kissing him, "of course
ne didn't, Father. I came on today by train, and met
him by appointment at The George. But he's not to stay.
He hasn't had a hot meal since he set out, and he slept
by the road last night."

"He's time for a drink, none the less," Adam said, and
bawled, more to express his elation than to disperse the
crowd, "Get on with whatever you were doing, the whole
lot of you! Damned thing won't run away. Jenkins, tow
it in the man-o'-war shed. And if there isn't room make
room, d'ye hear?" Then he led the way up the stairs
again, with George, Gisela and Edward at his heels, and
Edward, bright lad, didn't have to be told their various
tipples, bringing out brandy, sherry and ginger-beer
for himself. Alone among the latterday Swanns, Edward
had no head for liquor.

Adam said, raising his glass, "Well, here's to the two
of you, and I'm more pleased to see you than you can
imagine. Your mother hasn't stopped nagging me since
I took up this packload again and I'm re-abdicating
tomorrow, like it or not!"

But then curiosity overcame everything else as he
remembered those rice sacks and he said, "Just how much
freight did you haul? Edward said something about two
tons."

"Edward had it right. It's sample rice, from Monday's
Liverpool shipment. The other half set off by waggon the
same nour as me but I'll lay you long odds it doesn't get

invoiced until sundown tomorrow. And even then they'll have to hustle."

The calculated subtlety of it tickled Adam. It was the kind of trick he would have played on doubting Thomases a generation ago and he did not begrudge George his moment of triumph. "She came out of it well, then. Damned well, I'd say. A hundred and seventy-five miles in – what was it? – two legs of ten hours apiece? Well, you've proved your point, and I'll make sure everybody about here knows it. How long will it take you to build more of those snub-nosed monsters and get 'em into commission?"

"All of two years," George said, "but that will be Scottie Quirt's job as soon as I've approved the blueprints for modifications. There'll be Swann heavies on the roads for a long time yet."

"Ah, that's what you say. A sop to my pride, no doubt."

"No, it's true. We've got our lead and there's no point in going off at half-cock again. I nearly came a cropper twice and on both occasions I had more luck than I deserved. A man needs training to handle one of those on the open road and apart from production we'll have to school a team of likely lads as drivers," and he sketched his adventures, as much for Edward's benefit as his father's.

Adam could see the boy was exhausted and took Gisela aside, telling her to take a cab back to The George. "If only to wash all that grime from his face," he said, and to George, "You'll be coming on to 'Tryst' with me and the lad after we close up?"

"No, Gov'nor. Gisela's booked overnight at the inn. Tell Mother we'll be over tomorrow. How are the children? They haven't tired her too much, have they?"

"She'll not like parting with them," Adam said. "The old place is quiet these days." And then he noted with approval that Gisela was pregnant again, and this added to his satisfaction for it surely meant that that foolishness had been worked out of the boy's system and he told himself he could take most of the credit for that.

She must have realised what he was thinking, for when she raised herself on tiptoe to kiss him she whispered, "In October, Father. Tell Mamma for me," and they went out, with the enslaved Edward in their wake, leaving him alone with his thoughts that were among the most cheerful he had had up here since he was as young as the man who had just toted two tons of Madras rice nearly two hundred miles without a horse to haul for him. Provided, of course, one discounted the Percherons who pulled him out of the river.

He gathered up his papers and took what he thought to be his final valedictory look at the broad curve of the Thames and its procession of barges, tugs and lighters shooting the arches of a bridge that had spanned this point of the stream for centuries. 'And that's another thing,' he thought. 'They'll have to think about replacing that for the passage of brutes like that one below.' But it wasn't his business, thank God. He'd had his fill of problems and there were plenty over for the Georges and the Edwards to solve

*   *   *

The sun was setting in its familiar orange glow upriver as he crossed to the new, brick-built stable block to look the vehicle over. It was neater, and far more compact than either of its predecessors but it had none of the grandeur of a four-horse man-o'-war, a two-horse frigate or even a well-turned-out pinnace. It stood there looking sullen and impersonal, a tool rather than a partner in the never-ending struggle of man to save himself time and trouble and ensure that he claimed his portion of luxuries from the scrimmage. It was very difficult to visualise a day when the stink that still hung about it banished the prevailing odours of horseflesh, leather and trampled manure. But he had no doubts at all on the prospect now.

Transport would make another leap forward, almost identical to that of the 'thirties and 'forties, when coachman Blubb and his ilk grumpily dismissed Stephenson's locomotive as 'that bliddy ole tea-kettle'. And was it so surprising when you pondered it? The history of a tribe was and always had been the history of its transportation.

He went out and crossed to the main gate, looking about him at the rows of new buildings that surrounded his belfry like an army of youngsters bringing an old warrior to bay. Old George would have a fresh start at all events, for a great deal had happened here in his brief and busy St. Martin's summer as The Gaffer; his Swann-song as the local jesters called it. The insurance had paid for most of the rebuilding and old Sam Rawlinson's pile the rest, but although the layout was his it wasn't his yard any more. It was the domain of that engine in there and he had no authority over it now that George was back.

The weighbridge clerk had a cab waiting and he got in, riding the short distance to London Bridge Station alone, for young Edward wasn't to be found and he welcomed the solitude. Edward too was in the other camp now, and in a year or so he would be little more than a left-over of the century that had begun with cheers for Trafalgar and would go out with salutes from fourteen-inch guns and the cough and stutter of those snub-nosed replacements for Cleveland Bays, Suffolk Punches, Clydesdales and Percherons. He didn't mind, or not all that much. He had done what he set out to do and a little to spare.

3

Drumbeat

MUCH AS HE HAD ENJOYED BEING IN COMMAND
again of the affairs of Swann-on-Wheels, Adam was glad
to return to the peace of life at 'Tryst' with Henrietta,
and found plenty to occupy himself, planting a bed of new
roses in the garden, and studying the art dealers' cata-
logues. He was still a keen observer of the firm's activities,
however, and it gave him great satisfaction in the year
following George's historic journey from Macclesfield to
London to see his son tackling the problems still facing
him with such determination. Now George was re-
united with Gisela, Adam had no doubts in George's
ability as his successor. In spite of Adam's own doubts
earlier about a future for petrol-driven vehicles, he was
now convinced that it would be George's Swann-Maxie
which would ensure that Swann-on-Wheels remained the
largest and most progressive hauliers in the country.
Though it would take at least two to three years before a
complete change-over to petrol 'lorries' could be made.
There was certainly plenty to occupy George, improving
the technical performance of the new vehicle, and also in
planning out what reorganisation and re-routeing was
going to be necessary once the majority of long-distance
journeys were being made by Swann-Maxies.

They still sought him out in the last years of the old
century, coming singly for encouragement, for consola-
tion, or for a nugget of counsel from his bran tub of

experience, and he was sometimes amused by their deviousness for they often disguised their visits as duty-calls on Henrietta and needed a little prodding to come to the point.

Giles was a regular caller and the most outspoken, a man picking his path among Celtic caltrops sown for unwary Englishmen. George looked in oftener, with or without Gisela, giving a brash account of himself and his affairs but often seeking to draw him out on a choice of routes, the breaking-strain of an executive, or the credit-worthiness of a customer.

Hugo was not such a frequent visitor at 'Tryst'. For him it had been a frustrating and puzzling year, but it wasn't until several months after Lady Sybil Uskdale's nursing benefit sports meeting, in the Putney arena on August Bank Holiday, 1898, that he found it necessary to come to see his father for some advice.

*   *   *

It was a very fashionable event and Hugo, ordinarily disdaining what he would have styled 'a bunfight meeting', would not have been there had it not been for the fact that Lady Sybil, president of the Volunteer Nurses' movement, was a forceful and persistent woman, able to appreciate the drawing power of a track champion who held European records in amateur athletics for the mile and the marathon. At twenty-nine Hugo should have been past his prime as an athlete but he showed no sign of a decline during that first circuit, loping along with the measured stride that sports editors claimed did not vary by a centimetre and apparently in no hurry at all to prove he could lap the best of his opponents when the time came. But then Springer, the London harrier, crossed to the inside, inadvertently implanting a track shoe on the arch of Hugo's right foot and causing him to swerve in a way that disconcerted a knot of competitors on their heels. The result was a mix-up that steered the lamed champion into a marker post and the impact was violent enough to stun him.

When he opened his eyes, wincing with the smart of a lacerated foot, he was lying on a stretcher in the shade of some elms and Lady Sybil herself was ministering to him with that compound of authority, despatch and professional tenderness that made her so popular with photographers selling plates to the fashionable periodicals. On this occasion, however, she was not wearing her standard regalia of gleaming linen but a Paris creation of striped silk that emphasised, as her rustling uniform could not, the graceful contours of her figure with its high bust and impossibly girlish waist. This, together with a tiny straw hat, gently angled and worn high, made the very best of her plentiful blonde hair that was wreathed, German fashion, over her temples.

It was a very reassuring spectacle to a champion wincing with pain and aware that he had lost his chance of fresh triumphs in the tail-end of the season, and Hugo, forgetting his troubles for a moment, gazed at the vision with rapt attention, almost as though the track tumble had translated him to an Anglo-Saxon Garden of Allah where the queen of the houris awaited his pleasure.

The illusion faded, however, the moment the vision in striped silk spoke, saying, in a tone of voice that had never been challenged since nursery days, "Lie *quite* still, Mr. Swann, do you hear? You've had a nasty tumble and I feel entirely responsible for it. You must stay here until the doctor has examined that foot."

He blinked once or twice but then the pain of his wound increased, as someone out of his line of vision applied a salve, and had it not been for the soothing touch of Lady Sybil's white hand on his brow, he would have sat up and cursed the fool who had blundered across his path in that uncouth manner. Attendance at foreign sports stadiums had enlarged Hugo's vocabulary, and bystanders, held at a respectful distance by Lady Sybil's acolytes, might have learned an interesting variation of the British equivalent of, say, 'clumsy fellow, born out of wedlock'. As it was, there was no alternative but to lie still until a doctor arrived, going over him as though he had been the heir-apparent savaged by would-be assassins.

He heard Lady Sybil say, in a more peremptory voice than she had employed to him, "Into the committee tent! Move the chairs! Take the trestle table away! Bring the chaise-longue from the terrace! Cushions too, lots of them!" People scurried in all directions, two stewards lifting the stretcher and bearing him away, like a dying warrior king, across the trampled grass to the welcome coolness of the pavilion where, under Lady Sybil's expert direction, he was made very comfortable and given a glass of iced lemonade, held to his lips by the mistress of ceremonies.

Then, quite suddenly, it seemed, everybody except Lady Sybil disappeared and the sound of distant cheering came to him from the arena, rising to a climax as the winner, whoever he was, breasted the tape. He asked, a little petulantly, "Who won?" and she said, gently, "Never *mind* who won, Mr. Swann! You won't be concerned with who wins or who loses for quite some time. I'm having you taken to my town house as soon as the brougham comes round. I'm afraid you must regard yourself my patient until that foot has healed."

It crossed his mind to remind her that stunning good looks and extreme elegance did not entitle her to prescribe his comings and goings for as much as an hour but meeting the level gaze of her cornflower blue eyes all he could mumble was, "It's nothing, Lady Uskdale . . . a mere scratch . . ." She smiled down at him in such a bewitching way that he was deprived of the will to get up and limp outside to discover who had carried off the trophy he had expected to win at a canter. Instead he lay back among his cushions, wondering why a woman as celebrated and socially exalted as Lady Sybil Uskdale should make so much of a few foot punctures and mild concussion. Being Hugo, a stranger to the world of high

fashion, he decided it must be because she regretted having
enticed him to appear at a bunfight meeting and inadvertently eliminating him from more serious events in
the near future.

His surmise, of course, was a long way from the truth.
Nothing so trivial as a twinge of conscience had ever
prevented Lady Sybil Uskdale from acquiring anything
she coveted, and at this moment, having made up her
mind in a single intuitive flash, she coveted Hugo Swann
so jealously that he would have blushed had he discerned
her motive.

He was not necessarily stupid to so misread the situation. More sophisticated men than Hugo Swann had
pondered the secret motives of Sybil Uskdale for years
without arriving at any significant conclusions. The
eldest and by far the most decorative of the famous Uskdale girls, she was now within two weeks of her thirtieth
birthday and the only one among them unmarried.
And likely to be, so most London hostesses predicted, for
her hauteur was a legend, and all the eligible bachelors
she seemed to find repellent and she scared away less
exalted candidates with a mental superiority that was the
very worst card an eligible spinster could display in the
presence of a suitor. Even her detractors (among them
the frustrated mothers of a dozen or more spurned
eligibles) had to admit that Sybil had had her chances,
some of them splendid chances all the way back to her
coming out ball, twelve years before. Yet here she was,
within days of the spinster's Rubicon, still pottering about
first-aid posts, obsessed with some horrid plan of luring
nice girls from the real business of life in order to learn how
to alleviate the sufferings of the victims of road or railway
accidents, as if these things couldn't be left to the professionals and lower-middle-class girls who went in for
voluntary nursing in the hope of finding a husband. It
never seemed to occur to the most discerning of them that
Sybil Uskdale saw her vocation in precisely these terms.

In the course of her long, semi-regal passage through the

ballrooms and drawing-rooms of fashionable London Sybil Uskdale must have encountered a regiment of gallants who would have needed no more than a soft glance, a blush or a mere hint, to bring them to the pitch of proposal. Yet so far not one of them had been given the signal and the simple reason for this lay in the impossibly high physical standards Sybil Uskdale set herself when her thoughts turned to marriage.

It was not that she did not desire to be married. She did, and with all her heart. Indeed, had the more staid of her hostesses been granted access to her secret fantasies in this field it is doubtful if she would have received invitations into their homes. For the truth was Sybil Uskdale panted for a man, providing he was one who was neither a middle-aged widower or a member of the younger set that she thought of, in her eccentric way, as a 'pebble'.

The origin of this line of thought is interesting, illustrating her singularity in that closed society. As a child she had paid occasional visits to Folkestone, where it was fashionable at that time to rent a villa by the sea, and there she had witnessed a group of local boys diligently throwing pebbles at a shelving ledge twenty feet up a cliff overlooking the promenade. Every now and again a pebble lodged itself among a small pile but nearly all of them rebounded and fell among the gorse growing below. When, some time afterwards, she was introduced to the young men who were paraded round Belgravia's drawing-rooms like so many colts each season, she at once equated them with the pebbles flung by little Folkestonians in the hope of making a lodgment. She never had and she never could think of herself as anything so commonplace as a ledge, and throughout a succession of seasons no single pebble lodged with her but this was the fault of the pebbles not the pitchers. In a later era, when Victoria had at last made way for her more relaxed heirs, newspaper editors found certain labels for young men making regular appearances at these exclusive mating functions. They called them 'chinless wonders' and 'debs' delights'; and

Sybil Uskdale would have regarded the soubriquets as
very apt. Their chinlessness offended her estimate of what
a husband should look like. Not one of them had ever
looked remotely like Hugo Swann, as he lay concussed on
the stretcher under the elms at Putney on that hot
August afternoon. It was then that Sybil suddenly realised,
and with a sense of liberation so compelling that it required
strict self-control not to proclaim it aloud, that here was
the man she had been looking for all these years and that
her quest was now at an end.

She had always been attracted to athletes and was herself an ardent bicyclist and tennis player, so that she knew
all about Hugo Swann when she invited him to participate
in her nursing fête. It did not matter to her that he was
a prosperous tradesman's son, and the fourth in line at
that. The notion that like should mate with like was
passing out of fashion anyway, and it was now considered
almost chic to marry into trade, so long as the word was
elevated to 'commerce' and so long as the commerce had
resulted in wealth. All the Uskdale wealth reposed in
land, and, as everybody knew, land was at a discount now,
what with successive agricultural depressions, and millions
of pounds of refrigerated food were pouring into the ports
from the dominions and colonies. Far better a tradesman's
son with a beautiful body than a pebble with an uncomfortable country house, his father's mortgages and a
thousand unproductive acres in the shires. Particularly
a tradesman's son of Hugo Swann's splendid proportions,
who looked, she thought, like Achilles lying on his shield
as she ran her approving glance the length of his bronzed
body, happily open to close inspection in his singlet and
running drawers. A shaft of sunlight, striking through the
branches, teased his thighs, sown with short golden hairs
that grew all the way down to calves knotted with solid
muscle. A long ecstatic sigh escaped her as she contemplated those hairs, and the thicker growth just visible
above the hem of his singlet, and she had a vivid impression of what it would feel like to lie beside him and

feel the weight of that huge sword arm across her breasts. Then her fancy went further and she contemplated the extreme satisfaction it would give her to stroke those short, curling hairs and the limbs they grew upon and she made up her mind in a matter of seconds. Hugo Swann's days of bachelorhood were numbered.

*   *   *

Hugo came to see Adam a few months later when it had finally dawned on him that Sybil Uskdale was resolved to land him, weigh him and, for all he knew, mount him in a glass case and hang him on her boudoir wall, but because he was Hugo, childlike in a situation of this kind, Adam handled him gently, managing to persuade him that he had reached a stage in life where he would be well advised to settle for a rich, influential wife, who regarded him as a person of enormous consequence and would coddle him in a way that would compensate him for the sacrifice of bachelorhood.

"The trouble with your line of country is that it gets tougher in direct ratio to your weight and wind," he said. "You're what age now? Thirty, is it?" and Hugo conceded ruefully that he would not see twenty-nine again. "Well, then, you're past your prime, old lad, and may as well admit it. She's wealthy and well-born so they say, but not as grand as she pretends. Her grandfather was in Chilean nitrates to my recollection and *his* father was a Pennine weaver with a few bright ideas. However, that's neither here nor there. The important thing is, do you want middle-aged freedom at the price of lonely old age? Some men reckon it's the better bargain and for all I know you might be one of 'em."

It was the first time in his life Hugo had aspired to such an intimate level of conversation with his father and confrontation of this kind embarrassed him horribly. He said, grimacing, "I dunno, Gov'nor, I always reckoned I'd marry and settle down sometime. It didn't seem to matter when or how but Sybil, well, she's a rare sport for a woman."

"What do you mean by that?" asked Adam, relentlessly. " 'Sport' is an ambiguous word in that context, isn't it? Are you implying she was free with her favours among her kind before she met you?"

"Lord, no, Gov'nor, not that! She doesn't give a fig for polite society and never did, according to her sisters. They told me she could have married time and again but she wouldn't have anyone picked out for her, the way all those girls do." He shuffled a moment. "What I mean is – she, well . . . she doesn't *crowd* a man, and tag him along to all those soirées and at-homes. She's a top-class tennis-player, she's bicycled across France and can handle a racing skiff better than some of the undergrads you see at Henley."

"She sounds tailor-made for you, Hugo. Grab her while the going's good, boy. Your mother will be delighted, I'm sure, for it'll be a dressy wedding, no doubt."

"I haven't said a word about a wedding," protested Hugo but when he saw his father's twinkle he grinned and mumbled, "Well, everyone seems to *think* I'm spoken for tho' I haven't actually proposed so far."

"You leave that to her. She'll do it more gracefully than you and it's my belief she won't be long about it," and it seems that he had sized up Sybil Uskdale as accurately as he had been wont to take the measure of his customers, for the announcement of the engagement appeared in *The Times* the following week, and within twenty-four hours (another accurate prediction) Henrietta came to him wailing she had nothing to wear for the great occasion.

All of which, he supposed, was run-of-the-mill stuff, no more than his due as the father of nine.

*   *   *

It was otherwise with Alexander, when he looked in to ask his father to use his friendship with Lord Roberts in order to enlist him as an ally in the campaign to increase the number of Maxim guns per infantry battalion.

The prospect of button-holing anyone as celebrated as 'Bobs' (as everybody seemed to call him these days) and then preaching him a secondhand sermon on field tactics, was not one that Adam relished. There had been a time when this would have presented no difficulties to a man holding equal rank with the old campaigner, but that was so long ago that it belonged to another age. They had kept in touch over the last forty years but their correspondence had been intermittent and more or less formal, a matter of mutual congratulations mostly, although he remembered he had turned to Roberts for help once before, when Henrietta badgered him into using his influence to get the boy into a good regiment. Roberts had been kind and helpful about that, he recalled, and there might be no harm in an invitation to luncheon, at Pall Mall Club, to which they both belonged although, now that he thought about it, he had rarely seen Roberts about the place. He considered very carefully before he assented, however, saying, "You're absolutely sure you want me to do this, son? I don't mind getting snubbed, or not so long as I'm persuaded it's in a good cause. But if it got around that you had been using backstairs methods with a lion like Roberts it could spell trouble for you, I daresay."

Alex said, emphatically, "I don't mind a snub either, Gov'nor. I've already had more than my share in that direction, nor do I mind the backdoor, for they all use it whenever they can. That's why chaps like me, who take their work seriously, get more kicks than ha'pence. Ninety per cent of the men who outrank me got where they did by a word in the right ear at the right time, and the cavalry have the edge on all of us when it comes to patronage. Suppose you invited him to lunch, I was around and you called me in and introduced me when you'd got as far as coffee and cigars? That's all I'm asking. I'd play it from that point on."

And thus it was arranged, so blatantly yet so neatly

that Roberts went to his grave without knowing the 'chance' encounter had been stage-managed, and because Roberts was another man who took his profession seriously, he listened attentively, Adam noticed, when Alex paraded his hobby-horse round the most famous soldier in the Empire, showing it off like a nagsman at a fair.

Roberts said, when Alex excused himself, "Does you credit, Swann. More than you deserve, a straight-talking young chap like him. Sound on theory, and far more battle experience than most of the well-heeled youngsters you meet in the mess nowadays. How old is he?"

"Thirty-eight. Eight years older than I was when you and I parted company in India."

Roberts smiled and Adam remarked that, although his face was furrowed, and burned the colour of elm bark after half-a-century in the sub-tropics, his eyes were still young. 'And nothing remarkable about that,' he thought, 'for if they weren't so he wouldn't have given me the time of day after all these years,' and would have reverted to talk of scenes and companions of their youth had not Roberts said, suddenly: "Matter of fact, I've had my eye on him, Swann. Ever since you wrote and told me how he survived that shambles in Zululand. Did you know the subs dubbed him 'Lucky' Swann on account of that?"

"Yes, I did," Adam said, quick to seize his advantage, "but they have less flattering names for him now. One of them is 'The Barker' he tells me. I don't have to tell you that one pays a price for setting up as an expert before one's within a step of retirement, or that most professionals play at soldiers all their lives. Those who don't usually acquire reputations as mess-bores."

"And that's happening to him because he's refused transfers that meant promotion to stay on as a small-arms specialist? Well, that's you emerging in him, I daresay. You always were an obstinate cuss, Swann."

"No more than you, although your convictions were the more fashionable, even then."

"Not everywhere," Roberts said, thoughtfully. "My concept of Empire was rejected by you, if I remember correctly, but it's true that a majority of career men aren't interested in anything but polo, pigsticking and cutting a dash with the ladies. I wouldn't have got this far if I hadn't had more than my share of luck. Kitchener, too, I can tell you, and some of the others. We chaps need luck more than most and we're all going to need a lot more before we're much older."

"Where, particularly?"

"South Africa. Nobody will frighten Kruger into toeing the Imperial line and anyone who argues otherwise is a fool. You've read it all in the newspapers, I daresay."

"I've read a lot of bluff on both sides. The question is, if it did come to a showdown, who is likely to back Kruger? The German Kaiser wouldn't, and the French wouldn't. As for the Austrians and Russians, I daresay they'd have to be told who Kruger was. So who is bluffing who?"

"Kruger is bluffing himself," Roberts said. "That's his grief and ours, so long as those get-rich-quick Johnnies in the gold mines keep clamouring for the franchise and want us to take over the Transvaal." And then, as though his mind was off at a tangent. " 'The Barker', eh? Well, if I read that youngster correctly it's not promotion he needs so much as a backer or two on the staff, and that shouldn't be difficult to arrange. After all, he's talking sense. How many casualties did Kitchener's outfit suffer at Omdurman? Twenty-eight, and they killed ten thousand of the Mahdi. That was only achieved by automatic fire-power. I'll turn up the boy's file the minute I get a chance."

He sipped his brandy and they smoked in silence for a minute. Then Roberts said, "I've got a son about his age. Fine young chap who might go far, but not as far as your boy. Too amiable for one thing. I'm glad you put one of them in the army."

"It wasn't my choice, it was his own and his mother's. Tell me – that dream of yours about the destiny of the British. Does it look as rosy as it did to you then?"

"Can't answer that," Roberts said. "It's only half-fulfilled as yet. Need a century at least to bring something as big as that to full growth."

"But you must have a good idea how it's shaping."

"It needs pruning, I can tell you that."

"Ah, then you're coming round to my way of thinking. When I watched you ride by in that procession it crossed my mind that I was watching a lot of greedy children who had eaten enough confectionery to make 'em tolerably sick."

"They can do with a purgative," Roberts said, "but there's one coming and they'll be the better for it, so set your mind at rest as to that."

He got up, moving briskly as a boy. "Pleasure to see you again, Swann. We should do this more often. There aren't so many of us left nowadays."

They went out into the sunshine, a slim, short man loaded with honours and a very tall one, loaded with cash, and as they shook hands and took separate cabs, it occurred to Adam that they represented two sides of the national coin. Glory, a more mystical, less strident equivalent of the French 'gloire', and trade. The bray of the trumpet and the chink of the till, combining to produce a jingle that could be heard all the way round the world. 'Well,' he thought, 'I don't know what will come of all that in the end but something might. Can't but help the boy to have someone like Roberts behind him. Queer that . . . what he said about South Africa. Hadn't thought it was that serious myself, but he should know . . .', and he used the train-journey to Bromley to study the political correspondent's column in the *Pall Mall Gazette*, – 'that chap Stead's rag' as he still thought of it.

There wasn't much about South Africa there, only a paragraph announcing Paul Kruger's steadfast refusal to extend the franchise to the riff-raff that had invaded his

Old Testament domain once gold and diamonds had been discovered in the Witwatersrand, and he wondered what he would do in Kruger's place; bow the knee, to what most men would accept as the inevitable march of progress, or fight to the last ditch for the way of life adopted by the Cape Dutch after they had trekked north to their Promised Land?

The train ran into the station and he left his *Pall Mall Gazette* on the seat to beguile someone else's journey. The older he grew the more insular he became; the slow growth of his own cypresses and Himalayan pines interested him more than international rivalries these days. That was one of the troubles about growing old – one ceased to have any convictions about anything save those affairs, necessarily trivial, that lay under one's own hand.

2

Henrietta remembered other wars but never one like this one, with everyone, from scullerymaid to Duchess caught up in it, knitting, nursing, arguing, advising, one could almost say advancing against Kruger alongside the Yeomanry and any number of fancy volunteer units, all falling over themselves to singe Kruger's beard.

The earlier wars had been occasions for ceremonial for all who were not actually fighting, and so few had been in those days; hardly anybody one knew, more's the pity, for she had always wanted to be personally involved in an Imperial adventure.

There had been those colourful cutouts of Imperial warriors to paste on to nursery screens, awarded as Sunday School prizes; and reports in the weekly journals of last stands, broken squares and Highland pipers sitting on rocks puffing away at their bagpipes while shot and shell exploded all around them. But everything had always been at a remove, an intriguing succession of slides projected on to a magic-lantern screen.

Today, as the mother and grandmother of Imperial

soldiers, she knew that it wasn't quite like that, that sometimes men were speared and mutilated, as Alexander had
so nearly been at that Zulu battle with the long un-
pronounceable name, but she had no earlier experience
to guide her when Stella appeared at 'Tryst' demanding
to know how she could go about erasing young Robert
Fawcett's name from the muster roll of the Kentish
Yeomanry, after the boy had been silly enough to sign
on for the duration. Robert was still a month or two short
of his eighteenth birthday and had no business at all to
do a thing like that without consulting his father.

Stella was right to be angry, of course, and Robert,
senior among Henrietta's tribe of grandchildren, deserved
a severe scolding but she could not stifle a thrill of pride
at the lad's spirit, prompting him to go all that way from
home in order to confound the Queen's enemies. She said,
distractedly, "I really don't know how to advise you,
Stella. In my day wars were fought by soldiers, not
farmers' lads. Even Alex, only a year older than Robert
when he went off to fight the Zulus, was preparing to be
a soldier and Robert isn't, is he?"

"I really couldn't say," Stella grumbled, "but he'll feel
the weight of my hand alongside his ear the minute he
comes home. His father has learned to rely on him for he
does two men's work around the place, or so Denzil says."
Henrietta thought it odd that Stella should put Denzil's
crops and cattle before the honour of the flag. She was
therefore mildly shocked when Adam took an identical
view, dismissing Robert's gallant gesture as a piece of
schoolboy nonsense.

"He's absolutely no call to risk his skin in that quarrel,"
he growled. "The Boers are outnumbered by ten to one
to begin with, poor benighted devils." Although she had
always entertained great respect for Adam's knowledge of
public affairs she did not feel she could let this pass without
protest.

"But surely the boy feels he *ought* to do something,"
she said. "I mean, I think Stella is being very parochial

about it. She's got two younger boys and three lumping great farmhands . . ." But she stopped, seeing his brow cloud and feeling, in any case, out of her depth on a topic of this kind.

By then, of course, Alex had sailed, but this was in the natural order of things. Fighting the Queen's enemies was what he was paid to do and she had come to believe nothing much could happen to Alex for he obviously had a charmed life, like a sailor born in a caul. The situation grew even more perplexing when Croxley, 'Tryst's' second gardener, left at a day's notice, explaining that he was a reservist and had no choice. And after Croxley young Ricketts, the stable-lad, took himself off, also volunteering for the Yeomanry, so that Henrietta decided privately that Adam must be in error for once, for surely all these people would not be needed to deal with an enemy outnumbered ten to one.

The news, that autumn of 1899, seemed to prove her right. Nobody, it seemed, could get within singeing range of Kruger's beard and anyone who tried was shot down like a partridge. Defeat followed defeat and the sense of shame they brought spread outwards from London, like a wave of bitter-tasting medicine that everyone was obliged to swallow in droplets. Larger doses were on their way. When everybody was busy dressing their Christmas trees, news came of three shattering reverses in a single week, a week the newspapers called, justifiably in Henrietta's view, 'Black Week', for she could not recall a single occasion (apart from that temporary one at the hands of Zulus) when anyone challenging the British on the field of battle had come away the victors.

Adam, for all his lofty talk of the Boers being outnumbered ten to one, was clearly depressed, especially when he heard that his old friend Roberts had lost his only son, killed trying to save guns at Colenso. He said, gloomily, "Only mentioned him to me last occasion we met, that time I put in a word for Alex at the club. I gathered he was the gallant-idiot type. They invariably get themselves killed in the first skirmish. But how the devil do they expect a father, facing grief of that kind, to pull Buller's chestnuts out of the fire, now we're fully committed? Damned politicians should never have let it come to this. The country's gone mad and the whole world is laughing at us. Giles is the only chap I've met who takes a sane view of the silly business."

Henrietta was intrigued to learn that Giles, by nature such a quiet, studious boy, had taken the war fever, and said, innocently, "What does Giles think we ought to do, dear?" and Adam administered one of the biggest shocks of their married life by growling, "*Do?* Why, what any Government in their senses would do in the circumstances. Find a face-saver, pull out and let the Boers go their own way."

She did not think she could have heard him correctly. It was so uncharacteristic of all she knew of him to advocate such a craven course and concede victory to the enemy, just as if positions had been reversed and the British were a small republic facing an opponent with vastly superior resources.

"Pull out!" she gasped. "You mean . . . let them *win*?"

"Dammit, woman, they are winning!"

"But only temporarily. I mean, they're bound to be beaten in the end, aren't they?"

"Yes, they are," he said, "but we won't emerge with any credit. They've already given us the hiding of our lives and demonstrated that the only possible way to beat them is to wear 'em down, burn their farms and slaughter or capture every able-bodied male between fourteen and seventy. By God, if I met a Boer now I wouldn't have the gall to look the chap in the face. We're behaving more like Prussians than Englishmen."

She gave it up after that. Clearly he had got some bee in his bonnet about the Boers and was deaf to the opinions of everyone around him. She only hoped he would keep his mouth shut in the presence of any of her friends she invited in over the Christmas holiday.

There was to be the usual family party, with a coming and going of the whole tribe of children and grandchildren, and she wanted to make a special impression this year. Hugo would be bringing his aristocratic wife on Boxing Day, the first time she had been offered an opportunity of getting to know the exalted creature, for the brief introductory visit before the wedding didn't count and at the ceremony itself she caught no more than a glimpse of the bride among all those fashionably dressed guests.

* * *

As it happened, however, Hugo and his wife appeared long before Boxing Day, bowling up to the forecourt in a very elegant equipage just as she was emerging from the kitchen in a grubby apron, after helping one of the girls to unstop the clogged runaway of the well-trough. She found it hard to believe that even Hugo could be so dense as to spring the girl upon her without a warning and would have blushed scarlet if she had not had her mind switched by the vision of Hugo in a well-tailored uniform of dark blue, with a broad yellow stripe running down his trouser-leg. Daughter-in-law Sybil escorted him up the steps and presented him like an impresario introducing his star-turn.

"There now!" she cooed, "doesn't he look perfectly *splendid*? Aren't you proud of him, Mrs. Swann? My word, but that tailor did a wonderful job once I put a flea in his ear! 'Swamped with orders, ma'am,' he said, if you ever heard such nonsense. As if Hugo didn't take precedence over a queue of stockbrokers and pen-pushers! Kiss your mother, Hugo, I'm sure she expects it."

Henrietta wasn't at all sure what she expected, apart from the floor to open and engulf her after being confronted by the daughter of the Earl of Uskdale in a flowered apron and a sewing dress, two years old. She was seized in Hugo's bearlike embrace and lifted clear of the floor but Sybil did not seem to pay the least attention to her embarrassment. She had no eyes for anyone but Hugo. Henrietta had time to note the soft shine in her ice-blue eyes as she patted and prodded her exhibit, straightening non-existent tunic creases and flicking imaginary specks of dust from the frogging. And then, to make bad worse, Adam had to come downstairs, pause on reaching hall level and exclaim, "Lord God Almighty! What's he joined, a German band?" and she could have cracked him over the head with the sewing-room door-stop. Luckily his daughter-in-law was not only blind to everyone but Hugo but deaf to opinions that he looked anything but every inch a soldier. Then Adam moved all the way round him in a cautious circle and said, "That's a City of London badge, isn't it?" and Lady Sybil said that it was and that Hugo was now a member of the Inns of Court Volunteer Company.

"But how does that come about?" he protested, giving Henrietta a chance to doff her apron and stuff it behind a row of leather fire buckets that stood alongside the stair cupboard, "He's not reading law, is he?"

"Oh, I managed that easily enough," Lady Sybil said, implying that she could, if she wished, secure Hugo a seat in Kruger's war cabinet. "All it needed was a word here and a push there, and here he is, come to say his goodbyes before joining General Gatacre's staff as a supernumerary. We're both sailing on the *Empress of India* the day after tomorrow."

"You're going too?" Henrietta gasped.

"The entire nursing unit is going," confirmed Sybil. "Eighty-six of us, not counting the surgeons. Daddy telephoned me before it was released to the newspapers."

"But Hugo has had no training for staff work, has he?" asked Adam, whose face still expressed incredulity, "he's only fooled about in the Yeomanry."

"Does one *need* training for a post of that kind?"

"Well, military men are in two minds as to that, my dear," said Adam, his features relaxing somewhat.

Lady Sybil said, "I daresay they'll see you get trained

in the field, Hugo. And now . . ." she turned her best hospital-fête smile on the cringing Henrietta, "I really *would* like a cup of that nice China tea you gave us when Hugo first brought me here, and we've at least an hour for a gossip, because we aren't due at the Overseas Comforts concert until ten o'clock, and that will give us plenty of time to change. It's a nuisance really but I did promise to appear."

It was not Henrietta's idea of a gossip. She hardly contributed a word and Hugo said very little but sat there beaming at his wife as she described in detail how she had set the stage for Hugo's début as a national hero. When they were leaving, and Hugo embraced her again, Henrietta shed a tear or two, for the bovine Hugo had always seemed the most helpless of her sons. But then she reflected that he was in extremely capable hands and Lady Sybil's manipulations would almost certainly ensure that he climbed the military ladder at twice the speed of his brother Alex.

Adam, it seemed, had more sombre thoughts as they watched the brougham sweep round the curve that ran between the leafless limes to the gate. "I don't know, I never did credit Hugo with much grey matter, but I would have thought he had sense enough to stay clear of that shambles. That woman's a menace. And to think I urged the boy to marry her!"

"She's obviously very much in love with him," Henrietta said.

But he replied, glumly, "Is she? Is that love? I don't think it is. Not our kind of love at all events. She's using him as a kind of reflector, something to catch the public's eye and bend it in her direction," and he withdrew to his study without another word.

3

He could talk to Giles, had always been able to talk to him ever since he was a boy, with his nose stuck in all those heavy tomes in the library and his flow of questions about the meaning of existence.

Giles and Romayne were among the Christmas visitors and Romayne was far gone with child, and seemingly happily settled in that Welsh valley where Giles had at last found anchorage. He used this as an opening gambit when they took a walk together on the last afternoon of the old century, climbing the spur behind the house and crossing the bracken-clad slope towards the river that fed Adam's lily ponds. He said, "That wife of yours, boy, she seems to have found contentment that eluded her all this time. I must say I never realised she was genuinely interested in social reform. To be honest I always saw it as a bit of a fad."

"I don't think she's more than marginally involved in politics," his son told him, "or not in the way Debbie is. You're right about her adjusting, however. Our relationship has changed in Wales. I'm not saying we were unhappy before but . . . well . . . she always seemed to me to be looking for something."

"Want to tell me?"

"If I can."

They walked on down the gentle slope to the river where it split into two streams to form the islet that Henrietta always thought of as Shallott, a grey-haired man, born in George IV's reign, and his serious-faced son of thirty-four, who always seemed detached from everybody around him.

"She's identified with me now," Giles said, "in a way that's almost miraculous. Or so it appears from my standpoint. It was she who brought it about, you see, something she did without prompting from anyone, and it's made a place for her that didn't exist before. Given her a clearly defined purpose, I suppose, that was missing all the years she was growing up surrounded by lackeys and neglected by that old devil of a father. I've got to win that seat, if only for her."

"How do you rate your chances?"

"Fair to middling. Better now that I've taken L.G.'s line on the war."

"How can that be? It's a very unpopular line, isn't it?"

"Not among my people. They've been an oppressed minority for generations and some of them see Kruger as a South African Llewellyn, fighting for freedom. L.G., and all the other pro-Boer Liberals, have had a very rough ride these last few months but I haven't. I've had some rousing meetings and our party machinery improves all the time. If I don't win the next election I'll win the one after that, once reaction sets in and people begin to see that L.G.'s line was the right one. This jingo mood isn't a natural one for the British. By and large they're a fair-minded lot when they're sober. Right now, of course, most of them are blind drunk."

It was a good enough analogy, Adam thought, approving his son's clearheadedness. He said, pausing for breath, and looking between the willows at the winter flood swirling round the butt end of the islet on its way to the sea, "By God, I've seen a thing or two in my time, since I was a boy growing up in the fells. Railways lacing the country. Trade figures multiplying fifty times over. The nation swelling itself up like the frog in the fable and edging everyone else out of the sun. It took Rome five centuries to do what the British have done since Waterloo, yet how long is it in terms of the calendar? Eighty-five years. Just over a single life-span. Would you believe I once saw a poor devil hanged in Carlisle for setting fire to a barn? When I fought my first skirmish in India, Germany, as we know it today, didn't exist and most of America was a desert. It's the pace that makes one dizzy. The entire cast of society has been broken and remade since those days. Everyone's expectations are upgraded, even those of your miners, although you probably wouldn't get them to admit there had been much change in their standard of living. There has, tho', and I don't know where it began, exactly. Was it with steam-power and greater mobility? Or with the emergence of trade unions?

Or with Gladstone's compulsory education acts? Or a social conscience among an élite minority, with leisure and time to digest the philosophy of Tom Paine and company? Damned if I could pinpoint it, or predict its future course. It's like that river there, made up of a hundred streams welling out of the hills until it's strong enough to carry everything along. Can you make a guess where we're heading, lad?"

"I try every time I make a speech or finish a canvass," Giles said, smiling, "but I come up with different answers once a week. I suppose it depends on the calibre of the men on top, and what kind of course they've set themselves."

"What course are you setting after midnight? The end of a century is a good time for stocktaking, isn't it? Not at my time of life, mind, but certainly at yours."

"To adapt the new technologies to the needs of the average man, woman and child, I'd say. That's the heart of the problem. All those innovations you've been spouting at me aren't worth a damn if all they do is to help make rich men richer, and are used to browbeat sixty thousand Boer farmers into changing their way of life to please diamond diggers and gold prospectors. You can only work, argue and fight within the law. The law's very far from perfect and still bears down on the majority but less than it did. And, anyway, it's a lot better than a street full of people throwing bricks at one another."

They took the short way home across the bridge and through the five-acre ornamental landscape Adam had conjured out of the two paddocks, a few coppices and some rough pasture. He was silent as they climbed the rise but as they emerged in the forecourt he said, thoughtfully, "We'll be lifting our glasses tonight, when the village bells ring the old year out and the twentieth-century in. I don't know what the others will be drinking to but I'll raise my glass to you, boy. At least two of us speak the same language and that's a comfort for a man with a family as big as mine."

He went in, reminding himself that it was less than just for a father to acknowledge a family favourite but how could one avoid a preference, with five sons and four daughters of such diversity? He had a flash of insight then, concerning this particular son, his wife and that child in her belly, and all three acquired special significance in relation to this mellow corner of England that he had shaped and made his own, in a way that the network was not and never would be a durable monument to him. Alex had his career and George the business. Hugo had that extraordinary wife dancing attendance on him and the girls had their husbands and families. Something told him it was Giles and his successors who would live here some day when he was dust and maybe some of them would come to think of it as he was beginning to think of it, the only worthwhile legacy one generation could pass to another. Land, and what grew on it; contours, cunningly adapted to the eternal round of seasonal colours that nothing could change or distort, no matter how many cleverdicks came forward with their inventions. It comforted him somehow, a conviction that continuity was attainable, providing a man had patience to keep striving for it.

4

Sacrifice to Dagon

It was deemed a signal honour to ride on reconnaissance with Montmorency. The Empire, woefully short of heroes of late, had plugged holes in the Pantheon Wall with a hotchpotch of newcomers. Small fry, by yesterday's standards. Captains, sergeants, pipers and even bugler boys, but welcome none the less under the present humiliating circumstances.

Captain the Hon. R. H. L. J. de Montmorency was at the apex of this improvised pyramid, having, so to speak, secured a year's start over his competitors by winning the V.C. serving with the 21st Lancers, in Kitchener's Sudan campaign, in '98, and since added other dashing exploits to his credit, so that his name was familiar to the readers of every penny journal in London. It followed that anyone who rode with him was shortlisted for reflected glory.

Glory, after such a laggardly start, was rallying out here along the farflung battlefront. Times were already on the mend when Hugo landed at East London, and trekked north-west through Queenstown to the sector where General Gatacre was doing his best to wipe out the shame of earlier defeats on the central front. He was having some success too, or so it was rumoured along the route. The Boer generals, De la Rey and Schoeman, were already giving ground and falling back to the north, the price paid for their inexplicable failure to exploit the rout

237

of the British in this area when the tide of invasion lapped into Cape Colony.

The enemy moved slowly, however, far too slowly for Gatacre, who was now deploying his cavalry to chivvy them as the main offensive developed on the right flank. When Hugo received orders to ride ahead with Montmorency's column he was delighted, not so much because Montmorency was a popular leader but because he had a suspicion that the long and purposeful arm of Lady Sybil would soon reach out from her field hospital at Queenstown and keep him out of Mauser range of the Boers while he was, as she herself had put it 'easing himself in', a phrase that suggested a cushy billet well behind the lines.

He was not to know that his selection for a forward post was the direct result of a message Gatacre's chief of staff had received from the daughter of the Earl of Uskdale, informing him that the famous athlete she had married, and shipped out here along with her nursing unit, had no aptitude for paper work and would need careful coaching. It was an unfortunate admission so far as Lady Sybil was concerned. A staff officer, mounting a massive advance against an alert enemy, was not likely to fancy the job of coach to civilians in uniform and merely did what seemed to him the next best thing for a serving officer sponsored by the daughter of an earl. He attached Hugo to a proven hero, reasoning that this was the shortest route to newspaper acclaim and likely to please the lady concerned. Only that day he had received news that the Boers were pulling out at Bloemfontein. A token rearguard resistance was the worst Montmorency's column were likely to meet while feeling their way across the Kissieberg hills to Stormberg Junction.

Like so many others in the great arc of Imperialists between the Orange River and the Tugela that winter, Gatacre's reckoning was seriously at fault. The Boers were moving back certainly, and faster than his Intelligence had deduced, but they were determined to make the British pay for any gains they made. Montmorency's column rode headlong into a well-laid ambush that emptied fifty saddles at the first volley and the survivors, milling about in the wildest confusion, could not see so much as a hat to aim at after they had galloped for cover.

Hugo had been enjoying the ride up to that moment. Half-dozing in the saddle he jogged along, dreaming of conquests past and yet to come, seeing his presence here as little more than an exciting interlude in a lifetime of pot-hunting. He did not share the general view that an athlete approaching his thirtieth year was past his prime and should be casting about for the means of acquiring other laurels. After all, he was neither a sprinter nor a leaper, and long-distance runners often continued to compete well into middle age. An Italian, over forty, had just won the marathon at an international meeting.

Then, in a sustained crackle of rifle fire that reached him like the flare up of dry sticks on a fire, he was jerked back into the present, with wounded and riderless horses cavorting past him in all directions, dismounted troopers looming out of the flurry of dust and Mauser bullets going over him like a swarm of bees.

He did what seemed the only thing to do, wheeling and dashing for the nearest cover, a scatter of low rocks at the foot of a broken hill on his immediate right, and when he got there, flinging himself to the ground and making a grab at his horse's bridle, he was astonished at the scene of chaos that presented itself, not only along the track ahead but right here, in the shelter of the rocks.

Dead and dying troopers were everywhere among terrified horses, some of them hit and screaming with pain. Dust rose in a red cloud, obliterating the field of fire. Equipment, including a scatter of long, useless lances, lay everywhere. A sergeant sat with his back to a rock, trying to staunch a spouting wound in his thigh and his blood spattered Hugo as he stepped over his legs, making for a knot of unwounded men cowering behind a larger rock and emptying their magazines at nothing. He recognised none of them and this was not surprising, for he had only joined the column the day before. The only man he could have identified was Montmorency, now lying dead, someone told him, a hundred yards higher up the pass. His informant, another sergeant, had something else to say about Montmorency. "Led us right into a rat-trap," he shouted, above the uproar. "Didn't even scout the bloody hills with a flank guard, and we'll not hold out here for long the way those fools are loosing off!" Then, ignoring Hugo, he darted among the marksmen bellowing, "Hold your bloody fire! Wait until the dust settles! Save your ammo! For Chrissake, save your ammo!"

The dust was a long time settling and in the interval Hugo's horse rolled over, shot between the eyes and falling on its right flank where Hugo's carbine bucket was strapped. He only looked long enough to satisfy himself that the horse was dead before drawing his revolver and accosting the frantic sergeant again.

"Aren't there any officers left?" he demanded.

"Yessir," the man said, breathlessly. "Mr. Cookham over there. But he's plugged, I believe!" He pointed to another outcrop twenty yards higher up the slope where a group of about a dozen survivors were gathered round a young subaltern with a wispy moustache, who was supervising the erection of a barricade of loose rocks.

The rate of Boer fire had slackened somewhat by then, but it was still inviting certain death to venture on to open ground. Hugo decided to risk it and tore across the exposed patch, a bullet striking his spur and making a sound like a finger snapped on a wine-glass. He got there unscathed, however, and Mr. Cookham seemed relieved to see him. "You a regular?" he demanded and Hugo said no, just a supernumerary who had joined the staff earlier in the week. The sergeant was right. Cookham had been hit in the upper arm and his left sleeve dripped blood.

"Well, here's a how-de-do," he said gaily. "It looks as if I've got my first command." He glanced around the circle where the dead and wounded outnumbered the living by two to one. "Don't think I'll have it long, however. What's your name, Supernumerary?"

Although he had been in Africa less than a month, Hugo was well aware that any regular, even a nineteen-year-old subaltern, would hold the Yeomanry and Local Volunteer units in contempt. He said, diffidently, "Swann, Mr. Cookham. Hugo Swann . . ."

The officer let out a whoop and said, "Swann, the runner?" and at once transferred his revolver to his left hand, grabbed Hugo's right and shook it. "Heard you were around. A rare pleasure to have you here!" he said. "You'll set up a new record today if we get out of here alive," and the joke seemed to remind him of his duty, for he turned away and issued a stream of orders concerning the barricade, rate of fire, transfer of badly wounded to the patch of shadow under the tallest rock and several other instructions that Hugo did not catch, for a wounded horse, dragging itself round by its forelegs, struck him and sent him staggering off at a tangent as another bullet shattered his wrist-watch and grazed the skin along the joint of his thumb. It was no more than a scratch but enough to project him the far side of the dying horse at a bound. He landed on a dead lancer, spreadeagled behind the barricade.

Gradually the dust began to settle and the blue of the sky showed through the haze. A long outcrop of rocks some two hundred yards distant in the left foreground became visible, clearly the point of ambush, for intermittent flashes revealed where invisible marksmen were peppering them from two angles.

Cookham said, breathlessly, "Have to hump ourselves higher up. They'll pick us off one by one so long as we stay here!" And under his direction the ragged group of survivors began to claw their way up the slope in short, individual rushes, aiming for a bulkier outcrop thirty yards above their first position.

Most of them made it, although a trooper scrambling

up beside Hugo spun round and went tumbling head over heels down the incline again, his carbine making a tremendous clatter among the loose stones. Up here it was possible, by risking a bullet between the eyes, to get a grasp of the battlefield as a whole, a shallow valley with larger outcrops clothed with scrub on the Boer side and a long, steep ascent, bare of cover, at the rear of their own position. Cookham shouted, "How many of us, Supernumerary? Count 'em for me, will you?" Hugo, counting, said there were two dozen on the ledge and some lightly wounded still firing from below.

Cookham had his binoculars unslung now and used them to sweep the valley left to right at the price of losing his helmet that whipped from his head and sailed away like a clay pigeon. He said, "Well, it's better than I thought. They've only wiped out the head of the column. There's no firing for'ard. Murchison's lot have pulled back out of range, lucky devils! They'll have sent someone back for reinforcements and guns by now but that won't help us, frying up here." He paused, frowning with concentration, and Hugo was struck by the contrast between his outward immaturity and his calm acceptance of responsibility involving the lives of every man between the ridge they occupied and the floor of the valley. Images of two of his brothers presented themselves, Alex, a veteran soldier by the time he was Cookham's age (and very like Cookham now that he came to think about it) and Edward, at home beside the Thames, who was young enough to have been at school with Cookham. He thought, 'Either one of them could pull their weight in a show like this but I'm not much use, damn it. I feel like a passenger in a ditched 'bus, waiting for someone to tell me what to do,' and the thought of those rows of silver cups, urns and medals in the showcase at 'Tryst' returned to him, as though heliographing their puerility and trashiness across thousands of miles of land and water. He said, ruefully, "I can't even hit 'em with this, Mr. Cookham. And my carbine's back there, under my horse."

"None of us can hit 'em," Cookham said, cheerfully. "I doubt if we could even if we could see 'em. The sun is at their backs and their worst marksman could shoot the feathers out of our bonnets. Still, so long as they know we're here they'll hold off, and that'll stop them moving south and laying another ambush for relieving troops. Something else too – they can't even guess at our numbers." He bobbed up again and took another quick squint through the binoculars. This time a flight of bullets passed over, the Boers firing high and overestimating the height of the ridge for the bullets ricocheted from the rock face above.

"Checkmate," Cookham said. "We can't stir but they dare not hold that position for long. By that time the batteries will be up and they'll have to look lively getting away over that broken ground behind them." He sucked his teeth. "We're snug enough by that reckoning. There's no time for them to work around behind and fire down on us, but suppose . . . Pity you're a miler, Swann."

"Why?"

"If you were a champion sprinter we might have a sporting chance to nab them . . . Remember that track, branching left two miles back?"

"I remember it."

"I'll lay a pound to a penny it passes behind that range of hills. If the relieving force sent cavalry and horse artillery down it, and they looked lively, they could cut the line of retreat before the Boer pulls out. Look . . ." and he whipped a pencil from his notebook and propping the sheet against the rock face sketched the manoeuvre, a narrow sweep behind the Boer position, masked by high ground at the junction of the tracks.

"Won't they have posted lookouts above that track?"

"If they're as smart as I think they are, but no more than two or three men. Murchison could pin them down if you got word to him."

"How far back is Murchison's column?"

"Under a mile. But to get down from here you'd have

to move over the ground faster than you've ever covered it. Those chaps over there are the best shots in the world. I wouldn't order anyone to take a chance like that."

"You don't have to order me."

"You'd try it?"

"I'm no use up here, with a six-shooter, Mr. Cookham."

Cookham considered him gravely. "You're game, Mr. Supernumerary. We'll give you covering fire, but for God's sake raise the dust the minute you reach level ground."

"They won't stop me."

He knew, somehow, that it was his moment. All the pounding over the Exmoor plateau as a boy, all those circuits of tracks over the years, all those cheers and trophies that had come his way in the last decade had led to this, a dash down a valley whipped by bullets from the rifles of the deadliest marksmen in the world, carrying a message from a wispy-moustached boy to a rearguard picquet. He knelt half upright, stripping off his spurs, tunic and helmet.

"When you're ready, Mr. Cookham."

The boy said, slowly, "I saw you win the Stamford Bridge two thousand metres when I was on leave last year. You've got one hell of a stride, Swann. And more puff than a blacksmith's bellows. Good luck – sir."

He saw the 'sir' as an accolade, a singularly graceful compliment from a professional to an amateur. It brought him more satisfaction than any victory in the sports arena. They shook hands and Cookham passed the word along to give covering fire at rapid rate the moment Hugo left cover. Then, with a single prodigious leap, he was off, bounding down the slope and swerving at every obstacle in his path, dead men, dead horses, jettisoned equipment, loose rocks, everything between him and the brown surface of the beaten path over which they had ridden not half-an-hour since.

He had no awareness of being a target on the way down. His concentration was centred wholly on his swerves and leaps and the placing of feet encumbered by heavy cavalry boots. Then he was running south, faster it seemed than over any straight stretch to the tape. Once on the level he heard the impact of individual Mauser bullets striking the rocks in his path but none struck him and gradually the fusillade reverted to the odd whining plop as a spent bullet ricocheted into the slab-sided hillside to his left.

He came upon Murchison's rearward picquet behind an outcrop on the Boer side of the path, a little short of the distance estimated by Cookham, for he had run, at a guess, a little over half-a-mile from the point where he reached level ground. A man stood up and called, making a trumpet of his hands, and he changed direction, breasting a slight slope and leaping the low parapet into a shallow depression where a few dismounted lancers were huddled, commanded, it seemed, by a middle-aged trooper. He said, between laboured breaths, "Thirty survivors still holding out a mile back. Orders from Lieutenant Cookham in command. Boers occupying high ground on this side of the valley. Mr. Cookham says to find Major Murchison and tell him to send cavalry and guns behind the range to cut 'em off."

"There's a Boer outpost overlooking that track, sir. That's why we daren't move back."

Hugo thought, glumly, 'He's waiting for orders, for a direct order, and there's no one else to give it.' He said, "Take all three troopers. One of you will make it if you move fast. Give me your carbine and a bandolier. I'll climb higher and try to pin them down for a spell. I'll wait until they're firing on you before I move."

The man was an old sweat, conditioned by years of service to rely on an officer, even a volunteer. He called his three men by name, telling them briefly they were to make a run for it, one at a time. Anyone who got through was to pass the order on to Major Murchison. Then, his confidence restored, he turned back to Hugo. "Just how far for'ard *is* Captain Montmorency, sir?"

"Captain Montmorency is dead. Lieutenant Cookham's

commanding all that's left of the column. Tell them that too if you make it."

"Can they hold out long, sir?"

"Indefinitely. But the Boers will pull out by the time reinforcements move up. Get going, man."

The man handed over his carbine and unslung his bandolier. "There's around twenty cartridges, sir. Good luck, sir."

"You too," Hugo said and watched as, one by one, the four of them leaped from cover and ran a zig-zag course down the track. The old campaigner went last, in less of a hurry than the others and taking full advantage of the overhang of scrub this side of the path. One man fell but picked himself up again and Hugo had no chance to watch their further progress for he had to turn his back on them to scale the tumble of rocks screening him from the snipers' outpost on the crest.

The hill here was a series of small fissures and easily scaleable, partly on account of its milder gradient but also because every cleft was sown with a prickly, tough-stemmed growth sprouting leaves not unlike the umbrella plants that grew down by the ox-bow below 'Tryst'. He went up very carefully, hugging the slope, for the crackle of shots from above and a short distance to the left, told him the Boers posted immediately above the fork were still trying to pot the troopers as they made their way to the rear.

He had expected to find the summit of the spur open ground, with no cover worth mentioning, but as soon as he reached it he saw that he was wrong. For some reason there was more scrub on this side of the valley and the umbrella-like plants had straggled all the way up a donga that might, at one time, have been a tiny watercourse. There was no advantage in him making his way along the ridge as far as the outpost snipers. Sooner or later, probably the moment they saw a sizeable body take the left hand branch at the fork behind the Boer position, they would withdraw, moving at the double all the way along the crest to warn the main body. He realised the logic of Cookham's assumptions. 'Damn it,' he thought, 'that kid has more brains than Montmorency. If he'd been commanding the column we should never have run our necks into the noose like this,' and he opened the lowest pouch of his bandolier and found there five bullets, enough to fill the half-empty magazine of the carbine.

The sun was blisteringly hot and he lacked the protection of his helmet. By raising himself to his knees he could just see the track down which he had run, two dead horses marking the southern limit of the battle and the seam where Cookham's survivors were still holding out judging by the occasional burst of fire from one side or the other. He could have seen a good deal more had he stood upright but the tallest umbrella only grew to a height of about two feet and if his presence here was so much as suspected, all his trouble would have gone for nothing. The outpost party would fan out and fire at him from several angles, rushing him if they failed to hit him because they would see a warning to the main body as worth the sacrifice of some of them. So he lay very still, carbine thrown forward and ear to the ground listening for the scrape of a boot and trying to calculate how many Boers he would have to deal with. Presently, however, the outpost's rifles fell silent. Either they had accounted for the troopers or had reverted to their task of watching the ox-path a hundred feet below where Murchison or base reinforcements would soon be beginning the outflanking movement.

About twenty minutes passed in almost complete silence to the north and south, the cessation of fire implying that the main body to the north had already begun their withdrawal towards Stormberg. Then, quite close at hand, he heard guttural voices and the chink of metal on loose stones, but although the voices seemed to be approaching he could see no movement in the scrub when he raised his head above the cluster of parchment-like leaves at the top of the donga. He had just lowered it again when he heard someone shout an order in an urgent tone, and in the same second he saw his first man, a grey-bearded, thickset Boer, with a slouch hat and his rifle held at the trail, moving at a crouching run immediately to his front and already less than thirty yards from where he lay. He raised himself on one knee and took a snap shot, with no pretence of aiming and the man stopped in his tracks, his legs set widely apart and his free hand stretched out, as though to ward off the bullet.

He remained in that curiously rigid position long enough for Hugo to get an unforgettable glimpse of his expression. Not so much startled as abstracted, the expression of a man who, quitting his front gate for work, suddenly remembers something he should have done before slamming the door. Then, quite slowly, the Boer toppled sideways, his rifle dropping soundlessly into the scrub, his body falling away down the incline out of sight and sound as it rolled down the western slope of the hill and at that precise moment his following companion showed, hatless, beardless and with Mauser in firing position. The face behind the levelled rifle was that of a boy, fourteen or younger.

He was obviously firing blind for his shot went wide by yards and he had no time to work his bolt and press the trigger a second time. Hugo's second slug hit him squarely in the chest so that he staggered backwards, dropping his rifle and pressing his hands to the point of impact. Then he fell flat on his back in a small open patch so that Hugo, peering through the stalks, could see the upturned soles of his hobnailed boots.

A long silence followed, unbroken by the staccato crackle of fire higher up the valley, or by a rustle or boot-scrape further along the spur. The sun, now directly overhead, scourged his neck and sweat dripped in his eyes, blurring the sight of the upturned boots in a grey-green haze that undulated like a curtain in a draught.

The shot from the right and below almost did for him, ripping through the rucked up folds of his shirt and cutting the shoulder strap of his bandolier so that it fell free and would have bounced into the donga had he not made a grab at it. He swung half-right and fired twice but whether he hit anything or not he had no means of knowing, for at that moment a fourth Boer fired from the left, the bullet coming close enough to slice the scrub six inches from his nose.

He had to take a gamble then on whether there was a fifth or sixth Boer somewhere behind the dead boy, for there was better cover there in the form of a spur of rock. Once behind it the marksmen on the lower terraces would be in his sights. He half-rose to his feet and dashed forward and was within a yard of it, his left foot braced on the outflung arm of the boy's corpse when his head exploded like a rocket, painlessly yet with a kind of deliberate wrenching movement that stretched every nerve and muscle in his body.

*   *   *

He was still breathing when they found him, sprawled half across a spur of rock at the very summit of the ridge, with the dead boy touching his foot and the other man he had shot some ten yards lower down the western slope of the hill. Kneeling over him the stretcher-bearers debated among themselves whether or not it was worth their pains to carry him down to the ambulance behind the company of Devons now advancing in open order towards Cookham's survivors half-a-mile down the valley. On one side of his temples was the familiar small puncture. On the other, exactly opposite, a jagged gash, welling blood. The middle-aged trooper, identifying and reclaiming his carbine and bandolier decided the matter for them, saying, laconically, "Stop yer gab an' take the pore bleeder where he can snuff it in shade. But for 'im that bloody look-out detail woulder made it all the way back an' give their mates the tip. Looks like he got two of 'em before they got 'im." He moved on, walking upright to the spot about two hundred yards on, where the two other members of the outpost lay, one dead, shot from below at long range, the other holed in the leg and biting on a plug of tobacco while a medical orderly applied splint and bandages to the shattered shinbone. So Hugo's gamble had been justified in a sense. There could have been no fifth Boer crouched behind that spur of rock and one more bound would have won him the contest. The stretcher-bearers, grumbling at his weight, worked their way slowly to level ground and the wound was plugged pending closer examination, providing he survived the ride back to the nearest field ambulance tent. Two wounded troopers of the 21st Lancers, salvaged from among the casualties higher up the valley, tried to divert attention from the smart of their own wounds, by having a bet on the issue.

2

Sybil, eldest daughter of the Earl of Uskdale, currently directing her dynamic energy into the administration of the military base hospital at Queenstown, had two public faces. To her intimates, in the enclosed circle in which she had been reared, she was cool, sophisticated, uniquely purposeful and self-contained. To the public at large, particularly those who devoured bulletins from the war fronts, she was rapidly qualifying for a niche in the pantheon of English heroines alongside Grace Darling, Boadicea and Florence Nightingale. Both images were too facile to equate with the truth. To a great extent Sybil Uskdale's life up to this point had been a masquerade for, contrary to all public and private estimates of her character, she was a complex personality and her positivity concealed a canker of self-doubt.

There was logic in this. Rejecting, instinctively, the social strictures of her times and, more especially, of her class, she had not yet succeeded in filling the vacuum that renunciation implied and was still, in a sense, preoccupied with her quest for a credible alternative. Her obsession with nursing was one aspect of this search and her acquisition of Hugo Swann as husband was another, her most daring decision up to that time. Both spiritually and physically she yearned for fulfilment in a changing world where the tide was beginning to run against wealth, privilege and social protocol, and had long since set her face against the purely decorative, submissive role that most well-endowed women accepted with equanimity. But one does not slough off the habits and training of childhood and background at a bound, and there were times, particularly of late, when she questioned not only her ability to fly in the face of convention but her right to pursue the course she had set herself.

Physically, as a vigorous and exceptionally robust woman of thirty, she had coveted Hugo Swann ever since she saw him stretched out in that committee tent at the Putney fête. But so far the marriage had been oddly frustrating, for she soon decided he was really no more than an overgrown boy, disinclined, unable perhaps, to use her as she longed to be used. Awed by what he obstinately regarded as her social superiority his demands, so far, had been faltering and inexperienced, so that she had been forced back on her original resolve, that is to use him as a crutch and fanfare in her drive to develop into what she dimly realised might be a fulfilled woman. He was young and lusty and there was time enough ahead. But then, before she had time to come to grips with this new situation, the war had engulfed them both and she found herself running a hospital overflowing with maimed and desperately sick men, all of them young and full of promise, each calling to her to be nursed through a personal crisis involving stomach wounds, shattered limbs, devastating facial and head wounds and, more pitiful still, the ravages of enteric fever, now accounting for three out of every four patients brought in on the hospital trains. In the strain of facing up to her responsibilities she had almost forgotten Hugo.

The death rate was appalling by any standards. At

some hospitals, they said, men were dying at the rate of fifty a day from this scourge alone and the nursing staff and doctors were hopelessly inadequate to deal with such a situation. They did their best, God knows, and Sybil among them, working stints of up to twenty hours but with the advance to the north the rate of casualty increased and the strain thrown on the administration became intolerable. She was tough but she did not know how long she could survive the demands made upon her and then, a challenge that made every other shrink to insignificance, they wheeled in what was left of Hugo, shot through the head in a skirmish up in the hills and certain, so the surgeons said, to die.

*   *   *

Her immediate reaction was one of terrible guilt for she reasoned that, but for her, Hugo would be safe at home, jogging round the running track and turning up every now and again with another of those silver trophies. She saw herself, at that moment, as a murderess who had deliberately plotted his death and in her misery she wanted nothing else than to die herself and ahead of him.

But then, when he refused to die, when Udale, the chief surgeon, told her that he had a chance, she rallied, by no means shedding her crushing packload of guilt but finding sufficient resolution to set it aside, a parcel that would have to wait its turn to be opened, and gradually she not only reintegrated herself into the daily rhythm of the hospital but delegated herself Hugo Swann's guide back to the land of the living.

She had him isolated in her own quarters and although this isolation would be seen as an exercise of privilege on her part, she did not care. Hugo was her personal responsibility, the victim of her vanity and if, by sheer force of will, she could restore him to even partial health, nothing was going to be allowed to stand in her way.

These were her attitudes during the initial period, when

Hugo, head swathed in bandages, lay silent in his cot, a hulk with a fingertip grasp on life. Her first reaction was the deliberate postponement of the acknowledgment of guilt. Her second a resolve to atone for the terrible wrong she had done him and when Udale came to her to report the successful conclusion of his third operation she allowed herself to hope, after the surgeon, in response to her persistent badgering, gave it as his opinion that the patient's reason did not seem to have been affected by the clean passage of the bullet.

"How can you be sure of that?" she asked, breathlessly.

"He talked, more or less rationally, under the anaesthetic. For what it's worth that in itself is unusual with a wound of that nature."

"What did he say?"

"Mentioned a Lancer subaltern by name. 'Cookham' it sounded like. That, and a young Boer who pointed a rifle at him."

"Does that alone signify anything?"

"A little. For your sake I took some trouble to find out the names of officers involved in that scrap. A Lieutenant Cookham was the fellow who sent him on that run with the message."

"What about the Boer?"

"That might mean anything or nothing. Some fleeting impression of the battle that stayed with him possibly."

She derived some comfort from this and spruced herself up for her next spell of watching at the bedside, where she combined the office of nurse with that of general administrator. The mirror in her tented quarters showed her a gaunt, hollow-eyed stranger, quite unlike the bustling woman who had presided here before the Stormberg ambush. She even went to the lengths of using papier-poudres on the dark areas under her eyes, and a touch of rouge to her cheeks against the time when they removed his bandages for the first time.

But then Udale insisted on a fourth operation and the night it was performed, again successfully, he piloted her to a secluded corner of the convalescent sector and admitted the true source of his evasiveness during earlier discussions on the case.

"Someone has to tell you, Lady Sybil, and everyone else shirks it. He'll recover all right. Not much need to worry on that score. But he won't see again, not a glimmer."

It was as though a mailed fist had crashed into her abdomen and then the same assailant had grabbed her by the throat and squeezed until tears streamed from her eyes and she had the utmost difficulty in breathing.

"Won't *see*? He's *blind*? Hugo Swann, *blind*?"

He nodded, reaching out to steady her but she shook him off.

"But that's . . . that's monstrous! It can't be so! It can't!"

"You must have considered it."

"Never! Never once! I thought of everything but not that . . . *not that*!"

He said, his eyes on the scorched turf, "The bullet severed the optic nerve. Only vital damage it did. A pure freak. Chance in a million it didn't kill him outright, or leave him a cabbage." He took a silver flask from his pocket and unscrewed the stopper. "Take a swallow of that. Please, I insist!" and she took the flask and gulped down the raw spirit but it did little to steady her. She whispered, presently, "Go back to the wards, Mr. Udale. Tell everybody I'm not to be approached, not for any reason," and surprisingly he went, leaving her on the threshold of a little pergola they had built for sitting-out patients.

She stood there without moving for a long time, only half aware of the medley of background noises of the vast, tented purgatory, the dolorous squeaks of unoiled ambulance axles, the continuous murmur that rose from the huge convalescent marquee, housing men who were short of a limb, and permanently disfigured perhaps but not one, so far as she could recall, deprived for ever of his eyesight and reduced to the helplessness of Samson in the camp of the Philistines. There was a bitter analogy here. Samson Swann, noted not for his strength but his fleetness that seemed to her, indeed to all who knew him, the very essence of his being. Samson made a sacrifice to Dagon, the Philistine God. Not by his enemies, not by the Boer who had fired that freakish shot but by her, Sybil Uskdale, who had coveted him, won him and led him out to make sport for the multitude. Surely no woman since the world began had gratuitously laid upon herself such a mountain of guilt and shame.

And then, without warning, there burst from her a terrible sob that was like a soft explosion between her breasts, yet so violent that she sagged and almost fell, clutching the upright of the pergola porch and groping her way to the seat beyond. She would have given all she possessed, life itself, to be released into tears, but her eyes were dry and her throat, fearfully constricted, once more in the grip of that merciless fist. The thought of self-destruction came to her, warm and welcome as a fur-lined cape in winter, and she conjured with various possibilities – the row of bottles marked 'poison' in the dispensary, a razor at her wrists, a rope about her neck to anticipate the slow strangulation of the mailed fist. She considered them all, clinically and objectively, but neither one nor the other seemed adequate as a means of escape or retribution, and as she rejected them the idea slipped away like a rebuffed beggar and she was left with nothing but a tiny spark of defiance that had never ceased to glow in her from the day she put aside the frivolities and proscriptions of her caste.

She said, acknowledging as much aloud, "It was my doing and I'll finish it for no one else can," and she got up and walked jerkily to her quarters, lifting the tent flap and averting her eyes from the still, mummy-like head on the pillow. She sat down and looked in the mirror again, flinching but forcing herself to study the reflection, a small-boned woman in a starched coif with a blue, scarlet-lined cloak about her shoulders. A woman with good features and light blue eyes ringed by sallow areas below the lids. A wide mouth firmly compressed and drawn down at the corners. The famous Uskdale chin, small and resolutely pointed, jutting slightly out but softened somewhat by the central cleft. Behind her the man on the bed shifted and muttered, then relaxed as his breathing became heavy and regular. She said, again aloud, "I'll tell him and I won't put it off. No sense in holding out hope, in breaking it gently over a period. That's his due and my obligation."

3

She was there when they removed the bandages four days later and watched an orderly scrape away at his bristles, seeing the familiar face emerge from a cloud of lather and marvelling that the scars were so small and insignificant. A pinkish circle on the right temple, puckered and no more than a centimetre across. A zig-zag line like a small hedge tear in the left temple, where the bullet had emerged and the stitching remained to be cut. And about this second wound an area of heavy bruising, fading from dark blue to coral where new hair was growing in a ragged sideburn. They left the eyes covered with gauze and cotton wool, and then, as arranged, the doctor shooed everybody out and she waited for Hugo to speak.

He was talking freely then. Two days earlier he had asked them what had happened upon that ridge, whether young Cookham and his survivors were saved, whether the Boers had made good their escape and, at length, how long it would be before they removed all these damned wrappings from his head.

Mr. Udale told him what he knew of the battle. Cookham and his survivors had been rescued. He and Cookham had been recommended for decorations. The main body of the ambush party had slipped away but they had captured the rearguard, thirty-odd marksmen who came down off the ridge under a white flag.

As to his wound, his wife, Lady Sybil, would tell him about that, for right now, Udale said, he had too much on his hands and so, for that matter, had she. "All I can say is you're lucky, Swann. Couple of months and you'll be out of here and sailing for home."

Sybil fed him then, spooning broth into his mouth, crumbling bread between her long, slim fingers and jokingly pushing it between his bearded lips. He said, when she told him they were alone, "Odd, me turning up here so quickly. Seems only a day or so since I said goodbye and went off with the new draft. How long have I been in hospital, Sybil?"

"More than a month," she said, "but we'll talk about that later. Right now you must sleep. You were in very bad shape when you came in, dearest, but Mr. Udale thinks you've done splendidly."

"Where was I hit?"

"In the head. Just once but it was as the surgeon said, you were lucky not to be killed."

He lifted his hand to the bandages and canvassed them from ear to ear, from the crown of his head down to the chin. "My God, it must have come close," he said. "That chap lower down the hill. One of two of 'em, firing from either side, crafty devils. Simply never occurred to me they'd move off the crest." And then glumly, "Sorry about that kid, though."

"What kid, Hugo?"

"The one I had to shoot. Couldn't have been more than fifteen. Stood there bold as brass after I'd got the older one. Who the devil would want to kill a kid that age?"

"Don't think about it. The fault lies with the men who sent him there. Try and sleep."

She could have told him then, she supposed, but it seemed wiser to wait and build up his strength a little, and once they had the bandages off he made tremendous strides, so that she wasn't surprised when he sat up as soon as Udale cleared the tent and said, "When can I see you, Sybil?"

She choked at that and had to summon every scrap of courage to prevent herself breaking down there and then but at least he had given her an opening. She took his hand, lifted it and pressed it to her lips.

"Hugo, dear."

"Yes?"

"I've got something bad to say. Can you take a grip on yourself? Can you hear me out without . . . without shouting me down, trying to get up, making a . . . a fuss?"

His brow contracted. Clearly the statement puzzled him very much. She took a tighter grip on his hand, still covered with the tape they had put over the long bullet crease on the palm. He said, finally, "There's something else? I was hit somewhere else? But you said . . ."

"No. You've just the one wound but that . . . it was as bad as could be. The bullet went in one side and came out the other . . ."

"My face is smashed up?"

"No, dearest. You're as handsome as ever. The most handsome man in the world," and she kissed the freshly shaven face twice, still without releasing the hand.

"What then?"

She braced herself, as for a leap across an impossibly wide chasm.

"Your eyes, Hugo."

She felt him stiffen and at once extended her hold to his shoulders, drawing her chair so close to the bed that she was dragged sideways by his weight. "It was the optic nerve. It's damaged . . . enough to affect your sight."

He tore his hand free and lifted it, passing his fingers over the gauze.

"How badly affected?"

"It's very difficult to say. It might be a long time before we know."

It seemed best to tell a white lie, to leave him a ray of hope. He would need time, years perhaps, to adjust to the truth. Yet even now he did not cry out or give any kind of vocal reaction.

"That doctor. He said I'd be going home."

"You will. We both will."

"But if there's more treatment . . ."

"You'll get treatment in London. The very best there is. Far better than anything they can do for you out here."

"Then I might . . . might see again?"

"It's possible."

"*Possible?* Dear Christ . . . !"

The reaction came at last, a convulsive heave that lifted her clear of the chair.

"*Please,* Hugo! . . . You never know about these things . . . Surgeons nowadays can do amazing things . . . impossible things!"

"Like making a blind man see again?"

"Don't *say* that word . . ."

"Why not? Why not, if it's true? Oh, Christ! Christ help me! . . . Sybil, tell me there's hope . . . real hope. You must know . . . you're in charge here."

Little by little she was getting a grip on herself and it derived from a defiance of the kind she had cultivated and practised all her life. She said, "I'm matron because of whom I am, not because of what I know. I'm not a surgeon and I'm not a doctor. I was only playing at the job until I came out here, and saw what awful things can happen to people. But I know this. We'll go everywhere and we'll see everyone. In London and on the Continent. Maybe there's someone who could give you partial sight . . . I don't know about that yet, and can't even make proper enquiries from here, in this awful country. All I can say is your sight is badly affected and all I can be glad about is that you're alive and I'm here to help and will always be here, right beside you. Will you try and remember that, and never forget it, and think about it all the time, Hugo? Will you do that for your sake and mine? It's terribly important for both of us that you should. For me especially because . . . because I brought you here, I put you in the path of that bullet." Mercifully, at that point she began to cry, the tears flowing silently as she rocked to and fro, a woman racked with unbearable pain. A little of her stress communicated itself to him. Not much, perhaps, but enough to cause him to lift his free hand to her face and touch her eyes with the tips of his fingers. He said, "Don't cry, Sybil. Not now. Not yet. Just . . . just *be* there and talk . . . Say something . . . anything . . ."

"I'll always be there. Anything you need, Hugo, and all the time. Every day and every night, my love."

"Kiss me again."

She turned her head and drew her lips slowly across his cheek and mouth, enlarging the caress into a kiss and lifting his hand to the swell of her breasts under her taut bodice. In the year of their marriage she had never kissed him in that way or known how to, and her body quivered when she sensed the impact it was making on his senses, as if close contact with her flesh raised a barrier against the onrush of the murderous despair bearing down on him like a runaway express. She slipped her hand inside the loose linen gown that covered him and ran it lovingly over his massive shoulders and down the length of his ribs, consciously doing battle with the malign, destructive forces that were intent on destroying him.

"Oh, God, I love you . . . love you . . . I'll care for you . . . make it up to you somehow. *Trust me*, Hugo! Never stop trusting me . . . !"

An orderly appeared at the flap of the tent, glanced inside, hastily drew back and stole away, stepping quietly over the seamed earth of the parched compound.

5

The Fists of Righteous Harmony

TAPSCOTT, THE METHODIST MISSIONARY, BROUGHT
them the first hard news, hammering on their bungalow
door about an hour after dawn and almost falling over the
threshold the moment Rowley drew the bolts. Tapscott,
the little man who always reminded her of Peter the
Hermit, shorn of his zeal but pinned here, it seemed, by
dwindling hope that the Lord would finally take cog-
nisance of his settlement along the Hun Ho River, in the
apex of the Lu Hun and Peking-Tientsin railways, where
he ministered to a flock of two dozen converts.

It was not, of course, the first news they had had of the
campaign against the Foreign Devils, and their contemp-
tible converts, the Secondary Devils. All that spring
rumours had been creeping north from the Honan
province and west from Shensi and Kamsu, where the
Fists of Righteous Harmony, jocularly referred to by the
representatives of various sects in the Chihli province as
'The Boxers', had been promoting their hate campaign
for more than a year and were now openly threatening
to erase every trace of the foreigner from Peking to Hong
Kong and the vast hinterland of Mongolia. Their aim, it
seemed, was to restore the ancient culture of China and
the Manchu dynasty to the omnipotence it had enjoyed
before the scattered trading posts were established, and
the missionaries arrived with their gospel of a risen
Christ and their meddlesome opposition to the rituals of

a civilisation that was flourishing hereabouts when the Foreign Devils were living in caves on the other side of the world.

Rowley had showed her one of their propaganda posters, a drawing of a crucified pig transfixed with arrows and a Mandarin presiding over the execution of goat-headed strangers. She had dismissed it, as he had done at the time, as a crude expression of the almost total ignorance that predominated in this land of absurd contrasts. A land where female children were of so little account that many were left to die at birth, and an ex-concubine enjoyed absolute power over countless millions of idolators. But the breathless arrival of Tapscott changed all this, converting what had been a crop of rumours into indisputable fact. For Tapscott told of a descent on his settlement by men with red headgear and red ribbons at their wrists, who had butchered two of his converts and forced the rest to act as their labour force, pending an advance, they said, on the capital itself, where every foreigner who refused to leave would be instantly decapitated.

She was not really surprised by Rowley's reaction and realised the futility of reasoning with him. He said, "They mightn't take much account of our spiritual advice, Tapscott, but my experience is they've still got respect for our drugs and surgery. There'll be sickness down river, no doubt. And wounds to be dressed. Turning one's back on the situation will only make it worse for all the outposts strung out along the railway and river line."

"What alternative is there?"

"There's one. I'm going down there to find someone in authority and give him a piece of my mind, before they get too uppish. The legations in Peking are already threatening the Court, I'm told. Sooner or later the Government will have to act against these ridiculous bandits. You'll be safe enough here and you obviously need rest. Wait until I've something to add to your report before we go on to Peking and get an audience with the British Ambassador there." After which he issued orders for the saddling up of his riding and pack ponies, summoned his interpreter and set off while the badly shaken Tapscott was still soaking in his bath.

They were not in their usual location. When the temperatures began to soar they had moved south-west to within half-a-day's ride of Machiapu where they rented a summer bungalow and supervised an outlying post catering for the coolies working on the new railway branch to Paotingfu. Some Belgian engineers were camping five miles nearer the present terminus and there was no danger in his absence for a day or so. He kissed her gravely and rode away and she did what she could to counter the chattering rumours among the converts, set in train by the initial outburst of that fool Tapscott on his arrival. The heat was building up all the time, even here away from that stinking slum of a city, and she thought, 'I doubt if he'll want to return north when he comes back but if he does I'll put my foot down in favour of staying out here for another month or so. Right here we can at least keep to surgery hours and that's more than we can do in the city, where queues are still waiting at sunset . . . As for Tapscott, well, it's high time he was recalled and a younger man sent out. He's finished, that's plain to see. Another six months here will kill him . . .'

She did not mind the comparative isolation, having no taste for the society of the legations and the company of missionaries' wives in Peking, with their malicious gossip and outward piety, their eternal round of race meetings, amateur theatricals and sewing bees. In a way she half-sympathised with the unconverted Chinese, who regarded their presence here as an unwarranted invasion of privacy. The very rawness and brashness of Western civilisation was apparent to any thinking person who had spent a couple of years in China and the striking contrast between Chinamen and the East African and Papuan savages of previous stations was so demonstrative that she sometimes wondered why an intelligent man like Rowland Coles did not throw in his hand and demand a transfer back to settlements where the natives were children and could at least be relied upon to defer to the white man's right to call the tune. She could only suppose he had more or less withdrawn from all but the medical sphere and found his work here more absorbing and varied than it had been in less settled communities. She read a little from the latest batch of periodicals her mother sent out, took a long siesta, conducted an impromptu surgery at sundown, coping with a dozen or so simple cases, mostly dressings, and wrote a long letter to Joanna ready for collection by the first Belgian railway surveyor who called in at the post. Then, relishing her first lazy day for weeks, she ate supper with the worried Tapscott and retired to bed.

*　　　*　　　*

She was awakened by what sounded like a crash of glass and glancing at her watch in the thin morning light that filtered through slatted blinds and mosquito net, saw that it was coming up to five. The initial crash, half-heard beneath a blanket of sleep, did not worry her much and she dismissed it as a kitchen accident on the part of the cook, but then she heard the wailing voice of Tapscott right outside her door and she jumped out of bed, struggled into bedgown and slippers, and called, sharply, "What *is* it now, Mr. Tapscott? What's broken?" but the only response was a kind of squeak and she threw open the door and saw him standing there in his nightshirt.

He looked more like Peter the Hermit than ever in that get-up and was shaking from head to foot and jabbing his finger in the direction of the compound. She was aware then of a sustained buzz beyond the shuttered door, and, realising that it was early for the staff and converts to be abroad and making so much noise, she went back into her bedroom, held the blind aside and glanced out across the verandah. About twenty Chinese were gathered there in two groups, standing near the compound entrance, but there were strangers among them and she told herself again that Tapscott's nerve must have gone to let himself be scared to that extent by what looked like a quarrel among the staff, for she recognised Li-Yung, their major-domo, among the smaller group and he seemed to be making strenuous efforts to drive the others away from the gate. She said, impatiently, "Li-Yung has caught some-body stealing. Or it's a casualty brought in and he's trying to explain the Doctor is away," and she went out of the front entrance and down the steps to the compound fence.

They made way for her with great haste, scattering in both directions, all save the major-domo who stood rigidly against one of the gate uprights, with a curiously blank expression on his face. She said, "What is it, Li? What did they want?" but he made no reply only pointing across the track to a tethering-pole nailed to two stakes, each about five feet in height. Balanced on top of the further one was an object that she took to be a large round stone to which trailers of grey and russet-coloured moss were attached. She said, "What *is* it, for heaven's sake?", but still he made no reply so she hitched her robe and went out to see for herself. It wasn't a stone. It was a severed head, draped in bloodied hair and whiskers and she stopped short about five yards from the pole, gazing at it with a revulsion that paralysed her senses. Li-Yung shuffled closer to stand immediately behind her. "A horseman brought it, a Kansu warrior. Hai saw him and said he carried a Kansu banner."

She hardly heard him, much less understood what he was saying. She was slowly coming to terms with the frightful certainty that this was Rowland Coles' head and in the few seconds that elapsed between seeing it and identifying it she noted aspects of it that stamped them-selves on her memory like a brand on the flesh. The eyes were half-closed and the mouth open so that the expression was a parody of a man caught in the act of yawning. She marked this and several other aspects; the length of the iron-grey hair with its premature white streak; the thick growth of the beard below the high cheekbones; the fact that one ear was half-severed, as by a sword stroke that had all but missed. And then the wide landscape beyond the tethering pole heaved and spun and the pale sky merged with the brown folds of the plain as she teetered backwards and all but brought Li-Yung to his knees in his effort to prevent her falling flat on her back.

*　　　*　　　*

When she opened her eyes the room seemed to be full of Europeans, some of them in travel-stained white ducks, others in operatic-looking military uniforms and armed to the teeth with an array of swords, daggers, holstered revolvers and bandoliers. Someone, a young civilian, was holding a metal cup to her lips and she sensed the taste of brandy on her tongue. The civilian said, in near perfect English, "We haven't much time, ma'am. We're taking you along to Peking. Can you sit a pony?"

She pushed the cup away and nodded, holding at bay the memory of that grotesquely decorated post, for the sense of extreme urgency that dominated the room conveyed itself to her, sufficiently strongly to enable her to hoist herself out of the chair and stare about her, recognising the civilians as Belgian railway surveyors from the camp nearer Fentai and the armed quartette as foreign soldiers in battle array. The young man who had given her the brandy said, "The legations sent an escort. These men are Cossacks from the Russian Embassy guard. They were enough to get us out as far as here but we daren't waste a moment, ma'am. If you can ride we can move that much faster. If you hadn't regained consciousness I was going to harness up a cart."

She said, tonelessly, "The staff . . . the converts . . ." and he replied, indifferently, "They've gone. We had to threaten them with our revolvers to leave the horses behind," and they hustled her out into the open where Li-Yung and one other Chinaman were holding the bridles

of about eight ponies. The head, she noticed, had
gone from the haltering post. She became aware, on
mounting, that she was still in her nightgown, bedgown
and slippers but Li-Yung fastened her mantle about her
shoulders and they moved off at a trot, heading north-
east into the sun. The civilians rode in a compact body,
the Cossacks, carrying lances, rode in formation, one out on
either flank, the others fifty paces behind the cavalcade.
She had no other awareness of the journey than the painful
friction of her calves on the smooth leather of the stirrups.

2

The trauma isolated her for a long, long time, protecting
her to some extent from the stupendous happenings around
her; from the noise, heat, stench and deadly ennui of the
legations' siege so that, although present, and even,
marginally, participating now and again, she could not
have given a coherent account of what was occurring in
that city within a city. And this, to a great extent, was
responsible for the rescue of her reason, for she continued
to think of Rowley, and that object crowning the post
outside the compound, as totally unrelated to one another.

It was not that her memory was blurred in any respect.
Indeed, it was sharp and clear, more so than it had been
at any time throughout the monotonous months they had
shared out here. She accepted the fact that Rowley was
dead, that never again would she see his grave, bearded
face across the table, or lie beside him under the mosquito
net in some benighted corner of the earth, but he might
have died in a faraway land among strangers a long time
ago, and this meant that the identity of the head had no
significance. It was just a head, anybody's head. Something someone had left there because they were tired of
lugging it about.

She came to know the precise moment when she returned to full awareness, cognisant of their perilous situation here between the wall of the Forbidden Imperial

City and the Tartar Wall to the south, where the American
and German detachments manned the barricades. It was
about halfway through the siege then, the day the Imperial troops and their allies, the Boxers, mined the French
Legation and blew it sky high, together with some of the
garrison. The roar echoed clear across the city, from the
Tartar quarter in the north to the Temple of Heaven on
the southern rim of the Chinese quarters and probably
across the plain beyond. And at once the tocsin in the bell
tower began to toll and on its notes she found her identity
restored to her, that other Helen Coles, *née* Swann, who
had ridden her new safety bicycle down Kentish lanes
and laughed and danced and flirted and played endless
games of tennis at the old house in the Weald. She watched
everybody else run to the assembly point but she did not
join them. The sense of release and self-discovery was too
urgent for that. It was like watching oneself born. She
just stood by the canal that intersected the defences and
listened to the crackle of rifle fire coming from the direction
of the shattered French Legation and thought: 'I'll live
through this. I'll go home. I'll see 'Tryst' again. I'll
survive to see Joanna and tell her what having adventures
and escaping to the outside world is really like . . .' For
she recalled a discussion they had had on this very
subject the night she and Joanna conspired to switch
beaux.

But at a deeper level than relief was another, altogether
alien emotion and it had to do with this land and these
people. With their flies and their smiling perfidy, with
their teeming, gimcrack cities, boundless plains and
brown, sluggish rivers, and she could only identify this
as hate, an intensity of hate she had never felt for anyone
or for anything in the past. She wanted to punish every
last one of them for the misery and bitterness and frustration they had engendered in her and the terrible anger she
felt for them, and for the place they lived in, and her hate
was so compelling that it could only find release in action
of the kind the British Marines, and Cossack Legation

guards and the volunteers known as 'The Carving Knife Brigade' were taking at this very moment. She could not leave here without some act that would stamp the seal of her hatred on the country and its people and this would be more than a mere reprisal for Rowley's death. It would be the ultimate expression of all she felt about her time here and after that, purged and purified as it were, she would take passage home and put this part of her life behind her.

Slowly, a little more each day, she became interested in the plight of the beleaguered garrison, learning the geography of the various bastions of eleven nationalities fighting for their lives inside the shrinking perimeter. She knew the perilous handholds the Germans and Americans had upon the Tartar Wall, the battered Fu, where the forlorn Japanese garrison contested every inch of the area east of Customs Street, the half-ruined French Legation and its comic opera Ambassador, Monsieur Pichon, who was forever declaring that survival was a matter of hours and, above all, the central bastion formed by the crowded British Legation, with its bell tower and its hordes of sick, wounded and clamorous refugees. She identified with the rumours too. How soon the relief column from Tientsin would arrive. How long the rations of stewed pony and champagne would hold out. How many more casualties the garrison could afford before the attackers swarmed in to exterminate every man, woman and child assembled. She was aware of every desperate sortie there into the labyrinth of ruined buildings about here, the creeping advance of the Chinese barricades that were slowly enclosing them in a wall of rubble, the high courage of heroes like Captain Halliday, R.M., the poltroonery of absurd figures like Pichon, the French Ambassador.

But to know these things, to stand off and witness them was not enough, and neither was the offer of officious women in sweat-soiled dresses to stitch sandbags made of silk, satin and sackcloth, or tend the crowded hospital ward where men, women and children died every day. This was women's work, of course, but it wasn't *her* work. She had to do something far less passive, far more definitive and there was no prospect of a woman taking her place at the barricades, where she would be most likely to find her chance to assuage the terrible thirst for revenge and atonement. Whenever she went to one or other of the thinly manned posts she was quickly sent out of range by the officer or N.C.O. in charge, warned off like a venturesome child approaching a tree-felling party of woodsmen in the grounds of 'Tryst' and told, roughly but kindly, "Please to stand away, ma'am!" or "Please to go back, ma'am!" but it was through these persistent attempts to get within killing range of the Boxers that she at length acquired sufficient guile to circumvent their prohibitions. But that was towards the end of the siege, when the temperatures were well over the hundreds every day and the last of the ponies was marked for death and the stewpot.

*　　　*　　　*

By then, of course, she knew that the Boxers were not, in fact, within anyone's range, for someone told her they had proved utterly useless wielding their clumsy weapons against anyone but unarmed missionaries and terrified converts. The daily attacks were now mounted by Imperial troops, armed with artillery and modern Mausers, and sometimes she caught a brief glimpse of one of them, darting about behind their maze of barricades on the outer perimeter of the Fu, or slipping by under the Tartar Wall. Colourful figures, in blues and scarlets, greens and golds, with their inscrutable banners and whenever this happened the yearning to down at least one of them became so masterful that she could have dashed over the intervening barricades and flown at them single-handed. But then, towards the end of July, her moment arrived, so unexpectedly and in such mundane circumstances, that it had almost gone before she was aware of it.

She had found herself an approved job by then, carrying rations to men enduring long spells of duty at the loopholes, ordeals that lengthened in relation to the daily reduction of effectives manning the defences. It was in the Fu area, where the Japanese were sometimes helped out by some of the more spirited among the horde of Catholic converts, brought into the legations' quarter the day the siege began and within hours of the murder of the German Ambassador. By then the Fu was a scene of almost complete desolation, with buildings levelled and the open spaces where they had stood strewn with rubble concealing, and sometimes half concealing, Chinese soldiers who had died prising the Japanese from one position after another. The defenders had now retreated to a triangular position terminating in an apex pointing towards the north bridge over the canal, some fifty yards beyond the garrison's barricade and here they had built a six-foot wall pierced with loopholes, some of which were shuttered by hand-carved wooden blocks used to preserve the ancient works among the thousands of books housed in the Hanlin Yuan Library, the oldest library in the world someone told her, but now a gutted ruin, like everything else about here. The blocks were set beside the wall, ready for insertion every time a loophole was vacated. There were strict orders to this effect, dating from an occasion early in the siege when besiegers had used one to fire directly into the defences.

Some sort of attack seemed to be in progress at this moment. From the apex of the triangle came the almost continuous stutter of small-arms fire, punctuated every now and again by the boom of Imperialist cannon engaged in a one-sided duel with Betsy, the home-made gun used by the British marines. She had just crossed an open space carrying her pail of stew and was approaching the wall to make a delivery to the sentry standing there when the man, a Catholic convert, quitted his post in response to a shouted command for stretcher-bearers from the embattled sector. He left in such a hurry that he not only forgot to shutter the loophole but left his rifle leaning against the wall. The battle, at this juncture, was about eighty yards to the north but crouching there, close against the barricade, Helen heard no signs of activity beyond the cloud of smoke and brickdust that masked the sector, so she set down the pail of stew and took a quick peep through the loophole as far as the burned-out ruins of Customs Street.

It was then, without the slightest warning, that she saw her opportunity. A thickset Imperialist was inching along the outside of the wall in the direction of the dust-cloud and she judged him to be an officer of some kind for his uniform was exceptionally colourful and instead of a rifle he carried a revolver and a scimitar-type sword with a broad curving blade and two points, one set above the other. She did not hesitate a second. He was no more than five yards away when she first glimpsed him, but, seeing the unshuttered loophole, he half-turned and took two strides towards it. In that moment she grabbed the sentry's rifle and fired at point-blank range.

She had never fired a gun of any kind before but she had often watched her brothers potting pheasants and partridges in the coverts at 'Tryst', so that the act of levelling and aiming was instinctive. The gun went off with what seemed to her a disproportionate roar and the recoil was so fierce that it struck her shoulder like the blow of a club, causing her to stagger back clear of the wall. Even so she had a clear view of the officer who doubled like the blade of a jack-knife, spun round and then, with a kind of grace, toppled backwards over a block of masonry and lay still, his boots angled to the sky.

At first it did not seem possible that she could have killed him so effortlessly and she remained where the recoil had driven her, one hand holding the heavy rifle across her breast, the other slowly massaging her bruised shoulder. She could see nothing of him but his angled boots but his posture convinced her that he was dead. As dead as those other men half-buried under the rubble. As dead as the

English officer she had seen buried by the bell tower the previous evening. As dead as Rowland Coles, whose headless corpse was lying out there on the treeless plain.

The feeling of wonderment passed, replaced by an altogether different emotion that she could only describe as a kind of omnipotence. It was as though, by that single shot, she had emerged from the flesh, bones and spirit of the jaded woman who had stooped to glance through the loophole and reassumed the personality of the eager girl she had been when she married Rowley and went off with him to seek adventure on the far side of the world. All the bitterness, the frustrations, the disappointments of the last few years dropped away, discharged into the body of a middle-aged Chinaman now lying across a block of masonry with his boots pointing to the sky. She had a sense of repossessing herself, much as a proud woman might cross the threshold of a house where everyone waited to do her bidding.

Mechanically, and with no real awareness of what she was doing, she laid aside the rifle, shuttered the loophole, picked up her stew pail and moved along the wall towards the enveloping dust cloud where the defenders were grouped in the apex of the works and very confident, it seemed, of beating off the unco-ordinated attack mounted from the ruins of the Hanlin.

They saw her coming and a sprucely-dressed Oriental, whom she recognised as Colonel Shiba, came towards her and bowed. The gesture, in that time and in that place, made her smile. It was her first smile in months. Her manner, and perhaps her presence there, seemed to please him for he too smiled, revealing about twice as many teeth as a man should have, but he said, taking her pail, "You should not be here, madam. Not when there is firing. Please to withdraw out of range."

She turned back and made her unhurried way along the wall, then over the open ground to the Legation, bathed in a serenity that was balm to the spirit, and was at once reabsorbed in the fretful routine of the kitchens.

Everything that happened during the remainder of the siege was an anticlimax. Hope of succour came and went, fanned by stories of searchlights in the night sky to the south, by reports of distant gunfire, by the coming and going of couriers who seemed to make their way to and from the beleaguered legations with very little trouble. The truce came and then, in mid-August, the storming relief column, headed by the jovial Colonel Gasalee and his polyglot army of British, American, Russians, Japanese, French, Austrians and Italians. Nothing during those climactic days could ruffle her newfound serenity, not even the unconfirmed story from a fugitive that Rowley's body had been found and given Christian burial some ten miles down the river line from the spot where she had been rescued by the Belgian engineers and the Cossacks. Rowley was dead but then, to balance accounts, so was that thickset officer, shot through the loophole. It only remained to begin all over again. Not here, of course, not anywhere where temperatures soared to 110 degrees in the shade and huge, lazy flies swarmed about one's head and plate. Somewhere cool and green. A place where everybody spoke a familiar tongue and servants wore starched caps and aprons. She had no belongings to pack, nothing but a few souvenirs of the siege and the clothes bought with the grant paid out to survivors to enable them to travel down to the coast and await transport home.

They went out in convoy, the women chattering gaily and continuously of the horrors of the siege but although she listened it was in the mood of an indulgent parent settling to the prattle of children. No one among them had killed a man in a split second of time and because she had said nothing of her exploit they thought of her, she supposed, as a brokenhearted widow, one of so many overwhelmed by deep, personal tragedy. Or perhaps not even that. Simply as a drifter who had helped out now and again in the kitchens of the embattled legations.

6

Study in Black

WHENEVER HER MIND TURNED UPON SUCH THINGS
(it was not often, for Henrietta was a very sanguine person)
it struck her that, over the years, the clan had enjoyed more
luck than most. Not so much because they had prospered,
socially and commercially, but because every one of them
enjoyed splendid health and most troubles, she decided
after she reached the sixty mark, stemmed from sickness
and the disabilities that got between one and one's in-
dulgences.

Apart from that one frightful period in '65, when Adam
had lost his leg, 'Tryst' had never been a home of mourning. Unlike most women of her generation she had
succeeded in rearing the nine children she had borne
between 1860 and 1879 without a single procession to the
churchyard. Their illnesses, if you could call them that,
were trivial and transient and their luck held out in other
ways. Six of them were comfortably settled now and each,
in his or her own way, had found a partner that could, at a
pinch, be reckoned 'suitable'. Not, of course, a unique
being like Adam but someone who adapted to their several
idiosyncrasies and that, she supposed, was rare when you
thought in terms of half-dozens.

Stella had made that unfortunate first marriage, but
luck (plus her mother's despatch and sagacity) had put
that right in no time. Alex had survived any number of
bloody fields without so much as a grazed knee, whereas

the younger ones, although getting into innumerable
scrapes, all seemed to possess a degree of resilience that
equipped them to evade the full consequences of wrong-
headed decisions and the occasional folly. Even Joanna,
who had played fast and loose with young Jack-o'-Lantern
Coles, and got herself with child, had succeeded in dis-
guising a crass piece of idiocy as a romantic adventure.
Alone among them Henrietta was privy to the fact that
Joanna's eldest child, now eleven, had 'come across the
fields' as they used to say. Helen's future worried her a
little. It couldn't be good for health or child-bearing to
go trapesing round the world in the wake of a medical
missionary but it was her life and she had chosen it and
if, by now, she wished to change it, then she could use
her native wit to persuade that solemn stick Rowland to
abandon such unrewarding work, come home and buy a
lucrative practice in Kent, for the Coles were known
to have made a fortune peddling pills and Rowland,
eldest of the family, was likely to be rich when his father
died.

As for Giles, he seemed contented enough these days,
despite his eccentric approach to a war that had engulfed
two of his brothers, and that flighty wife of his had at last
succeeded in presenting him with a son, something Henrietta had thought unlikely after thirteen years of child-
less marriage. George and Edward were both as obsessed
with the business as Adam had been until recently, and
Margaret, the family postscript, seemed happy enough
mooning about the fields and coppices with her clutter of
paints and canvases.

There remained Hugo, the family clown, but he too
had had an astonishing run of luck so far, first being
granted licence to pursue athletics as a career (only a
father as tolerant as Adam would have countenanced
that!), then falling into the lap of that extraordinary
woman who made a positive fetish of a boy whom Adam
had often dismissed as 'fifteen stone of musclebound
bacon'.

All in all an unbroken run of luck, stretching over a period of more than thirty years and she saw no reason to suppose it would not continue, at least for as long as she retained her faculties and could keep a sharp lookout for squalls. For in a way Henrietta took upon herself most of the credit for this galaxy of achievement. After all, it was she who had borne the brunt of their upbringing, for Adam had always been immersed in that other family of his — the Swann network of depots and establishments that sometimes seemed to her to haul half the merchandise of the Empire from one point to another. If the children had turned out well then they had her rather than him to thank for it. And after her, she supposed, that dear, dogged Phoebe Fraser, who had served them so selflessly since Stella and Alex were toddlers.

As the seasons passed Henrietta came to assume that the Swanns were immune from the disasters and tragedies of less fortunate families and more and more, as she grew older and more prescient, she half-identified with that other matriarch at Windsor, whose even larger brood enjoyed the same ascendancy. It was therefore with a sense of appalling shock that she read the express letter from Alex, postmarked Durban, telling that Hugo, God help the boy, had been shot through the head in a Boer ambush, and although well on the road to recovery, was temporarily blinded. Alex stressed the word 'temporarily', pointing out that Hugo was scheduled for a long and complicated course of treatment on his return home but he added, as a kind of buffer against despair, that he was likely to lose the sight of one eye and have limited vision in the other.

For days after she had received this frightful news, Henrietta was stunned. Nothing Adam could say helped her adjust to it for Hugo, admittedly the slowest witted of the family, had been its prime physical product. Just as she took pride in Alex's invulnerability, George's cleverness, Giles' erudition and the girls' undeniable charms, so she basked in Hugo's rare beauty, seeing him as a reincarnation of a Greek demigod, described in

Mr. Kingsley's book, *The Heroes*. She simply could not picture Hugo as a big, helpless baby, led about by others and sitting mute while somebody cut up his meat or found his trousers. He had always possessed such an abundance of effortless grace and of all the boys he seemed the one less equipped to adapt to a terrible handicap of that kind. But as the shock wave receded somewhat her anger mounted against that bustling, rather overpowering woman who had landed him into such a mess. Adam had to take a stern line with her, pointing out that Hugo was a grown man and could have made his own decision about volunteering for active service. He was also harsh enough to rap her knuckles about her own contribution, saying sharply for him, "Listen here, Hetty. I won't have that! It's not the slightest use taking that line and throwing your dignity to the winds. I seem to recall you were among a majority here who clamoured for war with Kruger and his burghers. I daresay a good many of them have been shot through the head and lost their farms into the bargain. It's a terrible thing for a boy to face a handicap of that kind, and I'm in a better position to appreciate that than most, having stumped through half a lifetime with a tin leg on account of a fool who couldn't read a railway time-table. But upbraiding Sybil Uskdale and the Boers won't help any of us, least of all you. If people go to war some of them come out of it in worse shape than they went in and at least the boy's alive. Do you know how many men have died from enteric fever out there on that veldt?"

"I'm not the least bit concerned with them," she snapped, "for they aren't my sons."

"They're somebody's sons and they lost their lives in what I think a damned poor cause. Sooner or later everyone will come round to that view. Even Hugo."

"Is that going to help him?"

"No, but neither is adding to that wretched woman's tragedy by letting her know you lay the blame at her door. She's all he's got now for he'll never run again and if I'm not mistaken he'll realise that."

"I never thought to hear you talk so cold-bloodedly about your own flesh and blood!" she wailed.

"I'm not cold-blooded!" he growled. "I'm simply trying to make the best of what can't be altered. She'll make sure he gets the best treatment in the world and she's in a better position to do it than we are!"

It provoked one of their rare, smouldering quarrels that persisted right into early July, when a wire came informing them that a shipload of wounded was arriving at Southampton and they could go along the coast and meet Hugo and Sybil on disembarkation. There was no question of bringing him home. He was scheduled to go straight into a private clinic, supervised by Sir Oscar Firbright, the famous eye specialist, there to undergo further surgery for several months.

*   *   *

It was on the quay, as the wounded were being carried ashore into the waiting hospital trains, that she first questioned her attitude and began to reflect upon Adam's forthright advice. The change was not effected by the sight of so much suffering but by her first glimpse of Sybil during the brief interval before the hospital train pulled out.

The change in her was shattering. She seemed to Henrietta no more than a ghost of the brilliant creature who had bounced up the steps of 'Tryst' seven months ago, dragging Hugo in her wake like a barge towed by a splendidly equipped steamer. Her cold, classical beauty was all but gone. Traces of its sparkle lingered in the hard blue eyes but the cheeks were pitifully hollow, the full, sensual mouth dragged down at the corners, and the famous Uskdale bloom had been drained from her cheeks by the South African sun, the reality of war, or both. Her figure, Henrietta recalled, had been slight but very trim at that spectacular wedding at St. Margaret's. Now it seemed angular and graceless, whereas her voice, hitherto slightly hectoring, had dwindled to a murmur little above a whisper as she said, brushing Henrietta's cheek, "You don't have to berate me, Mama. I've been doing that for myself all these weeks. But the only thing that matters now is to get him well and in a frame of mind when he'll put his trust in his surgeons and doctors. That's *my* responsibility mainly but you can help if you will. Remind him he's so much to live for, even if it takes him a year to adjust to not seeing."

"Won't he . . . isn't he likely to see at all?" Henrietta had stammered. "I mean . . . isn't recovery a possibility?"

"No, it isn't," Sybil said, staring down at her elegant boots. "There's no point in lying to you or to myself any longer. The best we can hope for is a glimmer of sight in his right eye and I'll thank God to the end of my life if we can achieve even that. I have to go now. I'm travelling on with the unit. It was kind of you both to come all this way for a few minutes."

She boarded the train then, without a backward glance and Henrietta, eyes blurred with tears, accompanied Adam across the platform to where the civilian boat-train to London awaited them in a siding. He said, with something between a sigh and a groan, "Well, there's the war everybody wanted," but then, in a milder tone, "He's in good hands, Hetty. Something about that woman I like, despite everything. Spunk, maybe."

They had arranged to stay at the Norfolk overnight before returning home and as the cab dropped them off at the portals her eye caught a newspaper placard reading 'Peking: Massacre Feared', and her heavy heart gave a great leap and then seemed to subside well below the navel for she remembered Joanna writing to her only last week saying that Helen had written to her in May, telling her that she was based on Peking but sometimes accompanied Rowley to help out at out-lying surgeries. She caught Adam's arm as he was paying off the cabbie and said, "Look at that! It can't be that Helen and Rowland are involved . . ." and he said, gruffly, "Come inside and take tea. I can tell you more than you're likely to learn from the *Daily Mail*," and she went into the tea-room where he ordered tea and buttered scones with an air of gravity that warned her he must have been aware of Helen's danger for some time but had postponed telling her, probably on account of Hugo. She said, "Tell me, Adam. I've a right to know."

"Nobody knows anything for a fact. It's all guess-work so far. That, and the kind of sensation papers thrive on. You knew there had been unrest in North China, didn't you?"

"No, I haven't even glanced at a paper since we heard about Hugo. Every page was full of war news and it only made me more miserable than ever."

"Well, there's been an uprising of some kind. A secret society they call the Boxers has been working up a hate campaign against the foreigners, especially the missionaries. They've even killed one or two, but not in her province, somewhere a long way to the north and west."

"But it actually mentioned Peking on that poster."

"There's an unconfirmed report from Hong Kong about the foreign community there. A German diplomat has been killed and our Government has asked their Government to protect British nationals."

"Can't we find out anything specific about her? I don't think I could stand another shock of that kind."

He took her hand and pressed it. "Leave it to me. I'll find out somehow. I've got a good agent in Hong Kong and I'd believe anything he wired me but I can't do it tonight. I'll get the wheels moving first thing in the morning. I know roughly where that chap Coles operates and will put some feelers out." He paused, still holding her hand and regarding her with the vaguest suspicion of a twinkle. "Poor old Hetty, you are having a time of it! Haven't seen you this way for long enough. As a matter of fact, I can't remember how long."

"I can," she said, sombrely, "since the time of that rail crash all of thirty-five years ago."

"Well," he said, "we all get our turn if we hang around long enough." And then, "See here, we're not doing Hugo or Helen any good by moping. How would you like to go to a music hall and don't pretend it isn't 'decent'. It's the best way I know of holding trouble at bay for a couple of hours."

She said, unexpectedly, "I'll do anything to take my mind off Hugo. What time do they start? Is it after or before dinner?"

"Both," he said, grinning, "but I'd best take you to the first house. The second gets a bit rowdy."

She thought: 'That's the really comforting thing about him. He *knows* things. About what's going on in Peking and what time the curtains at music-halls go up. He knows me too, enough to give me that facesaver about the propriety of visiting a music-hall on a night like this . . .', and she finished her tea and went up to their room for a rest and a wash.

He knew the entertainment world too, it proved, for he chose the 'Star' where the bill included the great illusionist Devant and a galaxy of eccentric comedians and daring acrobats, the latter all foreigners, she noted, working in family groups. For two hours she all but forgot her misery watching pyramids of men, women and children in skin-tight costumes pile themselves almost as high as the proscenium arch, girls presumably sawn in half skip nimbly from gaudily painted closets shouting 'Hoi!' as they flashed wide, toothy smiles at the audience, short fat men in baggy trousers screaming abuse at tall thin men in evening dress, soubrettes who specialised in songs that would never have been tolerated twenty years ago but seemed now to delight the patrons and jugglers who whirled clubs so rapidly that it made one dizzy to watch. He said, as they settled into a hansom and made their way back to supper, "Well, Hetty?" and she kissed him impulsively on the cheek and then, quite irrationally, began to cry. Just a little; just enough to require a furtive dab or two between lamp-standards as they bowled down Fleet Street, past the Law Courts and into the Strand. He didn't notice. Or pretended he didn't.

2

As she had half-expected there was worse to come.

She never recalled a period as sustained and depressing as this, for the crisis in 1865, when they came to her for permission to amputate his left leg, had lasted no more than a few weeks. After that, with him absent and on the road to recovery, she was able to adjust, losing herself in his concerns at the yard and watching the calendar against his return.

This crisis needed more stamina and patience than she possessed. Wretchedness and uncertainty stretched into months, right through the remainder of the summer, the autumn and into the new year, when a mantle of sadness settled over the whole nation with the death of the Queen at Osborne.

It was September before they were called upon to face the fact that Hugo would never see again, that further surgery and visits to Continental doctors were pointless but, mercifully perhaps, the sharp edges of Hugo's tragedy were blurred by the long spell of agonised waiting for news of Helen and Rowley, and finally the shattering announcement that Rowley had been murdered by those Chinese fiends and that Helen had survived the horrors of a seven-week siege.

There was relief, to be sure, in the news that she was alive and was on her way home but Henrietta, entirely without experience of this kind of situation, was not in the least sure what she would do with the girl when she arrived. She was sad then that Helen had no children to take her mind off the tragedy and very relieved when Joanna wrote from Dublin saying that, as soon as her sister had rested, she would be glad to welcome her for an

indefinite stay. The two had always been very close and
Joanna's jolly household would surely have a more bene-
ficial effect on a young widow than a sojourn at 'Tryst'
just now, with everyone so cast down about Hugo.
Adam approved the plan at once, saying, "Best thing in
the world for her. There's only young Margaret here and
the age gap is too wide. We're in no fettle to cheer her
up, are we?" And then, advertising his lifelong detach-
ment from the brood once again, "How old is she now?
I never can remember the order they came in."

"She's thirty. Just a year younger than Hugo."

"Ah," he said, vaguely, "then I daresay she'll marry
again soon enough."

"I really don't know how you can say such things,"
Henrietta protested. "For heaven's sake don't mention
such a thing in her presence."

"I've a damned sight more sense than that," he said,
smiling, "but it's the best thing she could do for all that.
No sense in making a fetish of a dead husband like Queen
Vic. Oh, people are sympathetic for a year or so but after
that they go out of their way to avoid you. Just remember
that when I pop off, Hetty."

He meant it jocularly enough, she supposed, but she did
wish he would save his gallows humour for George and
his male cronies. The prospect of widowhood, even at an
advanced age, terrified her, notwithstanding a tribe of
children and grand-children, and she could never forget
he was her senior by twelve years. She said, "I daresay
you'll outlive me and I hope to goodness you do," and
went about her business, getting Helen's old room ready
in the west wing beyond the gallery and remembering, as
she entered it, how gay and hoydenish those girls had
seemed growing up here in the days when their safety
bicycles were novelties.

She managed at last to put Rowland Coles and his
horrid death out of mind. She could always do that with
people who were not her flesh and blood and when Helen
did arrive, in the last golden days of October, she was

agreeably surprised to discover that the girl, outwardly at least, did not appear to be devastated by her frightful experiences. She looked sallow and peaky to be sure but who wouldn't, after having one's husband murdered and afterwards enduring a seven-week bombardment in a fortress with temperatures into the hundreds, horsemeat for rations and the prospect of butchery held at bay by a few barricades and one's own fortitude?

Adam helped more than he realised, questioning her closely about the siege as soon as he realised she didn't mind discussing it, and as more and more horrific details emerged Henrietta began to feel a glow of pride in her daughter's hardihood. She was sure she could never have behaved so gallantly and upheld the honour of the flag in that way, not even if Adam had been by her side. She was shocked, however, to learn that Helen had not only killed a man but gloried in the fact.

"You mean you . . . you *know* you killed him? You weren't just . . . well, there, with a gun in your hand?"

"I killed him, sure enough," Helen said blandly, "and if you can bring yourself to believe it, killing him did me a great deal of good. I would have killed a few more if they had given me half a chance."

"Well, I can understand you feeling bitter and . . . well, full of feelings of revenge," Henrietta said, turning away from her daughter's hard, rather brittle smile, "but I mean . . . well . . . it couldn't have been a *pleasant* experience. Not even in the circumstances. And I really don't understand how it could make you feel any better about poor Rowland."

"Well, it did," Helen reaffirmed, "but as to expecting you to understand how, I don't think I could do that, Mamma. You would have to have lived in China and been there and listened to those savages howling for blood. Maybe Papa would understand, having served in the Mutiny and buried those women and children slaughtered at Cawnpore."

Adam understood and the curious change in the girl

interested him, bringing her a little closer somehow. He said, when Henrietta had excused herself on some domestic pretext, "Do you mind if I add something to that? Keep up the attack, girl. Don't ever let self-pity creep up on you. That's no road out of the woods, believe me. Came close to letting go myself when I had to learn to walk again at dam' near forty but I held on somehow. Matter of professional interest. What make was that rifle you used to swat the Chinaman?"

"A Martini-Henry," she said. "I found that out later."

"It had a devilish kick, didn't it?"

"It left a bruise on my shoulder as big as an orange."

"And popping that fellow didn't get into the official reports?"

"No. I never told a soul about it until now."

"That was wise," he said, thoughtfully, "for you're full young and can begin again. Go over to Ireland. Take it easy and look around. Ease yourself back into the mainstream as I did. It can happen. I'm proof of it. How are you off for cash?"

"I've still got your two hundred a year and I'll get a pension they tell me. Plus compensation for all we lost at the bungalow but it will take time to come through I suppose."

"I'll double the allowance and see that it's paid through our Dublin branch."

"That's very generous, Papa."

"Is it? I wouldn't say it was. Not for a girl who can tote a Martini-Henry and live seven weeks on horsemeat and champagne."

He kissed her absentmindedly and went out into the autumn sunshine and down the drive to his observation mound behind The Hermitage, pondering with the slow, massive strength of an ancestral tug. Swanns had been in the killing business for centuries and here it was, cropping out in a girl who was the daughter of a tradesman and reared in what most people would regard as genteel circumstances.

*　　　*　　　*

Lady Sybil brought Hugo on his first visit shortly after Helen had left and Adam read them all a brief lecture the day they were due to arrive.

"Don't treat that boy as a helpless invalid," he warned. "Nothing more irritating when you're crocked than people fuming and fussing about you, handing you this and that and telling you to watch out. God knows, you don't need hourly reminders of a handicap of that kind. Leave all the gentling to his wife. She's a professional and knows her business if I'm any judge."

She did, too, as he was very quick to note. She didn't let the boy out of her sight but her ministrations were wonderfully unobtrusive so that he gained the impression she was working round the clock to accustom him to routines that would build up his confidence. As to whether she was making real progress it was difficult to say. Hugo was very subdued and sat about mostly, like a big, ageing collie, too old and tired to frolic. Who could tell what the boy was thinking when he felt the sun on his face or the wind in his hair?

Adam had a private word with Sybil about his future and, as he had expected, she had specific plans for him. "He's going to take a course as a masseur at one of the big military hospitals," she said. "It'll keep him in trim and give him something to think about, as well as contacts with other handicapped men of his kind and age. I'm going to make sure he rides, too, on a leading rein, and I've engaged a retired sergeant-major as his personal batman. Truscott, he's called, formerly of the Duke of Cornwall's Light Infantry. I chose him because he was once a well-known amateur walker. He has as many trophies as Hugo I wouldn't wonder. He'll be reporting here tomorrow if that's agreeable to you, Mr. Swann."

"Splendid idea," he said, his approval of her increasing with each new encounter. "The more mobile he is the easier he'll adjust and after all these months in hospital he needs all the exercise he can get."

Truscott was an instant success, a sunburned man about

fifty with legs like saplings and a jerky way of carrying himself, as though he was forever on the point of breaking into a trot. He had the traditional parade-ground bark, even when he was trying to please and his yell of '*Sah!*' every time Hugo summoned him so intrigued the grandchildren that they at once incorporated him into their games. Indeed, within days of Truscott's arrival the game of 'Sah!' took over from hide and seek and prisoner's base and soon Hugo's batman was a firm family favourite.

Adam watched them set off one morning on their first tramp over the plateau that enclosed 'Tryst' from the east and noted with relief that sightlessness had done nothing to shorten the effortless stride that had carried Hugo to victory over so many miles of track and steeplechase course. He thought, seeing the pair move into the screen of elms that topped the spur, 'He'll do, so long as that woman sticks to him . . .' and went into his study to report on both Helen and Hugo in a long and explicit letter to Giles. Of all his children Giles alone shared his complete confidence.

3

On January 22nd the news was broadcast from Osborne to the remotest corners of the world, tapped out on countless telegraph keys, spoken over thickening clusters of wires that were beginning to enclose every sizeable city of the land, passed from mouth to mouth across the island that had once been marked as 'Tom Tiddler's Ground' on the Swann waggon maps, then over the Solent to the mainland, then out across the shires to the coasts of Donegal, Sutherland and the Empire beyond the seas. The impossible had happened. Victoria had slipped away on a grey winter's day and a curtain of black fell on an era.

It was as though nobody had ever died before. As though, to yield up the spirit, and be trundled away in a coffin, was a privilege extended to the very few, a singular dispensation by Providence as a reward for spectacular services on earth.

The face of the nation changed overnight. Every public building was hung with circular wreaths that looked like so many black lifebelts and many were shrouded in yards of whispering crêpe. Black crêpe was at a premium. Top-hatted city gents tied it about their arms, cabbies tipped their whips with crêpe bows and every woman who valued her neighbour's regard (and quite a few who did not) went into full mourning, including the ultra-loyal among the London prostitutes who continued, however, to ply a brisk trade among the thousands of provincials who travelled up to town for the occasion.

Adam, secretly amused, was among them, reminding himself that he had no business witnessing the event for he had been born two reigns ago and could recall wearing crêpe round his straw hat for Silly Billy, the Queen's uncle.

The ceremonial of the four tribes had always interested him, however, and he sauntered about glancing at solemn faces and hoping to catch one of them off-guard. He was unsuccessful. On a 'bus ride from London Bridge to Kensington he did not record so much as a single smile and even the Thameside costers looked as if they were losing money on every hot potato they sold in response to their dolorous cry of "Warm yer 'ands an' warm yer belly for 'apen'y!"

When he read that the royal corpse was being conveyed by state procession to Paddington for its final journey to Windsor he took a fancy to travel up again and avail himself of an old customer's offer to watch its departure from a hotel window overlooking the station approach. Henrietta declined to accompany him and not, as she claimed, on account of the cold, foggy weather. Her dismay was genuine, more genuine than even he realised, for more and more of late she had begun to identify with Victoria and there seemed no point in reminding oneself of one's mortality at this chilly season of the year. So he went alone, staying overnight at the Norfolk and booking an early cab to his vantage point where his host had a comfortable sitting-room with balcony and a supply of hot toddy to keep out the cold.

It moved him more than he would have believed, all those cloaked potentates marching behind the gun-carriage with its pall topped by the Imperial crown; the silent ranks of infantry standing with bowed heads and reversed arms between the cortège and dense phalanxes of Cockneys, Londoners without a speck of colour about them save the odd splash of undertaker's mauve. He had never liked the woman much (though he had always entertained respect for her dead husband), but he did not begrudge her her eight, cream-coloured horses. One had to admit she had stayed the course better than most monarchs and had even succeeded in pulling herself together somewhat after the first twenty-five years of widowhood.

He had plenty of time, as the cavalcade crawled past, to let his mind range freely back and forth across the decades, as it often did on occasions of this kind. Odd, irrelevant thoughts occurred to him, tiny tributaries of the national stream of history personally explored by him over many years. He remembered when the army had discarded traditional headgear in favour of the German pickelhaube, a curious concession to the widely accepted belief among military men that the Prussian army's performance against the French in 1870 entitled them to set military fashions, as though the design of a man's helmet determined his prowess in the field. He found it difficult to see the heavy, tired-looking man riding behind the bier as the future King, remembering, with an inward chuckle, all the fuss there had been about Bertie's frolics with the girls and at the gaming tables, that had earned him his mother's disapproval since he was eighteen or thereabouts and breaking out from the frigid mould she and Albert had cast for him. And on the King's immediate right he had more serious doubts about Vicky's unpredictable grandson, the German Emperor, wondering

if he was qualified to run a village skittles team, much less
a thrustful nation of eighty millions. He seemed on his
very best behaviour, however, reining back as they
approached the station entrance in order to allow Uncle
Edward to exercise his priority rights. He could see
nothing of the new Queen and princesses, in their closed
carriage pulled by a mere four horses, so that his mind was
free to conjure with the secret thoughts of the spectators,
wondering how genuine was their involvement in this
splendid panoply of death. Reasonably so, he would
imagine, but not for the obvious reasons. Very few of them
down there could recall any royal symbol other than the
little old woman on that gun-carriage, now on her way to
lie beside her beloved Albert so that they would see this,
he supposed, as a break in the continuity of their lives.
That would disturb many of them. The English did not
like their continuity broken, fearing changes in the national
pattern as much as the French and Italians welcomed
them. All their lives she had been there, as unchangeable
as a feature of English topography, the cliffs of Dover or
the curves of the Thames. Ever since childhood her
double-chinned silhouette had crystallised their awareness
of national prejudices and preferences, and whereas her
withdrawal, in the 'sixties and 'seventies, had made her
unpopular, the two Jubilees had restored her to her place
at the pinnacle of the royal pyramid. So that it followed
they were watching not *her* exactly but their own past, a
past transforming itself into a future, and that meant uncertainty for most. Especially those no longer fortified by
the arrogance of youth.

*   *   *

The kings, princes and flunkeys moved on and he sipped
a whisky, awaiting dispersal and a chance to make his
way back to Charing Cross and home. His old friend
Lord Roberts repassed below, his horse (black like everything else today) led by a groom, along with the horse

the King had been riding, and there came to him again a brief vision of the crossroads he and Roberts had occupied immediately after the Sepoy Mutiny, when Roberts had opted for glory while he had seen a military career for what it was – years of boredom and heartache for all but the mystics like Roberts. Instead he had devoted himself to what? To money-making or something more exalted? What was it exactly? Surrender to a compulsion that had nagged him since boyhood? To make a mark, to fulfil his own extravagant fancies in competition with other egotists? He didn't know. He never had known with certainty. Yet he was sure of one thing. He didn't regret his choice and given his youth he would do it again but sooner, much sooner. The real point was, where did one go from here, if anywhere? He was seventy-three and unlikely to see another royal funeral, unless Edward VII, fourteen years his junior, gorged and whored himself to death. The long years of striving were behind him and in the time left he could never be more than a spectator. A keenly interested one, however, not only of his own concerns but of the ultimate destiny of his race and he could make no more than a guess or two at that. They had passed their apogee, he supposed, a year or two back, when they involved themselves in this ridiculous war with a bunch of farmers but the country was still sound enough, politically and financially, so long as it stopped short of tearing itself in two unequal halves, the Little Englanders on one side, the Imperialists on the other. And that mightn't matter in the end. It was hard to believe that anything cataclysmic would result from this temporary schism for the people. Even those like Giles and his radicals howling for social reforms, were conservative at heart, trafficking mostly in compromise. It seemed more likely that the real challenge would come from outside. Not from the Germans as he had once thought – they wouldn't get far with that ass of a Kaiser raising dust everywhere he went. More probably from France that George said was leading the field in the new technologies,

or from that vigorous offshoot of the British across the
Atlantic that had its own way to make in the world. If
he lived as long as Vicky he might begin to discern some
of the answers. Whatever they were they would be interesting . . . interesting . . .

The penetrating cold tormented the stump of his leg
and he thought longingly of his own fireside and Henrietta's eager questions about the funeral procession. He
said his goodbyes, despatched an urchin for a cab with
the promise of a florin if he got one and went downstairs on
to the porch. The crowds were rapidly dispersing, already
forgetting the bier and its contents in search of something
to keep out the cold. The boy arrived with a growler and
he climbed in, sitting back in the musty interior saturated
with spectacle and turning his thoughts towards home.

PART THREE

Towards the Summit

I

Headstart

THE OLD HANDS ABOUT THE YARD – AND THERE were still some who remembered Adam Swann's heyday – exchanged wry jokes when it got about that the New Broom had retreated to the tower, the only section of the Thameside premises to emerge more or less intact from the fire.

It struck them as ironic that a man who preached the heresy that the horse was obsolete, and was threatening to supersede them by the spawn of that snorting juddering contraption he had driven down from Manchester three years ago, should choose a draughty, fourteenth-century belfry, approached by a narrow, twisting stair as the hub of his empire. In deliberate preference, moreover, to the new red-brick office block they had built fifty yards short of the Tooley Street exit.

It was out of character somehow. A man who had, as it were, forced upon them every kind of innovation in the last decade, was not a likely candidate for withdrawal to a lumber room lit by oil lamps and not even served by a telephone but equipped, instead, with the speaking tube apparatus Adam had employed all the years he had worked up here. In a way they saw it as a recantation, an admission that the new ways were, after all, inferior to the old and when he remained up there fourteen months, making but fleeting visits to ground level, they told one another that he had mended his ways and not before time.

They would have been outraged had they realised that what George was doing was to use his father's eyrie as a kind of Guy Fawkes' cellar, to hatch a plot aimed at erasing every familiar aspect of the yard and setting in motion shock waves that would be felt in every corner of the network beyond. Neither did they suspect that the tidal wave that followed would wash every last one of them into premature retirement, making way for newcomers who would talk a language largely unintelligible to them, who would think in terms of horse-*power* rather than horses and whose avowed purpose would be to reduce haulage schedules, routes and laden capacity to a series of formulae that made no kind of sense to them.

For all that, they were not entirely wrong about him. There was about his withdrawal a hint of the Adam of the 'sixties and 'seventies, a man who found it essential to commune with himself in solitude before he could focus his mind on the immensity of his task and solve a thousand closely interrelated hypothetical conundrums. For what George was doing in the fourteen months that succeeded the submission of his engineer's report that a fleet of motor-vehicles was costed down to the last detail, was to redesign the national arena in which the fleet would operate. Such a task, far more formidable than any his father had tackled in his up-and-coming days, needed not merely physical stamina but a very high degree of concentration. To say nothing of access to the hundreds of route maps and trade summaries built up over the forty-two years Swann-on-Wheels had been in operation.

No one else could have done it. No one else could have attempted it and there was a reason for this. George Swann, New Broom Extraordinary, was the firm's only real link between past, present and future. At least, the future as he saw it.

It was, he came to decide, a matter of gradients. Everything in his flirtation with power-driven vehicles over the past twenty years suggested that gradients were the key to every imponderable. Perhaps others would see it differently, would give priority to factors like wear and tear of rolling stock, centres of population, concentrations of industry, quality of road surfaces and other come-day-go-day aspects of the hauling trade. But George's experience equipped him to survey each of these factors separately and make a deliberate choice as to which of them demanded maximum attention. It did not take him long, after studying Scottie Quirt's report, to select gradients as the keystone of the exercise. Everything else was relative. Everything hinged upon a single, determinable axiom, viz: 'Can a Swann-Maxie waggon haul a given weight from point A to B if a gradient, in excess of a given limit, interposes between point of departure and point of arrival?' If it could, well and good. If it could not one might as well consign the whole complex of dreams to the wastepaper basket and indent for fifty thousand pounds' worth of younger horseflesh and new waggons, leaving the advancement of power-driven vehicles to the wealthy amateur with time on his hands and a bottomless pocket.

It looked at first as if the answer to this equation was negative. Swann's main routes, according to copies of Adam's maps (the originals still occupied pride of place in The Hermitage museum, at 'Tryst') established that a laden waggon, with flexible traction as regards the number of horses employed per haul, could be dragged over almost any terrain where business was to be found. All the initiator was required to do was to increase teams or change the nature of the waggon in relation to the load and the natural obstacles in question. Bearing this in mind the entire country was wide open and Adam Swann had proved as much forty years ago. Swann's frigates regularly crossed the Pennine Ridge and used unsurfaced cart-tracks in the remotest areas of Wales and the West-country. Its pinnacles, with one nimble Cleveland Bay between the shafts, threaded the most congested centres of the nation's cities, usually without loss of routeing time, for there was always a maze of side streets available. Even Swann's men-o'-war and Goliaths, eight-, six-, and four-horse vehicles, could, given a leisurely time schedule and diligent routeing, haul enormous loads clear across country, from North Sea coast to Cardigan Bay. But Scottie Quirt's report confirmed that one could not hope for such flexibility if one substituted power-driven vehicles for the drag-horse. Britain was not a level plain, served by modern bridges. There were always, God curse them, gradients, some a mere one in ten but often as steep as one in five, or even four, that could defeat, with a sneer-scream of grit or a flurry of liquid mud, the maximum thrust of a Swann-Maxie engine.

It had not needed his experiences on the trial run south to teach him this, although those experiences highlighted the two-edged sword suspended over the neck of the too-hasty innovator. Two-edged because it involved not only ascents but descents. Whereas it was a matter of routine to apply drag-shoes at the summit of a hill before tackling a sharp descent with a waggon, one now had to rely upon braking power and he foresaw that it might be years before some bright spark evolved a foolproof method of checking a fully-laden waggon on a one-in-four hill. One could not always rely on the presence of an amiable and inventive amateur, awaiting one's thundering descent into a ford, as had occurred early in the trial trip. Neither could one bank on the presence of an evangelist knife-grinder to straighten things out, as had occurred on his second day's run into London. He saw now, looking back, that he had enjoyed the devil's own luck on that trial run south. Who could hope for such fortunate encounters when Swann's new waggons were making daily runs from the Tay to the Channel, from the Wash to Cardigan Bay?

It was then that he began to regret his arbitrary abolition of the localised structure of the network. With the original seventeen territories reduced to a mere five, with the scrapping of the old patriarchal system, and the new (and so far successful) policy of centralisation, the initiative of the regions had been superseded. More and more hauls were planned and routed from Headquarters. Improvisation on the part of provincial viceroys was not encouraged. Indeed, in many respects it was frowned upon. The power of the men out there had been subtly curtailed as they had learned to rely more and more upon the guiding hand of Headquarters, less and less upon their own reactions to local problems and this policy had seemed to pay dividends. For one thing, it put a stop to regional jealousies. For another, it checked indiscriminate exchange of teams, waggons and even contracts between managers who liked one another and overall reluctance to co-operate between men who did not. It knit the entire enterprise together. It encouraged a variety of lucrative by-products, not least among them a far closer co-operation with the railways than any achieved in his father's day. But it had, as he now saw with dismaying clarity, a fatal defect. It introduced a system of long, interlocked hauls over all kinds of terrain, and Maxies could not adapt to such demands. In a month, he suspected, head-quarters would be swamped with reports of ditched vehicles, stranded loads of perishable goods, helpless drivers and infuriated customers. In bad weather half the fleet would be off the roads. And in six months Swann's forty-year-old boast, that he could haul anything any-where in less time than his liveliest competitor, would become a tavern jest. What could result from that but ruin?

It cost him a great deal to face up to this conclusion. His faith in the petrol engine was all but absolute and he never doubted, not even now, that a time would come when nobody but a rural baker's roundsman would invest a penny in a horse as part of his stock-in-trade. But geo-graphy was geography and, although extremely obstinate, he was not so pig-headed as to risk his own future, plus the livelihood of three thousand men, on a fiction that wishing it could reduce Britain to a level plain, like the old

Crescent Centre territory in Lincolnshire. At the same time, as in all human equations, there had to be an answer and he set himself to find it.

*   *   *

The answer, when it came, was so obvious that it hit him like a piece of falling tackle, projecting him nose foremost into the jumble of maps, sketches and half-finished sums that covered his desk.

It was there in that same summarisation of his father's maps that he had brought up here a day or so after receiving and studying Scottie's report, and it now lay buried under so much clutter that he had to dig for it.

There it was, a curious relic among all those figures and designs and memoranda, a scale condensation of the seven original maps Adam had drawn up in 1858, between them embracing every shire in England and Wales, for neither Scotland nor Ireland featured on Swann maps of the period.

He unrolled it almost reverently, a piece of parchment measuring about three feet by two, with every regional border sketched in and, what was more to the point, every railway line and contour marked in coloured inks. The old discarded nicknames were there – the Bonus, the Kentish Triangle, the Polygon and so on, and as he identified them one by one he was afforded a searching glance into his father's mind when he had split the country into so many irregular and disparate sections. For Adam, at that time, had clearly been beset by the identical problem – gradients, and what they meant in turns of profitable road haulage.

The key was there and he used it to unlock his memories, memories of a hundred conversations he had had with his father about the early days of the network. Some were sharp and clear but others needed to be chased into corners, and it was one of these that convinced him, without a shadow of a doubt, that the answer was almost within his grasp. Something about a railway engineer who had counselled Adam on the subject of investing his capital . . . something to do with natural obstacles standing between Swann and his destiny. And then, with a growl of triumph, he heard his father's voice speak across the years from a time when the two of them had been stuck in a fogbound railway coach on their way home to 'Tryst', when he was little more than a boy. The voice said, ". . . Fellow told me to fill in the empty spaces . . . whole damned outfit emerged from that." And in response to George's query as to the wisdom of staking everything he possessed in a single idea Adam's gruff reply, "Never had second thoughts about it . . . Believed in what was happening around me . . . Most people didn't . . . thought the industrial wave of those days was a flash in the pan. I knew it wasn't. That's why I kept ahead of the best of 'em . . ."

He got up and went over to the wall cellarette, pouring himself a brandy four fingers high and carrying it back to the table. It gave him a lift he did not need. He had his answer. *Re*-regionalisation, and to hell with his pride! A redivision of Swann's four big units into a score of smaller ones, each self-supporting and self-administered. Only this time what would determine the regional frontiers was not the curving lines of the 1858 railway system but the factor that had drawn them in that specific pattern when Stephenson, Brunel and all the other pioneers were assembling their gridiron. *And what was that but contours?* For railroads, even now, half-a-century later, were still the slaves of rock formations and river valleys, shoulders, marshes and plateaux that took shape when the earth cooled and the islands were subdivided by as many haphazard ridges as one could expect to find on a baked apple!

He cleared the desk of everything but the map and an atlas open at a page of England and Wales unscored by his father's inks and crayons. He overlaid the smaller map with a sheet of tracing paper and began to work, drawing

a kind of parody of Adam's breakdown with an eye that
never strayed from the light and dark brown shading of
the highlands, not even when he reached for his glass, put
it to his lips and sipped the undiluted spirit. And as his
pencil skimmed the tracing a new regional network
emerged with startling clarity, a minced and sliced version of an England ripe for conquest by Scottie Quirt's
fleet of Swann-Maxies, all but two of them still on the
drawing board awaiting Headquarters' go ahead. The
borders almost drew themselves, bondsmen of the
Cheviots, the Cotswolds, the Chilterns, the Cambrians,
the more testing areas of the Pennine Chain and the high
plateaux of the Westcountry moors. A few regions were
much larger than Adam's but most were smaller, separated from one another by gradients that a petrol-powered
waggon could never hope to climb unless it tackled them
unladen. And even then, in places like Shap, Dartmoor,
the Fells and the North Riding it would do so at risk.

Day after day he sat there, tracing, retracing, noting
down, calculating distances in relation to centres of industry where his customers were thick upon the ground,
siting motor depots with an allocation of light horse transport, and sub-depots on the lower slopes of the highlands
where, at a pinch, he could call on teams of draught
horses to help power-driven freight over a hump and ease
it down a steep declivity.

It was the evolution of this emergency scheme that
established yet another principle in his mind. It was no
longer a question of either/or, of retaining or banishing
the heaviest of his draught animals and settling for the
new at the expense of the old. For here, surely, was an
exercise in long-term phasing, of combining horse and
mechanical thrust to combat the freakish terrain of the
islands. If a haul necessitated the crossing of a frontier,
and that frontier ran along a high ridge approached by
steep hills on either side, then draught teams could be
whistled up in advance to be used in a haulage or braking
capacity. But the bulk of the journey, on both sides of

such a barrier, could be accomplished at three or four times the speed of an old-style frigate or man-o'-war and Swann-on-Wheels would thus enjoy the best of both worlds.

His fancy, and a sense of deep indebtedness to Adam, led him to conjure with a spate of nicknames for his newly-defined regions. The Mountain Square, generally speaking impossible terrain for a Maxie, was all but abandoned to the horse. So was the long central spine of England, from the Southern Uplands between Solway and the Cheviots, all the way down to the Peak area, west of Sheffield. He called this Pennine strip The Chain, pencilling in sub-depots at Appleby, Keighley, Penistone and Bakewell.

In the old Western Wedge he set about similar fragmentation, establishing sub-depots at Barnstaple and Ashburton commanding Exmoor and Dartmoor respectively. Between the Mendips and the Quantocks, where few really formidable slopes interposed between Taunton and the Bristol Channel, he formed a new unit, naming it The Link, for it served this purpose between the far west and easier territory that stretched away as far as the Thames estuary and the Wash where river roads were plentiful and surfaces among the best in the country.

Away to the east, in the old regions Adam had called The Bonus, and The Crescents, there were no sub-depots. The land was flat and rivers were well-bridged, all the way up from the capital to the Vale of York, then east again to the Humber and the Naze. In the main, this was ideal Swann-Maxie country, where teams could be freed by the dozen to earn their oats on the gradients further west and north. He named this two-hundred-mile section The Funnel because that, on his new maps, was how its shading appeared to him. Then, and then only, he addressed himself to Scotland, where motor-vehicles could operate without much difficulty in the Lowlands whereas the horse would likely hold its own for decades north of the Tay. The same, in a sense, applied to Ireland.

Broadly speaking Ulster, Leinster and Munster were open to the Swann-Maxie but there seemed no profit in sending them into Connaught or down into the far west.

When his maps were completed and neatly redrawn for the brochure he planned, he turned to costing, and after that to compiling a short list of candidates for regional control and the younger cadres who would be given their chance as managers of the sub-depots. He worked from a roll of names sent up on request by Accounts. Some were managers of proven ability, like Rookwood, Higson, Godsall and Markby, men who already controlled regions of their own, but in the longer list were a score of youngsters in their 'twenties, whose latent abilities showed up in last year's bonus slips. Finally he compiled a detailed report for Scottie Quirt, telling him to hold himself in readiness for conference confirmation of a fleet of sixty vehicles, to be put into commission as they emerged from the workshop and sent out to work the day they completed their test-runs.

He did not realise how spent he was until he had despatched the brochure to the printers. On the way down the spiral staircase he staggered and had to make a grab for the rail. He thought, 'By God, I need a break and I've earned one! I'll take it before I put it to the directors' conference. They'll need a fortnight to digest it and I daresay I'll have to spend myself all over again convincing the doubters. Some of them are getting set in their ways and I can't really rely on the backing of more than a few . . . chaps like Jake Higson up in Scotland, and Godsall, who has always been the most forward-looking of the originals . . .' So he made his decision on the spot. He would take Gisela and the children down to 'Tryst' for a few days and try it out on the old dog fox before the day set for the conference. It would be interesting to see how the Gov'nor reacted to a scheme that was, in essence, his cartographical grandchild.

2

In the very earliest days of his venture Adam Swann had seen himself as an isolated traveller with his eyes fixed on a far distant objective, separated from him by a wide and varied terrain. But the peak, despite distance and haze, had always been there, stark, clear, beckoning and infinitely desirable.

He did not think of it in fanciful terms, as the Celestial Mountains or El Dorado for he was not a fanciful man, rather a supreme individualist who, although well-endowed with imagination, had learned how to employ fancy to practical purpose, evidenced by the lighthearted nicknames he bestowed upon his vehicles and territories. He thought of it as The Summit and was not deeply concerned regarding the prospect it might offer him when he arrived there.

Very soon after setting out he was joined by Henrietta, then by his motley crew of privateersmen and finally, in late middle age, by his grown sons and daughters, all of whom, it seemed, had their eyes fixed on some adjoining peak, but there never had been a time, not even when he journeyed alone, when he regarded his odyssey as a private endeavour. It was one he shared, willy-nilly, with his tribe as a whole, for he always saw himself as a standard-bearer of the era travelling only one step ahead of his fellow-countrymen, the English, and their proven allies, the Scots and the Welsh. He discounted the Irish as a race of by-roads dawdlers, temperamentally unsuited to a haul of this length and complexity.

As time went on he drew appreciably nearer his goal, adjusting his pace somewhat and taking time to look around him as he progressed, but he was still untroubled by what lay beyond the furthest ridge. A man's life-span did not run to that, he would have argued. Somewhere along the road ahead he would, inevitably, drop out of the line of march, surrendering the vanguard to a seasoned successor and this successor could only be George, the

closest reflection, without his experience, of himself in his
early thirties.

Thus it was that he welcomed George when the boy at
last emerged from his hibernation period, guessing that
what he would have to say would concern, among other
things, the march-plan into the future. For George,
lucky dog, was young enough and strong enough to concern himself with the prospect beyond the summit.

He heard him out in almost complete silence, interject-
ing no more than an occasional question and that a shrewd
one, for the old man, George noted, still retained his fan-
tastic memory for terrain and regional potential. When
George had talked himself out he gave him another ten
minutes to concentrate on the maps and was relieved
when Adam at last looked up and said, "You came up
with this alone? Up in that old belfry? No clerks? No
brain-picking discussions with Accounts and Routeing?"

"I daren't risk that, Gov'nor. I didn't know the real
answers myself until a month ago and I've had my head
down ever since. It seemed . . . well . . . dangerous to
start gossip down in the yard. You know what they are.
It would have gone out along the grapevine in a matter of
hours. Do you approve of that?"

"I certainly do," and he gave one of his hard, tight
grins, "for whenever I had anything important on hand I
made damned sure I manoeuvred myself into a position
to anticipate their tomfool objections. They were a pig-
headed bunch in those days. Always had to bully 'em
into trying anything new."

"Well?"

"Don't rush me, boy. This is a revolutionary scheme.
Far more ambitious than anything I dared to hatch up
sitting overlooking that slum. What's your spot estimate
of the cost over a twelve-month period of transition?"

George took a deep breath. "A shade under a hundred
thousand. Say the round sum to be on the safe side."

"Four-fifths of the Reserve Fund?"

"We could scale it down and borrow from the banks."

"Why do that and pay their interest? The money's there, waiting to be used isn't it?"

"Then you approve?"

"It's a damned good scheme. It's got the smell of success about it." He paused. "Didn't you expect me to say that?"

"No, I didn't. I hoped for your approval in principle. No more than that. Will you show up at conference and give it your blessing in public?"

"Not me," said Adam, fervently. "You're running the show now. It's up to you to win 'em over. If you do it's a bunch of feathers in your hat. If you don't, it's your funeral."

"You think I'll have trouble convincing them?"

"You'll have trouble, boy, but you're completely persuaded it's a practical proposition, aren't you?"

"Absolutely. I've double-checked every figure, every mile of the routes, and even my estimates can't be more than two to three per cent out."

"Well, then, you dig your heels in. Damned hard. Don't budge. And don't whittle against your better judgment. A hundred thousand, eh? That'll rattle their teeth. I shall be able to hear their sighs from here."

"Can I do that? Can I stand by that scheme without compromise if the majority vote against me?"

"Legally yes. The Swann holding is still standing at fifty-one per cent, isn't it? At a pinch we've still got over-all control. When I made the network into a private company, and let those rascals invest their own money, I gave them half-a-mile of rein. I didn't throw the curb away."

"But it isn't as simple as that, is it?"

"No, it isn't. You couldn't make it work in the face of a really determined opposition."

"Suppose I do run into opposition on that scale?"

"You hammer away at it, week by week, month by month. And you exploit their rivalries shamelessly. That was my method and I always got my own way in the end."

"That could take a long time, Gov'nor."

"Yes, it could take time. A year, maybe two or even five. But I'll tell you something, boy. You'll win in the end."

"Why necessarily?"

"Because you're my son. Because you're a natural leader and they're natural followers, every last one of 'em. If they hadn't been they wouldn't be there, still in the fold. The best of 'em would have hived off long ago and set up on their own. Even the thrusters like Godsall, and that convert to the kilt, Jake Higson."

There came to him then a heightened appraisal of his father's unique talents. Not as businessman, a gambler and an innovator. These had been apparent to him even as a child. Rather as a superbly accurate judge of potential, especially the potential of men of action, with an ability to distil past experience into a series of considered judgments on any one or any grouping of his associates. It stemmed, he supposed, from the Swann genes, developed over centuries on a thousand battlefields, and in as many embattled siege works. It reached back to the first Swann who had adopted the profession of arms, somewhere around the first years of the fifteenth century or perhaps, unrecorded, long before that, and it had been running strongly in the strain ever since, clear across the patchwork of history and Imperial conquest, from the campaigns of Henry V to the plains of India during the year of the Mutiny. It must have revealed itself in colonel and cornet and in foreign fields and in dynastic clashes in English shires, under or opposed to chieftains like Edward IV, Cromwell, Kingmaker Warwick and Prince Rupert. It had found employment on the Plains of Abraham and in that sorry business when the Anglo-American colonists in buckskins sent Cornwallis' and Burgoyne's redcoats packing. It had helped to tip the balance at Salamanca, Vittoria and Toulouse, and plant the flag on the bloody ramparts of Badajoz and Ciudad Rodrigo. It had made nonsense of Boney's ultimate bid for Europe on a Brussels plain, where his own grandfather had left two of his fingers. He said, as a kind of admission of his unpaid ancestral debt, "I'd sooner have you behind me than the whole bunch of them, Gov'nor. That's what I came seeking. Your blessing."

The old man mused for a moment. Finally he said, with a shrug, "You don't need anyone back of you, George. Not really. Not when the cards are dealt. Edith Wadsworth, the woman they all thought of as my mistress at one time, once likened 'em to a bunch of privateers, planning a descent on someone's coast, and she was about right. But a privateer doesn't cast off without a captain it can trust, and even the share-and-share alike pirates sailed under a quartermaster. You'll do, boy. Always thought you would somehow."

He watched George gather up his papers, throw a knowing wink in his direction and saunter out, seeing himself forty years ago and feeling glad that his battles were behind him.

3

Of the twelve original managers who bought themselves in when Adam (tiring of having his policies challenged by men who claimed the right to hector him without risking their own cash) made a private company of the concern, only five still sat on as directors. The other seven had either died or been replaced by successors in the regions. George thought of these five as the hard core of Swann-on-Wheels, who had seen it grow to maturity and who regarded their stake, rightly or wrongly, as more than financial.

Godsall, once an army officer, had ruled in the old Kentish Triangle. He now controlled the whole south-eastern beat of the network. 'Young' Rookwood (George reckoned his age at fifty-three) was the Dick Whittington of Swann-on-Wheels, having risen from vanboy to the rank of viceroy in what was once known as the Southern

Square. His enlarged beat now extended north to the
Midlands and west as far as the rural territory of the late
Hamlet Ratcliffe, who had died at his post on the eve of
Victoria's Golden Jubilee. Ratcliffe's place on the board
had been taken by his nephew, Bickford, a shrewd forty-
year-old, known throughout the network as 'Bertieboy'
Bickford. Scotland was controlled by another ex-vanboy,
Jake Higson. The East Midlands were still under the sway
of the Wickstead family, the sons of Edith and Tom Wickstead, whose independence was tempered by their devotion to Adam, the only man in the network aware that
Tom Wickstead had once been a professional footpad.
Tom, ailing now, had been succeeded in the old Crescent
lands by his son Luke, a young man who had always seemed
to George excessively shy. Further north, between the
Yorkshire coast and the Pennines, Markby, a comparative
newcomer, had made great strides of late. Markby was
an innovator. It was he who had forced through a policy
of purpose-built vehicles and he could usually be relied
upon to put forward some constructive propositions at the
quarterly conferences. Over in the West, in the old
Mountain Square lands embracing all Wales, they had a
new viceroy in the person of young Edward Swann, whose
coming-of-age present had been a managership and a seat
on the board earlier that year. Edward would have to be
regarded as a new boy and expected to keep his mouth
shut on anything but topics concerning his own beat.
Clint Coles, representing Ireland, would also be ham-
strung by family ties, although George felt he could rely
on his brother-in-law's vote on a major proposition. Clint
(the Swann family still thought of him as Jack-o'-Lantern,
a soubriquet he had acquired when he eloped with Joanna
Swann) was a fine salesman and a very amiable man, and
he and George had always seen eye to eye.

There were two imponderables, Morris, once of the
prosperous Southern Pickings territory around Worcester,
and Dockett, a wayward character who had made a great
success in Tom Tiddler's Land, otherwise the Isle of

Wight. Morris was elderly now, and long retired, but he
had the keenest financial brain in the network and was
very active on the board, where he kept a sharp eye on
cash reserves and could bear down heavily on anyone he
suspected of relegating the profit motive to any notch
below number one on Swann's list of priorities. Dockett
was the reverse, a gambler who had no patience with men
who played safe. It was Dockett, who, as far back as
1863, had proposed specialisation in his own most profitable line, that of house removals, and had later initiated
the saucy slogan painted on all Swann's house removal
waggons, '*From Drawer to Drawer*'. He seemed a likely sup-
porter for a scheme as grandiose as George's.

He pondered them all separately, trying to assess their
reactions to the fat brochure, illustrated with maps and a
diagram of the Swann-Maxie prototype sent to all directors a fortnight in advance of the summer meeting, and his
conclusions were guardedly optimistic. Edward and Jack-
o'-Lantern were, so to speak, safely in his pocket. He
was almost equally sure of Markby, in the North, and of
Dockett, who now played a leading role in Swann's coastal
and Continental trade. That, with his own vote, meant a
nucleus of five but he needed support elsewhere unless he
was to face the long-term prospect of ramming the venture
down managerial throats. Between them men like Rookwood and Godsall could rally a great deal of support among
the relatively inexperienced men around the table,
youngsters like Luke Wickstead, known to be cast in a
cautious mould, so that it was with some misgivings that
he sensed restraint on the part of both Rookwood and
Godsall when they greeted him and he took his seat at the
head of the table.

In the old days the board meetings had always been
held in the original warehouse. Now, the warehouse
having gone up in smoke, they gathered in comfort in
the board room, south of the tower where the atmosphere,
although more comfortable, did not encourage the breezy
give-and-take of the old, privateering days. It was a pity,

George thought, that the Gov'nor had declined to chair the meeting, even in a neutral capacity. The most independent among them still had affection for him, besides deep respect for his judgments. He was also a terse but effective speaker, a talent George had not inherited. He lacked his father's sense of irony that had always helped to cool tempers and heal feuds. Accustomed to working alone he lacked the patience to reason with the querulous and suffer the windbag gladly. In his view a man who had not studied his subject matter down to the last detail had best remain silent and he was uneasily aware that no one around that table knew much about the vagaries or the potential of mechanical transport. Alone among them Godsall owned a motor but it was chauffeur-driven and as a first-class horseman he had a contempt for anything that went on under the bonnet. Indeed, George suspected that Godsall's car was maintained for reasons of social prestige rather than personal prestige.

He tried to compensate for this deficiency in his opening speech. After the usual preamble he developed a theme based on the dramatic headstart a fleet of petrol-driven waggons would give Swann-on-Wheels over its competitors. Mechanically propelled transport was not unique in the trade. Several rival hauliers ran steam waggons, double-crank Fodens mostly of the traction type, used for short, heavy haulage. A few were experimenting with the new ten hundredweight Albion 'dogcart' on suburban routes. But a fleet of sixty heavy vehicles, working from provincial depots placed at strategically sited points across the country, was something entirely new in the concept of road haulage. He was aware, of course, that the staking of almost the entire reserve fund on a single gigantic project entailed risk, but he argued that it was a carefully calculated risk. That was why he suggested a slow phasing out of the horse over a period that might extend into ten or twelve years. The limitation of power-driven vehicles to comparatively short runs in the initial years was, he said, designed to accumulate experience without the risk of slowing down deliveries and increasing insurance rates.

He sat down unconvinced that he had made the best of his case, and telling himself, rather petulantly, that a speech of that kind should not have been necessary. It was all there in the brochure for anyone but a fool to see and if any one of them had failed to understand the tremendous implications of the report that man had no right to be sitting here.

The long, uneasy silence that followed his invitation for comments gave him his second clue to the overall mood of the gathering. It was clearly one of extreme uncertainty and nervousness, based less on the general proposal than on the amount of capital demanded. It was difficult, he supposed, for ex-gamins like Higson and Rookwood to think in terms of a hundred thousand pounds, when they probably recalled the earning of sixpence as the hallmark of a profitable day on the Thames foreshore. He waited, glumly, for what seemed a long minute and then, at a nod from Rookwood, Godsall stood up to address the chair.

George had always enjoyed a good, working relationship with Godsall, seeing him as the most go-ahead of the viceroys, and he looked for a sign of this accord now. Godsall, however, avoided his eye, addressing himself to the wings rather than the head of the conference and his first words were a storm signal.

"For a long time now, gentlemen, it has been an open secret that the Chairman and I have seen eye to eye in most matters . . ." and George took this as an expiatory remark, designed to soften the impact of what followed. He was right, for Godsall went on, "However, at this early stage of the proceedings, I am obliged to confess that I find myself implacably opposed to the project so lucidly set out in the Chairman's brochure. Not, I hasten to add, in principle, but certainly in particular, but if I had to say why, in a few words, it would be difficult. It seems to me – as I gather it does to others present – that we are being asked to swallow at one gulp a meal that might, in the long run be very nutritious but, in the manner of taking, could so damage the digestion as to put Swann-on-Wheels on bicarbonate of soda for years!"

George, looking down at the table, did not see the titter that ran down both sides of the table for what it was, a release of nervous tension. To him, momentarily stunned by Godsall's polite perfidy, it was a barb signifying unanimity, or near unanimity, of their rejection and ridicule of the plan. In a flash he was a boy again, standing in a classroom holding a blotched exercise exposed to the usher's irony, and he thought bitterly: 'God damn him! He could have given me a hint . . . *One* of them could have hinted . . . written . . . questioned the practicality of the project before we assembled here and before I took it for granted any objections would be based on technicalities . . . !' But then, with a tremendous effort, he got his resentment in hand in order to give his entire attention to Godsall's devastating analysis of the brochure and form some kind of judgment as to the essence and validity of his dissent. He realised then that Godsall's opening admission had been honest. The man was not opposed in principle to the switch. He was merely rejecting its breadth and totality.

He had to concentrate hard to follow the drift of the speech. Odd phrases and deductions evaded him, slipping away and drowning in a sea of bile . . . "the Chairman is aware, as must be everyone sitting round this table, that I have never set my face against the prospect of an eventual phasing out of the horse in favour of power-driven vehicles . . . seen it as inevitable in the long run . . . will admit, unreservedly, that the introduction of, say, a few power-driven vans, as a very useful experiment offering guidelines to the policy of the years ahead . . . but what is proposed here is certainly not that! It is total committal that could put the entire enterprise in jeopardy at a prohibitive cost in order to prove -- what? That power-driven transport is on the way in? That it is

possible (as our Chairman himself has proved) to make a
two-day haul over two hundred miles with a load of over
a ton aboard? That a well-designed waggon, powered by
petrol or steam, can move over chosen territory faster than
a man-o'-war? Or even a frigate, pulled by the best team
in our regional stables? But surely, gentlemen, these
things don't need proving. Certainly not at the cost of a
reserve fund it has taken us years to accumulate against an
emergency or series of emergencies . . . !"

Every face was turned away from him now. Rookwood,
Markby, Higson and even Bertieboy Bickford and young
Edward were straining their ears in order not to miss a
syllable of Godsall's merciless rhetoric.

". . . No one here can point a finger at me as a man who
sets his face against anything new *because* it is new, but
to invest in power to this extent is to walk a tightrope from
one end of the country to the other, and for a very simple
reason. What is that reason? I believe the Chairman is
more keenly alive to it than any of us. His experience
with power-driven commercial haulage goes back years,
to the time of the earliest prototypes. He is one of the
pioneers and we respect him for it. But he will tell you,
if you ask him, that the performance of one of these
vehicles can be very impressive for two days running. He
would not guarantee that performance for ten such
vehicles over a month or a year. Or twenty. Or sixty
within the foreseeable future. To do that, while running
a day-to-day business hauling goods over every kind of
terrain, and under every kind of condition, is not so much
to put one's head in a noose as to trust one's weight to a
single rope, insecurely fastened. I am all for progress,
gentlemen, and the widest possible range of experimentation, but I am not prepared to face that terrible risk. Not
yet. Not until we have actual proof that the power-
propelled vehicle hauling over, say, ten hundredweights, is
not only faster but more dependable than a horse bred for
haulage."

He sat down rather unexpectedly and there was a buzz

of assent. At least George, glowering at the far end of the table, took it for assent, and when nobody seemed disposed to offer the first comment he said, quietly, "Do I take it you intend to move an amendment to the proposition printed on the last page of the brochure, Godsall?"

"No, sir," Godsall said, promptly, "not at this stage. Not before a full and free discussion."

"Very well, then let me put it this way. If Mr. Godsall's opposition to a fleet of sixty Swann-Maxies *was* couched in an amendment, is there anyone here who would second it?"

Rookwood rose. "I would, Mr. Chairman."

Somehow George had sensed he would endorse Godsall's sentiments. Unlike all the men around the table, with the exception of Jake Higson, his fellow waif, Rookwood had served Swann-on-Wheels in every conceivable capacity over the years, all the way up from urchin vanboy, swinging on a tailboard rope, to staid and highly respected manager of a huge slice of territory in the south. He was a humourless man, slow to make decisions, but when those decisions had been taken he was tireless, inflexible and unshakeably loyal to the interests of the undertaking. He said, looking directly at the chair, "Everything Mr. Godsall said made sense to me. My observation in this field has left me with the impression that petrol-driven vans are superior for light work in congested areas but inferior to reliable teams hauling full loads over long distances. I have even gone so far as to make checks in this respect, on haulage undertaken by Wetherby and Sons, in my area. They hauled a turbine down to Southampton Docks by mechanical waggon last February. The journey, allowing for breakdowns, occupied forty-eight hours. According to my calculations" – he glanced at a sheet of paper he held in readiness – "one of our Goliaths could have accomplished it in thirty hours, allowing two hours lost in city hold-ups."

"Wetherby uses steam-waggons." This from Markby, on Rookwood's immediate right.

"That's so. He operates two on my beat. Traction-engines, that can average nine miles an hour on the flat and the route he took on this occasion was flat in the main. Both breakdowns occurred on gradients. One of one in nine, the other a shade in excess of nine."

You had to hand it to Rookwood. He was a man who very rarely generalised and whose homework could never be faulted. George thought, glumly: 'I wish to God I had him on my side but that's asking too much of Rookwood. He's never taken a real risk in his life, and he'd probably tell you that was the secret of his success.' He looked carefully down both sides of the table. No one else seemed eager to commit themselves. He said, "We'd best give everyone a chance to speak. This thing is far too big for free and easy discussion. I rule we take it in turn. Down one side and up the other. What's your view, Bickford?"

Bertieboy Bickford, operating in the west where, so far, nothing but agricultural traction had been seen, much less used, looked flustered. He was, Adam would have said, a very likely successor to his uncle, the rumbustious Hamlet Ratcliffe, who had always succeeded in surprising them despite mountainous prejudices, a bucolic appearance and a buzzsaw Westcountry accent like Bickford's own. Ratcliffe, no doubt, would have set his face against an innovation on this scale but he would have stated his objections in a way that brought a whiff of humour into the proceedings and Bertieboy was equal to his uncle's memory. He said now, in a brogue that vividly reminded the long-termers of the man who had died hauling a huge statue of Queen Victoria over rough Devon roads when he was in his eightieth year; "They things coulden tackle the roads in my beat Maister, so that lets me out. I dessay the Chairman thowt o' that when he drew up this scheme. Some places you have to hitch four horses to a frigate to haul a load o' turnips over one of our humps and then be bliddy smart wi' the shoes to stop 'er backsliding. I take it these yer trucks would be used on the flat mostly. Did you 'ave that in mind, Mr. Swann?"

"Not entirely," George said, "as you'll see under the sub-heading dealing with branch depots. But you're right about your territory. I wouldn't risk them in the west as yet. That would be asking for trouble."

"Well, then, 'tis none o' my bizness, is it?"

"Yes it is. You're a shareholder, the same as everyone sitting round this table. And in any case, you've always kept your end up down there and I'd appreciate your opinion. Say whatever you've a mind to say."

Bickford frowned, slowly massaging the side of his long, thin nose with his forefinger. "Well an' good, Mr. Chairman. Well, yer's what I have to say. Time was when my Uncle Hamlet was called upon to haul a circus lion all the way down the Exe Valley and put Swann on the map doin' it, as some of you might remember. I was only a tacker at the time but I can tell you this. Uncle Hamlet woulden have coaxed no lion into one of they bliddy contraptions. That old rascal would've been running free on Exmoor yet if Uncle 'Amlet hadn't had a waggon an' team back of him."

It was enlistment with the opposition but George welcomed the comment for all that. It relieved the unbearable tension and went some way towards liberating successive speakers, inhibited by the bluntness of Godsall and Rookwood. Markby was for the gamble, pointing out that the reputation of Swann had been built on innovation and conceding George's claim that a fleet of sixty waggons, designed for heavy traffic, would give them an impressive start over every other haulage firm in the country. "A twopenny-ha'penny carrier on my beat has already captured the Whitby fish trade with one of those light vans," he said. "As time goes on we'll have to face up to stiffer and stiffer competition, not only with other hauliers but with the railways. I've got word they're talking about putting in two-tonners at Darlington, and one or two of the bigger distribution centres up north. I say let's take the plunge and be done with it!"

Young Edward took the same line although, operating

in hilly country west of Offa's Dyke, he had the same claim to neutrality as Bickford. He had read the brochure three times, he said, without benefit of private discussion with his brother, and it seemed to him, a new boy among them, that the entire future of haulage lay with power-propelled vehicles. He sat down, blushing, but then, against probability, Jake Higson came down on the side of caution, and so did young Wickstead. Not because either of them doubted the long-term prospects of motor haulage but solely on grounds of expenditure. A cheaper scheme, with the emphasis on experimentation should be considered, they said, for the virtual wiping out of the central reserve fund would leave every region at the mercy of a bad winter, of the kind some recalled in the past when half the roads in the country turned to slush, river valleys overflowed and an impossible strain was put on teams, waggons and waggoners.

Clinton Coles, speaking for Ireland, took a character-istic line. An inveterate gambler, he was for immediate expansion but his support did not mean as much as it might have done. Careful consideration had been given to the Irish terrain and there was far less competition over there than in the other regions, even in Scotland north of the Tay and in North Wales, where one-man carriers were thick on the ground.

When everyone had had their say, including half-a-dozen comparative newcomers who had nothing new to contribute, George asked Godsall to frame his amendment during a lunch break and put it when they reconvened at one-thirty. He did not join them for the usual convivial session at the old George Inn, judging it best to leave them to argue among themselves over their beer and beef sandwiches. Instead he took himself off to his tower, having no stomach for food but carrying his brandy over to the embrasure where he had a clear view of the Thames, shimmering in summer heat that seemed to slow the pass-age of the tugs and barges shooting London Bridge. He no longer felt like a schoolboy holding a blotched exercise but like a general facing incipient mutiny, and he longed with all his heart for his father's counsel. It was here, he supposed, in every cranny of the ancient chamber, where Adam had spent half his life, but he was too bewildered and too tired to locate it. His mind grappled with the verdict resulting from a show of hands. Markby, Edward and Jack-o'-Lantern were all he could count on. Plus, possibly, two or three of the newcomers, who had little to lose and were still sufficiently awed by his father's ghost to vote for his successor. Seven, more likely six, facing the landslide of hardheaded experience and prestige set in motion by Godsall, Rookwood and Higson, men whose support he desperately needed. It wasn't enough. It wasn't nearly enough. His father said he would win through in the end and so he would, he supposed, when it became obvious to every child in Britain that the horse would follow the longbow and the three-decker warship. But by then he would have lost his headstart and all a switch-over would mean would be a jockeying for position among the nation's leading transporters. He was not interested in that kind of campaign.

*   *   *

Godsall's amendment, promptly seconded by Rookwood, was lucid. It proposed a scaling down to ten Swann-Maxies, placed at carefully selected depots in favourable terrain, and limited the maximum expenditure to twenty thousand. After a two-year period the whole position could be reviewed. If the figures were encouraging he would withdraw all his objections. George saw the real sting was in the tail of his speech, however, when he said: "Thus restructuring of the entire network will be avoided, for what is this proposal but a return to regionalism? Do any of us want that, with all the wasteful rivalry it entailed in the old days? Let any power-driven vehicles we put into commission prove to us they can run independently of the horse. Don't let us set ourselves up as a target for a *Punch* cartoon, with lame-duck vehicles pulled home by horses, the way half of them are as yet." He sat down and when George did not immediately rise, he said, "I take it you'll exercise your right to reply, Mr. Chairman."

"No," said George, "I won't. Not out of pique but because I've said all I have to say in that brochure. We'll take the amendment. All in favour?"

Three hands went up at once, those of the proposer, seconder and Jake Higson. Two others followed more reluctantly, Bickford's and Luke Wickstead's. Then five of the six new men voted in Godsall's favour, a total of ten. Markby, Young Edward, Clint Coles and Coreless, one of the new men from the Polygon area, stood with George. Dockett, for reasons best known to himself, abstained. The amendment was carried, ten votes to five, with one abstention.

They broke up without the usual jocular exchanges. The tension of the meeting carried over into adjournment but Godsall approached him looking troubled and said, "No hard feeling, George? I only spoke out of my deepest convictions."

"That's your privilege," George said, "but you're wrong, for all that."

"I'm not that much of a gambler," Godsall said. "We've all come a long way since the 'sixties and for most of us it was a hard, uphill pull." Then, hands in breeches pockets, he lounged off, without stopping to confer with his supporters and in ten minutes all but young Edward had gone.

Edward said, falling into step with his brother as he crossed the yard to the tower: "I wouldn't take it that hard, George. Ten Maxies will prove your point in less than two years, won't they?"

"It's not the same, lad. The Gov'nor saw what I was driving at. It's Swann's loss that they couldn't or wouldn't."

"Will you be catching the train at London Bridge now?"

"No. Someone from the Midlands is waiting to see me. He wrote for an appointment four days ago and I told him I couldn't see him until after conference. He's only in town for the day." He took a card from his pocket. '*Jas. L. Channing. Birmingham Castings*'. Have we ever hauled for them?"

"No," Edward said, promptly, "but I've heard of them. Steel people, working exclusively on Government contracts."

George smiled, his first smile of the day. "You've got the Gov'nor's memory," he said. "Tell him how it went, will you? And say Gisela and I will probably be down for the inquest on Sunday."

"I'll do that, George," and he plodded off, with that curious Sam Rawlinson gait of his, deliberate, square-toed, vaguely aggressive, and George thought, 'He'll be a big man in this outfit before long. Bigger than any of us, I wouldn't wonder,' and turned to climb the steps to the turret, having been warned by a clerk that James L. Channing, whatever he sought, had already been appraised of the end of the conference and shown up to the eyrie. It was unusual to receive customers up here nowadays but George had no stomach for the main office, with its clutter of clerks and chatter of typewriters for the story would be all round the yard by now. The New Broom had taken the beating of his life. The wheelwrights and the farriers could breathe again. The turret drew him as a source of respite.

2

Snailpath Odyssey

HE WAS A TALL, ANGULAR MAN, WITH PIERCING GREY
eyes that gave George an impression of intense seriousness
calculated to reduce the most frivolous to instant sobriety.
The kind of man who would stand no nonsense from anyone, who could quell a riot by simply standing there.
Very erect, superbly self-contained and resolved to be
accepted at his own high valuation. A man of authority
and integrity, seldom, if ever, caught off guard. He said,
civilly, "Your business is completed, Mr. Swann? You
can spare an hour?" George said he was at his disposal
and apologised for keeping him waiting. There was only
one visitor's chair in the turret so George motioned him
to it, taking his own seat behind the desk with his back to
the light. It gave him a marginal advantage and Channing was clearly a man in whose presence one looked for
such advantages.

"Then I won't waste your time, Mr. Swann. It was
courteous of you to receive me at a time when you were
obviously fully extended. Birmingham Castings would
not mean anything to you as we have never done business,
but you will have heard of us, no doubt. We are a firm of
armourers, engaged with Government contracts. Naval
mostly but we do some commissions for the army. I know
your firm rather better, of course. It has an enviable
reputation."

His precise manner of speaking was disconcerting,

particularly after a heavy day, so that George thought, 'I was a fool to let the appointment stand . . . This joker will want action and immediate decisions and I'm not in the mood to break new ground . . ."

But the man plucked at his curiosity and he said, "Good of you to say so, Mr. Channing. What can I do for you if anything?"

Channing's thin lips twitched. It was probably as close as they ever came to a smile.

"Probably nothing. You were represented to me as my sole remaining hope. By a mutual friend, I might say, Gideon Fulbright. Your father, I believe, hauled for Fulbright over a long period. He seems to hold your father in great esteem, Mr. Swann."

"Most customers did. But my father has retired, Mr. Channing."

"So I understand." Surprisingly he broke off and shifted his searching gaze to the belfry.

"This tower was his office?"

"For forty years. He started here in the 'fifties and never cared to leave it."

"Interesting," Channing said and it was more than a formal comment. But then, with shattering directness, "I probably know a great deal more about Swann-on-Wheels than you know about my undertaking. I understand you are putting motor transport into commission."

"A limited number of vehicles, largely for experimental purposes," George said, more and more baffled by the man, "but none are on the road as yet."

"I see." He paused, placing the tips of his slender fingers together, flexing them rhythmically and breaking contact so that George saw it as a self-energising gesture, almost as though it was a means of lubricating the brain. "My business would hinge on that. Would you be prepared to tell me, in strictest secrecy, how far you are advanced in the field?"

"I don't mind telling you. As a matter of fact it's generally known in the trade. I have two vehicles ready to run up in Manchester. Another eight will be commissioned later in the year. I planned a fleet of sixty but my associates are not prepared to commit the firm to that extent. That's what we've been discussing all day."

He could not have said why he was unburdening himself to a total stranger, and a very unforthcoming one at that, but it slipped out and somehow, in the oddest way, it comforted him, enlarging the area of communication between them. There was something about Channing that suggested he was in the presence of another pioneer, another gambler even. Someone who, like George, was not only able to drive himself but would back himself into the bargain and that down to the last halfpenny in the petty-cash box. He said, "Might I offer you a brandy and a cigar, Mr. Channing?"

"Thank you, Mr. Swann. That's very civil of you," Channing replied.

George busied himself with the drinks and while he was pouring, and reaching into the back of the cellarette for the cigar box, he heard the rustle of stiff paper. When he turned Channing had spread a draughtsman's tracing on his desk. "There's my problem, Mr. Swann. It could be yours too. In passing, are you able to identify it?"

"It looks like part of a gun turret. For a heavy calibre gun, I'd say."

"Thirteen point five. The largest they fit. It's not strictly a turret. It's the cupola, the crown of the mounting and I am bending the rules more than somewhat by showing it. However, I can hardly ask you to haul something of that nature two hundred miles without returning the confidence you have extended to me. That drawing, one could say, represents the biggest single humiliation of my professional life. You see, I'm here in the capacity of a supplicant, Mr. Swann, but my pride and reputation might yet be salvaged. With your help. Your good health, Mr. Swann," and he raised his glass and emptied it without seeming to move his lips.

George picked up the drawing and studied it carefully,

a three-dimensional sketch of a squat, wedge-shaped block measuring, at a rough guess, twelve feet across and six feet in height.

"What's its overall weight, Mr. Channing?"

"Without mountings? Something in excess of six tons. That's confidential, of course."

"You're asking me to haul a six-ton load two hundred miles by a power-driven vehicle? That's impossible, Mr. Channing, even over the flat."

"But you have two such vehicles. Would it be at all practicable to couple them?"

The idea was revolutionary. Even George Swann had never contemplated coupling Maxies in an attempt to double their thrust. But *was* it so unthinkable? With some kind of platform to take the bulk of the strain linked to the sources of power. A flat-car, coupled between two railway box cars?

He said, "Give me a minute, Mr. Channing. Enjoy your cigar," and took a sheet of foolscap drawing paper from the pile he had used for mapping the new network.

For five minutes or more he was sketching, drawing freehand but using the ruler to calculate the overall length of the fanciful cavalcade. The maximum load of Scottie Quirt's prototype was around three tons but, as ever, that hinged on gradients. To drag a load like that up a one-in-eight slope was out of the question, even with a six-horse team of Clydesdales in support. It was a challenge of a kind he had never faced before and it went against the grain to resist it, but only ignominy and danger to man and vehicle could result from a jaunt of that kind. He threw his pencil aside.

"If it was a five-ton load I'd risk it. Six is one over the odds, Mr. Channing."

"Can you tell me why? In layman's language? I've had no personal experience of power-driven transport."

George explained why. It was a simple matter of engine thrusts and gradients. "I could risk hauling around two tons in excess over the flat, but you couldn't climb with that weight at your back. You would need vehicles with caterpillar wheels and even then it would be a chancy operation. Where does it have to be hauled from and to?"

"From my foundry, in Bromsgrove, to the naval yard, Devonport."

"Why can't it go by rail?"

Channing was silent. Finally he said, sourly, "I wouldn't be here, throwing myself on your mercy, Mr. Swann, if every other means had not been considered and rejected. The Admiralty, very properly, won't co-operate. Why should they? The original section that this will replace was delivered and fitted, then found to have a twenty-three-inch fissure. It was my product, personally guaranteed by me. To get it to the nearest port, Avon-mouth, would require a longish rail haul and no railway will handle it. It's not a question of weight, you under-stand, but rather of width. There is up-traffic to be con-sidered and lines would have to be cleared over the entire journey. The Government can arrange that on special occasions but it requires two months' notice. In fact, that's our regular route. For the replacement, however, I have just one week in hand, Mr. Swann."

"Why is it so urgent?"

"The ship is due to begin trials on the twenty-second of the month. The flawed part has already been stripped and discarded."

"Couldn't its replacement be fragmented?"

The lipless mouth twitched. "You may be a pioneer in motor-transport, Mr. Swann, but casting a gun-mounting of that size and quality is even more specialised. I've been at it, one way and another, since I was a boy apprentice in Armstrong-Whitworth's workshops. If it could be done, and reassembled on board, I assure you I wouldn't be here begging favours. Any haulier worth his salt could get it to Devonport piecemeal." He rose and slapped his gloves, a gesture of resignation. "Thank you for giving me your time, Mr. Swann. It isn't as if I was a long-standing client of your firm."

"Don't go, Mr. Channing."

A thought occurred to him, emerging from the jumble of the past where mental lumber rooms were crammed with network trivia. Two or more years ago he had watched carpenters at work on a ditched Goliath in the old Polygon headquarters, at Salford. He remembered them using a crane to fit the huge central beam into its sockets and hearing how the Goliath, hauling an ill-secured generator into Rochdale, had fouled an archway and held up traffic for two hours on the main Manchester road. A Goliath, specially braced, could support a six-ton load, providing it was professionally bedded-down. But it would need, he would say, a team of a dozen horses, with post changes every ten miles or so to drag it over that distance. No waggoner, however experienced, could control a string of that size over two hundred odd miles of tortuous English highway from Warwickshire to the Tamar. Everything could happen and everything probably would. The team could become unmanageable in medieval streets, heavy with traffic and presenting any number of right-angled turns and bottlenecks. In the history of the network no vehicle had ever set out from base with more than seven horses in the traces. Yet the memory of that long, lean Goliath persisted. Somewhere, in this jigsaw of factors, there was a place for it, and his imagination conjured up a vision of an improvised cavalcade, a horseless Goliath, sandwiched between two Maxies, one pulling, one pushing from behind. He took up his Atlas and opened it at the two pages portraying the Midlands and the West.

"When you came to me, when you thought the haul might be possible, did you have a road route in mind, Mr. Channing?"

"I did indeed." He took a slip of paper from his wallet and passed it over. It was not a map but a list of place names with notes alongside. Bromsgrove, Worcester, over the Severn at Tewkesbury, Gloucester, down the Severn

escuary to Bristol, north of the Mendip slopes to the flat,
negotiable country around Bridgwater, due West through
the pass between the Quantocks and the Blackdown Hills.
Then on to Exeter and the right bank of the Exe, and
thence, hugging the coast, a probe for practical gradients
across what George thought of as the udder of Devon to
Plymouth Sound. It was possible, given minute planning
and any amount of luck, with himself and Scottie Quirt at
the wheels, and Young Edward following on with the
steadiest Clydesdales they had in the stables. It *might* be
achieved, with outriders and civic co-operation in every
town they traversed but progress would not average more
than five miles an hour. Say, sixty miles a day. And
again given extraordinary luck. A four-day haul, leaving
him three to make his preparations and join Scottie in
bringing the Maxies from Manchester to Bromsgrove.
Time could be saved by borrowing a Goliath flatbed from
the nearest Swann depot, Birmingham, no doubt.

He said, trying to keep the excitement from his voice,
"You wield some sort of Government authority. Could
you get me an hour's clearance through places like Worcester, Tewkesbury, Bridgwater and Taunton? That's
imperative with a haul of this kind. We might – *might*, I
say, manage on the open road, and I'll plan a route bypassing every impossible gradient. It would mean extra
mileage, of course, but given cooling-off time we could
run from dawn to dusk."

"I can get clearances," Channing said. "We've done
that before in emergencies by appealing to the local Chief
Constables. Plus a certain amount of wire-pulling, I might
add. The mountings could go by rail. But I can't get that
overall load below six tons."

"That's a risk that has to be taken and I'll take it. My
pride is involved too, Mr. Channing. Only today my
associates as good as told me I'm living in a dream world
on their money and this challenge is tailor-made for a man
in my situation. Get those clearances. Send on the mountings, and have tackle ready to load the turret on to a

waggon I'll have on your premises by this time tomorrow. I can't guarantee the time schedule as yet. It depends on how long it takes to strip excess weight from my two motor vehicles and get them down from Manchester. Probably Wednesday, to be ready to move out on Thursday." He paused. "I'd be right glad of your company but I can't risk passengers."

"I'll be on hand," Channing said. "Good day to you, Swann." And then, glancing round the octagonal room, "Fulbright was right about your firm. 'Adam Swann,' he told me, 'would haul away the dome of St. Paul's if he was given a free hand and a guaranteed contract.' We've said nothing about mileage rates."

"How can we? Until my father has been consulted as to routeing I couldn't calculate it to the nearest fifty."

"Then your father still has a say in things here?"

"No. He just happens to know every bridlepath between here and the Grampians."

He went down the turret steps behind Channing. The yard was closing down and the skeleton night shift were lounging about the weighbridge hut at the Tooley Street entrance. "There's one other aspect, Mr. Channing. Publicity. Is that out of the question, having regard to the nature of the haul?"

"I don't see why. The cupola will ride under laced tarpaulins, I take it? I might even be able to help in that respect. We have a useful relationship with some sections of the national press." He looked at his watch. "I should be able to catch the six-forty-five from King's Cross."

He clamped his tall hat on his head and moved across the yard to his waiting cab, a tall, angular bird, who moved like a heron searching a river margin for the next meal. George stood a moment, deciding the priority of his consultations. He could be in 'Tryst' in just over the hour, spend two hours with Adam, and still catch the express north by midnight. Gisela would have to wait for a wire telling her he would be absent for upwards of ten days. It wouldn't bother her overmuch. There had been many times of late when his dinner had gone cold and been fed to Laddie, their labrador.

2

The composite vehicle, although outlandish enough to be certain of exciting curiosity wherever it travelled, was yet unlike anything he had envisaged once the cupola was bedded down and shrouded in its tarpaulin.

He had forgotten that the two Maxies, coupled fore and aft, would have to be stripped of their excess chassis fittings, for they would be used exclusively for propulsion and would carry nothing at all. Tailboards and bolted sides were removed within two hours of his arrival in Manchester and it was two very skeletal vehicles that set off on the morning of the sixteenth for Channing's foundry in Bromsgrove.

They arrived without incident and young Edward, bless the boy, was there to meet them, with his Goliath and team of eight Clydesdales, plus a plan to collect fresh teams, if necessary, at two stages en route. Edward had done some weight shedding on his own account, having shortened the central beam of the long vehicle by a good six feet, a mutilation he would be called to explain when he returned the vehicle to Melrose, the waggon-master in this area of the network.

There was no time, unfortunately, for George to get more than a quick rundown on Scottie Quirt's refinements to the Swann-Maxie since that first trial run south, more than three years ago, but he saw at once that they greatly increased his chance of hauling that terrible weight southwest over Adam's devious route, carefully traced on his maps, a job he had been able to do on the night express that rushed him north on the night of the fourteenth. The system of force-feed engine lubrication had been improved, and the rear springing greatly strengthened, but by far the

333

most important improvement was the new water-cooled braking system. One of his greatest fears had been a brake fire in the original fabric-lined footbrake. Now Scottie could assure him that the latest tests had established a safety margin in descents up to one in six, the maximum gradients they were likely to encounter on the route planned.

The route itself had all the hallmarks of Adam Swann's famed familiarity with British highways and byways. Wherever a detour could avoid a steep hill, up or down, Adam had devised one, and had also paid particular regard to the width of bridges they were obliged to cross. There would be no difficulty, he told George, in negotiating main-road bridges, like the bridge over the Severn at Tewkesbury. They were all crossed regularly by haywains as broad in the beam as the Goliath, but it was possible he would pay a high price for the unavoidable detours over second-class roads that had never, at any time in their history, carried a four-in-hand of the pre-railway era. The odd bottleneck, he warned, might well present itself here and there (he had ringed one over a tributary of the river Parret, at a place called Withypool) but his guess was that the leading edge of the load would clear the parapet, providing care was taken to load high.

The warning, in fact, presented George with his first major problem. He had to strike a precise balance between the danger of making his load top-heavy, thus courting disaster in the form of a spill on uneven ground, while providing the clearance he judged necessary for stone walls and parapeted bridges encountered during one or other of the detours. In consultation with Channing he compromised, settling for a clearance of four feet four and a half. The turret was then bedded down sideways, giving them an overall reduction in width of four inches either side and while this, in itself, reduced stability, it was a risk they had to take. A saving of eight inches on some of the stretches of second-class road included in the itinerary was essential, despite the headshakings of Channing's foreman loader.

As to fastenings, apart from four short lengths of chain securing the base of the turret to the staples of the Goliath, he used rope in preference to steel cable. High quality hawser rope offered a certain amount of flexibility. The strain imposed on a chain would prove a source of danger at every pothole and dip in the road.

The cavalcade, when it was lined up, resembled nothing within his experience. Fore and aft were the snub-nosed Maxies, that did not look like first-generation descendants of the vehicle he had driven south with a couple of tons of rice aboard. With their hooded cabins and naked chassis they suggested a couple of half-demolished covered waggons, of the kind American pioneers hauled across the prairie, whereas between them the foreshortened Goliath looked more like a raft than a waggon. In reserve, in charge of two Welsh waggoners Edward had recruited in the Mountain Square, were the eight Clydesdales, four harnessed to a man-o'-war, four more tethered behind and all looking, George thought, ashamed of enlistment in such a caravanserai. The man-o'-war they pulled was laden with stores and tools, including the tool kits of the Maxies, thus saving a little more weight. Edward said, "The team could make the whole journey with that light load at your likely pace, but I've wired for reserve teams to be held in readiness at Gloucester and Taunton. It depends how much you're likely to demand of them."

"I hope to God nothing at all, lad," George said. "They're insurance and nothing more on this kind of haul, but I'm glad you're along nevertheless. Ride in the waggon. Channing has taken upon himself the job as outrider in his Daimler. He'll keep five miles ahead and arrange clearances in the towns."

*   *   *

They moved off in the early afternoon of the sixteenth, with more than five days in hand and at the last minute Channing sent word by one of his clerks that the Admiralty had given them an extra twelve hours, reckoning that the fitting of the cupola, in Channing's presence, could be accomplished in three days. The deadline was thus set forward to one p.m. on Monday afternoon, by which time they were expected to pass the dockyard gates.

It was a perilously tight schedule, even with the twelve-hour bonus, for it allowed for no more than twenty hours for stoppages during travelling time. Quirt, after inspecting the cargo very thoroughly, said, "Could we no' travel nights, Mr. Swann? It would add a good deal to the margin, even if we moved at half speed," but George said he had set his face against night travel. The moon was in its first quarter, and the route was far too involved to risk a wrong turning or too swift a passage over rough ground. "We'll need strict march discipline," he told both Quirt and the waggoners. "At dusk we'll camp and move off again at first light. Thank God it's a June haul. At five miles an hour we could never have made it at any other season of the year."

"Will you be heading us?" Quirt wanted to know and George replied, "No, Scottie, that's your honour. I'll drive number two where I can watch that load. God help us all, it's like travelling two-fifty miles carrying a juggler's end-of-the-act pyramid. At the least sign of trouble I'll give you a long blast on the horn and when you hear that brake, but do it as though you were stroking a crocodile."

"I'll mind that," Scottie said, "and here's my signal to you for synchronised braking," and he reached into the driving cabin of the leading Maxie and showed George a pennanted lance. "When you see that flag, brake. It'll show on the offside, I've tested it."

It was twelve miles to Worcester over the first and largely experimental leg of the journey, and he was thankful there were no detours marked on Adam's route. The surface of the old Worcester–Droitwich coach road was good and apart from Rick Hill, that slowed them to a nervous two miles an hour, they covered it without incident. The load seemed steady enough and the engines behaved well. Positioned immediately behind the turret George could not so much as glimpse Quirt's vehicle but every now and again, on gentle slopes, he could feel its slow, insistent tug that became, over the miles, a kind of Morse code regulating his speed. He thought, thankfully, 'That chap is steady as a rock. I wouldn't have cared to play this cat-and-mouse game with anyone else as a partner. I don't think he's given a damned thought as to what could happen to him, if the load ran away, for I couldn't hold it . . .' But then he made a supreme effort to put such gloomy thoughts out of mind and glanced over his shoulder for a peep at Edward's man-o'-war trailing them by some fifty yards. They passed through Wychbold and Droitwich about tea time and he calculated their progress at a little short of six miles an hour. Men, women and children stopped to gape and shoppers pressed themselves back against the façades of the buildings as they trundled past. Everything on wheels gave them the widest berth possible and one drayman, after a single startled glance, cut a corner over the pavement into the nearest side-street. The traffic here was light but George knew this would not be so in a more populous town like Worcester. He could only hope that the local authorities had responded to Channing's demands for clearance.

It seemed that they had when the outskirts of the city were reached. The road was empty of everything save knots of interested bystanders and with his back to the westering sun a photographer, using a tripod, took a picture of them on the move. The river was crossed at a snail's pace, George noting with satisfaction that there was ample clearance of the low parapet and they took the left-hand fork beyond the Cathedral, clearing the city by six-thirty and heading south for Tewkesbury. Malvern gradients tended to slow their progress now so, at eight o'clock, George gave the signal to halt and a farm cutout enabled them to pull off the road. Scottie's engine was running hot, although his own was still behaving well and while Edward, who had elected himself quartermaster, was seeking the farmer's permission to camp and co-operation as regards stabling, he called Scottie down.

They had checked load and engines by the time Edward returned with news that they were welcome to sleep in the barn and later their host ambled out, a pipkin of a man with a complexion as streaked and rosy as one of his own Worcestershire apples, to stare thoughtfully at the halted cavalcade and wrinkle his nose at the unfamiliar stink of the petrol fumes. His phlegm endured until George, thanking him for his hospitality, told him they had covered the twenty-two miles from Bromsgrove in a little over four hours. The information impressed him. "From Bromsgrove? In under five ower? Wi' that hump aboard? Why, you woulder had to pass the city, then?"

"We got police clearance," George explained.

"Arr, you'd need it, I reckon," and he continued to stare thoughtfully at the nearest Maxie until George, feeling some further courtesy was required, asked him if he would care to look at the engine under one of the bonnets.

"Not I," he said, and retreated into his yard with such precipitation that even the dour Scottie Quirt smiled.

"So far so good," George said, "but we'll have to step up our average tomorrow. I've just worked it out. It's four point six."

"If we can hold it at that I'll no' complain," Scottie said, taking a bottle and two tin cups from his luncheon-box. "Those Taffies are brewing their tea but you'll tak' a drop o' this, will you no'?"

"I'll tak' both," George said, calling to Edward to join them.

*   *   *

It was too good to last, of course. Around midnight when all five of them were snoring in the barn, thunder rolled down from the Malverns and presently it came on to rain, a heavy downpour on the roof sending Scottie out to check on the tarpaulin bonnet covers draped over the engines. By first light the storm had passed but when George went outside he saw to his dismay that the ground under the Goliath was soggy and an offside rear wheel, where the crushing weight of the cupola bore heaviest, was buried to the rim. They fetched straw, cinders and brushwood and after a warm-up tried to move back on to the road but the wheels of Scottie's Maxie spun dangerously and it was no help to bring George's vehicle round from behind to double the traction. Edward said, dubiously, "Maybe the horses could do it better, pulling on a long trace from firm ground," but all George's experience told him no trace could stand that kind of strain. Time was passing. The sun was up now and they had already wasted over an hour. "We need a solid platform under that wheel," George said. "Planking would do, providing it was heavy enough." He was on the point of seeking help at the farm when Edward said, "The man-o'-war has an iron plate on the waggon bed. It's one of the old type, before we fitted slide rails. Have you got a heavy screwdriver in your kit?"

It was worth a try. After ten minutes' tussle with deeply embedded screws they had the plate off, an oblong of sheet iron worn smooth on its topside by the passage of innumerable crates. They scooped a layer of red mud from the leading edge of the embedded wheel and hammered the metal under the rim with a sledge, too busy to snatch more than a few mouthfuls of the fried bacon the Welsh waggoners, Morgan and Rees, had prepared. Closely synchronising their acceleration they applied maximum power and with a long suck and a rattle the Goliath was heaved back on to the road. George thought, watching Edward plod away to his waggon without comment, 'Damned if he isn't a chip from a couple of old blocks, the Gov'nor and Sam. And that's equal to anything, even a two-hundred-mile haul with this weight aboard.' They moved off under the clear sky, passing Hanley Castle on their right, then heading down the old coach road to Tewkesbury at a good seven miles an hour. They were ninety minutes behind schedule.

Channing was waiting across the Severn and jumped on the step of George's vehicle, shouting above the clank and rattle of the procession, "Don't stop, Swann! I've clearance as far as the Abbey. Is she riding well?"

"Better than I hoped," George roared. "The delay was my fault. Pulling off the road on to soggy ground. Won't happen again. Learned my lesson!"

"Will you detour this side of Gloucester?"

"Yes, at Longford. I'll look for you where we rejoin the main road at the Tuffley junction." Channing stepped nimbly off again and they passed through Tewkesbury before the streets of the old town were more than half awake.

Channing was as good as his word. Constables held horse traffic at every junction and the passage was accomplished in under a quarter of an hour. He had time to glance left at the Norman Abbey, guarding the western approach to the town, then right towards Bloody Meadow, scene of the last Yorkist triumph, reflecting, 'A Crown Prince came unstuck about here more than four hundred years ago but it won't happen again at this spanking rate of progress,' and he calculated they had come just under eight miles in sixty-five minutes. It went some way towards compensating for the unnecessary delay back at the farm.

Nine miles on, at Longford, they made their first deviation, swinging left on to a flint road towards Barnwood and aiming to cut a wide semi-circle round Gloucester, seen in the near distance.

Their route would take them over higher ground on the northern slope of Robinswood Hill and their speed was necessarily much reduced here, for the road was narrow, its surface gritty and the summer foliage thick enough to swish the tarpaulin of the turret that he now thought of, in the farmer's terms, as 'The Hump'. Drops of last night's rain slashed his windshield, blurring his vision, but they made steady progress through Barnwood and were within three miles of the Tuffley junction when Scottie's lance signalled a halt. He climbed down to discover that the linked vehicles completely blocked the road, with drainage ditches, half-full of storm water, on either side. Scottie said, "Look yon," and gestured ahead.

A huge oak, growing in the nearside hedge, spread its branches overhead, making a green arch and he saw at once that it was far more than a matter of brushing through a screen of twigs and leaves. A low slung bough, thick as a weaver's beam, reached clear across the lane. It would strike The Hump at least two feet below its summit and further progress, pending its removal, was impossible.

He understood then the full hazards of detours and they seemed to him, at that moment, far in excess of narrow city streets, when they could at least rely on police co-operation. Out here was nobody, not even a handy farm to seek assistance and a longish halt could play havoc with their time schedule. He was standing there fuming when Edward nudged his elbow and he turned to see the boy – he still thought of him as such – holding a large bow saw, with powerful, widely-spaced teeth.

"That chap Morgan was a woodsman before he joined us," he said, equably. "He'd make short work of that, George."

"Where did you get that saw?"

"It's standard kit in my beat," the boy said, and looked mildly surprised that his brother, Managing Director of the network, should need to be reminded of such an elementary detail. Morgan, a middle-aged man with a wall eye, came forward diffidently, saying, in his singsong brogue, "Have it down, I will, in no time at all, Mr. Swann. But she'll have to be hauled clear and it'll take horse-flesh to do it."

He was right, of course. The bough, sawn near the trunk, would fall athwart the road and form a kind of chevaux-de-frise into the bargain. Once again George felt his basic policy vindicated, a partnership of horse and machine, for he would have baulked at using a Maxie for such a purpose in this enclosed country. Even so it was not easy to accomplish. The cavalcade all but blocked the road, the horses would have to be brought forward from the rear and the hedges were high and thickly sown. He said, "Get it down, Morgan. Edward, tell Rees to bring the Clydesdales forward on the nearside. It's just about possible to squeeze past if he uses the ditch. If it isn't we'll backtrack, find a gate and breach the damned hedge higher up."

It was early afternoon now and apart from their hasty breakfast at dawn none of them had eaten. His own contribution was to light a fire, brew tea and lay out home-baked loaves and local cheese he had bought at the farm. Before the kettle was boiling the rasp of Morgan's saw ceased with a long, splintering crash and the road ahead was choked with foliage. But by then three of the Clydesdales had been dragged slithering through the narrow gap, their huge hooves making a ruin of somebody's drainage system. Morgan, in need of a breather, climbed down from his perch in the bole and took charge of the tea while the others went forward to fix drag ropes to the branch, fastening them to the severed butt.

It was even larger than it looked and at first the Clydesdales couldn't budge it, but then Morgan called to Rees to stop fooling and cut away smaller branches, and they went to it with the saw and axes until the main trunk could be prised from its hold on the soggy banks. They had to drag it forward three hundred yards until they came upon a field gate and desperately heavy work it was for man and beast, but within just over an hour from the time of halting they cleared a path through the debris and moved on, munching as they drove, forcing a two-mile-an-hour passage through the lane to more open ground beyond.

The detour still held an unpleasant surprise. Within a mile of the main road the ground rose steeply as it wound

under the scree and their rate of progress became even
slower as the two engines wrestled with the weight of a
load he was beginning to hate like a mortal enemy. It was
past five o'clock when they met an anxious Channing
striding up and down the road with his hunched, heron's
gait, and George made a spot decision to take advantage
of an open quarry entrance with a hard-packed surface
and call it a day, over-ruling Channing's advice to push
on.

"The motors have taken a terrible beating on that incline," he told him. "There's no sense in pushing our
luck. We'll give them a good going over while your
chauffeur runs my brother and the waggoners to the
nearest inn. They've earned a hot meal and a night's
rest."

"There's a good inn at Whaddon, a mile or so further
on," Channing said, deferring to him. "Will you join us
for dinner?"

"Not me," George said, "Quirt and I will stay with the
load. We can make do where we are," and Channing,
thankfully a man of few words, moved off.

They gave the engines an hour to cool off before going
over them part by part, tightening nuts, checking the
braking systems, refuelling the twenty-gallon tanks with
the aid of a funnel. The long drag had been wasteful of
petrol and it was difficult to estimate how much the drum
had in reserve. Probably enough to see them through,
George thought, for he knew he could not count on the
certainty of a fresh supply. Between them they fed and
watered the horses, rigging up an improvised corral at the
face of the quarry. They were docile giants and would
come to no harm in there and when they were dealt with
he reckoned up his mileage as a mere twenty-one, the
product of eleven hours on the road. It wasn't good
enough, and for the first time he felt a prick of doubt.
Scottie Quirt, knowing his moods so well, voiced it when
he said, "We'll need a clear run tomorrow I'm thinking.
Will you risk passing through Bristol?" and the words of

his father came to him, saying, after a long squint at his sheaf of maps, "The Avonmouth route is the flattest but that means a snarl up in that city and a stiffish climb out of it to the west. If it was me, with that weight aboard, I'd detour via Keynsham. That's not a bad road, or wasn't in my day."

"We'll take the long way round," he said. "The Gov'nor usually knows what he's about between here and Pentland Firth," and making a pillow of a bag of oats he stretched himself on the waggon-bed and slept.

3

His confidence had returned by the time they moved off, shortly after six the following morning. Channing must have been astir even earlier, for he brought Edward and the waggoners to the quarry by the time the engines were warmed up and George moved out ahead of his rearguard, not imagining he would make such good time over the next leg that they would have difficulty keeping convoy.

It was another fine, clear morning and a chorus of blackbirds and finches whistled them good luck as they swung back on to the main Gloucester–Bristol road and went trundling down the lush green strip between the two cities, sometimes holding the cavalcade at a speed of approaching nine miles an hour and moving over the best surface they had encountered as yet. Just beyond Almondsbury they branched left to begin the wide detour of Bristol, finding the country more built over, and the roads much firmer and broader than during the Gloucester detour. They stopped for a cool-off and a bite to eat in Stoke Gifford and just as they were moving off again Channing drove up with news that Edward and his team were at least three miles behind. "He seems to think you'll want to press on," Channing said. "You aren't likely to need the horses in this area, are you?" George told him no and gave him a careful note of the proposed

344

route as far as Burrow Gurney, where they were due to
rejoin the main road. By ten o'clock they were under way
again, probing through Kingswood to Keynsham and
encountering no bad gradients, although three slowed
them to under two miles an hour.

The Hump seemed to be behaving with great circum-
spection. Its lashings remained taut and it cleared four
Great Western railway bridges with inches to spare. He
thought, 'That's another astounding aspect of the Gov'nor's
memory. Is there anyone else in the country, even a
veteran railwayman, with his kind of memory for low-
level bridges?' He wondered briefly how Adam had come
by it, for there must have been many changes in the railway network since he reconnoitred the country's high-
ways and byways on horseback, with his little red book on
hand to note down every feature of the landscape likely
to feature in a haulage estimate. It was really no wonder
the Swann veterans still held him in awe, even now, when
he was more concerned with his tulips and cypresses than
the nation's business. He knew all their beats far better
than they themselves knew them and neither was his
knowledge for trivia confined to topography. Near here,
where the Kennet and Avon and Wilts and Berks Canals
converged on the river, he recalled Adam throwing out
one of those stray pieces of information that enlivened any
journey or discussion with him. "It was the scene," he
had told George, "of the first real clash between King and
Parliament, at the very start of the Civil War. The
Cavaliers, so-called, caught their opponents on the hop
and got the impression, poor wights, that the war would
be won at a blow." They pushed on through Whitchurch
and Bishopsworth to the Great West Road, making good
time over narrowing roads. By noon they were back on
the broad highway, having covered upwards of forty miles
in just under six hours.

At Burrow Gurney they took another breather but
Edward did not show. Instead Channing reappeared,
like a daemon in a pantomime, with news that the waggon

team had headed straight through the city to save time
and were now leaving it by the western approach. George
thought, 'It's damned tempting to push on but I daren't
run too far ahead. The long stiff climb at Churchill is
less than ten miles ahead and before that I'm going to
need the horses as brake-insurance at Lulsgate Bottom.'
He was glad then that Edward had showed initiative in
taking a short cut and held their speed down to a crawl
over the next stretch, halting again at the head of the
incline and biting his nails until Channing and Edward
showed up almost together and he could use the armour-
er's Daimler for a preliminary survey.

The hill into Lulsgate was steep, certainly, and would
have to be tackled with excessive care, but the road surface was better than average and Channing agreed to
drive ahead producing, to everybody's amusement, a
large red flag of the type all motorists had been compelled
to carry until the 1896 Act of Parliament had been
rescinded.

He said, attempting a joke, "Anyone who sees that will
assume you've been in purdah for the last five years," but
Channing, although taking his point, did not smile.
Clearly the trip was playing havoc with his nerves and
George thought, 'That's the difference between planners
and doers. He's a planner and can design superb weapons
in that foundry of his, but I wonder how would he behave
if he was called upon to use 'em in action?'

He came back to the stationary cavalcade resolved to
use the drag chains, with the man-o'-war shoed on both
rear wheels and acting as a holding force. They moved
off in bottom gear, inching down the long slope at a slow
walking pace and he was very relieved when they arrived
at the dip and could unhitch the waggon and take advantage of the flattish stretch towards Bridgwater. Channing,
scouting ahead, said there was a cutting sown with flints
this side of East Brent and reaching here George decided
to curb his exuberance and call it a day. They had come
fifty-nine miles in under twelve hours, bypassing one of

the largest centres of population in the country and
tackling one of the toughest descents on the route map.
He helped empty Scottie's bottle of whisky to celebrate.

*   *   *

Their luck seemed set fair now. They moved off to a
quick start on Day Four, to tackle the Churchill climb
and take early advantage of Channing's traffic clearance
in Bridgwater. At the summit of the slope he deployed all
eight Clydesdales on chain traces, climbing the hill at a
crawl with the draught animals strung out ahead but they
kept moving and reached Bridgwater before many carters
were abroad.

After that it was flat, easy country to Taunton, eleven
miles further on, another town where they were shown
every courtesy. The Taunton–Wellington stretch slowed
them down, proving hillier than he had expected, but
they tackled every ascent with the greatest caution and
had no recourse to deployment or the waggon-brake on
descents. Edward kept up well and Channing roved
ahead with his blood-red flag. By mid-afternoon they
were in Cullompton, an hour and a half later in Pinhoe,
only a few miles short of Exeter. There was still plenty of
travelling time. He pushed on the odd four miles over the
lowest crossing of the Exe at Countess Wear and found a
halting place in a section where the county authorities
had all but completed a road-widening project just beyond the Great Western Railway's coastal stretch on the
west bank of the estuary. Their progress, he told them
with glee, had been spectacular. They had come, at his
reckoning, seventy-one miles in a smooth, uneventful
haul. They still had a day and a half in hand to cover the
fifty-odd miles to Devonport.

By far the most direct route to Plymouth was inland,
heading for Newton Abbot, but the main coach road ran
over two very formidable hills, crossing the Haldon escarpment and George, having had personal experience of

them during his occasional forays into the Western Wedge, recalled that they were not only steep but tortuous. His father had urged the longer way round, following the coast as far as Teignmouth, then turning sharply inland and moving up the Teign estuary to Newton Abbot.

At many places the road ran beside the railway, said to be the most expensive stretch to maintain in the country, and there were several sharp laps approaching and beyond the little seaside resorts that had grown up under the red bluffs. They reached Newton Abbot without incident, however, and took the road to Totnes, tackling a stiffish slope out of the town, and from there, moving very slowly in this undulating country, heading for South Brent, where the range of tors indicated impossible motoring country to the north.

It came on to rain after they rejoined the main road and he had all he could do to keep moving, with Dartmoor drizzle reducing visibility to fifty yards, but they kept going and were within hailing distance of the Great Western Railway crossing at Wrangton when Channing, scouting ahead, came back signalling a halt. He said, tersely, "What do your maps say about the bridge yonder?" and George, making a check, said there was a twelve-foot nine clearance.

"Somebody is behind the times," he said. "I've just measured it, and it's an inch or so under twelve. Come and see for yourself."

They went down towards the bridge and it was just as Channing had said. New pointing had reduced the clearance below the minimum and even with the tarpaulin stripped off there was no prospect of passing The Hump under the arch. It would foul the bridge two inches or more below the summit.

"Have you got a detour pencilled in?"

"Yes, but the Gov'nor queried it. There's a road bridge on the lower road and the surface is unmade. However, there's no help for it, we'll have to try the Ugborough–Ermington loop."

It was still raining when they nosed their way down a narrow country road south of the main route, then headed west again over an atrocious surface where their speed was reduced to under two miles an hour. He thought, sourly, 'With ordinary luck, yesterday's luck, we could have made Plymouth tonight. We'll never do it now,' and he sent Edward ahead to reconnoitre the bridge.

The boy was back in ten minutes looking glum. "It's even lower than the rail bridge," he said, "and there's only one way of passing it. We'll have to lower the road level by six inches or more."

He went forward to see for himself. The bridge, an old one, had once given haywain clearance but that was long ago. Winter rains had worn away the banks and there was actually a slight incline up to the arch where the road was surfaced with hard-packed rubble.

"It's a pick and shovel job," he told Edward. "Get Morgan, Rees and the tools."

"We'll need more than one pick and shovel to shift that in the time. How about local labour?"

"Is there any to be had at short notice?"

"Farms, I daresay. I'll look around," and he plodded off into the seeping mist while George, momentarily forgetting him, set to work with Scottie and the two waggoners, scrabbling at the surface with such tools as they had.

They had hardly broken the surface when Edward was back in a blue farm-waggon driven by a moorman with straw-coloured hair and a brogue so thick as to be all but unintelligible.

"Us iz zendin' ver Bain," he told George, after a long and hostile scrutiny of the cavalcade. "Youm bliddy well mazed, maister, to bring that gurt contrapsun round yer. Anyone knows you carn taake a wain from Yuish to Ivy-bridge this road." He made no reference to the rail bridge at Wrangton. Presumably local men had adjusted to both underpasses.

"Do you know what he's saying?" George demanded,

irritably, and Edward said, "We don't have to. He understood me the moment I offered him a sovereign an hour for his labour and tools. I had to show him the money, however. No flies on these boys."

'Bain' (subsequently identified as 'Ben', senior hand at the nearest farm) arrived a few minutes later, with two mute assistants and a load of tools. With a labour force of nine they made rapid progress, carting soil and rock chippings away in a wheelbarrow that had an excruciating squeak. Darkness closed in, however, long before the section was cut and levelled, so that George sent for storm-lanterns to hang in the hedges and the work continued in the soft yellow glow, lighting both sides of the arch.

When they were down to a uniform ten inches, and both approaches had been levelled off to some extent, he sent Edward in the moorman's cart for planking, busying himself with Scottie and the waggoners stripping the tarpaulin from The Hump. He took his time now, covering the dip with carefully placed planks two inches thick and it was well past midnight before they were ready to move. Channing appeared out of the murk, a heron with bedraggled plumage, who was already acquainted with the cause of the long delay. Rumour circulated quickly in this kind of country, he said, and Ivybridge was alerted as to their presence a mile south of the main road. "I've sent my man on into Plymouth with a letter to the authorities at Crownhill," he added, breathlessly. "We'll get every co-operation in the city. Will you wait for the light now?"

George told him no. All he wanted was to be out of this bottleneck without further delay and Channing, perched in the dripping hedge on the Plymouth side of the bridge, watched them pass through and tackle the incline towards the main road. The bridge had claimed something in excess of eight hours.

He curbed his impatience then and splashed up a muddy lane to the farm where the farmer's wife, whose brogue rivalled the carter's, made tea and beef sandwiches, and he paid Bain and his team for their labour and took his turn to wash under the kitchen pump. Dawn was lighting the eastern sky now and they made a fresh start about five, crawling into Ivybridge an hour or so later and pushing through it without a stop. Despite the early hour half the town assembled to watch the procession.

The final leg, some twelve miles from Ivybridge to Devonport, occupied them close on for three hours and it was nearly eleven-thirty when they trundled through the dock gates and saw Channing again, miraculously spruced up, who agreed to superintend the unloading and find someone to take care of the horses. He said, after a taciturn naval officer had inspected the naked cupola in its waggon-bed, "You realise how close we came? Another ninety minutes and they would have refused delivery," and George, stifling a yawn, replied, "They would have had to haul it back to Bromsgrove under their own steam for I wouldn't make that trip again for a king's ransom. We all need a hot meal and twelve hours' sleep. Did you book any lodging hereabouts?"

"Not me," Channing said, wrinkling his lip in the second smile George had seen him attempt during their brief but eventful acquaintance, "but I'm led to believe your father did."

"*My father?*"

"He's waiting in a local hotel. I forget the name. It's a half-timbered building, a stone's throw from the dockyard gates. Arrived yesterday, I hear." Suddenly, and with what was clearly an effort for so reserved a man, he extended his hand. "I won't forget this, Swann. I'm uncommonly obliged to every one of you. Will you give this to your men to share?", and he passed over an envelope, later found to contain a cash bonus of a hundred guineas.

The naval officer summoned him then and George was watching the mobile crane go into action when Edward

351

plucked his sleeve, pointing to a spare figure in a grey frock coat, standing squarely on the cobbles immediately outside the gates. "You can't keep the Gov'nor away, George. I think he's ruffled you didn't ask him along for the ride."

"I did," George said, "and he laughed in my face. He's nicely placed nowadays. All the fun without any of the grief. I'm beginning to think there's a lot to be said for getting long in the tooth."

They went out together and Adam, deliberately laconic, shook hands with each of them. "You cut it fine, boy," he said, as they crossed to the grill room of the hotel, where Scottie and the waggoners were already wielding knife and fork. "What kept you so long over the final leg?" and George, suddenly recalling his father's stories of old coachman Blubb, the Kentish Triangle manager who had once driven the 'Lord Nelson' coach and four north from the Saracen's Head in Snow Hill before the railways threw him on a scrapheap, said, "You could call it 'that bliddy gridiron', Gov'nor. I daresay old Blubb would have had something quaint to say about it."

"Ah, I daresay," said Adam, "but he would have been equally foul-mouthed as regards your means of traction." He unfolded a *Westminster Gazette* dated four days earlier, indicating a somewhat blurred picture of the cavalcade, moving through Worcester. "I've sent for the negative of that," he said. "We'll use it in the autumn advertisement programme. It should help to win you a handsome majority at the next conference. You'll talk them into going ahead with the fleet of motors, I imagine?"

"Scottie Quirt is travelling north tonight to put the original plan into action as soon as he's caught up on his sleep. They'll be approving a *fait accompli* when they finally get around to it."

"Ah, that was my way," Adam said. "Democracy? It's well enough in theory but it's no substitute for the committee of one, boy."

* * *

Adam Swann, whom few would have described as a family man in the literal sense, was none the less an interested observer of family alliances. Down the years he had pondered each of them objectively, feeling that there was something fresh to be learned about people in the shifts and loyalty patterns that went on under his nose. Perhaps it was this curiosity that enabled him to draw what he regarded as the really important lesson from George's two-hundred-and-fifty-mile haul with that bloodless chap's gun-turret.

It was not a reaffirmation of his unwavering faith in George as a pioneer, the only male of his brood in whom he saw himself in the splendour of his youth; neither was it the certainty that George, although moving at a snail's pace, had managed to whip the carpet from under the feet of his colleagues at the board table. Rather, it was a new relationship that had flowered under stress between New Broom and New Boy, his youngest son, Edward. For George, until then, had seemed not to need an ally within the family, whereas Edward (whose reverence for George had been evident since infancy), had been waiting in the wings for a long time now and had at last been summoned, to savour the bliss of what seemed, to Adam, a full and equal partnership. Overnight as it were. Somewhere between Bromsgrove and Devonport Docks. And under what circumstances? The factors contributing to form this interesting new alliance teased Adam all the way home, so much so that he took the very first opportunity that presented itself to satisfy his curiosity, when Edward, leaping out to lay claim on a cab as the express slid into Paddington, left them alone for a moment or two.

"How did the boy shape, George?"

"Edward? To have along on a trip of that kind? First-rate, Gov'nor. Absolutely first-rate." George hesitated a moment, standing with his back to his father and his hand raised to the luggage rack, and in the compartment mirror Adam saw the wide, familiar grin light up his face. Then George turned, heaving at their grips. "Damn it, I'll go further. Why not? Maybe I'm getting woolly. Maybe he's a marriage of your patience and Sam Rawlinson's bullheadedness. I'll come right out with it. He saved our bacon twice over. Without him I'd never have made it. Is that what you wanted to know?"

"I'll own to it, too, George. It's what I suspected and wanted confirmed."

3

Confrontations

IT WAS TIMES SUCH AS THESE WHEN, DROWSY AFTER an interval of tenderness crowned by a lovemaking he had dropped away into sleep, that the sense of identity came to Romayne. A presence, half-shade, half-fancy, yet almost tangible, standing beside the bed like a fairy godmother or like the jovial ghost of Christmas Present in *A Christmas Carol*. Warm and munificent, a personification of the benedictions of a lifetime, so that she was aware of a fulfilment that had eluded her since childhood.

It had grown a little, this presence, ever since they settled here, in this scarred monument to greed, with its tips and its skeletal pithead gear, its undulating seams of dwellings etched against a ragged skyline, its long tradition of toil and deprivation. Not a presence one would be likely to associate with ugliness and desecration but at home for all that, far more so than it would have been in the pampered circumstances of her earlier life and the difference lay, she imagined, in her personal contribution to the serenity of their sojourn and the reality of their newfound comradeship.

For ever since coming here she had seen him grow, a little every day, as he moved about among his miners and their cheerful, extrovert families, healing their small feuds and weaving their isolated protests against fate into a force and fervour that would one day carry him to Westminster as their champion. And it was the very certainty of this that enlarged him so that, looking back to a time when he was dabbling in trade, he seemed small, baffled, blighted and insignificant, with no outlet for his brimming reservoir of compassion.

She acknowledged, proudly and cheerfully, her role in this enlargement. Yet all she had done, when she came to think about it, was to point him in the right direction after so long in the wilderness although her claims in another, more private, area were more substantial. Not only had she brought him a son, and was soon, she felt sure, to bring him another, she was there to offer succour and revitalisation when he came home tired and used up, nurturing him as a lover in this nondescript room when rain came slashing in from the Atlantic and the wind roared down from the mountains, re-inflating his ego in a way that revealed to her not only his innermost secrets but those of every man and every woman who had ever sought and found deep, personal fulfilment in physical fusion. It taught her something vital about the relationship of men like his father and women like his indomitable mother who had, as it were, fed upon one another's being in a long and fruitful association and she was so happy that she feared it was too rich and rewarding to last out their lifespan.

Thus she no longer thought of herself as Romayne Rycroft-Mostyn, the spoiled and wilful child of a money-mad industrialist whose despotism extended over mines, dyeworks and chain foundries. Here, within the easy freemasonry of an enclosed community, where four out of five families wrenched a living from the seams deep under the mountain, she was plain Rosie Swann, the candidate's wife, and she rejoiced in the title. She had come home, out of the long, growling storm.

She withdrew her free hand from the blankets, half-turned and ran her fingertips across his chest and down over his warm belly to the groin, smiling secretively at the limpness and insignificance of her discoveries and wondering briefly if he was capable as yet of re-enacting the climactic surge of an hour ago and dreaming it possible if he was sufficiently encouraged. But then, turning away, she remembered he would need rest for tomorrow's winter foray into the Chamberlain citadel at Birmingham, beside his hero and sponsor, David Lloyd George, for whom their son had been named. She did not fear for him or his mentor on those Midland battlements, despite gloomy warnings of party wiseacres and newspapers, who said the Brummagers would make good their threat to lynch any pro-Boer who ventured among them. Giles Swann and Lloyd George could be relied upon to give a good account of themselves on any battlefield where their deepest convictions were challenged. In the end, despite slanders, violence and mob hysteria, they would win the day.

2

Giles, stepping out into a flurry of sleet on New Street platform a few hours later, did not share her confidence, being under no illusion what kind of opposition they would be likely to face up here and what excesses a Brummagen mob were capable of committing whipped on by the scourge of partisan-patriotism. Patriotism, he thought, was a word that should be expunged from the dictionary. It had become pitifully debased of late and was currently being used to justify every kind of outrage, both here and on the veldt where, so they said, thousands of Boer women and children had already died in Kitchener's concentration camps. A necessary price Tory newspapers claimed, to be paid for denying the enemy access to areas of recruitment and supply. Such facts, if they could be believed (and the latest underground intelligence from the Cape persuaded him they could) dishonoured not only the perpetrators, but the entire nation; especially a people whose boast it was that their homeland was the power house of freedom.

He wondered how his brother Alex would answer such an indictment. Or his mother. Or Hugo, poor devil, whose life had been shattered by impulses set in train by that same word. Surely war against the dependants of a gallant and already defeated minority was indefensible, even when British soldiers were dying at the same rate in tented hospitals behind the blockhouse wire. The entire war was indefensible, had always been indefensible and his loathing for it welled up in him afresh so that he hunched his shoulders against the December sleet and set off, grim-faced, towards the Liberal Club, there to seek the latest briefing on the Town Hall rally where Lloyd George, despite police appeals and a flood of warnings from his own supporters, had pledged himself to speak that night.

He found the sense of foreboding had spilled out of Headquarters into the streets. Police were everywhere, mounted and on foot. Shopkeepers were boarding up their premises, as against a siege or street battle. The very air was charged with strain, the tensions releasing themselves in the thud of hammer on clapboard and the bravado of the party workers, one of whom told him that, although entry to the Town Hall was strictly by ticket, thousands of tickets were known to have been forged and violence was a certainty. Lloyd George himself, he learned, was not yet in the city and his method of entry, and progress to the Town Hall, was a closely-guarded secret, but that he would appear as promised nobody doubted, least of all Giles, for here was a situation the Welshman would relish. All his life he had been moving towards this kind of climax and his personal courage was equal to any of the men who had sworn to silence him, hopefully for ever.

By mid-afternoon, under a sky heavy with snow, he had threaded his way through dense crowds to Victoria Square, where the Town Hall stood on an island, already besieged by patriots, so that Giles wondered how any legitimate ticket-holders could expect to get in without being manhandled. Here again scores of police were on duty but there was little, seemingly, that they could do to control the dense crowds and on a piece of waste land in

Edmund Street he saw a huckster doing a profitable business selling bricks at three a penny 'to chuck at Lloyd George'.

It took him nearly an hour to work his way round to the committee-room entrance, where the presence of over fifty policemen succeeded in keeping open a narrow gangway along which ticket-holders ran the gauntlet of the Chamberlain mobs, screaming abuse and obscenities at everyone whose ticket was accepted as genuine. He thought, on reaching the relative sanctuary of the hall, packed with supporters, 'What the devil has happened to the country? In the old days party rivalry was rumbustious but there was a schoolboy element about its clashes . . . It was never vicious, or never on this scale . . .' and he wondered if it might not have been wiser to cancel the meeting after all, for if the mob broke in something far worse than broken heads and bloody noses would result, and, even if he escaped, Lloyd George's obduracy would be deemed responsible for the carnage.

But then, his confidence returning as he looked at the massed ranks of the faithful and the knots of prowling stewards, he thought: 'Damn them all . . . David is right! Someone has to show the real flag. Someone has to make a stand for free speech and democratic tradition, and who better than him?'

*   *   *

He slipped in quietly and unobtrusively about seven o'clock, almost unrecognisable under a heavy peaked cap and a rough, workman's overcoat. Utterly composed, and with the familiar twinkle lighting his eye as he said, seeing Giles, "Well, Johnny Peep? How's this for a peaceful exchange of views? A little livelier than a House debate but more productive too, if I'm not mistaken. How is your wife? Did she come along for the fun?"

"She would have if she hadn't been pregnant, L.G. She sent her regards, and said I was to tell you we'll make it next election. We came much closer than I expected last time."

"And she's right, tell her. The mood of the country is changing, despite this welcome party. This is no more than a local fracas, the natural outcome of our Go-For-Jo campaign. Next time we'll give them the shock of the century," and he moved off to chat to Birmingham supporters among whom, Giles noted with some apprehension, were a number of women, already dishevelled by their passage into the hall.

The roars outside beat upon the isolated building like prodigious breakers on a rock, wave after wave of baying that made speech between individuals difficult and would certainly prohibit a public address. Giles shouted, in the ear of a rosetted official, "He'll never make himself heard against that," and the man, his face flushed with excitement, shouted, "He *knows* that! We *all* knew it! It's *being* here that matters!"

It was true enough, he supposed, and Lloyd George, the Welsh Cœur de Lion as they had christened him since the Bangor riot, was already dictating a speech that he knew he would never deliver, seemingly unperturbed by the terrible uproar caused by the use of heavy noticeboards torn down from across the Square now being used as battering rams on the doors. News filtered in, all of it bad. The baying mob had burst through the outer police cordon. The outer doors had yielded to assault. Infiltrators were trickling into the body of the hall. The meeting could only end in bloody chaos, unparalleled in this century.

At seven-thirty Lloyd George led the way out of the committee room on to the platform, fronted and flanked by a phalanx of police. It was soon apparent that the pessimists were right about infiltration. His appearance was greeted by a howl that blotted out the continuous clamour from the Square. Volleys of bricks crashed through the windows as the speaker, leaning forward to address a word to the press bench, was assailed by a boarding party who swept up to the platform in a body, overwhelming the press box in such numbers that it collapsed and precipitated a wedge of pressmen on to the floor. The reporters scattered, notebooks flying. The police and stewards counter-attacked and the storming party was seized and thrust down again. Arrests, in these circumstances, were impossible.

Half an hour passed. Stewards fought, police fought and the mob fought back, drunk and delirious with hate but all the time, slightly in advance of the shrinking party platform, Lloyd George stood there, relaxed, half-amused, fascinated it seemed by the tempest his presence occasioned. Police whistles shrilled, glass continued to shatter along the full length of the hall and the body of the building was jammed with a heavy, scrambling mass out of which rose a cacophony of screams, yells and hysterical appeals for help. The gesture was made and it was time to retreat. Shepherded by police the platform party edged back into the committee rooms, where barricades were instantly erected and all lights were extinguished on the orders of the Chief Constable. Slowly, fighting for every inch of ground gained, police and stewards regained control of the hall but outside the mob now ruled unchallenged. According to police instructions it had been reinforced and the Chief Constable, reappearing, said he could no longer guarantee the safety of the party. There was only one means to extract Lloyd George from the beleaguered building. He would have to pass out under the protection of a policeman's cape and helmet. As for the others, plans were being made for a retreat across the road to the Midland Institute offices, where they might wait until time and falling snow thinned the mob.

Giles watched him don the disguise, protesting that it was ridiculous but submitting, as he explained, for the sake of the Chief Constable's professional reputation. He said, as Giles sidled across, "How do I look, Johnny? Like someone from the chorus of Gilbert and Sullivan?" and Giles said, gravely, "Don't ask me until you're clear of this, L.G. We can joke about it later." They shook hands and as Lloyd George took his place in the line he called, "You were here, Johnny! I won't forget that, lad!"

They passed out in a marching file, heading for Paradise Street and Easy Row and ultimately, Giles learned later, the sanctuary of Ladywood police station clear across the city. But for the platform party the problem of exit remained and would do so as long as it was believed L.G. was still inside.

The respite was temporary. Soon a police inspector arrived from the main battle area, grunting that the line could only hold for a few minutes. At the committee room exit, a carriage and pair, assailed from all sides, and escorted by flailing mounted police, drew the attention of the main body of assailants. Before it was realised that its interior contained not the arch-traitor but police reinforcements, the stragglers had made their dash across the street under another police escort. They were only just in time. Giles, one of the last to leave, heard the mob storm back into the hall, climb the platform and range through every room, smashing and overturning everything in their path. They were not ejected until the Riot Act was read and a baton charge could be mounted.

Outside snow was falling in heavy flakes, mantling the stark outline of the civic buildings and muffling, to some extent, the roars of the disappointed Brummagers. The riot petered out. Ambulances collected casualties and those who could found transport home. Giles walked, shouldering his way through the stragglers to New Street, where he caught the night train to Newport, reminding himself that he lacked L.G.'s ebullience. To him the evening was bloody, raucous proof of the nation's sickness and it occurred to him to wonder how long it would take to cure. L.G., as spokesman for the minority who saw the war as an exercise in national degradation, had outfaced the patriots on their own ground and there was, he supposed, some satisfaction to be derived from that. But divisions, of a kind he had witnessed here tonight, must run clear across the country, driving wedges between man and wife, father and son, and as he thought this he reflected bitterly on his own situation, with one brother away fighting Cronje's commandos and another maimed for life by a stupid, vainglorious quarrel. It was not a happy thought, especially as he and Romayne had promised to keep their Christmas at 'Tryst'.

2

It was not often, nowadays, that Henrietta Swann had an opportunity to bask in her role as matriarch, a privilege she had enjoyed since the eldest of the brood had married and started a family of her own some sixteen years ago. As time passed, and each of them assumed responsibilities in various parts of the Empire, homecomings to 'Tryst' became intermittent and there never had been an occasion, since Christmas, 1888, when she had all of them assembled round her at one time.

This year, however, promised to be a great improvement on recent reunions. All but Alex and Lydia would be returning for Christmas Day and Boxing Day, and even Jack-o'-Lantern and Joanna had promised to appear, bringing Helen home after her recuperative holiday in Dublin.

Adam, permanently home-based at last, took a keener interest than usual in celebrations, personally selecting the Christmas tree and garlanding of the house with holly, ivy and mistletoe, but grumbling, as he worked, that "They owed all this fussy fiddle-faddle to that brace of prize sentimentalists, Prince Albert and Charles Dickens!" He made an impressive job of it. Henrietta never recalled the house looking more festive and welcoming, and when the first of the grandchildren scampered in (George's brood from nearby Beckenham) she was rewarded by their squeals of glee and the grave congratulations of her Austrian daughter-in-law, Gisela, the acknowledged family expert on the Teutonic Yuletide, refashioned for British hearths by that brace of sentimentalists, Albert and Charles, God bless them.

The following day, before luncheon, Hugo and Lady Sybil arrived, with Hugo's soldier-servant in tow, the latter stamping about the waxed and gleaming floors bellowing '*Sah!*', in anticipation of his master's requirements. Hugo, she noted, looked surprisingly fit and Sybil said, in a whispered aside, "The dear boy is adjusting, much as we hoped." Yet it was painful and pitiful to see him so stolid and stationary unless chivvied by that drill-ground sergeant or his wife, and a comfort to reflect that Giles would be along soon, for he and Hugo, she recalled, had been very close as boys during their shared sojourn at the bleak school up on Exmoor. She made a mental note to have a private word with Giles, whom she regarded as the family wiseacre, about a suitable occupation for an athlete who had lost his sight. Lady Sybil had been speculating on a variety of pursuits, among them model ship-making and fashioning things out of potter's clay, but somehow they did not suit Henrietta's notion of Hugo's need. It would have to be something far more positive, especially when Sybil's child arrived, claiming a share of its mother's time and attention. Giles would think of something for Giles always did. And Hugo would likely need him more than anybody.

Romayne, she noted with satisfaction, was holding on to that second child, due in the early spring they announced. A disappointing late starter in the Swann grandchild stakes the girl now seemed to be making amends, for David, their first-born, had only just celebrated his first birthday.

Then the Irish party arrived with a trunkful of presents, all prettily wrapped and ready to hang on the tree, and on Christmas morning Stella, Denzil and their tribe arrived from Dewponds, so that the old house crackled with hilarity and creaked under the impact of so much horseplay, the tenor of good cheer broken every now and again by a short-lived quarrel among the younger cohorts and a constant demand for umpires.

Twenty-six of them sat down to Christmas dinner at eight o'clock that evening, including the senior grandchildren. Upstairs, sleeping it off in readiness for Boxing Day brawls, were half-a-dozen toddlers and three babies, so that even 'Tryst', that had always seemed such a barn of a place with only Edward and Margaret at home, was hard taxed to provide accommodation for the clan. It was a long time since this had happened, Henrietta recalled. The last occasion had been that of Stella's second marriage, when Adam had shocked the county by filling the place with hirelings gathered from all over the network.

Early on Boxing Day Henrietta had another unlooked-for surprise. Deborah, her journalist husband, Milton Jeffs, and their little boy arrived from the Westcountry and she saw Adam's face light up, knowing the soft spot he had always had for the child he brought in like a spaniel out of the snow all those years ago, rescuing her from a convent where she had been lodged, poor mite, by that dreadful father of hers, Josh Avery, whom nobody had set eyes on since he ran away with all Adam's capital.

Two of the children had to be evacuated from an east wing bedroom and accommodated on truckle beds in the sewing room in order to make room for the Jeffs but this was soon accomplished and they all trooped out to watch Stella, Jack-o'-Lantern, young Edward and George's two eldest boys ride off for the Boxing Day meet at Long Covert. With them, at a steady trot, went Hugo and his rough-riding sergeant, who had recently taught him to ride on a leading rein.

"He won't *hunt*, of course," Sybil told her, "but he can poke about the coverts happily enough and I entirely discount the risk weighed against the good it will do him. We tried him out in Rotten Row a month ago and it was a triumph. I couldn't keep the photographers away, unfortunately, for it was regarded as very sensational by all the newspapers and he didn't take kindly to that. I've since warned everybody not to tell him his picture was in *Chambers's Journal*. That's understandable, of course."

But to Henrietta it wasn't, although she thought better of asking her aristocratic daughter-in-law to elaborate on Hugo's excessive modesty. Heaven knows, to her way of thinking, the loss of one's sight in action against the Queen's enemies (hardly anybody had adjusted, as yet, to thinking of them as the 'King's enemies') fully justified the pocketing of any kudos that came his way and she was still puzzled by Hugo's extreme reticence to discuss the war, even impersonally. He had never minded discussing his athletic triumphs and surely they were very small beer matched against what he had achieved, almost single-handed, against those wicked spiteful Boers. She could only suppose it had something to do with Lady Sybil Uskdale's aversion to the vulgar popular press and that she had drilled Hugo into regarding the mention of one's war experiences as putting on side.

All but Young Edward, a rare thruster, were back by mid-afternoon, spattered with mud and well laced with stirrup cup, and they formed an impatient queue at the bathroom Adam had installed adjoining the kitchen wash-house, calling loudly to one another to hurry on out and look sharp about it. Nowadays, she heard, people were actually installing bathrooms upstairs but the plumbing at 'Tryst' would never run to that, Adam said, not without having all its floors up and who knew what might result from that in a house advancing into its fifth century?

Just as dusk closed in over the leafless copper beeches of the drive and all the lamps were lit, there was a vast commotion in the forecourt and George appeared bellowing, "It's old Alex, by God! With Lydia and their girl, Rosie! You never said a word about their arrival, Mother! I thought they were still in South Africa and Rose was at school!" and Henrietta, feeling quite faint, replied, "So did I, and so did your father! But, that's *wonderful* . . .

wonderful for it makes us complete don't you see? And for the first time in I don't know how long!" She hurried into the hall where Alex, in his dress uniform, was helping his plain little wife to shed her mantle and their grave-eyed daughter, Rose, was hurriedly unpacking yet another batch of Christmas gifts.

If she had favourites among them Alex qualified for a place at the top of the list. Aside from Hugo, whose spell of soldiering had been so brief and so tragic, Alex was the only one among them who fulfilled her girlish dream of mothering a race of scarlet-clad warriors but she was fond of Lydia too, whom she realised had given him purpose and direction in his chosen profession. It was more than two years since she had seen them although Rose, their eldest child, had stayed here for the summer holidays, a quiet, well-mannered girl who had inherited, thank God, her father's looks and stature and promised to be quite handsome once she outgrew her coltishness.

Lydia said, kissing her, "Alex was due for another step up and was posted back to Colchester. We didn't write because we weren't sure but it was confirmed while we were at sea. He'll be gazetted lieutenant-colonel in the New Year."

"Why, that's splendid, my boy. Congratulations," Adam murmured, privately wondering if the promotion stemmed from his long-standing friendship with Lord Roberts, also home again after straightening out the mess the army had got itself in out there, and Alex explained that he was to be seconded to an embryo force being assembled at Woolwich for the purpose of consolidating all the experience gained in the field with heavy machine-gun units.

"There's a rumour that we're to be issued with two to a battalion," he said, between greetings, and then, a little uncomfortably, "Is Hugo here?"

"Everybody's here," Adam told him, "George, Giles, Hugo, Young Edward and all the girls, including Helen. You won't have seen her for years, will you? Not since she was last on leave, with that poor chap, Rowland Coles. But I wrote you about that shambles."

"Yes," Alex said, rather absently Adam thought. "It was a shocking affair but I understand Helen came out of it very well. Is she herself again?"

"No, she isn't," Adam told him, "but she's on the mend and looks fit enough. So does Hugo. Surprisingly so. He's been out with the hunt today."

"*Hunting? Hugo?*"

"On the leading rein. That wife of his is a trier and he's got a rough-riding sergeant who bullies him into taking regular exercise. But come along, meet them all yourself . . ."

But instead of following him into the mêlée in the drawing room, where tea was about to be served, Alex hung back saying, "Hold on, sir. I . . . er . . . I don't quite follow. You say Hugo *and* Giles are here? Both? Under the same roof!"

It says something for Adam's ageing reactions that he realised at once what Alex was hinting at and made an immediate response, heading off a squall that could shatter the conviviality of the occasion. He said, quietly, "Come in here a moment, before we get embroiled," and edged his eldest son into Henrietta's sewing-room, now doing duty as a spillover bedroom. He said, shutting the door, "You'll have differences, I daresay. But here and now isn't the place to air them. For mine and your mother's sake. This is the festive season, isn't it?"

"Not as festive as all that," Alex said, tight-lipped. "I confess I don't understand what's happened to Giles, or how he could show his face in Hugo's presence. Damn it, the fellow's unrepentantly pro-Boer, isn't he?"

"Come to that I'm not anti-Boer myself, son," Adam said, mildly. "A lot of people over here think the hammering should stop. We should have made a generous peace with the poor devils by now."

"That's the politicians' business."

"Giles *is* a politician, Alex."

It seemed that this was all but new to Alex. He frowned, as though finding the news distasteful and said, in the same flat voice, "He's also the brother of a man who lost his sight in action. I would have thought that should give him second thoughts about standing on a public platform and supporting that damned traitor, Lloyd George."

He saw the dilemma and a very unpleasant one it promised to be. Not only for Giles and Hugo but for all of them, especially Henrietta, who was riding so high just now. He said, "You'll have to call a temporary truce, son. I can't go into it now and I'm not even sure I'll want to later. You're a professional soldier and Giles is working to become a legislator. You don't have to remind me of the opinion the soldiers have of politicians, 'The Frocks' as you chaps call them. I held those opinions myself in my soldiering days, until I discovered how fiendishly difficult it can be to find a compromise between private convictions and the outlook of men paid to do what they're told to do, no more and no less. Things are getting very complicated as the world moves on, son, but for you chaps there's no question of taking sides. You get your orders and you carry 'em out, best you can. It's not that easy for others. Civilians have to find their own way through the maze and a damned tricky business it is, I can tell you, for anyone with a conscience. And Giles always had more conscience than any of us."

At least Alex paid him the compliment of reflecting a moment but he remained unrepentant. 'War does that to the best of us,' Adam thought. 'Once you've seen men you respect dead and dying you tend to judge everything in black and white and if you didn't you wouldn't be much good at your job.'

Alex said, presently, "That's all very fine, Gov'nor, but surely to God what happened to Hugo would cause a fellow to think twice about getting up on his hind legs and giving aid and comfort to the men who shot his brother's sight away? That's what Giles is doing if I hear correctly. I confess I've publicly disowned him in mess and I'm damned if I'll shake his hand now, even for your sake and mother's. He and Hugo used to be thick, didn't they?"

"Very," Adam said, "and they still are. And Hugo isn't bitter about what happened to him. If you can get him to talk about it, which I doubt, he'll probably express concern at making several Boer women widows before they got him down. Kitchener wants peace, doesn't he?"

"We all do," Alex said, "and you don't have to preach to me about the cost of war. I've been through half-a-dozen. But a man's loyalty should rest with his tribe, shouldn't it?"

"I'm not so sure about that. There have been reports here that some Boers are coming over to our side, and wishing to God Cronje and his commandos in hell for prolonging the agony."

"Well, as to that, I think no more of them than I do of Giles," Alex said, stiffly. "I'll keep out of his way, that's all," and he went out quickly, his tall boots striking hard on the stone flags as though to emphasise his flat rejection of pro-Boers, Frocks and Boers who were eager to compromise.

Adam thought, gloomily: 'Now here's a how-de-do, to be sure . . . I hope he has enough horse sense to limit his prejudices to a scowl or two. We don't want a family shindig on a day like this . . .' He looked out into the hall, caught one of Stella's boys hurrying past carrying a pyramid of muffins hot from the kitchen and called, "Hi, there, lad! Find your Uncle Giles and tell him I want to see him in the sewing-room. Tell him it's urgent and he's to come whatever he's doing," and the boy said, "Yes, sir!" and scuttled off while Adam, retreating into the little room again, lit one of his favourite Burmese cheroots and puffed at it gratefully until Giles came in, closing the door and saying: "You don't have to break it to me gently. Romayne was bothered about it the moment they showed up and she's slipped away to pack. If Martindale can run us over to Bromley we could get an evening train into town."

He said, sullenly, "I won't have that! You're under my roof and your mother's."

"Wouldn't it be better all round? I've got two choices. To tell Alex and Lydia what I felt about that war or back down and apologise for myself. I couldn't do that, Father."

"I'm not asking you to, son."

"Then what?"

"Let 'em both stew awhile. Bury 'em under a load of paper, in this case Christmas wrappings. I don't ask that for my sake but for your mother's."

"Suppose Alex raises it with Hugo and Sybil?"

"I've ordered him not to and he'll mind what I say. Meantime, steer clear of him, as he means to of you."

"What a mess it all is," Giles said, dismally.

"Nothing new about it, son. It always has been a mess one way and another. That's your problem if you ever get into Parliament. Find a way through it, treading on as few corns as possible."

"Compromise? With people like that mob who tried to lynch Lloyd George a week ago?"

"Not compromise, wait. Give 'em a chance to cool off. They will, if someone throws 'em another bone to gnaw. They'll soon be hurrahing L.G. and throwing their brickbats at Joe Chamberlain. Some people would call that proof of national instability, I suppose, but it never struck me as that. It's the way a democracy functions. The public take the soundings and you chaps trim your sails to the wind, the way the Frocks do in a free country. It oughtn't to warp your private convictions. Never did mine."

Giles smiled. "You're a wise old bird," he said.

"Not wise, son," Adam replied. "Wily. And I should be. I've had time enough to learn. I've always got my way in the end, and I promise you that you and the fire-eater L.G. won't have so long to wait for a swing around in public opinion. You'll sweep the board at the next election, then everyone will scramble to get on the winning side. You'll have to search for a man who owns up to ever having wanted to wring Kruger's neck."

"You really believe that?"

"I believe it. Seen it happen over and over again in the last fifty years. Go up and tell that gel of yours to leave her packing until tomorrow. You'll leave with the rest of 'em and keep the peace meantime."

And so it might have been but for an unlucky chance the following day when Giles, carrying his grips out to the carriage that was to run Romayne and himself over to the station for the first leg of their journey home to Wales, passed under the horse's head at the entrance of the courtyard archway and came upon Alex at the precise moment he was riding one of the hacks into the forecourt for a canter across the Downs.

There was no way they could avoid one another, short of a deliberate attempt on Alex's part to ride his brother down. He reined back, staring hard over Giles' head to the leafless trees of the avenue and looking so pompous that Giles had to smile. He said, on impulse, "Come, Alex, can't we even shake hands? None of us hold a thing against you chaps. We're opposed to the fools who sent you over there to protect city interests," and when Alex did not respond he shrugged and stood aside, giving Alex room to pass under the arch. He would have passed, no doubt, had not everybody's luck been out.

At that moment Hugo's sergeant emerged, leading Hugo's hack and Hugo himself came out of the tackroom carrying his crop and hard hat. Alex said, glancing at him, "How about Hugo's interests? Don't they count?"

"Good God, of course they do! Do you imagine I get any satisfaction out of what happened to him in a rough and tumble for South African gold and diamonds? He lies as heavy on Chamberlain's conscience as the women and children dying in those damned camps you fellows have set up Try and see it from the human angle!"

"I'm not concerned with one angle or another," Alex said, slowly. "Only as the difference between one man, doing his duty as he saw it and another, trailing round the country preaching treason," and he gave his mount a sharp cut and cantered off across the forecourt.

Hugo called, urgently, "Hold on, Giles . . . !" and Giles, roused now, tossed the grips in the carriage, stalked round behind the vehicle to where Hugo was standing with an expression of pain on his broad, good-natured face. He said, in a low voice, "I couldn't help hearing that. I'd like you to know I don't see it that way, Chaser."

The use of his forgotten nickname, 'Chaser', acquired after their schoolfellows had learned that he was the son of the Swann whose Western Wedge manager had cornered a circus lion on Exmoor, touched Giles. So sharply that it brought him close to tears, evoking as it did a halcyon period twenty years ago when he and Hugo had loped across the moor together, building calf muscles that were to earn Hugo so many trophies yet lead, ultimately, to the incident that had cost him his sight. He said, "Don't let it worry you. We're well enough used to that kind of abuse, Hugo."

But Hugo muttered, "Take my hack and unsaddle him, Sergeant. I won't be going out on the rein after all."

"Now, sah!" the sergeant protested, "m'lady won't care to hear you've dodged the column! What'll I tell her?"

"Tell her I've gone for a walk instead. With Mr. Giles. Give me a hand, Giles," and Giles took his hand and led him into the forecourt.

"Go up behind, on to the hill. It's a rare place for blowing the cobwebs away."

They went slowly up the winding path, worn into the rocky outcrop behind the house, heading for the wooded plateau where old Colonel Swann had spent so much of his time painting indifferent water colours from the up-ended whaler on the summit. The old, makeshift shelter was still there, its timbers seamed and split by a thousand south-westerlies. They sat together, Giles looking over the winter landscape. Hugo said, at length, "You never heard it, did you? Not the real story?"

"I heard how you got word from an ambushed column and tackled a Boer outpost singlehanded. It was in the papers, the time they pinned the medal on you."

"Ah, the medal."

Hugo moistened his lips and sat very still, hands resting on his enormous thighs. "The Boers didn't traffic with medals, did they? If they did that kid would have earned one, I daresay."

"What kid, Hugo?"

"The kid I shot, just before I was hit. Last shot of the battle barring this," and he raised his hand to the bluish circular depression at his temple. "The last I'll ever fire. Thank God."

"Tell me if you want to, Hugo."

"Don't know how, really." He smiled. "You were the one who always did the telling, Chaser."

That was true, of course. All through their time on Exmoor Hugo had come to him with questions. Questions on every conceivable subject, and had been content to accept any answer Giles gave as the voice of the oracle. To Giles he still seemed pitifully young to carry such a cross but his helplessness and unwonted stillness was beginning to work on him, as though, for the first time in his life, he could sit in one place long enough to think things out and form independent judgments.

"I've come to believe it was tit-for-tat, Giles. My stopping that bullet, I mean, a second or so after I'd shot the kid. I didn't know he was a kid until I looked at him. We'd heard they were using kids that age but I hadn't believed it, not until then. He was about your age when you first went down to West Buckland. I had a quick look at him lying there. Just a second or two. Then it was curtains. Matter of fact, he was the last person I saw. You get to remembering that, you know. At least, I did, sitting about and night times." Then, very levelly, "Do you still believe in God, Giles?"

"Some kind of God, Hugo. I'm never sure what kind."

"Not one that looks out for folks, the way they tell you in the church?"

"No, or not the way they tell you in church. And God is only a word. A useful word but it can fool people, to my way of thinking."

"How about your kind of God?"

"Maybe it's a plan, a providence, with good and evil roughly balanced. Part of the plan is how we tip it, one way or the other and it's our choice. Otherwise there's no sense at all in any of it. But you don't have to go on blaming yourself about that youngster. He was trying to kill you from cover. How were you to know how old he was? The fault lies with the men who gave him a rifle, and sent him out to do a man's job. And even more with our people, who drove those chaps into a corner where they had to fight or hand over to a lot of city sharks. The fault certainly doesn't lie with you, so get that into your head, once and for all."

"Ah, *she* said that. The only other person I ever told."

"Sybil?"

"Yes." Then, "She's a wonderful person, Giles."

"I know. I've watched. You're glad about the baby, aren't you?"

Hugo smiled and seemed, fleetingly, almost himself again. "You bet I am. That's a turn-up for the book, isn't it? Sybil's thirty-three."

"Romayne was almost as old. I daresay you'll have a string now you've started."

"Can't imagine. Me being a father, I mean. Don't think I was cut out for one."

"Neither did I but you'd be surprised when it happens."

They sat in silence for a spell, Giles fighting an impulse to take his big hand and squeeze. It was a long time since he had been so close to tears. Finally Hugo said, "You remember that dream I told you about once?"

"The one you kept having? That dream where you

were lapping everyone else and there was a lot of cheering?"

"You remember it that well?"

"I remember it."

"Funny thing. I never had it once I left school and that kind of thing began to happen all the time. Then I had it again, the first night I was back here, only it was different. I was sprinting across the veldt in those damned great boots, and they were like ton weights, dragging me back. I got there, though, and there was that Boer kid at the tape. Cheering and waving his hat like mad."

Tears began to flow and nothing he could do would stop them. What did one say to that? What was there to say? And anyway Giles could not trust himself to speak. Hugo said, after a half a minute had elapsed, "Does that mean anything, d'you reckon?"

"I . . . I'd say it did, Hugo."

"What, exactly?"

"That the kid understood, sympathised even."

The heavy features relaxed. He said, sniffing the air, "Maybe. Glad I told you." Then, "I always liked it up here. Especially early on, when I was out training before breakfast. I'll get that chap to teach me the way up here on my own."

"You do that, Hugo."

He took his hand now and drew him up. Together they moved off down the twisting track to the forecourt and Adam, standing musing at the long window of the drawing-room, watched their approach. He thought, 'I'm damned sorry Alex isn't here to see that. Might loosen him up somewhat.'

4

Dreams at 'Tryst'

WHO KNEW HOW MANY DREAMS STILL HIBERNATED
under the russet-coloured pantiles of the old house? How
many and how varied, but they were there all right. They
waited in odd corners. Distilled hopes, suppressed hatreds,
thwarted and fulfilled loves and secret fears of ten generations of islanders, all waiting for a chance, maybe, to slip
out of the shadows and find a new post. For the house
itself was the product of a dream, old Conyer's dream of
dredging enough loot from the Lowland banks to build a
home under the crag that had been his trysting place with
the Cecil girl when he was a nobody.

Adam had dreamed there often enough, and so had
Henrietta, but Adam and Henrietta were rarely oppressed
by dreams and when they awoke it was not often they
recalled their substance. No more than an elusive expecta-
tion of the good luck or bad they could look for before
the sun set again.

All the children had dreamed here in their growing-up
days and sometimes Phoebe Fraser, nanny to nine, had
been awakened by a cry and hurried in to them, soothing
them in her broad Lowland brogue. Now Phoebe was
past all that, even though she still regarded Edward and
Margaret, the two youngest, as children. She was not
qualified to interpret Hugo's dream, or hoist Helen out
of the slough of the dreams she had had since returning to
'Tryst'

377

Phoebe Fraser might, conceivably, have gone some way towards interpreting Hugo's dream, but Helen's would have shocked her half out of her spinsterish mind, and this was predictable. Phoebe knew much of boys but nothing of men, and her deep Calvinistic convictions had long since succeeded in repressing any stirrings of the flesh, stirrings she would have accepted as subtle overtures of Satan. In all the years she had worked there nobody had ever seen her so much as flirt with a man, much less lie down in a ditch with one, as some of the maids had when it was high summer and they were out of sight and sound of the house.

Helen Coles' dreams of public ravishment would have struck Phoebe as evidence that she had grossly neglected her duties in the process of Helen's upbringing for a woman, even a married woman, had no business with dreams of that kind. They belonged, if anywhere, in the mind of a harlot. Certainly not in the subconscious of a widowed Christian missionary.

And yet, in a perverse way, Helen welcomed them, for they replaced something more sinister. A recurrent dream she had dreamed often on the long voyage home and during her first weeks in Ireland, surrounded by Joanna's jolly family. In this dream, from which she awoke moaning and shuddering, she saw Rowley's head perched on that gate post, but there was a difference that made her flesh creep. It leered at her, in a way that was altogether uncharacteristic of Rowley, even when his head had been firmly attached to his shoulders, and the dream persisted, with variations, for a long time, so that she grew to fear the prospect of sleep.

But then, settled in the midst of the noisy Dublin family, her night fancies took a sharp new turn. Rowley, and Rowley's severed head, had no place in them. Instead they were dominated by the courteous, businesslike presence of Colonel Shiba, the Japanese military attaché. He who had made such a gallant showing in the Fu area of the legations during the siege. Yet Colonel Shiba's recurrent behaviour in Helen's dream was not gallant. Methodically, as though dismantling a barricade prior to a planned withdrawal, he stripped her naked and smilingly conducted her to his couch. A makeshift couch of sandbags sewn in patchwork. And there, with the same quiet deliberation, and in full view of the entire garrison, he ravished her, night after night, with a skill and despatch that Rowley had never once displayed, not even after they survived the awkward, experimental stage of the earliest days of the marriage.

The act of ravishment, taken in isolation, was by no means abhorrent to her. Indeed, once she had recovered from the shock of finding herself stark naked in the presence of a passive audience, she offered him no resistance. But when, at the climactic moment, he vanished in a shell-burst, she had a sensation of having violated not only her body but her entire conception of decency and the civilised code and this was reinforced by the mournful gaze of some European defenders at an adjoining barricade. Including, unfortunately, Miss Polly Condit Smith, the pretty American girl who was the toast of the garrison.

It might have been with the prospect of keeping such startling dreams at bay that she drank far more than her quota at the 'Tryst' supper table during her Christmas stay. Adam kept a good cellar and a particularly fine claret, so that she sometimes went to bed gay, flushed and temporarily at peace with the world, feeling herself secure in these familiar surroundings where everyone behaved towards her as someone sorely in need of a little cheering up. But no sooner was she asleep than the businesslike Colonel Shiba appeared and went to work, methodically, on the hooks and buttons of her bodice, and now there was an added embarrassment for, in addition to the silent garrison, her brother-in-law Clinton Coles was watching.

One night early in the new year, when all but the Irish party had packed up and left (Clint had stayed on to attend the January conference) the dream was particularly vivid and she awoke from it, less than an hour after lying down, with the virtual certainty that she had indeed been ravished. The claret had left her mouth parched and her head throbbed as she sat up and when she was fumbling with the candle she had a distinct impression that its glow would reveal Colonel Shiba stretched beside her.

But then, coming to terms with the familiarity of the room, and the night sounds from the coppices that were inseparable from 'Tryst', she realised that it was not Colonel Shiba's ministrations that had awakened her but the rumble of voices in the room adjoining hers, a room occupied by Clint and Joanna. She heard Clint's boisterous arrival, guessing that he was the worse for drink, then Joanna's mellow laughter following a stumble on his part, and the sounds, together with evidence of such cosy intimacy on the far side of the wall, renewed in her a desperate awareness of her own loneliness and deprivation, whirling her back to the days when she and Joanna were the conspirators on this corridor, flitting in and out of one another's rooms in order to giggle and gossip about their beaux. So poignant was the memory that tears began to flow and a sense of terrible injustice bore down on her, projecting her from bed to window, there to contemplate the western prospect of the slope bathed in moonlight as far as the blur of woods where Adam's Hermitage sat on the knoll marking the northern boundary of the estate.

It was a prospect that might have soothed her had it not been for the persistent rise and fall of voices in the next room punctuated by Joanna's ripples of laughter. Evidence of such accord and conviviality increased her melancholy, so that she was suddenly aware of an overpowering need to make closer contact with human beings untroubled by her terrible sense of isolation. It was then, with a suppressed cry of excitement, that she remembered the cistern telegraph, a device she and Joanna had sometimes employed when the rest of the household was asleep and they had secrets to exchange. An array of super-

annuated leaden pipes, that ran the length of the western
wing, had long since ceased to serve any practical purpose.
They were a relic from an earlier tenant, installed some
seventy years ago as a crude means of conveying stored
rainwater from the huge cistern in the loft to a few of the
more important bedrooms on this side of the house. Adam,
reorganising the entire plumbing system soon after he
bought the place in the early 'sixties, had done little to
disturb the existing network, judging, no doubt, that its
dismantlement would do more harm than good to the old
structure, and the girls, discovering a practical purpose for
this in their early teens, had often used it to communicate
with one another after they had been granted the privilege
of separate and adjoining rooms.

By removing oaken plugs in the section of pipe that ran
under the window, it had been quite practical (and very
stimulating!) to communicate with one another, and it
now occurred to Helen, standing in her nightgown and
listening to the amiable sounds from the next room, that
she had only to put her ear to the pipe to be certain of
hearing more, if not all, of the exchanges between man and
wife.

Ordinarily it might have struck her as a Peeping Tom
device but in her present mood she did not give a row of
pins about such niceties. She had her ear to the pipe
within seconds of remembering its presence and it was just
as she thought. Although, presumably, a plug was still
in place next door, the voices became distinct and she
could hear everything that was said, as well as every
movement about the room.

*   *   *

The relationship of Joanna and Clint had been genial
and uncomplicated from the earliest days of their association and marriage had simply broadened and deepened
it. Joanna, by now, had few illusions about him, seeing
him as an amiable, overgrown adolescent, particularly

when he was in liquor, but Joanna did not look for rectitude in a husband. Of all the Swanns she was the least exacting. Clint was kind, easygoing, fond of the children, a good provider and a roystering, affectionate lover. What more could a woman expect of a man, seeing that few men matured in any case?

From time to time, in the early days of their marriage, she had been bothered by his extravagance and hurt by his over-fondness for lively company, male and female, but he always returned to her after a brief lapse and she had a serene conviction that he was glad he had married her. Marriage not only provided him with an anchorage, of the kind all men of his stamp needed. It also enabled him to sidestep the gloomy certainty of inheriting his father's pill business, leaving him free to throw in his lot with the free-ranging Adam. When she looked back on their absurd elopement (she thought of it as that although it had been mounted and stage-managed by Henrietta after she had confessed to being two months pregnant) she concluded that Clinton Coles had been a beneficiary rather than a victim of embarrassing circumstances.

On this particular night George had been over again, plotting family tactics for the forthcoming January conference and when Clint and George hobnobbed they could make substantial inroads into Adam's wine stocks, so that she was not in the least surprised when Clint appeared, about one-thirty a.m., drunk as a fiddler and falling flat on his face when he tried to slip his braces and trousers off. He became clumsily amorous the moment she slipped out of bed to assist him, landing a hearty slap on her bottom and grabbing her by the waist as she bent to seize his trouser legs. Together they rolled on the rug, Clint taking advantage of the frolic to hoist her nightgown but he seemed incapable of pressing his advantage. She said, not minding this horseplay in the least, "*Wait*, Clint! For heaven's sake, boy. Stay *still* a minute while I get you to bed!" where she would almost surely have accommodated him, as the quickest method of getting a good night's rest, had she not, at that moment, heard a sound close at hand that drove all thoughts of him out of mind.

It was unmistakably a sob. A long, dry sob, indicative of acute wretchedness, and it came, unaccountably had she been a stranger to the house, from the direction of the window-seat. She scrambled up then, leaving Clint in disarray on the floor and hurried across the room where, on the instant, she identified not only the source of the sob but the way in which it had been relayed to her. It came from Helen's room next door via the old cistern telegraph they had used as girls.

It sobered her on the instant. She felt neither shame nor resentment in the realisation that Helen had been eavesdropping. Only pity and concern that she should be driven to seek such a means of sharing an intimate moment of a man and woman whose lives, in contrast to her own, were so free of strain and misery.

Although excessively outward-looking she was by no means insensitive, particularly as regards Helen, her girlhood ally. She had been all too aware of her sister's taut nerves since her return home and had done everything she could think of to comfort and relax her, introducing her into the uninhibited Dublin scene in the hope that, sooner or later, she would form an attachment with someone that could lead to remarriage and a chance to forget her frightful experiences in the East. She was a generous soul and her sincere affection for her partner in so many youthful adventures had survived their long separation. She had a certainty now that Helen's marriage had not been a success, or not as she understood the word. Rowley had been a worthy, solemn, self-opinionated old stick, so dedicated to his work that he would have neither time nor inclination for frolics that made married life so agreeable, despite the tendency among men, even men like Clint, to dismiss women as frail, fluttering creatures, entirely dependent on their mates. Perhaps alone among the Swann girls she had taken accurate soundings of her parents' marriage, particularly her mother's approach to her father. A woman – a wise woman that is – did not quarrel with the fact that it was a man's world. She set about making the best of it and one certain way of doing this was to pander to male appetites, giving them free rein everywhere but in the kitchen. This, at least, kept them even-tempered and any woman with an ounce of sense could manipulate an easygoing man wholly pre-occupied with his own concerns that were limited, in the main, to food, bed, counting-house profits and the raising of progeny, approximately in that order.

She turned away from the pipe, jerked Clinton's trousers free, removed his shirt, underpants and shoes and took a firm grip under his armpits, saying, "Now get to bed and sleep it off. I won't be a minute."

His renewed clutch at her was easily evaded and he flopped back on to the bed, grinning foolishly, and saying, in the assumed Irish accent he adopted for these occasions, "You're a *foine* woman, Jo! Said it often and say it again! . . A *foine* woman!" But by then she was gone, not even waiting to slip into her bedgown and had hurried into the gallery and along to Helen's room where, as she half-expected, she found the candle burning and her sister sitting on the edge of a rumpled bed, the very picture of melancholy.

There seemed no profit in beating about the bush, so she said, sitting beside her and throwing an arm about her shoulder, "I heard you at the pipe. Don't worry, love. Clint didn't. He's far too bottled. Now, what *is* it, Helen? How can I help?" She was rewarded by a convulsive embrace on Helen's part and another sob, stifled this time, that released a steady flow of tears.

They sat there for a long time until Helen mastered herself sufficiently to say, "It was unforgivable . . . Me eavesdropping like that . . . I . . . I don't know what's come over me lately . . . I remembered the pipe and then . . well, you're so happy, Jo! And for me everything's so sour and wretched. There's no end to it and when I'm alone and have those awful dreams . "

"What dreams, Helen?"

"The one about Colonel Shiba, the Japanese attaché. And sometimes the frightful one I used to have before about . . . about seeing Rowley's head on the post. Not as it was but alive."

Joanna tightened her grip. She knew all about Rowley's head but the name of the Japanese attaché had no significance for her. She said, "Tell me about the bad dreams then." Helen made no response. "Just saying things, just putting them into words. It makes them less important, Helen. Goodness, it's no wonder you have terrible dreams after what you've been through. Anybody would. Most women would have gone out of their minds."

"Maybe I have."

"Not you. Tell me. Tell me everything."

Outside in the coverts one of the resident 'Tryst' owls hooted. It was a mild night for January and the wind, crossing the Weald from the south-east, went to probing the barley-sugar chimney-pots but without the savagery it showed throughout most of the winter. Joanna draped a blanket over their shoulders without releasing her grip on Helen's shoulders and Helen said, "I don't have the worst one now, or not often. But the new one is almost as bad. It's so real. I can feel it happening to me. And so silly, too, for that man never behaved towards me in any way but correctly. He was a gentleman and brave as a lion. Everybody thought so."

"The Japanese colonel?"

"Yes. He was there when I shot that officer through the loophole."

"What happens to you in the dream, Helen?"

She told her, shamefully and haltingly, but forcing herself to describe both dreams in detail. She told of the macabre leer on the face of a decapitated head. She described the firm, expertly performed ritual of a public ravishment on a couch of sandbags sown from quilts and blankets.

"Do *you* think I'm going mad, Jo? Surely that's a mad dream to have time and again, isn't it?"

"No, it isn't mad. And I think the dreams are linked in a way. One's come to blot out the other." And then, without diffidence, "Tell me about Rowley. Tell me about your life together *before* he was killed. How was he? How did he treat you?"

"He was always kind, or tried to be in his funny, absentminded way."

"I didn't mean that. How did he treat you as a woman?"

"He didn't, not really. Whenever he did I . . . well . . . I had to encourage him, to remind him I was his wife even. He wasn't like any other man I've known. You remember how most men didn't need much encouragement that way. Clint still doesn't, does he?"

"No, not Clint!" She came near to chuckling, despite what seemed to her the terrible poignancy of her sister's plight. "But Rowley was never in the least like Clint, thank heavens. Sometimes I used to think Rowley wasn't a man at all, just . . . just a kind of . . . well, a saint, if you like. But saints shouldn't marry, should they? And this one did. It must have been awful for you. I don't know how you put up with it all those years and in all those awful places."

She thought hard, trying with all her might to relate the stray images and conjectures that occurred to her and arrive at some kind of conclusion that would lead her to comprehend Helen's present state of mind. She tried putting herself in her place, not as a woman who had survived unbelievable terrors and hardships, but as a wife lying beside a husband night after night, unable to awaken more than a token emotional response in his body. It was very difficult but because she was her mother's daughter, and because, instinctively, she turned her own sensual nature to very good account, she could get some glimmering of the truth, and in the wake of that truth she saw a possible solution. Or the means of promoting a shock, physical and spiritual, that held promise of a solution. Love and pity rode roughshod over her upbringing, and

all the canons of so-called civilised behaviour, for here
was her own sister, who had dragged herself home from
the threshold of hell, and was now defeated by the clamour
of her body and degradation of spirit that Rowland Coles's
indifference had invoked. Innocently perhaps, and from
the highest motives but mercilessly none the less.

She said, "Listen, Helen. Wait here. I'll only be gone
a moment. Wash your face and put a comb through your
hair while I'm gone," and she took her sister's hand,
jerked her up and pushed her towards the wash-stand,
pouring water from the jug and dipping a flannel in it.
"Go on! Make the effort, for everybody's sake," and she
hovered by the door until Helen began to lave her face.
Then she slipped away, moving barefoot along the gallery
to the stairhead where Adam left a fixed oil-lamp burning
all night in the deep niche beside the sewing-room
door.

She went down and stepped gingerly between the two
truckle beds inside, then through into the wainscotted
dining room, pungent with cigar smoke. In a sliver of
moonlight she found and lit a candle, carrying it to the
sideboard where, among other decanters, stood one containing Adam's choice port. She poured a beaker and
carried it back, lighting her way up the stair to the door of
her room and peeping inside to see Clint sprawled naked
across the bed. She pulled back the sheets and rolled him
in and although he muttered and opened his eyes the lack
of focus told her he was still asleep. She went out again
and into Helen's room, where her sister was sitting in
front of the mirror brushing her long dark hair. She
seemed calmer now although her hands trembled violently.
Jo said, handing her the port, "Drink it down. Drink all
of it. It's what you need. It'll do you good," and Helen,
after a single look of bewilderment, began to sip. A little
colour returned to her cheeks.

"You're very kind, Jo. You always were the best-
hearted among them. I'll manage now."

"Until you sleep you'll manage. Then you'll dream

again, one dream or the other. There's something else you have to do, Helen, and no one can do it for you. No doctor, nobody, you hear? Go into Clint now. I'll stay here until you come back."

"*To Clint?* Me?"

She slammed down the glass so hard that the stem snapped and the bowl rolled across the dressing-table as far as the pincushion, leaving a small pool of dregs on the polished surface. "You can't mean that, Jo. You . you *can't*!"

"But I do mean it! You need a man more than any woman I ever saw and I mean to get you one of your own the minute we go home. But you can't wait that long, not to feel . . . feel *wanted* and needed. Not to feel a woman again. You needn't worry about his side of it. He's bottled and won't know providing you use your wits. Just go to him, like I say. Just this once."

"But it's wrong, Jo. It would be terribly wrong with anyone's husband, but yours . . ."

"It's not wrong unless I say it is and I don't! I say it's right. Just this one time. As I say, he's drunk but not so drunk as he won't stir the minute he feels a woman's arms around him. I should know. There's nothing I don't know about Clinton Coles."

The colour in Helen's cheeks flooded back. She sat twisting the ribbon of her nightgown, her eyes fixed on the smears of port on the dressing-table surface.

"How can you be so sure? I mean . why would a thing like that help?"

"I don't know why, I only know it will. Maybe it would break that awful sequence of dreams and, anyway, you'd come alive again and that's what's important right now. Besides, what harm would it do? Do you remember how we schemed to switch our beaux that time at Penshurst? Well, it would make you feel young again, ready to start over again. Good grief, Helen, how long is it since a man held you in his arms?"

It was a question she could not answer. Eight months

had passed since Rowley was butchered but long before that, ever since the first refugees came in ahead of Boxers rampaging in the west and north, Rowley had been preoccupied, wholly absorbed in his work as healer and comforter in the field. Maybe a year or more had elapsed since he had used her in that way and much longer since she had felt herself a wife to him. And remembering this the prospect of lying with Clint did not seem so outrageous, for she began to discern a kind of logic behind Joanna's reasoning. The mere thought of lying beside her jolly, ever boyish brother-in-law and of feeling his arms about her quickened her blood and breathing. What deterred her, however, was the cold-bloodedness of such a proposal, surely unique in the relationship of sisters. She said, wonderingly, "Don't you love Clint, Jo?"

"I love him in my own way. The way he likes and the way I'm used to. But I love you too and I won't see you reduced to this, with no one to help, no one to turn to. Besides, he's had other women since we married. Not often, and never seriously, but he's had them. Believe me, I know what I'm doing, Helen."

"But if he's drunk . . . if he's asleep now . . . ?"

"He'll come half-awake and then he'll drop off again, thoroughly fuddled. As soon as he does slip out again. I'll wait for you here."

She got up, both hands still fidgeting with the length of ribbon. "How do you *mean* exactly? A thing like that bringing me peace? Helping me to forget?"

"You'll see. Do it, Helen. Just do as I say."

She got up, realising that some act of physical propulsion was needed and taking Helen by the hand she opened the door. The gallery was in darkness, apart from the faint glow of the lamplight that touched the head of the stairs. She could hear Clint's snores, the only sound breaking the heavy silence of the night. Then she led the way along to her room, entered it ahead of her sister and blew the candle out. She said, in a normal voice, "Shift over, Clint," and surprisingly he obeyed, his snores ceasing as he stirred. "There, get about it, girl," and she groped her way out, closing the door.

Helen had no certain knowledge now whether he was awake or asleep. She could hear his irregular breathing and it caused her to hesitate a moment longer, telling herself that if he said one word she would turn back and tell Jo that such a thing was not to be thought of. He did not wake and presently she crept carefully in beside him, settling herself so close to her edge of the bed that she barely touched him. She could feel her heart thumping a rival rhythm to his swift, short snores as minutes passed before the warmth of his body communicated itself to hers and she turned, again very stealthily, lifting her right arm and groping for him where he lay just within her reach. She touched his exposed shoulder and fingertip contact with his flesh made her shiver so that instinctively she drew a little closer, touching him lightly with her knees and breasts.

Warmth and comfort seemed to pulse from him, communicating itself to her in a way that soothed rather than excited her but the enlarged contact was enough to increase her rate of breathing so that soon, growing a little bolder, she enlarged her grip and pulled him half round so that he lay flat on his back. He moved sluggishly, almost unwillingly at first but then, or so it seemed, a tiny flicker of initiative passed to him and he flung his arm across her, drawing her closer as his volley of snores ceased abruptly.

Suddenly, outrageously it seemed to her, she wanted to giggle, the sheer absurdity of the situation inflating inside her like a large, coloured balloon, but she mastered the impulse and lay still for a moment, revelling in her own audacity and remembering a time – a thousand years ago it seemed – when she had first shared a bed with Rowley Coles as a girl bride who had entered marriage so confidently but had discovered, all too quickly, that her limited experience as a flirt counted for nothing with a groom cast in his solemn mould.

Time passed. It seemed to her an age had elapsed since

she had joined him between the rumpled sheets and a sense
of anticlimax stole upon her as she faced the fact that it
was more than likely Jo had been mistaken about the
certainty of him making the most of his opportunity. It
seemed more than possible that he could lie there snoring
until morning and it was the prospect of advancing daylight that prompted her to summon up her courage to
resolve the situation one way or another. She could, she
reasoned, rely on a few seconds' grace if he was sufficiently
roused to open a conversation. She could slip away while
he was still bemused and tell Joanna to return at once.
She could be clear of the room before he had found
matches and candle but in the meantime she felt she owed
it to herself to put Joanna's theory to the test. Cautiously,
an inch at a time, she lifted his arm and placed it against
her breasts, holding it there and was rewarded by the slow
glow of satisfaction it brought her, as well as an insignificant signal that his senses were stirred inasmuch as he
drew a little closer, stretching out his legs and turning on
his side, this time facing her. He did not wake, however,
although his snores diminished to heavy, regular breathing
and it was this, perhaps, that emboldened her sufficiently
to turn her face towards him, and kiss his cheek. Lightly,
almost teasingly, as though he had been one of those awkward young men who competed for modest favours in the
far off days when she and Jo had been county belles with
half-a-dozen swains at their disposal.

The kiss, light as it was, had a disproportionate effect
upon her. He was sporting a growth of dark bristles
announcing that, with the prospect of male company that
evening, he had not bothered to shave for dinner, and the
mere touch of his bristles on her lips was a sharp reminder
of the contrast between Clinton and Rowland Coles, for
Rowley had never needed to shave more than once a day
and his whiskers were as soft and downy as a boy's. It
emphasised, somehow, Clint's heavy masculinity and
awareness of this, together with the weight of his hand on
her breast, quickened her desire in a way she would never

have thought possible a few minutes since. The initial shame that had restrained her from the moment Jo pushed her into the room fell away like shyness dispelled by a genial greeting and she suddenly felt free and untrammelled by guilt, not caring, in that instant, whether he was awake or asleep. She withdrew her left hand and used it to encircle his head, cradling him closer and kissing him again, more purposefully this time so that his grasp on her breast tightened, then fell away as he made a half-hearted attempt to pluck at the join in her nightgown. He was too impatient or too sleepy perhaps, to loosen the neck ribbons but the effort at least succeeded in banishing the last of her scruples. She plucked the bow loose herself and half shrugged herself out of the shift, her heart pounding like a steam hammer as she bared her breasts and enfolded him, showering his face with kisses now and straining towards him with a fervour she had never once displayed during Rowley's perfunctory embraces for somehow she had always sensed a demonstration of this kind would embarrass him. Asleep, awake or somewhere between the two, Clinton responded, reaching down to grasp the hem of her half-shed nightgown and hoisting it to her thighs. Then, so swiftly that she had no real awareness of the transition, the initiative passed to him and he half-rolled on her, muttering unintelligible words only two of which she caught but she could not have sworn that they were 'fine woman'. Then, with a kind of unconscious expertise he bore down on her and under the stress of his weight and clumsy handling she uttered a low cry, half an expression of protest, half proclaiming an intense physical release akin to the moment of waking after the methodical ravishment by the courteous Japanese colonel. Seconds later he was done with her and sleep reclaimed him again, his fuddled brain suddenly unequal to the struggle against the fumes of all the liquor he had shipped. He slipped away, rolling over on his back again, and his snores recommencing, his inert hand resting on her belly.

She lay very still, aware once again of the night sounds in the coverts and the pale glow of moonlight, almost blue it looked, shafting a gap in the curtains and touching a corner of the bed. Her body continued to tremble but her mind was inexplicably still. She knew then, savouring the knowledge with a deep sense of fulfilment, that Jo had been uncannily right after all. Not only about Clint but about her errant peace of mind.

R. F. DELDERFIELD

Give Us This Day

Book II   Reconnaissance

The second of two books that make up the
enthralling third part of the world-famous
Swann saga

With the same majestic sweep and brilliant narrative as he
evinced in *God is an Englishman* and *Theirs was the
Kingdom*, Ronnie Delderfield carries through his epic
saga of the Swann family on into Edwardian times.

The First World War is close to hand, the Victorian age
has given way to the Edwardian. There is trouble at
home with all the arguments about protectionism; there
is trouble in Ireland. And within the heart of the Swann
family there are the usual familiar troubles that seem
likely to cause disruption within 'Swann-on-Wheels'

'A pattern which innumerable readers will find deeply
satisfying'

Sunday Times

'A great sweeping entertainment of a book, full of life,
passion and excitement'

Daily Mirror

R. F. DELDERFIELD

To Serve Them All My Days

Book I   Late Spring

Here is the first part of Ronnie Delderfield's bestselling
story of school life during the earlier part of this century,
displaying yet again all the author's high qualities and
standing as another 'testament to his industry, his
passionate love of history, his stalwart belief in fair play,
tolerance and loyalty'

Evening Standard

David Powlett-Jones had survived the dreary carnage of
the Western Front, a young man whose attitudes had been
bitterly hardened by harsh experience in the violence
of war.

Now he found himself master in a remote school, in
charge of people barely younger than himself, with an
influence that was bound to touch upon and change the
lives of the hundreds of boys who might pass through his
care. It was a responsibility that demanded compassion
and foresight, honesty and commonsense – qualities that .
he was to nurture and develop in the exciting times that
were to lie ahead.

R. F. DELDERFIELD

To Serve Them All My Days

Book II   The Headmaster

No longer the shell-shocked young man fresh from the
front, David Powlett-Jones had now become a schoolmaster
of rare talent – able to change with the times and
understand their varying stresses.

As the age of strikes and hunger gave way to the years of
pre-war apprehension and wartime glory, so did David's
life change. Marriage blissfully came and tragically went;
headmastership came, bringing with it new responsibilities;
and always changing were the faces and manners and
attitudes of the people under his tutelage, drawing from
him all the understanding and compassion that he
could muster.

'A warm, humane and very able craftsman writing in the
panoramic manner that is natural to him'   *The New Yorker*

'So assured'   *The Sunday Telegraph*

'A reminder of his substantial qualities as a writer'
                                          The Guardian

A TOP SELECTION OF CORONET NOVELS

R. F. DELDERFIELD

A Horseman Riding By

☐ 04360 1	Book 1—Long Summer Day	50p
☐ 04361 X	Book 2—Post of Honour	50p
☐ 12971 9	Book 3—The Green Gauntlet	50p
☐ 15092 0	The Dreaming Suburb	50p
☐ 15093 9	The Avenue Goes to War	50p
☐ 15623 6	God is an Englishman	60p
☐ 16225 2	Theirs Was The Kingdom	60p
☐ 02787 8	Farewell The Tranquil Mind	35p
☐ 17420 X	Seven Men of Gascony	40p

To Serve Them All My Days

☐ 17599 0	Book 1—Late Spring	40p
☐ 16709 2	Book 2—The Headmaster	40p

Give Us This Day

☐ 18819 7	Book 2—Reconnaissance	50p

NORAH LOFTS

☐ 17826 4	Charlotte	40p
☐ 19352 2	Crown Of Aloes	40p

KEITH ROBERTS

☐ 18805 7	Boat Of Fate	60p

ELIZABETH GOUDGE

☐ 15105 6	Green Dolphin Country	75p
☐ 15104 8	Scent of Water	40p

NIGEL TRANTER

☐ 16213 9	Montrose—The Young Montrose	50p
☐ 18619 4	Montrose—The Captain-General	50p

All these books are available at your bookshop or newsagent, or can be ordered direct from the publisher. Just tick the titles you want and fill in the form below.

....

CORONET BOOKS, P.O. Box 11, Falmouth, Cornwall.

Please send cheque or postal order. No currency, and allow the following for postage and packing:

1 book—10p, 2 books—15p, 3 books—20p, 4–5 books—25p, 6–9 books—4p per copy, 10–15 books—2½p per copy, 16–30 books—2p per copy, over 30 books free within the U.K.
Overseas—please allow 10p for the first book and 5p per copy for each additional book.

Name...

Address...

....